THE
FOURTH
WALL

THE FOURTH WALL

SCOTT PETTY

atmosphere press

Published by Atmosphere Press

Library of Congress Control Number: 2021920344

Cover design by Josep Lledo

Atmospherepress.com

GLOSSARY

AAR – After Action Report

ACH – Advanced Combat Helmet

ACU – Army Combat Uniform

AO – Area of Operation

AWOL – Absent Without Leave

BND – Bundesnachrichtendienst, German Federal Intelligence Service

CG – Commanding General

CID – U.S. Army Criminal Investigation Command

COA – Course of Action

CONOPS – Concept of Operations

COP – Combat Outpost

D20 – Twenty-sided die

DCG – Deputy Commanding General

DFAC – Dining Facility

FOB – Forward Operating Base

FOIA – Freedom of Information Act

G2 – Intelligence Staff

GOMOR – General Officer Memorandum Of Reprimand

HQ – Headquarters

HVT – High Value Target

IED – Improvised Explosive Device

IO – Investigating Officer

ISAF – International Security Assistance Force

KC – Kandahar City

KLE – Key Leader Engagement

LZ – Landing Zone

M9 – Pistol used by U.S. Armed Forces, made by Beretta

MAAWS – Money As A Weapon System

MEPS – Military Entrance Processing Station

MOS – Military Occupational Specialty

MP – Military Police

MRAP – Mine-Resistant Ambush Protected

OBE – Out of Body Experience

OER – Officer Evaluation Report

PX – Post Exchange

RPG – Rocket Propelled Grenade

SAW – Squad Automatic Weapon

SIGACTS – Significant Activities

SIR – Serious Incident Report

SM – Service Member

UCMJ – Uniform Code of Military Justice

VBIED – Vehicle-Borne Improvised Explosive Device

PART I

FIRST
TASTE

"You look like you just got kicked out of fairyland and landed in the real world. Was everything gumdrops and cherry trees for you? One minute you're in fairyland, the next minute...BAM, welcome to Afghanistan." The airman repeated BAM for effect. The comment was likely scripted, something he liked to say to all the new arrivals. He was a BAM kind of guy. Or maybe he just wanted to pick on me. After all, he was Air Force, I was Army. It was his grin, his lips glistening in the red glow of the cargo hold of the plane. I was his superior officer, but his grin said I was just like everybody else. Or maybe he wasn't talking to me at all. He was talking to the thousands of military personnel and contractors who had streamed by him over the months. This giant transport plane was his domain.

The airman's voice was out of sync with the motion of his lips. He liked hearing himself talk. He flexed his arms and laughed. I couldn't watch much more of his show. I had bugs in my stomach and bugs in my head. I hadn't slept in two days, and I was already thinking of home, even though home was history, before I ever left. For good reasons, I chose to spin new wheels of fortune and adventure. I was bent on fusing earth and heaven.

My mission in Afghanistan was to work with local leaders

to help build infrastructure and transition to the next stage, whatever that was supposed to look like, or so I was told. The mission was more sinister than advertised, which could be said of all missions. The powers-that-be said a lot of it would be left up to me. I had some ideas. I was living comfortably in Houston, building my law practice and serving in the Reserve, and then I got the call one afternoon. My name came up in some random conversation far away. With all my experience in law, military intelligence, archaeology, and knowledge of the occult, I was the one. Had I not been drinking wine and painting a landscape when I got the call, I might have said no. I was really into the landscape, not my first oil painting but the first of its kind. I was exposed and dreaming, dreaming about having an adventure. Accepting the mission to Afghanistan was, at that moment, magic in its purest form. I imagined something then willed it to happen. That night, for some reassurance, I deeply meditated and had an out-of-body experience that took me across the world, across time. I saw my older self at a desk, writing this story, no longer in the Army, but on the front line of a different kind of war. Afghanistan was only the start of my epic adventure.

I was not planning to experiment with magic right away, but standing there, packed in with a bunch of other soldiers in the U.S. Air Force C-17 Globemaster, I couldn't help it. I needed to be seen. I had to know just how psychically connected I might be to my new brothers and sisters in arms. Would their own nascent psychic abilities respond to the powers I'd developed over the years? Could they also, to some degree, experience the sensation of being in two places at once? Wasn't that the life of an Army Reservist? I closed my eyes and took deep breaths. I could see nothing but a black void surrounding the transparent outer shell of my body, then an orb of light appeared and moved toward my feet. Breathing deeply, I sucked the light orb into my body through my feet. I took deeper breaths. The light filled me from bottom to top, all the way to the top of my head. I projected my mind into the liquid light and lifted away from my physical body and floated above the group. I looked down and saw myself. The major standing next to me nudged my arm. Even though I was several feet away, I could still feel his touch.

"Are you all right, Captain Jett?" said the major. We didn't know each other. He read the nameplate on my uniform.

"I'm fine, Sir." My voice sounded far away.

"You look a little green. First time in Kandahar? It's the birthplace of the Taliban, you know."

I felt green, plus red and all sorts of mismatched colors. I felt suffocated by a new, big system I didn't yet know. I floated further back into the plane's cargo hold. Onboard were soldiers coming off leave and soldiers just arriving in theater, like me, fresh and just as green, and a few civilian contractors. I kept silent, along with everybody else. No one was talking. Everyone looked helpless in the red glow. Everyone was going their own way in their dreams. No one knew each other.

"Get ready!" yelled the airman. He loved saying this, I could tell. He took a headcount. Everyone groaned as they stood up. The soldiers who weren't already wearing helmets started putting theirs back on, though I petted a couple of sweaty heads. The people didn't seem to notice. I looked back at my physical body. I could see myself putting on my ACH. I could feel the curvature and hardness of the helmet, down to the Kevlar weave, and the padding inside, which I had to assemble myself days earlier in Georgia, which seemed like so long ago.

I voyeuristically looked at me, standing there, bunched up with the others. We were shards of a broken form, about to reassemble into a grand story in a warzone. We were all fragments of another reality about to be dragged into a more surreal world. I took a good look around me. Most of the soldiers were young enough to be children of the senior officers, the ragged-looking men looking very eager to make another go-round with war, ready to face the monsters again. Oh, yes, there were monsters. But the men looked tired. In the strange light, they hid. Everyone looked so tired before the start of the game. I wondered if I looked as tired as the others. A kid was still asleep, drooling on his shoulder. His buddy punched him, but he did not wake. I floated right up to his face, close enough to smell the ghost of a Clif Bar he'd eaten. I felt a deeper connection with this young man. His aura was light pink, almost white, and a tendril of this light was slithering down his arm, across his hand in his lap, then it penetrated my own astral space, right up to my face. I didn't remember seeing him in the holding area at Bagram Airfield before we got on the plane, but I was so nervous during the long wait there. I kept to myself.

I waited in the holding area at Bagram for five hours before my flight to Kandahar. When I arrived at Bagram from Kuwait, I had little information about my contact. I was given a name. That was it. But I didn't shout the name in the terminal, instead I shouted out, "I'm Captain Thomas Jett!" The place went silent. Everyone was looking at me, spellbound. I felt ashamed for the way I came gusting into the room, like an awkward spy.

A young sergeant ran up and helped me with my gear. Before the next bird south to Kandahar, he drove me to the DFAC for some midnight chow. I ate a scorched burger, which had likely been sitting there waiting for me a long time. The sergeant was a chirpy guy, maybe twenty-two. I apologized to him for having to pick me up in the middle of the night, but he said he normally worked night shifts. I never saw him again, but I heard he was killed by indirect fire. What an unlucky, kind kid. Before going back to the terminal, he drove me around the base in his little truck. The roads of Bagram Airfield were as choked with traffic as Tokyo or Tijuana, and I choked on the dust and didn't stop choking till the end of my tour in 2012.

It was time to move. My physical body was tugging my astral form back. I could feel butterflies in my stomach and could even see them, down to their flight paths, rising and falling like musical notation. I looked again at the sleeping man, an E5 sergeant in his mid-twenties. Behind their lids, his eyes were darting side to side. I tuned out the movement of other soldiers and the noise of the plane's turbofan engines and focused on seeing this one man's dream. The scene was at first hazy, but forms appeared, neon colors, cars and people on a city street, and animals that don't exist. It was something the painter Salvador Dali might have dreamed. I looked at the soldier's nameplate: Ramsey. "Wake up, Sergeant Ramsey!" I yelled with the loudest astral big-boy voice I could manage. His eyes popped open wide, looking straight into mine.

"Yes, Sir," Ramsey whispered. He rubbed his eyes. He looked up and down, trying to find me. His aura went from pinkish to red flaked with gold.

"What?" said his battle buddy.

"Nothing," said Ramsey. "I was having a bad dream."

The next moment I was back in my body. The tail door of the C-17 hadn't yet dropped, but the engines stopped. I stroked the M9 I kept strapped across my heart. I closed my eyes. I heard voices—sentinels from beyond my dreams. *For Christ's sake, enjoy what's coming.* It was a first taste of the transcendent experience I had been seeking for a long time: to better understand what is beyond four dimensions, three of space and one of time, to transcend the fourth wall shared by all mankind and experience another dimension, a place I was not yet able to access through dabbling in astral travel, a place not adequately described in any of the ponderous grimoires I'd collected over the years. Though, with millions of words so minuscule, perhaps I just wasn't reading closely, dear reader.

There were fifty-something other soldiers waiting to get off the plane. Some would stay in Kandahar. Others would catch birds to FOBs and COPs throughout RC-South, my assigned territory. We shuffled closely, like armed cattle. There were other sounds of confusion. We wedged together. Our gear tangled. The local time was 0630 hours, 25 October 2011. It smelled like human waste, but I was prepared for this. Maddox told me I would smell Kandahar Airfield before I saw it. He went on and on about a lot of things like he had a lot to get out, whether I was listening or not. He told some war stories. As he described death, I imagined people dancing. I didn't see their faces, though. I just heard the music. This was due to the singsong way Maddox described his adventures.

I shared a tent in Kuwait with Lieutenant Colonel John Maddox. He was going on his fourth full tour. He had been to various other places in the Middle East forty odd times. He said he once became nauseous of the smell of Kandahar Airfield and threw up on a soldier standing next to him. He said he would be joining me in a few weeks. "You'll do fine," he said. He grinned like a fox then went back to reading his pulp western novel. Maddox was an older version of me, physically, except he was four inches taller. He had streaks of gray in his blond hair. Maybe it was why he called me 'pup,' because I looked like him as a pup. I could see what he did back in the day. His past was in his sharp, blue eyes. I didn't feel like I could keep up with the visions I had of Maddox. I could see he was a monster and a bit of a dickhead. Right when I met him, I believed he was responsible for piles of dead bodies. He spoke of his twin daughters. He talked to me like a son.

The tail door of the plane slowly dropped, revealing the gray stage of my new world, a world I had spent years conceiving. Layers of time were peeling away, backward from the future. It was a world already a part of my dreams, then and there. Like a child afraid of entering a dark room, knowing everything was going to become bizarre, I did not immediately walk down the ramp, but then I realized all roads in my life were leading to this point in time, to passing through this barrier, my elusive fourth wall, and none would lead back. I said a quick prayer, just jumbled words. My words conveyed a sense of immediacy. I hoped someone was listening, but I knew war was listening, and all her monster children, and that maybe I would pass through the fourth wall via the creeping madness of modern, asymmetrical warfare.

I took a deep breath and walked down the ramp, ready to begin the game. It was all bearing down on me. The land was flat and brown in all directions, all the way to the jagged mountains across the northern horizon. I never noted the names of those peaks. Has anyone? Who cares? My delusions of quantifiable satisfaction and straight explanations were destroyed the moment I arrived, soon to be replaced with a more complicated universe.

A group of Black Hawks was close by, about to take off. They were the angriest looking entities around. A few A-10 Warthogs were lined up a little further. The toothy-painted grins on the noses of the jets were the only grins around, except for the airman's. Ah, the dutiful voice of the airman. He thanked us for our service after we departed the plane. He disappeared into the plane and the tail door closed and we all stood around a bit.

"Who knows what you're doing here?" asked the same major next to me.

"Nobody," I said, "and you?"

"Nobody."

He talked as if he'd done this before. By "this" I mean drink from the magic fountain, act on warfare's vast stage, something apart from reality in a mystical, abstract realm beyond the fourth wall, a realm where will is manifested as reality. He wasn't acting like he was in charge, but his eyes revealed inner strength and knowledge. "This war will hand you your ass," he said. "Just be ready." I was not crazy about that major.

The desert wind grabbed my throat with its putrid fingers. The divergent images all around were beautiful. We marched down the flight line toward the rising sun. Celestial forms danced along next to me, I swear, or perhaps I was delusional with fatigue.

NIGHT
VISITORS

I talked to the sky a lot when I was a kid. My brain wanted my body to lift very gently apart and away from the earth, so an angel could dive in and replace my body. I'd look straight up and talk about my days and my dreams and all the players in those dreams. I was a creator, going back and forth in the cosmos.

On my last night in the states, I went drinking at a bar near Ft. Benning, Georgia. I was at Benning at a processing center for deploying reservists. I went through four days of in-processing for war. It wasn't just soldiers going to Afghanistan. Some were going to Iraq, some to the Horn of Africa, the Democratic Republic of Congo (DRC), and a few were off to Germany, and it made me miss my tour in Germany, just a year earlier.

The bar was between a used car dealership and a strip mall where the only thing still open was a Mexican restaurant. Military police were in front of the restaurant, along with some civilian police, and several individuals were face down in the parking lot. One looked like a soldier. His head was shaved. Whether he was drunk or not, he was cooperating. The other two were definitely not soldiers.

The bar was a rough place. It was off limits to soldiers under the base commander's orders, a fact I learned the next morning. There were about thirty people in the bar, mostly men. I tried not to talk to anyone. I didn't want to explain why I actually wanted to go to war or hear anyone else's horror stories. I wasn't looking for glory, and I wasn't looking for medals. I was looking for an experience that would clutch my dreams for the rest of my life. I had demons to deal with, like everyone. Unlike most people, I wanted to deal with mine face-to-face. Most people don't like facing their own ghoulish children. They like simple exchanges, *entrances,* and *exits,* and I decided months earlier I didn't want to continue going back and forth between the two, that experiencing war might bring the worlds of nonsense and purpose together into a sum of all questions and answers, the patterns of the universe explained. Perhaps the idea was a little deformed, a little fuzzy, but I wanted to build a new house, with new walls, and I could live inside and outside of those walls, at the same time. I was thirty-seven years old and had only been in the Army five years, only an officer since 2008, but I felt I was mature enough to handle such a house.

A young woman was sitting next to me at the bar. "You look tired," she said. She looked a little beat up herself. I could see she had competing lifestyles and schedules. She was wearing too much fake jewelry, and her hair looked like an animal which might scurry away any second.

I responded in a polite way, not a truthful way. "I am tired."

"I'm Lady Mist." She smiled sweetly and pulled a card from her pocket and showed it to me. At first, I thought it was a playing card, but it was bigger, with a picture of a knight on a horse. "This man looks like you," she said. I didn't think so, but he looked gallant and serious about his business, and people tell me I look pretty serious, and I guess that's what she meant. She invited me to follow her. I swallowed the rest of my whiskey and left the glass on the bar and followed her through a door in the back of the bar.

We went down a long hallway. *LM, where are you taking me?* I kept my nose in the game, but there was sawdust on the floor, and I sneezed when I sniffed. She led me to the rear of the building. I could've left, but I didn't. It's not like I paid her money. I didn't feel ripped off. Maybe I feared she would later leap into my nightmares, which of course she did. *LM, you're bad...but I'm starting to like you.*

We entered a small room with a card table set up in the middle of the room. White lace cloth covered the table. It was a cheap presentation. The room was dimly lit by a large candle on a brass stand in the corner, the kind of candle you'd find in a church. I shut the door behind me, but this didn't keep out the voice of Dwight Yoakum, and when a phone rang somewhere down the hall, Lady Mist took a big step toward me, as if trying to distract me, as if she was crossing an invisible line and being closer to me was going to generate energy. She assessed me, head to toe.

I could see Lady Mist was a witch. She was not my first witch. LM brought back old memories of...I forgot her name, if I ever knew it at all. I never met her in person. We carried on a digital friendship for a year, off and on. She sent me only a couple of pictures, and they were blurry, so I never got a clear picture of what she looked like. She would talk about having the ability to stalk around at night in different animal forms, that it was an ancient trick, but the trick was more about extracting energy from other dimensions, other planes of existence. I learned a lot from her. No-name-witch wasn't fat, but I started picturing her with fat cheeks until one day (the very day we planned to meet) her face exploded in my mind, and that was a sign not to meet her. The universe sends signals.

Lady Mist lit a candle and placed it on the table. I melted into the room. I started feeling more comfortable. I took my mind off everything else. Lady Mist looked different in this light. Her face was ashen, her smile gone. "What are you doing?" I asked her.

"Don't you believe in manipulating events here in the earthly sphere?"

"Others have written spells on my behalf, if that's where you're going," I said. "I've tried to practice them. I don't have a knack."

"That's what you think," she said. "You're blushing. Let's go ahead and establish further contact with a Tarot reading, for starters." Maybe I was blushing, but she had that same, blank expression.

I sat at the table. I needed whiskey, but I was ready for all her sideways comments. I'm sure she had many soldier-clients. It was the way she was looking down at me, despite that she was so young. I was ready for all her experiments. If she started levitating, I was ready. I cleared my mind. She spread nine cards on the table: eight in a diamond formation, with one card in the middle. She started turning over the cards. She explained the significance of each one.

"Why are you running?" she said.

"I'm not running," I said. I couldn't read her the way she was reading me, despite my psychic nature, and it bothered me.

"Demons are chasing you," she said. "I mean that literally, and I think you know exactly what I mean. They visit you night and day."

You're not the kind of person I'm going to vent my terrors to, LM. She turned over another card. An electric-blue spark struck my cheek. On the card was a picture of a burning tower, with a figure in free fall next to it. "None of this is looking good," Lady Mist said. She started whispering. She looked away. She saw something or someone, but I saw nothing.

"Who are you talking to?" I said.

"My spiritual coach. Her name is Dove." Lady Mist's voice was calm and sure.

"Was Dove a living person at some point?"

"You see, I knew you know what I've been talking about."
Lady Mist took a deep breath. Her breasts heaved. "You asked
the right question. Dove was my grannie. She's been in heaven
for three years, but she visits me whenever I ask her to. I was
with her when she passed. Her skin lost all color in seconds."
Lady Mist went off to some dreamy place. She paced around
the room.

"Does she visit you when you don't want her to visit?"

"She is responsible for all the bumps in the night." Lady
Mist's eyes were so sincere. Those bumps in the night gave her
total freedom, I just knew.

Since she opened up, I decided to reveal more. I stood up.
"One more bump in the night and I will flip out," I said.

"Do you mean it this time?" She held my hands. Her face
twitched. She was linking up with all her witch sisters on the
astral plane, learning whatever she could about me. Her
mouth was agape. I just knew she wasn't going to figure out
anything good.

I unleashed some whiskey talk. "There are ghosts in my
house. They are playful for now but are becoming more
ruthless."

"I can help," said Lady Mist. She pointed at the cards.
"Let's sit down."

Her eyes were glossy. Full circle, we went back to being
bashful. "Ok," I said. We sat down at the table.

"I have my own night visitors," she said. "You're not done
telling me about yours."

I continued: "They keep finding me. It's because..."

"It's because of your powers. I don't know you, but you're
going from one war to another."

"I volunteered to go to Afghanistan, you know. Am I
running away from something?"

Lady Mist turned over the eighth card: a picture of an old
man, but the card was inverted, not a good sign.

"He looks wise," I said, "and don't say he looks like me."

She didn't laugh. "He's a prophet," she said, "but in this case, he doesn't have good news. Whatever happens next, it's not my fault." She turned over the last card: a picture of a magician standing behind a table. He was wearing a flowing red robe, and in his raised hand was a wand. On the table were a sword and golden cup and other magical tools.

"What's wrong?" I said. "It's fine."

"You shouldn't have followed me back here," said Lady Mist. "You shouldn't have come here at all." She started crying. "Don't be mad at me," she said. She stood and backed away from the table. Then I understood. The card was upside down. "I'm sorry you found me. Just leave. Go where you need to go and come see me when you're back in Georgia. Please, do that. That way I'll feel better knowing I was wrong."

"About what?" I said.

"About everything."

"I'm not going to get into trouble," I said with a lump in my throat.

"Trouble will find you," she said. She left the room.

I looked for Lady Mist in the bar, but she was gone. I looked up at the moon while walking back to Ft. Benning. My heart was pumping, struggling with counter-currents of awe, fear, more than fear: terror. A cool wind washed over me, through me, like a liquid omen. I could hear distant thunder. It was a sign of a great storm brewing in the future. It was both a big, fat fuse and a portal for personal exploration and growth, not just my own. *I forgot to tell you, LM, that I stole your magician card. No, I'm just borrowing it, only for a bit. I'll return it one day. I promise.*

TURN ON
THE LIGHTS

The inbound terminal at Kandahar Airfield looked like the Alamo, with bullet holes all over the walls, inside and outside. Two soldiers were waiting for me. Major Twigg was tall and skinny, while Chief Snow was shorter, closer to my size. I was so tired I nearly passed out during the welcome briefing. The main message during the briefing was how to react to a rocket attack. Everyone had to practice by lying face down on the floor, stretched out, with arms covering face and head to protect themselves from flying debris. After the briefing, Snow and Twigg threw my bags into a little truck and drove me to the transient tent. Major Twigg said I had some time to rest and clean up before reporting to work. I was sure I had seen him before, but I couldn't figure out when and where. This is not uncommon for military personnel.

"You're a pinup boy, captain," said Twigg. "Look at that perfect haircut." I thought it was an odd thing to say, and it was quite a coincidence. It was the second time in two months that someone complimented my hair. The first was a crazy lady in front of the civil courthouse in downtown Houston. She told me I looked like a Nazi. She asked me how many lives I had destroyed that day. She told me to say hello to Hitler. Then she said I had a cute haircut. It was the first time since junior high anyone said such a thing to me. Snow and Twigg knew something I didn't. I kept quiet. They had several months of experience in this place, and I didn't.

They dropped me off at the transient tent. I pulled aside the outer canvas flap and entered the transient tent, dragging my duffle bags. It was totally dark. I had my flashlight handy and stumbled along and tried to be quiet. I could hear others stirring and snoring. From the amount of all those intersecting sounds, I could tell the place was huge, with hundreds of bunks. I could hear errant laughter somewhere in the back of the tent. The sound of those amused ghosts echoed. They stood out in my mind. I can't forget the sleazy smell of all those men. I found an empty cot and dropped my gear next to it and opened a bag and pulled out my sleeping bag and spread it out and crashed. I fell asleep right away and slept harder than I had in a long while, and when I woke up the ceiling lights were on and I was able to see the true size of the place. It was as vast as it sounded in the dark, with row after row of metal bunks. The two seconds it took me to remember where I was felt like ages. I was on a beach. I was in space. I felt so lost and free, without the dense fear of the unpredictable perils ahead. That shrill bugle call was coming.

Two soldiers were playing cards in the next bunk. "Did your mother teach you that trick?" one of them said. "No," said his buddy, "yours did. Right after I nailed her." I reached down and felt for my wallet in my back pocket. It was the gut-flinch reaction of a man who's awakened in too many strange and questionable corners of the world. My M9 was where it was supposed to be: touching my skin. I didn't have a name for the weapon. At Ft. Huachuca I named my assigned weapon Baba, which in Russian means "peasant woman." I pulled my sleeping bag over my face to block the harsh light, the harsh sight, and I slept for another hour, and when I woke up one of the card players was still there, a private named Derringer. He was from Cleveland. "I better not be in here much longer," he said. "My tent caught fire while I was sleeping off my night gate duty, and I was the only one inside. I was having a nice dream about being at a cookout with my girl back home in the park, and then I smelled smoke and it wasn't from meat cooking. It was my tent cooking. I jumped out of bed and grabbed my blanket and ran outside and started beating on my tent to put out the fire, but it was too late, so I went back inside and saved whatever I could. I don't know how it started. Maybe it was the Taliban. There are Taliban on this base. Could be the man who sells you a rug on the boardwalk, or it could be the man who cleans your toilet. They're watching your movements. They watch how traffic moves. They come up to you and say they're your friends, but they're not your friends. Then they go home at night and tell their buddies where to aim their rockets but thank Jesus they can't aim for shit. If I ever see one of those guys taking a picture of anything on this base, I will take his camera and beat him with it. I know you're a captain, and I'm just a private, but you just remember, Sir: You just never know who's thinking about killing you behind that smile. When I leave here, I'm going to follow in my grandfather's steps and become a preacher. This place has made me a believer." Not the last time I heard such a comment. Derringer fashioned his arms into a cross, as if he was trying to block something.

I nodded. "Exactly," we both said at the same time. I snapped my fingers.

A young man sat down next to Derringer. "You new here, Sir?"

"Don't poison the captain's mind, Louv. Here it comes, Sir. Get ready."

"There's tunnels beneath this place," said Louv. "You can hide down there. You can do anything you want. There's a whole world underground." I must've been giving him a look, because he said, "Not that I would go down there and hide. There's plenty to do up here in the real world. I don't even know where to go to find the tunnels. Honest. Don't look at me. No, Sir. I'm just saying this base is huge, and there's a whole other world. But you look like you could find them, Sir. You have that sophisticated look."

"Let the captain do his business," said Derringer. "I'm sorry about Private Louv, Sir. He's just getting wound up." Derringer reached over and delivered a fake punch to my stomach. This woke me up. I was high-speed. I punched him back, a little too hard, maybe. Derringer was sort of a composite of two guys I knew in basic training, just five years earlier. Sometimes I missed being an enlisted soldier. I wasn't young then. I turned thirty-three my third week of basic. I wasn't the oldest in my group, though. Less than two years later, I got a direct commission as an officer. As I often say: the Army didn't make me a man, but it made me a better man.

I watched Louv and Derringer and others in the transient tent. I kept thinking of basic training. I'd kept up with a few of the guys and through them heard horrible stories about some of the others. I laid on the bed and closed my eyes. I thought of what the war would be like for me. It was before me like a wall of smoke. I pulled out the magician card I'd taken from LM. I studied it, performed a concentration exercise where you slowly scan narrow sections top to bottom then shut your eyes and redraw the card in your mind, to build memory. Going in reverse, I redrew the card, starting with the table and the magical tools, proceeding right to left, then left to right, the robed man filling in the scene. When I got to his face I started to feel dizzy. I took deep breaths. I could feel the cool air outside, hear jets and helicopters taking off and landing. The next moment I was flying among them, but not by choice. Then I was in the bar in Georgia. *Are you bringing me back so soon, LM?*

Sitting at the bar was Wilson, a man I knew in basic training. He was twenty-five but looked forty. He was out of shape. He couldn't run or even do five pushups. I didn't like the guy. We all suffered because of him. He saw me enter the bar. He nodded at the stool next to him. I just stood next to him. I didn't sit. He looked at me without speaking, though I could hear what he once told our drill sergeant, that his unit was going to Iraq, but he was a trucker and wouldn't be fighting. Drill sergeant laughed and said truckers were getting killed all the time in Iraq by IEDs and ambushes. Wilson's eyes got big and his face turned pale. Years later I heard that Wilson was killed in Iraq, two weeks before he was supposed to end his tour, on his last long-haul mission. An IED exploded under the cab of his truck, right beneath where he was sitting. The blast-force shot straight up through the cab, incinerating everything. All they found was his headless torso, sizzling. Because he was wearing body armor, his torso was intact. Everything else was gone.

KAF

Kandahar Airfield was a massive complex heartbreakingly stranded in the desert of southern Afghanistan, south of Kandahar City. It resembled a wooden boomtown out of the American Old West, with rows and rows of metal Conex shipping containers and tents, big and small, and thick blast walls everywhere. The military complex grew out and far beyond the old international terminal, built in 1962 by the United States. It was home to more than ten thousand people. When I learned that the base was situated in a flood plain, I prayed I would never see rain, and I didn't for a while. The weather was dull at first. The sunlight was dull. From the looks of it, it could've been really cold or really hot, but it was neither. It felt like southern California, but the stink of raw sewage and warfighting human beings took some getting used to. Every odor was full and crept in from everywhere. A sickly shade of beige touched everything in Afghanistan. Even on a clear, sunny day, the sky was more brown than blue, with all the dust that stirred and covered everything, inside/outside. I could cup my hands and let it pile like falling snow.

It was my first day in Afghanistan, and I already missed Lieutenant Colonel Maddox, a man I'd only talked to a few minutes here and there. He was supposed to arrive in Kandahar any day, so he told me in Kuwait. He had been to Afghanistan more than once. He said he was an advisor assigned to a reconstruction team. We were under the same command. He wasn't straight with me about his work history. I could tell he was holding back and tweaking information. He'd probably killed more people than cancer, though I didn't ask for specifics. He didn't seem malignant or cold-blooded, but his eyes said it all. He spit a little when he talked, and his lips quivered when he wasn't talking. He could get to talking pretty fast.

When I met Maddox in Kuwait, he seemed happy with his place in the world and in war. He walked with his head high as if he possessed some secret knowledge. He talked to me the way a teacher would. He was not very charismatic, but he had a dark side that could draw you in. In war, he would make a confident companion and confidant, but outside the walls of war, he would have no star power. This was my initial impression.

In Kuwait, I asked Maddox what it was like being under fire for the first time. He looked beyond me. His eyes were livid. "Any description I can offer would be hopelessly inadequate, maybe inappropriate. Whether it's the first time or the hundredth time, it gives the same rush, like shooting heroin, and that's one reason why these young soldiers keep coming back for more and more. It exorcizes all your fears and failures, puts them before you so that you have to deal with them. You have no choice. Any small obstacle in your mind becomes a demon. I've looked into the face of evil many times, and by now that face is familiar to me. Anytime you leave the wire you feel, in this sequence, large butterflies, then your stomach will ache, then you may throw up, and that's ok. It's normal. You wipe your mouth on your sleeve then do your job. You'll get focused, and quick. You are weapons hot, red. You are hunting and being hunted, and that brings an intense feeling. You want to be objective-oriented. Kill before being killed, because if you don't you won't reach your objective. And remember: A sense of poised insanity can help keep you alive.

Learn to walk the fine line between calm serenity and panic."

He smiled, entertained by his own story and glad to cause some fear. At that moment I saw that, like all men, he was on the lunatic fringe, and the voice of the devil was never far behind his own. He was grim, like me. Maybe he had a magician card, like me.

I had a few hours before I had to report to HQ. I left my bags at the transient tent and explored KAF. I walked down a busy road. The road curved. There was a berm to the right. I climbed the berm and before me was a foamy brown disc bigger than a couple of football fields side by side: the poo pond. The color was more disturbing than the smell. I wanted to draw my weapon. God only knows what monsters were lurking in there. No one else was around to ask questions about the pond's origin or its future. It was just little me. I was shocked when I later learned that a Special Forces soldier swam in the poo pond on a dare. It was just another urban legend, probably. It was a poetic moment for me, standing on the edge of doom, gazing out at a toxic nightmare.

I walked to the boardwalk, the large square complex of shops and food stands. I passed a long line of vendors, hawking all sorts of things. An Afghan man tried to sell me the pubic hair of a virgin, with the assurance that it would protect me from harm in battle. He waved a little plastic bag in front of my face. "You will see, you will see," he said. I said thanks but no thanks. I found Tam Tam, a hole of a place, but they had good kabob and other local dishes. It was a good place. I ended up going there often. The owner was a young guy named Gul. He was a good cook and was just a genuine guy. After my meal, the incoming fire alarm sounded. I hit the deck and covered my face, just like I was taught. I heard the high pitch of a rocket flying above my position. It fell a couple of blocks away. It sounded like a car crash. I felt a thud. I got up and found a concrete bunker behind the boardwalk and stayed put until the all-clear siren.

"The rockets are supersonic," said Maddox one night back in Kuwait. "That means they travel faster than the sound they make, which means that if a rocket finds you, you'll be dead before you hear it coming." Maddox explained how the bad guys would put a block of ice on a trigger mechanism, and the ice would melt and release the trigger, so when the rocket fired the bad guys were long gone. That was just one of their many murderous tricks.

Maddox told me about one of his buddies who was lying on his cot in his tent in Iraq, and the guy sat up and took off his shirt and stretched, then he laid down again and started reading a book, and a rocket burst through the side of his tent to his right. It flew over him, so close that one of the rocket's pylons sliced across his stomach. The rocket went out the other side of the tent and into another tent and exploded, killing a sleeping soldier. Or his story of finding a friend with his hands and feet cut off, next to several others who suffered the same fate. While he told the story, I thought it must have been in Iraq, but Maddox said it happened outside of Las Vegas, Nevada.

Maddox's stories seemed random, but they weren't. They were proof. They provided a glimpse of what I was about to experience in Afghanistan. I could feel it. All the beige (and the big brown pool) was a first proof: proof of nature's inertia, proof of structure, even in war. I walked back to the poo pond. I wanted to get a last look. I knew my tour was going to fly by and I wouldn't be back that way. It doesn't smell so bad when you're standing on the shore. I kept an aerial photograph of the base pinned to the wall near my desk at the office. The pond was pleasant to look at, from above. It was a pleasant shape, a perfect circle.

A shape of energy itself was forming in my mind, behind sharp, sudden headaches. *Maybe I've tried to do too much, too soon, psychically, LM. I'm fresh off the plane, and I've got this card in my chest pocket, and the headaches aren't because of you. They're left over from the wine-drunk afternoon weeks ago when I agreed to this crazy mission.* Standing on the shore of the poo pond, I needed something less real. I felt like an interloper, soon to animate, waiting for the rapid sequence of my next instructions. It would've been nice to have a blueprint. I just wanted to know that at the end of it all I would have some memories and dreams. *Maybe I should have thought all this out, LM. So soon, reality does not feel all that real. The wall between illusion and reality is more of a curtain.* Day by day, that was the basic theme I grasped. You may have two sets of people, two sets of situations, sides that oppose each other. Their aims and values are mutually exclusive, but it is necessary to explain both and view both objectively, in order to fully describe the battlefield, whatever the battlefield might be, whether a physical place or just behaviors that yield images and patterns that play out together.

Everyone hated the pond. They wanted it gone like they wanted to be gone and back home with their families, but I saw the pond as a necessary poison. The smell was part of my communion with reality. For what it was, the size of the pond was unreal, like it was all that was left of some prehistoric crime scene, dinosaurs buried beneath the toxic desert. I squatted on the shore. What a place. In a way, the poo pond was the first monster I encountered on my tour.

MAJOR
PAULSEN

One day, Major Paulsen disappeared. Then I appeared.

On the north side of the RC South headquarters complex was a line of shacks. The one at the end of the row was my office. Major Twigg guided me there. I must not have looked too happy. "There will be light at the end of all this," said Twigg. He gave me my key to the shack. I found a couple of chairs and set them outside my door, creating sort of a front porch.

Twigg was on the right track. He wanted me to achieve a certain frame of mind in that little shack. He wanted to set me up for success instead of throwing me into a romper room of nation-building/career-building field-grades. Twigg worked around the corner of a line of T-walls and down at the far end of shacks and concrete bunkers. He took himself a little too seriously, though.

"I'll have some follow-up to all that work," Twigg said, pointing at the stack on my desk. He gave me a crazy look and left me alone.

Specialist Henry showed up shortly after Twigg left. Henry was baby-faced. He was tasked with helping me set up my office. Henry brought me a pile of papers and files to add to what was already waiting for me.

"What's that?" I said.

"These papers belonged to Major Paulsen, who worked in here before you. When he left he gave them to us. He was working on something."

"He left in the middle of something big?"

"He went home suddenly. I heard he was fired."

"Why?"

"You'd have to ask Major Twigg, Sir. I don't know."

Henry left me alone.

I found printed emails in a folder. I read each one. Some were love letters to his wife. I didn't find any replies, but I found other emails that talked about her death. I had to read through the emails twice to figure out it was the same woman. Paulsen didn't reveal much about what he was doing, but there was a certain sinister undertone in his words. He was a decent sketch artist, as well. He left more than mere doodles. There were drawings clipped to map fragments.

Major Twigg was a rage monkey. I learned this with time. He had this rage style. I could see him getting crosswise with Paulsen. I didn't see this at first, except in the way he smiled at me after he gave me the key to my shack. He had a string of secrets, I was sure. He hadn't told me a thing about the dark side of my mission. I was picking that up in piecemeal fashion, through hearsay and wicked little crumbs of information.

THE
UNDEAD

I couldn't sleep the night before my first mission. Around 0300 hours I got out of bed and dressed and left my shack and went for a walk. I had a flashlight, but I didn't need it. The moon was high and bright. There were just two clouds in the sky. They changed shape at a seemingly impossible rate, reaching out to each other like lovers being ripped apart. Perhaps that picture was on my mind because earlier I overheard a soldier talking to his girlfriend back home, saying that he wished he could be there to look after her. He said they were a great team and were meant to always be together. I stopped listening. I felt like a thief or snitch.

I walked toward Little Romania, where there was a little church standing out among the field of tents. The church had once stood in Romania and was brought here in pieces. Whoever put it there had a great idea, and I applaud the mutineer, a real dreamer of angels in faraway skies. Whoever it was, they weren't a big fan of war or KAF. I was drawn to the church like a jewel. It was a tiny anomaly, like me.

I moved with the kind of stealthy velocity you only have at night. I felt a psychic tug. I turned a corner and passed a long row of MRAP vehicles. At the end of the row in a patchwork of shadows were three people. All I could make out were the outlines of their bodies and the whites of their eyes. They saw me but said nothing. Their sex and age were indeterminate. I stepped closer. Their skin was gray. They were pre-human, reptilian, but this was their turf. They would be lesser creatures in the daylight, just as the undead. It doesn't take an out of body experience to understand the material world we see is just one of many.

I was in San Francisco again, 1998, at the end of Pier One near Fort Mason, where I encountered the same group of subterranean escapees at midnight. They followed me through time and around the world, those gloomy night staffers. I made it out of the San Francisco encounter alive, only to witness the aftermath of a murder in North Beach the next night, one of the simplest and most gruesome deaths I've seen to this day. I walked out of a shop and found an Asian kid with his head blown apart, his brains and blood too bright pink to be real, and for a few seconds, I floated above him, the only one who knew anything, the only one in the world. I whispered to him that everything was going to be ok.

I wasn't so sure of my chances to escape this Kandahar reunion with what I feared to be a dangerous crew. I had heard about the population of homeless people that roamed the base, people who had come to KAF making one last, desperate reach for some opportunity in life. The kind of opportunity that only war can bring...the same reason I went to Afghanistan, except they had already seen what was beyond the fourth wall. Not me. But I was ready for these creatures. I wasn't just a casual student of various martial art systems. Krav Maga. Kung Fu. Karate. I considered them as one deadly self-defense system. When in that world, I moved freely, as if I was flying.

Fears and memories were piling, copulating as they tend to do, but I was in the moment. I pulled my M9. My training kicked in, and I became mission-ready. I remembered everything Maddox told me. His lecture on carnage was brief, but I got the gist. I was ready to go in for the cold kill on those weird little ghosts, just as those ghosts could've killed me back in '98. *LM, I am not about to go my own way and let them go theirs. I love the world, but these creatures are not of this world. Protect me from their evil eyes.* Those thoughts stirred, from the lowest tier to the highest. They bloomed, like a disease. They grew exponentially.

A siren blasted. It was close, much louder than what I could hear where I was living. Those poor, sleeping Romanians. It was another rocket attack. I scrambled for shelter, but my new friends didn't join me. They bunched together. I don't remember their faces well. They are shards, like those '98 ghosts. They kept coming at me in new ways. They were the undead. After this encounter, I started carrying LM's magician card with me all the time to counter the alternate forms of darkness descending with speed in my life.

MISSION ALPHA

I barely got any sleep. My shack mates were all up before me. I didn't tell them I was leaving the wire. They did it all the time. I rolled out with Major Twigg and a civil affairs unit in a six-vehicle convoy. No one spoke of the rocket attack during the night. It was as if it never happened. I learned the reason for this was the frequency of rocket attacks, so they weren't much to talk about unless someone was killed.

We took the A75 north toward Kandahar City, then east on the A1, Afghanistan's "Highway to Hell," a frequently ambushed road. After a few clicks, we exited onto an unpaved road. Every bump made me jump, inside and outside. I had no desire to look out of the tiny windows of the MRAP. The world outside was all sludge, and I felt like staying put. I felt safe with my brothers, crammed together, with all the swarming ants outside.

We went to a village ten clicks east of KC. It was a pleasant day, the kind of day you'd want to spend at the beach or hiking. Our destination was a single-room mud hut. When we got out of our vehicles, people were standing around watching us. I thought, what was a kid's real chance to get out of a place like this? I had a quick vision of those people, splayed out and bloodied. I tapped my brow like the vision was evidence of a glitch in my brain. Only a few of us went inside the hut.

Everyone else pulled security or distributed chocolate to kids. Inside the hut, four men were flanking their elder, a man named Hafez. His men didn't say much. He did all the talking. We sat on the floor and drank tea. A young man passed around a plate of almonds and grapes. Hafez and Twigg talked like old friends. Twigg had been in theater eight months. He was already talking about his next assignment at the Pentagon. He introduced me as the new guy in town, but he touted all my experience. "Man of the people," laughed Hafez. His eyes gleamed cold. "I like America," he kept saying. His smile was cold. It gave me hope to hear his enthusiasm after so many years of war, and Hafez had probably been dealing with different Army people year after year about the same issues: services for the population, supplies for families, medicine, and the Taliban. The room darkened as Hafez described one particular man:

"Abdul Gulzar Malak was among the first Taliban. He killed my cousin and raped his daughters. He took my cousin's house and used it as his own. He let all his men use it when he was not present. He speaks five languages. He works with Iranians. I do not have the proof to show you, but I know it." Major Twigg nodded in agreement. "You must trust me. Look at his face, and you will know fear. Look at his eyes. They are black. His heart is black. He is an evil man, Captain Jett. When I last saw him, he threatened to torture our people if we worked with Americans, and while I am afraid of him and know he will go through with his threats, I am more afraid of the dark future for my children if this man and his kind are not driven from this land. The Taliban are foreigners, like you, but they are not helping us, and you are, and that is why am telling you these things, but you must trust me."

Major Twigg kept nodding. I nodded along with him.

"But there is more," said Hafez. "I do not want to scare you. I have said enough for today."

Twigg had heard all this before. The old man was

repeating it for my sake. "We must trust each other," said Twigg. Hafez and Twigg laughed.

Several boys were peaking at us through a window, but I felt like I was being watched by something more sinister. On the way back to base I studied a map of the area. "Let me see that," said Twigg. The MRAP bounced. The road was so bumpy. Twigg grabbed the map. "We're visiting towns all around here," he said, drawing a half-moon. "But right around there is what the villagers are talking about."

"Is that what the old man was talking about? He said there is more."

"There's a possible connection," said Twigg. "For now, I just want to stay focused on this place." He pointed at the map again.

"What is it?"

"That's the heart of darkness," Twigg said, making a not-so-subtle literary reference as he brushed his finger over a circle drawn near the Arghandab River. "We believe Mars Station is around here."

After we got back to base, I assisted Major Twigg with the After Action Report for the day's mission. I asked him about Mars Station. "We aren't sure where it is," he said, "but it's a nest of Taliban and death."

"That's your theory?"

"It's more than a theory," said Twigg. "Our intelligence says it's a weapons production site surrounded by bombs and full of tunnels. It's a place where the Taliban take civilians for torture and killing, and we suspect it's where the Taliban have taken some of our own personnel. I think there's more to it than that. Maybe I've been in this country too long." Twigg meant it. I could feel his inner heat.

"Where is our information coming from?"

"You're asking the wrong guy. I'm not in that business. Maybe Colonel Maddox can fill us both in when he gets here. It's why he's coming."

"But there's more, Sir, like the old man said."

"Yeah, but I don't understand what it might be," said Twigg. "That's where you come in."

Maddox discussed none of this when I met him in Kuwait.

.

MEGALITHS

I was drawn to a cluster of ten-foot blast walls arranged in a clumsy formation down the road from my shack at KAF. In a couple of hundred years, the blast walls will stand out as the only things left to mark the American presence in Afghanistan. It was my first day outside the wire, and at the end of the day, I was in a dark, lonely place, feeling more like a cutout image of a man than a real man, as if I was acting out a part in a play, except I felt like an interloper among the rest of the players, including all the villagers I encountered, and especially the children. They were welcoming, but it did not feel right to feel welcome. Twigg's tease at the end of the mission got me thinking, which was the point. And I could get some thinking done in the shadows of those walls, how they loomed like megaliths in a Scottish moor. Their extreme geometry, their ninety degrees of presence, testosterone flushed in cold stone. For me, the blast walls were symbols of the false structure of war, like a house of cards. We live in a house of cards, and despite all man's efforts, and certainly despite the digitization of our culture and our politics and our wars, our footprint will be revealed by an archaeologist's spade, and what will that person say?

That night I dreamed I was walking behind a captain who was leading a patrol of two fire teams. They had just left their FOB and were passing a line of blast walls. The soldiers were taking baby steps, going lightly across the wide field, which had been well-engineered. All the trees and brush had been bulldozed in order to create a spacious field of fire. I was talking to another soldier, telling him about my recent training in karate, how I was starting to learn more advanced techniques, getting into free-form fighting and five-step combinations. An RPG shot through the air launched from the distant tree line. I saw the round moving in slow motion, as a bug would see it. My field of vision was more than human. I could see in all directions. Neon light trailed the grenade.

The grenade caught the captain on its downward trajectory. In the dream, he kept talking. The round cut across his shoulder then tore through a soldier a few feet behind him. It exploded as it tore the kid in half. The blast wall behind him was painted red with blood and smashed with tissue, and with gravity working the way it ought to, all the bloody bits tumbled down, down, down.

The next morning I found the religious center. It looked like any other shack. Inside was one, big room. On the far side of the room was a balding British officer. I had already learned which country was which from the camouflage patterns on their uniforms. His sleeves were rolled up, like all the Brits, which was not something the U.S. Army did. Though balding, he had a good amount of hair in the horseshoe. His face was so pale, bright. He didn't look like he'd been in the desert long.

The chaplain stood and greeted me. "I'm Major Nichols," he said. I didn't go straight to him. I checked out the literature spread out on the small table up front. There were several Bibles and prayer booklets, along with a Koran and even a copy of the Bhagavad Gita. Next to the table was a cart of books. There were all kinds of titles, a couple of western novels and odd, old sci-fi works. I found candy: twenty, thirty martial arts books and magazines.

"What sad soul left these?" I said.

"Those were here before I arrived," said Major Nichols.

"You're probably wondering what I'm doing here," I said.

"Not at all. Make yourself at home. The books are for taking. Please."

"Where's home for you, Sir?"

"Manchester, England."

I chuckled. "Let me tell you about a weekend I had in Manchester, Sir."

"Do I want to hear this, young captain?"

"Of course you do." I grabbed a few martial arts books and sat at the table.

The story involved a weekend with a witch in 1997. She taught me about seeing into the spirit world and being seen by other spirits, even if it meant them poking a little fun at me. Manchester was a decent place for such an encounter, and lots of fun people came in and out of her flat. She had some witch friends, and she had crazy ideas for crazy concoctions, "and spit works fine for lots of spells," she said. It was April. It was gloomy. The more I talked about Manchester, the more shocked Nichols was. I pointed out many of things about his town that apparently he didn't know about.

MATTER

One day I started writing a letter to Lady Mist back in Georgia:

Lady M, There was very little you could've done to help me prepare for this place. Don't try to contact me. Let me do the talking. Everyone walks around with dazed looks. I'm one of them, but my command gave me a big mission. I can't say much about all that. It involves some people I don't know much about. So for now they just live in my imagination. It's easy as that. God help them. How are you, my witch? I could use your help. I thought it might be ok to write you. You didn't seem totally repelled by me, or anything. Some are. It's understandable. Wish you could be more than just a memory, but there's distance between us. I know you must help lots of soldiers, but have you ever found yourself in the same mess as them/us? Probably not. Some guy told me the other day that the angel of death appeared before him but kept moving. He was sure the angel came for him, he said. He said he felt like he was next. He said he was ready. He laughed. He was a charmed guy. Charmed by whatever would not get in the way of him going home in one piece, but I didn't have the heart to tell him that he was marked for death, in my eyes. It was his aura.
  I wish I would've run into you back in early 2007 before I joined the Army. Maybe I did. Was that you painted on the wall

near Wall Street? You looked good, but you didn't say much. I gave you a good, long look, from painted feet to painted lips. You could've shown me the ways of the world.

Maybe that's when this soup started, when I sparked to life, not by a lightning bolt or a bolt of luck, but from merely positioning myself within entropy's path, to be swept away by it, transformed by it. Like a plant...or any lifeform with an external source of energy...once placed in this confined environment of pure conflict, my whole being was restructured, and I became a different form of matter, with a new swagger, rejuvenated, Captain Jett 2.0 so to speak...not a slave to it, no way.

My head hurts. I can't tell you why. I'm not getting enough sleep. Or it's a headache from the future, a portent. I can tell you that it feels right, that I am on the right path. Was this the path you predicted or intended? You might direct some psychic energy my way, and I will do the same toward you. Don't be surprised if we bump into each other on the astral plane. Or just write. I would like to get a real letter, not an email. Can you make that tiny-tiny adjustment?

Each day here feels like a surprise. I wish I had the psychic power to go back to where it all started: fourteen billion years ago when matter formed. It was all some higher entity's dream. Higher than what? Or lower than what? I believe our universe is a piece of a bigger picture.

It troubles me that I can't go back to beginning times, hundreds of thousands of years after time itself began, back to the time of the first atoms. It troubles me that I won't ever know what will become of all this. I believe it will all dwindle back to the nothingness where it started, and that is where God can be found. So in order to find God, we should be looking forward to where we're going, and not backward to the beginning. God is in the game. God is the devourer and the devoured. Comments? Suggestions? Fire away.

YVONNE

There were a couple of barbershops near headquarters, one on the main boardwalk, another was in a sad little two-story building behind the boardwalk. The shop was downstairs. The barbers were either Russian or Cambodian. We were together in this mess, old Cold War buddies in a disturbing little scheme.

I got a cut from a Russian woman. She was in her mid-twenties and small and slender and wore her hair in a ponytail. I could speak a little Russian, so I made some small talk. Her name was Yvonne.

She blushed. "I will give you a nice Russian haircut, popular with all the boys." She slowed down her work. She took a step back and gave it some thought. She worked her fingers into my skull. I sunk into the seat. She was like me, in an anti-logic place in her life, larking about. "Tell me about America," she said.

"I can tell you about it sometime," I said, "but much of it I've never seen."

"It is like Russia. Most of it I have never seen."

I inhaled the smell of gel and my own sweaty hair from her palms each time they passed my face. I closed my eyes, but I could still see her moving around me. Her aura was yellow, an indication of deep intellect. "Why are you here?" I said.

"For work, of course," she said. "I must survive. Why are

you here?"

"It's complicated. Work, of course." I stopped her from cutting my hair too short. I wanted to return soon. As I was leaving, her aura changed from yellow to crimson.

I still had to stop by the post office and deliver my letter to Lady Mist, and now here she was, a copy of Lady Mist, here at KAF. She was a real angel, a standout among all the strange elements. I told her so: "I had a dream of a mysterious figure with wings. I think it was you."

"Dreams mean your mind is trying to tell you something. Dreams mean you are alive. Dreams can be dark, but you have nothing to fear."

She finished the haircut by leaving the front strands a little longer than the rest. She spiked up the front.

"Now you really look like a boy," Yvonne said.

"I don't know if I like this look," I said. "Time will tell."

"Time tells everything," Yvonne said. "Time will tell if you ever come see me again."

ANTI-MATTER (KA-POW!!!)

Lieutenant Colonel Maddox was just in time for murder and mayhem. Nothing new for him. He would quickly settle into it. His first day in theater was a long, long day. One day was actually two days. Day one started out fine. Even before waking, I carved out my day in my dreams: generic scenes of war coupled with the surreal and unexpected. This was war.

I had slept in my clothes again. My clothes were stiff with sweat. I was so dirty, just from being out in the world, the hidden world I'm attracted to, the one that landed me in Afghanistan. But I did an about-face in my dreams. I decided that I was going to let my hair grow out as long as I could get away with it. It was a grand plan: I was going to just cruise by the barbershop regularly and show Yvonne everything she was missing, while wiping away my long bangs.

When I woke up, my shack mate, Lieutenant Patrick "Patty" Vavak, was shaving. I didn't like him shaving in our room. The latrine was down the hall. Patty had a wild look that morning. He confided in me that he had a bad dream in which dead bodies were asking for help.

Since the murder and mayhem happened the same day Patty told me about his bad dream, I've always associated those first memories of the murders with Patty. His big phrase was "ka-pow." He said "ka-pow" after each little story. He said "ka-pow" after telling me about the dream. Patty was connected to lots of recent upper-echelon actions, or so he said. Maybe I would've been closer to him instead of Maddox if Maddox didn't take me under his wing.

When I showed up at my office, I received an incident report that almost made me lose the Luxembourg DFAC breakfast I'd just eaten: eggs and fried toast and stewed tomatoes and baked beans. Thirty clicks west, in a village now dubbed Sugarbush, since the recent trend was code-naming hot spots after American ski resorts, village elders were reporting at least thirty deaths. It was an estimate, based on dismembered limbs, and, in some cases, torsos, with equal numbers of men, women, and children. The elders reported seeing wraithlike shadows and hearing things that weren't human. I attended a briefing with Division-level leadership. Twigg was at the briefing. "Welcome to your mission," he said. He assigned me to the investigative team. I rushed back to my shack and grabbed my gear and double-timed to the airstrip.

Maddox was underneath a tent with a few others, waiting for a Black Hawk. When I saw him, I felt better right away. Maddox saw me and waved. There were other soldiers between us. There were a couple of full-bird colonels, along with plenty of captains to carry the load. The flight line was too loud for any conversation. Maddox was wearing aviator sunglasses, so the glint in his eye didn't show, but there was his smile, and his prickly voice was in my head, from memory. While I should've been trying to enjoy my first helicopter ride over the white-slime desert, Maddox's Kuwait babel was in my mind.

The landscape below was smooth at first, then turned to mountains, and we crossed over those mountains and hit some more nameless mountains. I was disoriented. Maddox was moving his mouth. Piles of dead people weren't going to bother him. No way. I don't know who he was talking to. Probably himself. I later asked Maddox why he was in such a giddy mood that day, despite the murders. He explained that it had to do with his car getting stolen and held for ransom by a gang in Amman, Jordan: "We played nice with the guys at first. They didn't know who we were. Turns out some police were even helping them. The police didn't know who we were, either. It turned out to be a bad day for all of them. The car turned up just fine." Maddox spoke softly when he spoke of the misfortune of others. Feral sounds punctuated his comments. I've seen how people make adjustments for their psychopathy, and he fits the mold.

The LZ was well away from central Sugarbush. At least two squads were pulling security around it. Maddox and I exchanged a few cordial words as if meeting for the first time, then he got down to business, as did I. We went our separate ways, though we soon came together again in Sugarbush. I tried to bring some order and symmetry to the situation, which was coming at me like a strong wind, a new dimension, a new geometry within a previous geometry. There was more to the space before me. Three-dimensional geometric structure couldn't apply to it. This wasn't just a random thought or experience. I was drawn to a certain future coherence, something waiting at the wild edge. Things were happening so fast that I didn't think about a more metaphysical approach, whether an OBE or using the magician card in my pocket to establish some psychic connection.

It was the day I met Kochi, one of the translators recently brought in from Kabul. He was a good kid, glad to be working at all. Kochi and I met with a village elder, then a man named Asad showed us around, but he didn't seem too willing. He looked puzzled and kept looking over at the kids hiding behind the elders and women, but we listened to him because he seemed knowledgeable. Kochi asked him for more details about what happened. Asad's explanation was confounding Kochi. I only understood a few words of Pashto. I understood their body language better.

"This man says a monster did this," said Kochi. "He said the monster terrorized the whole village."

"A monster?" I said.

"A creature of smoke and fire. He grabbed the weakest and the slowest with his giant claws. Then he tore them to pieces. The man said it was..."

"Yes? What was it?"

Kochi had a grave expression. "He said it was a *jinni*."

"What do you mean?"

Before Kochi could explain, Maddox found us. "This way, Captain Jett. Bring your crew." Maddox had already heard the monster story. I followed Maddox to the last house at the end of a row of small mudbrick houses. Maddox pointed out the blood left and right along the way. He didn't talk, just gestured with his hands. Maddox had to lean forward to clear the doorway. Body parts and blood were everywhere. I had a coppery taste in my mouth, just from breathing too deep and fast. My heart was pounding. There was a poster on the wall, a picture of an old woman holding an AK-47. I felt lost.

"Is this real?" I asked Maddox. "Where are their heads?"

Maddox didn't respond. He took a deep breath. "How many?" he asked Asad.

Asad and Kochi were talking. These were their own people, but someone or something outside their sphere was responsible.

My whole life had brought me to this bloody crossroads. I was in the shadow of mystery. I wasn't trying to figure out the impressionistic painting before me, I was thinking about my past, everything that led me to this point.

"Every federal agency except the IRS is going to be here soon," said Maddox, "even some you didn't know existed. We've got guys at every road, keeping any of these people from leaving and keeping any others from coming into town."

Kochi was breathing normally, but I knew he had come

face to face with a curse. Here we were in the same situation: what was out there to destroy, and how would we destroy it? Kochi was a sensitive kid. He had to go outside to vomit. There was even a designated bucket for that, set up and used by locals before we arrived, so as not to taint any other evidence on the ground. I later vomited also, just from getting a whiff of the vomit bucket. Scientists and soldiers and chaplains alike were going to have an interesting time with all this. They were going to get to start from scratch and get un-stuck from their little worlds. Theirs was a false linear approach to an even more false geometry, the three dimensions of length, width, and depth, subject to a fourth dimension of time. The whole 3D world was becoming just a shadow of something else, beyond the fourth wall. Such hostility, yet such harmony. The hostility was a part of the harmony, one required the other. My whole life to this point was based on false hubris, based on an incomplete picture. This whole idea of the fourth wall was something I envisioned, perhaps in a different way, long before then. It may sound odd. I just had some general idea that grew from my previous brushes with the supernatural. How was I supposed to deal with it? How does a man just walk into a new dimension and claim ownership? How does a man face the world of curses? Now I was beginning to see that just to understand the false geometry of this world we can see and touch, to understand and survive the chaos of modern warfare, I would have to cross into a darker place to view what I came from.

Weaving around in all four dimensions, looking for the fifth, and so on and so on, without ever touching, we are energy events, we repel, we do not attract. I did not intend to leave my body, but another power pulled me from myself and into the clouds. I could feel hands upon me, pulling me into space, and then pushing me through the universe. I raced by stars, thousands of them. I could see a thousand instances of this scene at once, like a fly with compound eyes. I'd never had an experience like this. It was not my doing. I stopped moving. I floated a moment, breathing rapidly. A cloud of tiny star-forms was around me, going in and out of my mouth with every breath. My body felt warm inside. I was comfortable, and I soon was breathing normally. Just when I was about to drift to sleep, I was pulled back across space and time into my body.

Kochi joined me. "Are you good, Captain Jett?"

I coughed, releasing a luminous cloud. Kochi saw the sparkling micro-droplets. His eyes grew wide.

I paid attention to the cadence of my breath. I didn't notice how close the mountains were before. They had grown jagged fingers that reached up all around the village like ancient megaliths. Maddox joined Kochi and me. He was smiling, like when we met.

"I told you, Jett," said Maddox. I was still in a daze. Maddox distracted me by showing me pictures of his twin daughters. They had the same icy blue eyes as him.

I saw Patty when I got back to base. I didn't say a word about the murders, but he knew all about it. "Ka-pow!" he said.

I looked at my magician card before going to bed. The lights in the shack were out and Patty was snoring. I didn't need to turn on my flashlight to look at the card. It was covered with a layer of shimmering stars as if all the stars on the other side of the universe I visited were condensed into a few square inches. I dared not dust off the card. I carefully put it in the drawer of my nightstand, next to my M9. From then on, the card would stay as close to me as my M9.

JOHNNY

I had a feeling, backed up by little intel, that the scoundrels who ran Mars Station were involved in the killings. I started asking soldiers whether they'd heard of or visited Mars Station. Most didn't know anything about it. Others heard stories, like me. Lots of shrugging. "It's not the kind of place you just go check out," said one soldier. "It's a black hole, a doorway to hell. Do you want to visit hell?" I thought, Hell must be a neutral place. Everyone's damned with nowhere to go and nothing to do but suffer. One of the soldiers I interviewed was named Johnny. He was a sniper. I only remember his first name because of his dog, which was also named Johnny. It wasn't his own dog, but he gave it a name, anyway.

"When I first saw Johnny he was eating dead flesh," said Johnny. "This was in Kandahar City. The dog went after a man I killed just moments after I killed him. No one else was going toward the body to assist. Nothing to assist. It was a headshot. There was still a firefight going on, but this dog, which had three legs, went into the bullets, and if a round hit near him he paused a second, but then he still went right after the bodies." Johnny said he watched the dog get its fill and move on, but on subsequent overwatch missions in the same area, he saw the same dog. "You couldn't miss this sad-looking beast, because he was king of his little kingdom. So I started calling him Johnny, in my mind. I didn't name him after me. I named him after my father, who lost a leg in Vietnam. Johnny just wobbled along. And then it happened again. I was tracking a target, and I saw Johnny hanging around, and I thought that might be a bad sign that a firefight was coming, and I was right. The target I was tracking went into a two-story building about a hundred meters away. Johnny was pacing back and forth in front of the building. A minute later, our cover was blown and we started taking shots on the rooftop where I was positioned, but whoever was shooting at us was a terrible shot. Nothing was even close, so I crept up on the ledge and took aim at a shadow in a window and pulled off a round and my target went down. I waited a minute for a secondary target, and I noticed that Johnny did, too, and we were both right. Another dark form appeared and started shooting at me, but this time the shots were closer. I waited till the burst of fire was finished. I fired another round and that guy went down. I took a breath because I knew that no one would be stupid enough to pick up their buddy's weapon and start shooting at me, but I was wrong this time. Someone else appeared in the window and started shooting. All the rounds were off. It didn't take long for me to kill the target. I waited for another guy, and so did Johnny, but after a few minutes, I didn't see anything. I packed up my gear and went downstairs and ran to the building. I think I was skipping, actually. I was happy that I got my guy and looking forward to a day off work. When I got to the building, Johnny was gone. Sniper Team Two joined me. We cleared the first floor. When we got upstairs, there was Johnny with his mouth around the neck of a dead teenage boy. The boy looked about fourteen years old. The boy didn't have a chance, thanks to me, so I just watched Johnny nibble, but I couldn't stand to watch the dog eat the boy's face. I had to kill that dog because if I ever saw him again, he would be a living reminder of all this. I missed the first time. He jumped back. I was shaking. I didn't want to kill Johnny. The first time I saw him, I liked him. He was a fighter, a survivor, but I was able to put a round in him before he ran away. Nearby was my first target and another boy about ten. Those boys were my sons' ages. It was like killing my own family, but they were shadows in a window when I shot them. They were shadows who were trying to kill us."

HALLOWEEN
JIFFY POP

I left work early around 2200 hours. Walking back to my shack via the KAF boardwalk, I saw Captain America sitting at a picnic table. He was perched alone, scanning the boardwalk with a tired but determined look, like he had been there all day. He was waiting for someone or something which wasn't going to come. He knew it. It was in his face. I walked by. His costume hung limply upon him. Soldiers and Afghans alike started coming up to him to get their picture with him. But he couldn't fly like me.

"Iron Man was here earlier," an airman said to me. He was black with a slim build and wearing glasses.

"Chase him down. Tell him we need him."

"The name is Nathan Haines."

"Nice to meet you. I'm Jett. And your rank is…" I wasn't familiar with Air Force patches.

"Technical sergeant."

"What brings you here?"

"Right now I'm waiting on a buddy. He's at the boardwalk. This isn't our neighborhood. Air Force is on the other side of the airfield. So if you're ever near Hangar 4D, that's where you'll usually find me."

There were a few Afghans dressed as Mexicans. They wore ponchos and sombreros and fake mustaches over their real ones. It was Mexican theme night at the Luxembourg DFAC a couple of days earlier. They served Mexican pasta and tortilla chips smothered in ballpark Day-Glo orange liquid cheese sauce, alongside dried fruits and nuts and spicy rice pudding, and I enjoyed the meal. These men were still celebrating.

"See you later, Haines." I continued along the boardwalk. A place that was a rug stand the day before was now stocked with costumes. A Harry Potter cloak, red and gold scarf, and everything, was front and center. And then it hit me: it was Halloween. I had forgotten. I had already dismissed Captain America as the cotton candy of war. I continued looking around the store.

"I'll be with you in a jiffy-pop," said the Afghan shopkeeper. A second later he came at me with a grim reaper costume. He stretched out the faux skeleton arms before me. "Here I am," he said. "In a jiffy-pop, like I said, but do not fear me. I am not the devil." He slapped my shoulder with a skeleton arm.

The man wanted me to play, but I didn't want to play. He was going for the sale too hard. He wanted me to follow him into his world. Just that morning, I watched a live video feed of enemy bodies being tossed into the air after successful indirect fire. I didn't want to watch, but I had to.

The man put away the grim reaper costume and came back with another Harry Potter costume, this one was Professor Snape. "You look so serious," he said. "This must be for you." I was not amused.

I gave him three dollars for the costume. He wrote my name down in a book and wrote 'Snape' next to my name. "Put it on," he said. "Put on Snape and become two people."

MOTION DIAGRAMS

All of war's energy behaviors neatly fit into a physics lesson. Perhaps war is best described by chilly lines and formulae. Fear and human invention come together in destructive ways. Even today, I can't visualize war without seeing waves and patterns, a whole matrix of odd elements that come together in a single form, forcing out chaos, replacing it with its own special chaos.

Men set free all types of caged things, in great panic events, with long pauses between, and their flight can be described as points and angles and acceleration, and those points are constantly appearing and disappearing. I started to visualize war as a motion diagram, where the loathsome and the sublime bump and push toward some end. Visualize with me: Every moment is a frame in a film. A man is a dot on that film. He is surrounded by other dots. So many dots, so many vector lines. Every thought and action determines acceleration. Dots collide with the other dots. It is just a matter of time. Time is never on your side. It is the humming of the world. War is proof of frequencies handed down through the ages. War is proof of the integrative forces of the universe, distilled into terrible ecstasies. Listen to all the dark voices.

I hoped to be able to connect the bones of all these disconnected events. I could feel the crunch of constant evolution, with long periods of stillness followed by stress. I started drawing again, inspired by an old girlfriend who liked to draw when she was under stress. I started seeing lines that I'm sure didn't exist. The mind plays tricks. It displays congruence in the universe, and I believe that congruence exists, but it is elusive, despite that it shines like sunshine. Early in my tour, I could visualize being centered and at peace, with the acceleration vectors always pointing directly to the center of a circle, illuminating it. Peaceful existence is a centripetal acceleration. Unfortunately, gravity gets in the way, and we are its slaves. Therefore, there can never be peace, as acceleration vectors pointing straight down demonstrate.

I went to Afghanistan to invent something, to discover universal truths, but I kept finding darkness within darkness. I found things I could never invent, nothing I intended. The fourth time I left the wire, fate found me. Maddox and I ate breakfast that morning at the British DFAC (we usually ate at the Lux). They had some gooseberry cobbler, which we both ate. Maddox was still working on tasks related to Sugarbush. He didn't tell me what he was up to, exactly. He was the one getting to do all the monster hunting. Twigg needed my help doing other things. I was tasked to help deliver supplies somewhere north of the base. I asked Maddox to talk to Twigg about some of my assignments. He said he would. Then he went to his convoy, and I went to mine.

The semi-illusion of my life in that place was just getting started. I was starting to smile, starting to care a little less about every little thing, and just going along. I was still running in circles in my head from a joke I overheard just before we started out. I went over my simple role in the larger mission that day, and it had nothing to do with Sugarbush or Mars Station. We were to maintain good relations with village elders, see who was home, count the children, distribute supplies accordingly, adjust fire as necessary, and scout out a good location for a new school. I'm not sure which direction we were heading, but we turned off a main road to a smaller road, then another small road, like the hand of the Lord was pulling us along. My mind was also on the Sugarbush monster...an idea quickly becoming just another distorted Fourth Wall thing.

Then the whole vehicle crashed in upon itself, right before I heard a boom. Like I was declared to be an intruder upon the world, like the world had figured me out, so it was getting rid of me. Right away, I went into survival mode. I knew I was about to embark on a real journey. I decided that whatever wreckage fell onto me, I was going to push it away and live to see the day when I could look back and smile. Except right away I was grumbling to myself about what I would look like. Was I already a ghost? Would anyone be able to see me at all? The rest is a mash-up of sights, sounds, and smells.

Blood and dirt were stinging my eyes. I still feel the sting sometimes. When I think of how short life is, I feel that sting. A quick, strong wind triggers it, along with the rest of the memory: I was deaf, at first, so my sense of touch was immediately heightened. I could feel it in my chest first...the thump of fate. My limbs were intact, but I felt a deep sensation around my heart and lungs, and I thought the only thing I was at that moment in time was a head and torso. I'd already heard stories of losing all arms and legs at once. I thought I might be just a stump. I couldn't see anything. I could see a buddy's head, but I wasn't sure if it was attached to a body (it was...). Then the event started replaying before it was done with its first play. It was like this new memory consumed all others, particularly the visual disturbance of the blast wave, before the loud explosion. Then it was quiet a minute, all the sound sucked away. I thought I was dead, but felt so alive and free, seeing the ground beneath me. I thought I had become an angel, then I realized it was the blast force lifting me several feet into the air. I was floating. No longer held by gravity, I had transcended something but couldn't put my finger on what it was. The whole world was floating. Then the shock of the event returned. I couldn't breathe because of all the dust, and the air was knocked out of me. That was nothing. Gravity came back, all the way. The world came back. I was going to be in the news. I would enter celebrity life. The vector diagram of the rest of my life would be very neat and predictable. I went through the displacement calculation in my head. This step was part of my beatitude. I never envisioned such an apotheosis, but this was going to be my new reality.

While flying through the air after the blast, I realized I had lost my power to fly out of my body at will. My old way of doing things was gone. Long I dwelt in a land where I was a master of mysteries. I was now in the hands of a type of chaos I had never known. To get the magic back, I was going to have to fight these new monsters or guide them toward some other end.

EXPOSURE

Three guys were killed by that IED. Three names: Rayburn, McDowell, Turner. The gunner, Stanley, lived. He lost both legs, but he lived. I wrote their names down in my journal, so I'd never forget them. I just ended up with a small bandage on my head. My head bled a lot, but that's because it was a superficial wound. It would heal fine. Still, my brain felt fuzzy. It still feels fuzzy some days. I was more impatient about everything after that day. I was edgy. Then those dead guys started coming to me in flashes of grief. They've never gone away.

The blast got lots of Army attention and some media attention. There was the investigation under Army Regulation 15-6, same as with the Sugarbush massacre, though the nexus between the massacre and Army activity was still a big question. I gave a written statement, but I didn't have much to say. It was an attack on my former self, or a welcoming into a new world, though I didn't know that at the time. I did have a new sense of my limitations. I went about my regular courtesies and training, even my martial arts training. I was systematic. I kept proper form, despite the new pounding in my head.

Twigg and Snow left me alone. Snow brought a space heater to my work-shack without asking. He was in good spirits after learning there was a character on the popular new series, "Game of Thrones," with his last name. It wasn't cold, but it was about to be cold. Thanksgiving was coming up in a few days. There was a sense of love in the air, but I didn't feel it. Maybe a little for me from Twigg and Snow, in the way that cats love. I still hadn't told mom and dad about what happened. They were off in their own world and did not need to be introduced to the new details of my new hell.

I was still just half-awake in this new world. More was coming. Chaos was at work upon me, staring me full in the face (with its bloodstained face). Chaos, the true order of everything. Growing, as it grows, the one thing that can be said to always grow in a closed system like war. I didn't see the chaos right away because of its complementary nature, the non-mirror-image nature of it. The pure-malevolence nature of it. It was early in my tour, and the fourth wall was towering before me, but my eyes had lots of adjusting to do, still just tiny parts of a complex system, a system in which my own will and imagination must play larger roles.

My office walls were covered with maps. I even put up a few leftover Major Paulsen doodles. These types of artifacts were essential to my kinetic experience of war. Everyone's offices were the same, with maps of varying types of classification on the walls. Despite all the high-tech gear, people loved paper. I had to add strings and slips of thin paper. This was the infancy of my vector wars. The lines brought a sense of peace because they displayed some direction, some decisive element of the universe.

"Lines of communication are important," said Maddox. It was our first time together since the blast. He meant in war and in home life. We were at the Lux eating breakfast. I was having my favorite: fried toast smothered in baked beans and stewed tomatoes. We were talking about his daughters. I think they were why he had such a sly grin, even during the bad times. His eyes turned gray. I preferred his blue eyes. Maddox loved his daughters, but from the way he talked of war, I think he loved war more. And whenever he spoke of off-center encounters, like the story about getting his car stolen in Jordan, he conveyed deeper secrets. He loved talking this way. It was his way of being powerful, his way of declaring himself Beast. And yet Maddox talked so coldly, and I guess that was how he loved and how he killed.

My thoughts turned to the literature left stacked on my office floor: comic books, pictures of people interacting with each other, showing the basics of right and wrong, but I was no moral authority. Voices were coming to me, but I wasn't there yet. Still, the Army tasked me to distribute the stuff, and that's what I planned to do, I just didn't love the idea. I loved the idea of magic in the world, but I didn't always like the idea of constructing a place for it. I tried to meditate. I tried to reach out with astral limbs, but I couldn't disconnect from my body. It was frustrating, and the endgame was so far away.

THE RED
HAND

I didn't write letters home, other than my scribblings to Lady Mist. I didn't have time. Explaining all the madness to family would've been like painting an abstract picture. Even now, blood and bits are broadly sketched in my memories, inviting me to play and play again. There's still the electrically charged aftertaste of what I consumed, some nights the same as when I was in Afghanistan, where the nights were generally quiet but always twitchy, always chilling.

Intel about Sugarbush was coming to me via Twigg. Maddox was helping with the investigation because he had dealt with this kind of thing before. Maddox wasn't delegating any tasks to me, yet. I was going to have to make my own adventure. So I took an old-fashioned approach. I just started asking around, but thanks to the blast, things were getting more and more blurry. I couldn't keep short-term and long-term memories separate. Things that happened twenty years ago felt like they happened yesterday, and vice versa. I started formulating ideas about what may have happened at Sugarbush. I was no stranger to the realm of abstract discovery. I had been there before. I had built several memory palaces in such places. One was underground. Another was above ground, stacked floor upon floor like the Tower of Babel. I didn't visit that place often. I built it in such a flimsy way, even the stairs creaked. Bats flew at me...memories getting the hell out of there.

One day, I was working out at the Prison Gym. The Prison Gym was full of muscle heads, guys that looked like they would be doing nothing but lifting weights, if they were in a prison, which we were. I noticed a few guys, each wearing a t-shirt with a picture of a red hand, and beneath that, it said 'We Are Dead People.'

I listened to their conversation a minute. They were Irish. I selected the soldier with the loudest mouth and said, "What's with the shirt?"

"Red Hand Defenders," he said. "It's a loyalist group in Northern Ireland."

His name was Ellington. After some chatting, he seemed a rare kind of soldier, sort of a poet/butcher. I saw great kindness and cruelty in him. His buddies were Butler and Redmond, all with red hair to match their shirts.

We were kindred spirits. The Red Hand started providing me little bits of intelligence, enough to get me started on the mystery of Mars Station, plus other things. Ellington was the strong-arm element of the group. He wanted to go back to Ireland and become a professor of philosophy. He was no older than thirty-five and still had time for that kind of thing. He went off a lot, especially on Butler and Redmond, but he would apologize. Ellington was red all over, from his thinning red hair to his thick arm hair.

When he talked of the dead, colors gushed through him, and when he talked of the dead, he talked of home. It was part of his version of home life, along with disgust and frustration. "I learned all my skills growing up in County Down, Northern Ireland," he said. "I watched my older brother, Michael, strangle a cabby once, though he let the man live. The man was my friend, but he was no friend of Michael. As a group, the Red Hand had disbanded by then, but some of us were still being trained by the older boys. I admired that they didn't want to give up on a cause, even when the others had given up, so I adopted their cause first then learned about it second. I figured with a lull in that movement I could use some different training and a chance for some different killing, so I joined the British Army and came here. I followed Michael, but he's already gone home to God. The Taliban cornered his unit in a mountain valley one day and killed half of them. It made all the papers. Michael's ghost haunts me."

Butler and Redmond were just boys. They worshiped Ellington. They saw what I saw: here was a man who had been beyond the fourth wall. He was comfortable with the ever-changing metaphysical environment, in that world and this one. Butler and Redmond were fired up. They were so hooked on Ellington's energy. He was a man who refused to wither away. He loved all kinds of commotion. He stood upright in the face of long odds. That was the Ellington I came to know over time. Butler and Redmond, also, but they didn't tell Red Hand stories like Ellington.

The way they joked together. The synergy. The universe belonged to them, not just vice versa. These were the kind of guys who could've painted a picture of war for me right away, instead of the piecemeal madness I was witnessing, peppered with all the stories I was hearing. The Red Hand wanted to hunt down the Devil and then go further.

They had a deeper understanding than me of what was beyond the fourth wall. That's why I was drawn to them. Conflict was in their blood. It was rising in mine. I noted the following in my journal around that time: "The governing dynamics of the battlefield are beyond physical matter, often presenting itself as magic. There is an air of the experimental. On the battlefield, the principles of a market economy are in play. Everyone is in a little laboratory bottle, within a glass chamber with the rest of the world looking on. People are interested in finding ways of doing more with less. I've been writing so many reports, trying to explain my observations in terms of straight lines, but I'm conducting my business in ways opposed to a straight-line approach. The world can accommodate it, but can humans?"

I just wanted to disappear into the night, disappear into a future that may not even include me in this place. So early in my tour, I was running on empty. I was going to have to reach out for help, for the Red Hand, or Maddox, or anyone. It wasn't just the warfare, which I'd signed up for, it was the behind-the-scenes stuff, the beyond-the-fourth-wall stuff, which I'd also signed up for but was just starting to see: the dreamscapes, the merging traffic patterns of madness and nature turning-turning. Icy smiles all around, and smashing and crushing. Maybe with lightning, maybe not. I had a little courage but could use a little more. That, too, was disappearing into a different night.

I needed to come up with some good work product soon, regarding my positive contribution to this conflict. "Just check the box and make it home alive," Maddox told me. "Wherever you are."

I could no longer fly, but I had other strange physical spaces to work in, such as Sugarbush and Mars Station, still just a circle on a map. I had enemies and friends, or the idea of them, at least. I had Yvonne and Lady Mist. I had Malak and ___. That part was blank, but things were about to change. And now I had the Red Hand.

THE CREATION OF A DETECTIVE STORY

Maddox was in good spirits in the days before Thanksgiving. While we were walking together on the boardwalk, Maddox pointed out a poster. It was a picture of a turkey wearing digital green and sticking its tongue out. It looked like a dead turkey, marching forward. Below the picture was an announcement about a special Thanksgiving dinner at the British DFAC.

"Doesn't look very tasty," I mused, "but I'm intrigued. Afghans are cooking a feast to celebrate an American holiday, being served in a British dining facility."

Then I had a big idea, a lightning bug in my throbbing, blasted brain: I would mingle ghosts and humans in my work. Lady M. and Yvonne were already encouraging such a move, and with the Sugarbush massacre, the time was right. I needed to open new doors. It would be like opening several books and reading them at once, multiple detective stories. Several dead cities would come alive at once. Ghosts/humans/garbage in garbage out/getting tangled in the tendrils of life, tearing each other apart in the process.

I had to take a different approach toward the investigation, toward the whole war, as a survival tactic. I wanted to shave away the waste, and I believed I could. The gritty stuff was yet to come, but I knew a wicked narrative would save me. So I started shifting the shapes of Kandahar Airfield. The turkey wearing digital-green was just the first in a long line of stimuli. A digital-green dream. That's how my plans came to me. They melted into me. They approached me as apparitions, dodged me in the way of apparitions. Then, in good-logical-linear-American fashion, the beings around me were no longer real, not even Maddox. They became data forms. I started referring to fellow soldiers and Afghans alike as 'players,' as in a game.

I created Emal Khan Mangal out of this mindset, walking along the KAF boardwalk with Maddox that day, feeling a chill Central Asian wind. That night I drew a picture of Mangal. He had rough elephant skin and grit all over his eyes and mouth and razor blades for fingers. He had to look at one mangled, ugly face every morning in the mirror. He was the murderer of all those good Sugarbush people. He was a smack addict and forced Afghan villagers to plant poppy fields. He was like me, trying to create his own little universe. Maybe there were actually two or three of him, jockeying for dominance, but he was real, in my book.

Growing up in Uvalde, Texas, I was intrigued by stories about local psychics and witches. As a student at the University of Texas at Austin, I majored in archaeology and anthropology and met people who opened my eyes to a different plane of existence, where thought and reality merge. When I moved to Houston for law school, I met a witch. She taught me to leave my physical form, to see myself as others did. When I signed my Army enlistment contract, I had an out-of-body experience. I hovered under the ceiling at MEPS in Houston, watching as I electronically signed one form after another. I didn't hesitate at all. My MOS was 96B, Military Intelligence Analyst (which would later be renumbered as 35F). It seemed like a big adventure and a great escape.

Though I joined the Army at the height of the war in Iraq, I didn't think I would make it to either Iraq or Afghanistan. I was just going to be a reservist and work stateside and try to do training and missions for extra money. I thought I might crisscross flyover country and visit places like Ft. McCoy, Ft. Leonard-Wood, Ft. Leavenworth (which I did). That was the plan, and I went into it with a full heart, but it was a trap. In time, the idea of experiencing modern warfare attracted me, the complexities of it, with no definable battlefields and no fronts. War was hybrid, with conventional and irregular forces, combatants and civilians, kinetic activity, and information warfare, all intertwined, creating a fantasy narrative. I was drawn to all these elements, like a minnow drawn to the light.

With the coming of December and winter deepening, the war became more curvilinear for me. Well-established vectors started tangling in my mind. My future was turning to goo. One sure axis led to a different one. I was having another simple, recurring dream that just got worse as it became colder: I dreamed of a neighbor's kid back in Houston who shot himself. It was a sad event for me. I called the boy Alex in my dream, though that was not his actual name. I invited Alex into my home. He said he was happy because he no longer had anything to hide. He said it was either watch his mom clean up his brains or walk around the old neighborhood.

I met Yvonne for dinner at Tam Tam. We ate beef kabob and drank tea. Conversation was difficult for me. I was having headaches. I told Yvonne little bits of my plan, about Mangal.

"That is magic," said Yvonne. "You conceive of something in your mind and you make it real."

Yvonne was at KAF to create a fiction of her own. I was a part of it, but I didn't know what to give her. I had met plenty of bland, lifeless people, but she was not one of them. War presented plenty of dark paths, nasty-looking paths. She presented a beautiful pause in my war life. She was thoughtful and sensitive and could be funny, too.

"Is something the matter, Yvonne?"

She was gazing at the soccer field in the center of the

complex. A few soldiers were doing sprints.

"My father," said Yvonne. "He is trying to contact me."

"You've never mentioned your father. What is his name?"

"Nikolay," she said.

"How is he trying to contact you?"

"He..." Yvonne started, "I cannot explain."

"He is trying to psychically contact you, isn't he? I do understand, better than you realize."

"Yes, but also no. It is through events...through this business of the missing soldier."

"What missing soldier?"

My Russian barber knew more about current events than I. She recounted what she heard in her shop while cutting a captain's hair. He was grumbling about having to deal with a missing soldier. Yvonne described a notebook on the captain's lap with DGR scribbled on the cover, so I named the soldier Digger in my mind. Digger just walked right off the airfield, according to the captain. He cut some wires and left the base altogether. KAF was a huge place, so that took some swagger. Digger sounded impulsive, but maybe he wasn't at all. He was taking an existential journey, like me.

"It is not what you think," Yvonne said. "He is meddling with dangerous forces."

"And your father is involved?"

Yvonne nodded. "I know he is, which means I must now be involved."

I was intertwined with all the forces beyond my control, but this was a new twist. It was way beyond me, higher than my mission.

She changed the subject. "I do not want to talk about my father now," she said. "Let me tell you about an Afghan woman I know in Kandahar. She told me her deepest secret. It was this: she had been in the Afghan National Army."

"What is her name?"

"Pari."

"Let's drink to Pari," I said. She told me more about Pari, and I realized that Yvonne was not so lonely and trapped on KAF, after all.

By the end of the day, the base was buzzing. Twigg and Snow were involved in the hunt, acting as liaisons between Digger's company and headquarters. They found Digger's phone in his barracks, along with his sketchbook, full of drawings of two-faced figures and double-helixes. One face was monstrous, the other was normal and resembled him. There were other drawings of monsters next to diagrams showing strengths and weaknesses, like characters in the roleplaying game, Dungeons & Dragons. CID thought he was somehow abducted right off KAF. They did not subscribe to the theory that he left on his own. I said nothing about Yvonne's ideas about her father.

I later visited with Major Nichols at the religious center. I told him the truth: that I was having more trouble dealing with others who were dealing with the missing soldier, instead of praying or thinking about the well-being of the soldier.

"That's not such a bad thing," said Nichols. "Most come to see me because they find evil thoughts invading the space of their prayers, so they're out fighting all day, then fighting themselves, perhaps fighting God, at night."

"Perhaps he discovered his own God somewhere out there," I said. "Maybe Digger is alive and well. God, too."

"Ah, I've heard the stories. Are you saying you don't think someone took him? That he's adventuring on his own free will outside the wire?"

"Whatever is going on, Digger is out there being presented with a new truth on his own terms. Maybe he wants the hardship that goes along with such a search. Sometimes it's good to go lower in order to get higher. I'm a little envious, actually. If I could only fly to him."

"Fly? What do you mean?"

I could see a gray/black aura surrounding Nichols at that moment. I've seen it with others. I had a theory that it meant they were choosing to divert from the long road toward death, whether to grow and save themselves or die young, who's to say. "Speaking of death," I said, "I have this theory about the Sugarbush murders." I told Nichols about Mangal, about how I believed he was a junkie building junkies, murdering anyone who defied him because he was the kind of man who thought he would be fine without other people. "I wonder if Digger was somehow involved in Sugarbush."

"Intriguing," said Nichols, "and imaginative."

When I got back to my shack/office, Major Twigg was waiting for me. "Good stuff is coming up, Captain Jett," he said. He looked so comfy-cozy when he talked like that. "It's on your desk." Was it a ticket to Houston? No. More like a time bomb. It was not good stuff. It was a list of computer equipment. I was irritated, but it wasn't just Twigg. It was his whole plan. He was selectively feeding me information. It was his prerogative as a superior officer. I was becoming increasingly frustrated with the plan's execution on his end and higher up the chain of command. I wanted to go higher in the mission, not lower. When we delivered more computer equipment to Taos (a good mountain town, in New Mexico and Afghanistan) the previous week, we found previously delivered equipment still in boxes. They were in the middle of a power outage. It happened all the time, the Taos elders explained. Their mouths were full of flies. I was unafraid by then, or at least indifferent. I was used to mouths full of foam and flies, us and them. So I continued to take interest in the bizarre. What was real in the war had become marginal. I was seeking entertainment in different ways. So a mission to deliver computer equipment didn't deliver a punch of excitement.

Maddox came by my office that night. "I just talked to Major Twigg. You're coming with me tomorrow. We're going back to Sugarbush." Maddox laughed, just a little chuckle.

"What's funny, Sir?"

"I've got something else for you." Maddox handed me a leather-bound journal. "It was Sergeant Ramsey's. I'd like your take on it."

"I didn't know you were involved in that investigation as well." I thumbed through the journal. It had fewer drawings than his other one, but there were topographical maps. "Does he mention anything about Sugarbush or Mars Station, Sir?"

"Just read the journal. It gets interesting. You know I like pulp westerns. He writes like that. I'm already a big fan." Maddox chuckled again. "See you at nine hundred hours."

EXCERPT FROM JOURNAL OF SERGEANT DANIEL G. RAMSEY, U. S. ARMY (ADVENTURE NAME: HISTORIANS)

The Red Bat touches down on the red surface of the planet Decrex. The Red Bat is a boxy-looking ship, but with a semicircular aft section and cockpit atop the largest box in the mid-section. The planet is similar to Mars and sits on the edge of the galaxy. TYDO and REMVI exit the ship. Tydo is a human. Remvi is a Lansar, a reptilian creature with scaly skin and a forked tongue. Before them is a vast red desert. Tydo removes his blaster from his holster. Remvi takes the lead in their trek toward Outpost Bekun (pronounced beh-coon, stress on second syllable). Tydo has heard rumors of a group that collects ancient artifacts with powerful qualities that defy known physics. Remvi, a bounty hunter, is being paid to find GREMSIK, a warlord, also a Lansar. Semi-retired, Remvi still has debts to pay, and the price on Gremsik's head is large. Remvi is not even sure of Gremsik's crimes. Remvi hitched a ride here with Tydo, who is a well-known explorer of this part of the galaxy. Tydo wants to find Gremsik also. He believes Gremsik can lead him to the collectors.

Ahead are two robed humanoid figures, tall and skinny, with gray skin and pale, yellow eyes.

Stop, says Tydo.

(Dice roll for Tydo: Perception check: successful)

I've seen these two before.

The one on left: Hope

The one on the right: Fate

I call them the Bishops, because they have such a reverent appearance.

BUILDING
AN EMPIRE

When I left the states for war and adventure, people were actually jealous. They had their own ideas. They were cruising along some false vectors. I thought: do you really hate your own life that much? People said they wished they were going. People with six-figure incomes actually said that to me. What I couldn't explain at the time were the various reasons I was going. They assumed I got "called up," whatever this means. Civilians often use the expression. I suppose I did get called up, technically, but I already went over this on page one, reader. Let me be clear: I invited myself to the war. I saw war as a path, a puzzle, an experience, all of those things. I saw it as a vehicle for metaphysical growth.

Even today, I stick to this approach. I've built my own little empire in this way over the years. After reading Digger's journal, I could see he was of a similar mindset. He created vast worlds, empires of his imagination.

Before meeting Maddox and his crew and rolling out for Sugarbush, I met Ellington and the boys for a workout at the prison gym. I got Ellington's first name: Sean. He also said his nickname growing up was 'Cruiser,' so I started calling him that. Then his soldiers started calling him that, following me. Cruiser talked about his family in Dublin. His wife and boy were living with his parents. His wife's parents were dead.

"You're going back to Sugarbush?" Cruiser said. "We've got a different name for that place, but I know what you mean. We were on patrol near there once, and I watched one of my Hands get split in half and thrown straight up by an IED. The boy landed in four different spots: a full leg here, a half leg there, an arm there, and then his torso. But he lived a few minutes more. After I gained my senses back, I sprinted through a spray of small arms fire to reach him. I applied a tourniquet as far up his leg as I could, but it didn't do much good, so I tightened his belt. He bled out fast. He was proud to die that way, in pieces. I could see it in his smile."

Cruiser scratched his chin. He squinted. He looked lost. "I believe in God, but that's because I've seen the Devil," he said.

Butler and Redmond weren't even listening. They'd heard it all before. Cruiser was a father figure. They needed him. Cruiser and I cut our workout short and walked back to our shacks. His shack wasn't far from mine.

"It's a nice day for a mission," said Cruiser. "A little cool, but you've got some nice sun. Steer clear of dead animals. Go with God."

Cruiser stopped and framed a line of blast walls with his fingers. He had the same fascination with them as me. "This place will look like Stonehenge one day," said Cruiser. "By the way, don't call me Cruiser anymore. It's an old name. Just call me Ellington."

And that was it. I never called him Cruiser again. After all, Maddox kept calling me 'Pup' instead of 'Captain.' I preferred the latter.

When we arrived in Sugarbush, villagers were spread out everywhere. Tactically this was not such a bad idea: spread out so if a bomb goes off, everyone isn't taken out all at once. As we stood around, waiting for some direction from Maddox, my imagination wandered. I was bewildered with how much more distant the people of the village seemed, versus during my previous visit. It was as if the universe was trying to tell me a different story. I represented a big galaxy; they represented smaller ones. That's where my imagination wandered.

"What do you think these people see in us?" I asked Maddox.

"I don't think they see us as much as they see this," said Maddox, tugging his rifle. He waved to Kochi. Maddox took Kochi aside. Two other translators joined them. Maddox opened his pack and pulled out a bunch of files and gave each translator a file.

Maddox told all the soldiers within earshot to hang back near the vehicles. Half these guys had already been injured in one way or another. They didn't need to be told how to behave. I noticed some pick-up trucks on the other side of the village. State Department workers drove the same type of trucks, CIA donations from a long time ago, when I was still in junior high school. After a long spell of sunlight, it got cloudy and cold. A couple of the translators started arguing. They got physical. Their auras were flashing. I sensed sorcery. I hadn't felt this kind of input from my surroundings since the morning I arrived in Afghanistan. Whatever happened I was going to let happen, just to feel a psychic tug, but Kochi broke up the fight. It was standard operating procedure to not put hard-case, mercurial-type Afghans side by side, but these things weren't concrete matters. Maddox had to interfere. He pulled more paperwork from his pack as if to remind them of what was really important. Then Maddox came over to me.

"What's in the files?" I said.

Maddox showed me. Each was a dossier about Digger, the missing soldier. There wasn't much written information, but there were several pictures. I took a close look at his face and it hit me: he was the same young man I woke up in the transport plane when I arrived in Afghanistan. He looked right into my eyes when I wasn't physically in front of him. Our minds connected. I had a sharp pain in my temple. Maddox noticed.

"You all right, pup?"

"Fine, Sir. That's why we're here again? To find out what these people may know about this Digger guy?"

"Everyone is calling him Digger, now," said Maddox. "Is that thanks to you? It's not just here. We've got teams spread out all over Kandahar Province."

But it was a logical choice for our team to go back to Sugarbush since we were there right after the massacre. The people looked ill and tired, and no children were running around. The lack of children said it all.

I was right about the trucks, the State Department. Through Kochi, we learned that two SD advisors were in Sugarbush when our team was there, doing the same kind of interacting I might be doing if I wasn't involved in tracking down our missing man. Since Kochi was logistics-minded, he gave us numbers and breakdowns of the population, plus foreigners, plus Taliban intrusions, all since the murders. Maddox and Kochi entered a shack without me, along with several village elders. Maddox came out holding a bunch of papers.

"New photos," said Maddox. "New information about the murders provided by the State Department."

"Why did the State Department wait so long to exchange intel? Maybe they have something on Mangal."

Maddox gave me a look. "Who?"

I remembered I hadn't yet introduced him to Mangal.

"You mean Malak," said Maddox. He was still focused on a known enemy: Abdul Gulzar Malak, the Taliban leader.

"Roger, Sir." But Mangal's hands were all over Sugarbush, as far as I was concerned. This was his land, a broken land. He was out there, watching us from the mountains. It was anybody's guess when he would reveal himself. All those children, so sorrowful and lost, were his children, and he was raising them to destroy...us, but mainly they were destroying themselves. I was starting to see them beyond the fourth wall, the little vectors of their lives, all their liquid moves guided by just their senses and false hope and perverted ideologies. I had a little false hope going on, that day. I just didn't feel like getting too close to anyone. I was frightened. They were good people. I could see ghosts among them, controlling them. I could hear high-pitched laughter.

But as far as I could tell, the people of Sugarbush hadn't seen Digger. Maddox confirmed it.

"They don't know our man," said Maddox. "All they want to talk about is that cloud of death that came during the night."

"I thought you already had that all figured out, Sir?"

"I do. Kochi is getting into it, also."

I kept hearing the laughter of Mangal. There was no end to it. This was not what I was used to doing. I was not used to keeping guard during a KLE, but it allowed my mind to wander. I had a certain concept of the next American Empire, and it would be based on mystical vectors and other kicked-up dream ingredients, wrapping around the world, folding other cultures into its own, creating an interior fully reflecting the exterior, sort of a fourth-wall-friendly state, not full, not empty.

"You're white as a ghost, Captain Jett," said Maddox.

Not to mention all the commotion deep inside. Maddox was inches taller than me, but at times I felt tiny next to him and stuck in naiveté, some days. Some days it pissed me off, like that day. He was on the inside of the shack, and I wasn't. He was one step ahead on intel, good and bad. Maddox provided appropriate commentary on Sugarbush at that moment in time. "What a fucking mess," he said. The SD workers got in their trucks and sped off, leaving us in the dust.

That night back at KAF, I could hear Patty in his bunk beneath me. He was talking dirty to his fiancée back in South Carolina. He had just bought a big video monitor at the PX. The monitor was pulled up close to his bed, but I could still see the screen if I leaned over far enough. "What's going on down there? Show me your panties," Patty said. I lay back and stared at the ceiling. Through the ceiling, I could see stars. I watched bigger galaxies consume smaller galaxies. I envisioned a universe composed of webs of dark matter. And here I was, in the midst of war, learning my place in this universe. It was as if the universe was telling me to take a cloudier form, something immune to all the nonsense on my side of the fourth wall, a journey different from any other out-of-body flight I'd experienced. I thought of the magician card, still in the breast pocket of my MultiCam ACU top. I imagined the magician was me. I pictured myself in another age, on another world. "Ka-pow, baby," said Patty.

I had no perverse fascination with any of this, by the way. "How are things going down there?" I whispered. Patty turned off the monitor and the room got quiet. I couldn't sleep. After a few minutes, I climbed down from my bunk and retrieved Digger's journal from my pack, and got back in bed and read by flashlight.

EXCERPT FROM JOURNAL OF SERGEANT DANIEL G. RAMSEY, U. S. ARMY (ADVENTURE NAME: HISTORIANS)

Rhoknol and Peruvia, both human, are aboard the Fury, flying through Yostar Sector. Their ship is not very furious. It is an old medium-transport, F Series. The most notable item in the ship is the Ilix: a polyhedron-shaped object, the size of a human brain, complex as a human brain, not fully understood by its owner, Rhoknol. Rhoknol is sixteen years old. He doesn't seek to fully understand the Ilix. He seeks to sell it at a high price. Is it a fragment of a universal mind or universal psychology? Peruvia is ten years older than Rhoknol, but she has been part of his life for all his life. She is employed as a guardian by Rhoknol's father, Trismokin. She sees the Ilix in a more limited way: it is an ancient technology, specially engineered for some particular domain, such as language, vision, or movement. Rhoknol believes it is all of those things. The Ilix eventually starts getting inputs, but from where? And to what end? It starts vibrating. It glows yellow.

A CONVERSATION WITH MY RUSSIAN BARBER

Mid-December. I worried it was too late to send Christmas cards. Mail to and from Afghanistan took two weeks. I met Yvonne at Tam Tam, though I had already eaten dinner. She ordered steak and ate rapidly, slumped over. I brought her some Christmas cookies from the Lux.

"I promise I will not cut off your ears when you come to my shop," Yvonne said. This kind of playful banter had been going on since we met. She wasn't a fan of Christmas. It brought back memories of her sister. This was a memory that really absorbed her. Yvonne had a celebrity moment years ago when her little sister killed herself live on the internet. She was in her room at home in Moscow. She hung herself from a hook above her closet doorway. Her body was bruised. Yvonne didn't know how it could've been so bruised, but she suspected it was related to a biker gang her sister was involved with. Yvonne said she felt guilty because she helped her sister install the hook, understanding that it was to be used for an art project. Yvonne showed me videos on her phone of old interviews following the death. It made big news in Russia and Europe, all over the world, Yvonne said, though I didn't remember seeing anything about it. Even after Yvonne explained, I didn't have the urge to look anything up. I asked about the rest of her family, her parents, but she wouldn't talk about them. Yvonne sounded like she needed a break. She wanted to go for a walk. We walked around for an hour. I let her show me parts of the base I didn't know existed.

We had lush conversations that night. She talked about people at work. She was troubled by an Indian barber who fled his country due to extensive persecution by his government for his failure to deal with mosquito breeding in his own backyard. She was tormented by the mere possibility of getting sick from this man. She was a wreck. She weaved tales of terror with her present circumstances, and I understood her need for magic better than my own need for it. I didn't approve of her past. She knew it. I made oblique comments about her family, trying to get her to talk more about them. Her issues were with her father. Through layers of commentary, the hieroglyphic aura of her crazy, bad-girl life was showing.

Trying to take both our minds off work, I showed her a picture of people from headquarters after the final run of the physical fitness test earlier in November. Even Maddox thought it was a terrifying picture. We were so dirty and vulnerable looking, happy with both. God only knows what the bug-eyed kid on the front row was thinking. He was wearing barefoot running shoes. He wasn't even part of our group. I'd never seen him and didn't see him again during my tour. We were sweaty and disgusting but smiling big. Major Twigg posted the photo on the Army's website for the world to see. At least I got a laugh out of Yvonne.

I needed her full spirit. At that time I would've done anything. I was prepared to summon spirits.

I told Yvonne about Lady Mist and what happened the night before I left the states for my tour of duty, about drawing the magician card.

"This lady," said Yvonne, "she was feeling bad that she could not watch over you. Now I will take up that cause. While you are out there watching over me, I will be here, watching over you."

I think she meant that we would be in it together, from that point on. She took me deeper into the KAF netherworld. She took me to a place she had discovered and laid claim to, a little nook between Connex boxes, a secluded space about thirty-six square feet, half-covered by a tarp. A wooden board atop an upturned plastic box served as a table. A couple of folding chairs were next to the table.

"I am going to help you," said Yvonne. "You know that I can." Her hair had a red tone in the semi-darkness.

"I'm not going to stop you," I said. "This is not a first."

"A what?"

"It's an English expression. A first time."

"Nor is it my first time," said Yvonne.

She opened her backpack and pulled out a small box and opened it. Inside was a deck of cards. She dropped the cards. I helped pick them up. They were Tarot cards, brown and tattered, vintage-looking, with too many fantastical creatures to describe here.

"The cards have been in my family for generations," she said.

"Did they walk around this part of the world? Your family, I mean."

"The dead ones tell me they did," Yvonne said, "but sometimes I do not believe them. I do not even believe they were my family, some of them."

We sat in the chairs. Yvonne started spreading the cards in a dual-diamond shape on the box. She was serious. She spread the cards as far apart as she could. She laughed when she drew the magician. Both her laughter and the card startled me. I reached for my sidearm but stopped short of completely drawing it from its holster. Either she didn't see this or my overreaction did not disturb her. For a half-second, I didn't know her at all. After all, she drew the magician, and I still had a magician in my pocket. She had to know things I didn't know.

Her reading was as muddled as her English, but only when performing the reading. After that her English was fine. Yvonne sounded insane, but I think her heart was in the right place. Ahh...the wild beating of her heart. The growing strength of my attraction would prove itself true in the missions to come. I was further away from three-dimensional space and becoming better adapted for anything other than that. Like the butterfly effect, perhaps my attempt to further complicate then consolidate this space would yield positive results. There were my vectors, spreading into areas uncharted by American forces, unfolding into a pile-up of evil omens.

That little space between Connex boxes, with Yvonne in it, was the first room in my Afghanistan memory palace. Everything grew from there. I associated memories with the mere idea of some crazy colonel finding us, rooting us out like dual diseases who didn't belong, and we really didn't, if you think about it. We were both lightning bolts. During those initial moments of building a new memory palace, memories from other places infiltrated my thoughts, fictional places.

"Yvonne, did you ever see the movie, *Time Bandits*?" I could see from her expression she didn't know what I was talking about. "The 1981 film about a band of dwarf robbers? And the map of time and space they stole from the Supreme Being? No? It was one of my favorite movies when I was a kid. If I only had such a map."

A couple of days went by. I missed Yvonne's fingers on my skull. We planned to meet Friday. I had a feeling it would be sooner, and it was. It rained Thursday morning, just a bit, but enough to create pools of water that dotted the base. I had a horrible dream that morning about the murders in Sugarbush. I woke up with a headache. There was just too much crime, too many crime vectors.

I went for a long walk before reporting for duty, intending to get rid of my headache and make another attempt to leap into the sky and see this place from high, but I couldn't push through my skin. Unsure of Yvonne's work schedule, I showed up for a haircut, but she wasn't there. Major Nichols was. A fat Russian man was cutting his hair.

"Ah, Captain Jett," said Nichols.

"Good morning, Sir," I replied. "Where's Yvonne?"

"Yvonne is resting," said the Russian barber. He gave me a malignant smile. He knew me. I knew he knew me. Maybe Nichols was talking about me before I arrived.

The barber was finishing up with Nichols. Nichols looked pale. His long hair was all gone. He still had some stubble. "You coming to see me soon?" he asked me. That smile, backlit by a real grasp of something he believed in.

"I ought to, Sir. I need to."

The barber turned Nichols' chair to face me. They both had brooding, dark auras which started pulsing in sync. I felt like an intruder, all of a sudden. I walked backward out the door.

Major Nichols followed me outside. He was hovering there, still smiling, his dark aura getting bigger, turning darker.

"Take a cue from..." Nichols said then exploded into several pieces. Less than ten. The blast threw me back. It was another Time Bandits moment. Several people exploded in the same manner in the film. By some miracle no blood or bits got me. Flesh flew into a nearby fence and hung there.

The incoming alarm sounded, too late. I got to my feet and looked at the smoking crater where Nichols had been standing. I found Nichols' head. His mouth was twisted a full one hundred fifteen degrees behind the rest of his face. His teeth were loose and going every which way between strips of flesh. Just from observing his displaced features, you could get a good sense of the strength of the blast. My ears were ringing from the blast, not as bad as the first time that kind of thing happened to me.

LM, I've got a man's head in my hands right now, but it's

a deeply spiritual moment. He's got a wicked smile. Not Major Nichols, but some other entity, something else present. The trouble is I don't know what to believe, and the road ahead is dangerous. The city ahead looks dismal. I'm supposed to preach certain values, stuff that I haven't found yet myself. They are taking their time, just crawling toward me with worried looks. I've seen a big, skeletal finger pointing at the exit, but it's far-far-far away. I can see myself becoming an insomniac when this war is done. Looking at these dead eyes will give me nightmares that I don't want to experience. They'll come.

Look at Nichols, LM. I don't want my final vision of him to be his dead eyes and his pale cheeks, blood-streaked. He had such rosy cheeks in life. I want to see something different...to keep the madness away, I'll have to...that's it! A Eureka moment, LM. You just gave me another big idea. I'm going to come up with other stories and lives, entirely different from the ones I'm learning. It's in Nichols' dead eyes, too. He's telling me to go this way. You presented me with sights and sounds unfamiliar to me. War has done the same.

Chaos itself, the chaos of the moment, was to blame for this talk, like maybe one of the angels of chaos did this just for my sake, for the sake of adventure and discovery and various disastrous effects. I saw Lady Mist as a different kind of angel and started talking to her more and more after this attack. I needed her to help me connect with the other side of the fourth wall. The total momentum of the system at that moment was against me. You could say it was a form of communication, if purely physical, as in all war: elements of fire combine with elements of maneuver to produce the desired effect. It was my area of expertise, as a soldier. I was trained to find optimal levels of symmetry among time and knowledge and resources. The point of victory in life and war and space lies within those axes, within the umbrella formed by that bloody crucifix. War encourages this optimization, but it is as if it is purposeful in keeping the players from achieving it. It transforms achievements into something else until the terms themselves have changed. But ultimately the death of Major Nichols helped in my fourth wall approach: I realized that I must accept that I could design and command complex systems, whether physical or metaphysical, and then carry through with the mission, be less of an observer, content to leave my physical form and journey through astral space. No. I was destined for more.

By the time Yvonne showed up, Nichols' body had been removed. She turned pale when she saw the blood. She didn't ask what happened, at first. I told her what happened. She was emotional, whirling and whirling. She offered some guidance, but I didn't need her guidance. She cried. She felt like a sister. I already knew what my next steps would be. I started hunting on my own, not fetching for others.

INTERACTIVE DOSSIERS

With confidence and little memory of the events of that morning, I spent the evening making a new list of high-value targets and other persons of interest, trying to be as specific as possible in my descriptions, physically and otherwise. I didn't hold back, using my imagination to fill in gaps.

Twigg had been feeding me all sorts of intel on the murders. He gave me a computer tablet, filled with intel. So many new leads were coming in that it was going to be impossible to track everything without a good system. Twigg greedily smiled when he plopped more stacks on my desk. Snow would do the same, with the same kind of smile. They were both just messing with me. Whenever I saw someone new, I added that person to my list. To make things more interesting and spark my imagination, I connected names on the list, whether al-Qaeda, Taliban, or their Pakistani intelligence (ISI) sympathizers, with role-playing games characters of my own creation, a la Dungeons & Dragons. Some had divine powers, others didn't. For instance, a bomb-maker in KC became a wizard, someone with the ability to cast spells and create potions.

Maddox visited me. He was so tanned. His tan was much deeper than mine. So my first Taliban characters were tanned and healthy, inspired by Maddox. My new pantheon went way beyond Mangal (or Abdul Gulzar Malak, if he was involved at all, and were the two connected? I wondered). I created a ton of new monsters. Just calling them monsters is so cheesy and cliché, I know, but these guys were cutting off people's heads and such. 'Enchanted' is not a better term. 'Monster' is better. They were reaching out from the fifth space, beyond the fourth wall. The abyss portion of that space (sort of a sub-universe, as I saw it at the time) was reaching for me, and I responded. With this different approach to war, and considering I was thinking of the Mars Station mystery, I wasn't in a "how am I ever going to get through this" frame of mind. I was more entwined with the future.

I started laughing more, though the darkness of the world was turning deeper and deeper. Maybe I seemed lost to others, but I wasn't feeling that way. I was starting to say things just as I wanted to say them, according to my visions. I imagine that fine soul, Sir Isaac Newton, had similar feelings when he was interacting with other scientists, defending his revolutionary theories of motion in nature and time itself. God or no God, a man needs to spend time on an island in order to become a better man.

My little D&D plan was not too far off the mark: such a wacko plan would stimulate creativity and clear mental roadblocks. My intention was to manage uncertainty. I recalled my intelligence training at Ft. Huachuca. Developing a dossier, some sort of kill-package, was not beyond my training, if it was a bit beyond my actual experience. So this was by-the-book stuff, but more. At the same time, I started writing a book based on information I learned about Major Paulsen, who was in my office-shack before me, and a man named Sultan, an Army sniper. I called the book *Gift Rats*.

This is the progression: start with a name or a face; find his/her friends and start a dossier with their name/face; build a history; establish patterns and routines; pinpoint within a certain degree of error where the target is at a certain time;

brief interested parties; capture or kill within parameters authorized by people who have power over your own career. As a reservist and a lawyer by trade, I had it a bit easier than the intelligence career man. People like that moved around not only as apparitions in the field but as apparitions among themselves. Hunting and killing wasn't my trade or interest, but I did have an interest in the overall mission, and the spooky development of it, and I had autonomy (Twigg liked to communicate via stacks of paper on my desk). I was going to write a new book to get 'mission complete' if necessary, by God. The book was in my head, though (not talking about *Gift Rats*), sort of an interactive dossier that pulled together bits of fantasy. So far, it was going in all sorts of directions. My brain was fertile. I drew from Digger's methodology. I had to make my own because others weren't helpful. Interrogation logs were limited and mostly contained talk of Sugarbush. Except for the one I had, Digger's notebooks were with CID. Then, somehow, they ended up with G2 for a deeper analysis of what intelligence they might contain (for extraction by G2, not out of some sense of preservation by CID).

How did I know this? There were several layers of security I had to go through each day to get to all the tech and reports I needed to do my job, layer after layer of doors with card readers and code boxes and soldiers at desks checking in everybody. I got to see the Bluebird Big Board, filled with matrices so full and twisted I could see every HVT Bluebird was tracking, right down to their friends' friends' friends. Some were noted as being captured or killed. It was a dirty parade, much bigger than my own list. Bluebird was my moniker for the higher intelligence community, as a collective whole. Bluebird is a modified Blue Falcon, a common Army expression that means Buddy Fucker. Insert here: kakawww...the sound of a hungry falcon. (The Army loves all this imagery.) The letters AGM (Abdul Gulzar Malak) were in several places on the big board, and was that Maddox's handwriting?

It was a big show by Bluebird, real and cheap in its presentation, very low-fi, and a little disturbing by the way, but it was a necessary part of the presentation of modern warfare. For Bluebird, it was a big picture war, but the further down the chain it went, everything got smaller: smaller tracking devices and probes and drones and more and more robots were on the drawing table, the next generation of soldiers. Even I had a big bug-drone plan that I intended to one day reveal to Big Army. But Haines beat me to it. Haines was the Air Force Technical Sergeant I met on Halloween. I hadn't seen him since Halloween, but there he was, standing beneath the big board, showing a couple of soldiers a glass box. Inside the box were what appeared to be two fireflies. Haines didn't see me. He looked like he was making a sales pitch. Between the fireflies and all the other lights, my mind was swimming.

Later that day, I started writing an email to the CG. I didn't hold back. I cc'd Maddox. I would later brief the CG, but at that time I really didn't have his ear, so I decided to turn over a new stone and took the imagination route, *like my sidebar comments to you, LM*, with my letter for a start: Dear Sir, I have some concerns to lay out, north-south-east-west, not three dimensions, not four, think <u>five</u>, plus a new methodology, based (in part...perhaps 'inspired' is the better word) on some good advice from a certain missing SM and a superior officer (not missing) and a civilian or two. I got cold-cocked by a local Russian woman and a witch back in Georgia. It's the truth. It's in the <u>fifth dimension</u>. Ya'll have got me on a track to craft my own future, in the form of new enemies. Lightweight entities for now (the Russian girl thinks I'm seeing ghosts). I'm working on a good intel product at the moment, but I just have to let you know this path is leading to an unhealthy outcome, for everyone involved, and it makes me cringe. I don't want to be just gliding along when this is all done, numb, my strong spirit merely a chalk outline. It's the children I worry about. I see their bright faces, but they come at you with greedy hands and hungry grins. I give children coloring books and crayons. I don't give them pens. They'll take them apart and use the components to make bombs. I know that. And some are lookouts, and they'll report on the size and strength of our units to their Taliban buddies. They don't do it because they want to. It's a matter of survival, like they have guns to their heads, all hours, all the time. So we've got to target their minds in order to save this place. The mind is where any revolution begins. The mind heaves and heaves and backslides then heaves again, till it explodes. I have a headache. Since you are my senior rater, Sir, I just wanted to explain some of these things. More later... CPT Jett

I studied Digger's notebook. He was working on multiple role-playing games. Two were set in outer space. One adventure featuring Rhoknol and Peruvia, another following Tydo and Remvi. Another adventure followed a man named Baz Beuttner and took place in Los Angeles in 1998.

I'm becoming as connected to Digger as you, LM. His man, Baz, is a crazy loner who lives on North Berendo in Los Angeles, the same street where I lived, and I lived there the same year. What a crazy coincidence. Listen here: Baz Buettner: mystic, psychic investigator, occasional actor. He makes his money ghostbusting, mostly for Hollywood royalty. He's on the payrolls of some big-time people.

Here's how the adventure starts: Baz slumps deeper into the old recliner. He could move into the big, empty house, but he likes living in the garage. His dead parents haunt the house. He'd rather deal with all the other Monsters of Los Angeles (MLA). The television's light turns the garage blue. His Transformers shine on his dresser, and Voltron. The Dodgers are leading the Mets by two runs...

He calls Central Casting to see if any parts are advertised. Just as he settles into his recliner to finish watching the game, his plants start choking him. They wrap their vines around his neck. They reach underneath his arms and pull him back, over the back of the recliner. It is his own fault. He has gone too far experimenting with his plants. At the same time, he has a vision: a monster is trying to communicate. Baz throws off the vines and starts playing his Pointer Sisters cd. He knows the plants hate this.

Digger's writing style was a bit dry but amusing. At the time I didn't know much about what kind of work he was doing for the Army, but I imagine he wrote a lot of reports and would've rather been writing stuff like this.

It goes on, LM: Baz receives a call from DISPATCH on his new cellular telephone. He has never even met the woman. She has told him she is twenty years old. He thinks she sounds older. They have never met in person.

BAZ: Go ahead.

D: Downtown, midnight. In front of the U.S. Bank Tower.

BAZ: I've got something I want to ask you about.

(It's usually not a two-way flow of information. Baz is just the recipient of information.)

BAZ: For some odd reason, while my houseplants were trying to kill me, a vision of a Shoktor popped into my brain.

D: All I can do for now is crosscheck past encounters with the MLA.

BAZ: Please. (He bites his thumbnail.) It's a big book. This could take a while.

It sounds like Baz has to go out into the city of monsters, once again. It is who he is, even though he would rather stay home and watch the ball game tonight.

This means something, LM. I haven't tried to fly in a while. This man, Digger, can fly. I saw it in his eyes on day one...

The magician card was on my desk next to a stack of field manuals that belonged to the shack's previous occupant, Paulsen. I picked up the card. Does Digger have one of these? I thought. Maybe his is more powerful?

Maddox barged into my work-shack before chow. I turned the card facedown. "I read your email," he said. "Congratulations. You've got a date with the CG, you crazy bastard."

BRIEFING RC-SOUTH COMMANDER ABOUT MARS STATION

Maddox and I caught the CG just before his bedtime. Maddox gave me some advice while we were waiting: "Captain Jett...Thomas...You're doing well so far, but this man is going to want to know facts. Let me handle that. He's going to want to know where we stand on the murders, and Digger, and the fact is I don't have much on either."

"Is that why I'm here?"

"You're here because you've been working on all this."

"In my own way, Sir." I noticed all the little grooves in Maddox's face. He got in my face.

"You're a piece of work, Jett. Your theories...I've seen your notes. You think the whole theater is filled with ghosts."

"Not exactly, Sir"

"Have you been having headaches?"

Before I could answer, a sergeant entered the room. "General Williamson will see you now."

I had not met any generals in my brief career, but Williamson didn't strike me as general-like. He was lanky, with sort of a goat face. He was a three-star Lieutenant General. He had his little catchphrases, like all generals. "I've got my money on you boys," he said to us, calling both of us 'boys,' despite our age difference.

"We've got this guy Malak," LTG Williamson continued, "and we're hot on his trail, and then there's Mars Station. Love the name. Yours?"

"Major Twigg's, I believe, Sir," I said. I wasn't sure. I'd never asked. "It's a freakish place, Sir," I said. Maddox nudged my elbow.

"It's what?" said Williamson.

"I'm just trying to paint a certain landscape, Sir."

"You figured that I'm an art lover?" Williamson smiled. He showed us the painting behind his desk. We were living in a desert. Why would he have a painting of a desert in his office? "I had it shipped over to make the place a little more like home." Again, strange man.

I kept going. I folded in all sorts of puns, anecdotes, theatrical gestures, subtle references to his childhood, which I was making up in my head, the way I did with our Taliban foes, as Digger did with his own theoretical world. I laid out my vision at that point, which was also a product of my dreams. Explaining my dreams would've been too complicated. Williamson was more interested in methodology.

"Interrogations, Maddox?"

"Ongoing, Sir," said Maddox. Maddox and Williamson talked as if they went way back.

"Impressions, Captain Jett?"

"It's not about extracting a ton of information, it's about the right kind of information. As far as Mars Station...I just think there's more going on than what you realize or imagine."

"But not more than you imagine," said Williamson. He smiled. At that moment, I knew he was on my side. "Who's running the place?" he said.

"Could be Malak," I said. "Could be any of his people. We should keep an eye on all of them."

"Malak is the easy choice," said Williamson. "Don't you

think, Maddox?"

Maddox nodded.

"And there's Mangal," I said. Maddox nudged my arm again.

"Who?" said Williamson.

"Another theory of mine, Sir. I've been wargaming this for some time. There's Mangal. There's a group of players..."

"You're thirty-something, Captain Jett?" said Williamson. "You look as young as my grandson."

"You don't look old enough to have a grandson, Sir." It was an attempt to escape future trouble.

"Who is he under again?" Williamson asked Maddox, pointing at him with a bony finger. "He's not one of yours?"

"Major Twigg is his first line."

"I see. I want you to take a more direct role in this man's future, Maddox. I know you're not in his chain." Williamson winked at me. He maintained dominance, he just did so with a wink.

"Yes, Sir," said Maddox. They were setting up some complicated tricks, with me at the center, but I didn't pick up on it at the time. Some for good, some for bad.

A map of the Arghandab River Valley was on the wall. It was marked up, top to bottom. "May I show you, Sir?" I pointed at a grid-square along the river.

"Nothing is around there," said Williamson. "I've been out that way many times."

"I think we ought to take a second look," I said.

Williamson smiled with half his mouth. "I've got a President and a Congress that wants me to focus assets on other things, like getting out of here smoothly, not digging in deeper. That's what you're asking, right?" Williamson was clinging to the idea of linear movement through time and space. I had to fix that.

"Captain Jett would never ask such things of generals or the President or Congress," said Maddox. He had been dragged across the carpet by too many generals. He was getting cynical.

I don't know if it was Maddox talking off the top of his head or the general having fun with us before his bedtime, but my mind strayed. Some other ideas popped into my brain. "What if these people we're trying to change are just pawns of a higher power we can't imagine?" Maddox gripped my shoulder. I didn't like who he became in the presence of this general.

"We're all pawns in one way or another," said Williamson. "We've had over-watch positions around there for weeks. There's been no unusual activity. Why should I give a shit about it? I'm not convinced I should."

"There's been no unusual activity that you can see, Sir," I said.

"You're so concerned with Taliban you don't even know exist," said Williamson.

"I'm not the only one who sees the war this way, Sir. I've been studying Digger's notebooks. He was on the verge of discovery."

"Digger?" said the general.

"He means Sergeant Ramsey," said Maddox. "The missing soldier."

"The AWOL soldier, you mean," said Williamson.

"His creative methods and analytical skills are different than mine," I said, "but I've reached a similar conclusion. There is a side of this war beyond what you see with your own eyes, almost beyond belief. Consider what happened at Sugarbush. It's not just Taliban and al-Qaeda out there, Sir. We're dealing with monsters. I've had experience with this kind of thing." I couldn't be sheepish about my ideas.

"What experience?" said Williamson.

"Yeah," repeated Maddox. "What experience?"

How would I explain? If I said too much too soon, they'd compound the words coming out of my mouth with the well-documented pain in my brain post-IED, and that would be the end of my adventure. "I have a diverse background. I'm a lawyer, Sir. The kind of people you deal with..."

This set LTG Williamson off. "Oh, don't get me started about lawyers. Legal reviews are holding up missions, even some weapon systems I've played a part in creating."

I found a better way in. "You don't say, Sir. I create weapon systems also. Well, on paper."

"Like Leonardo da Vinci," said Maddox.

"Such as?" said Williamson.

"The Fourth Wall," I said. "Sometimes I simply use T-4-W in my notes."

Williamson sat at his desk. "Describe this T4W."

"I can't fully describe it," I said, "because I don't know what it is yet. That's where you come in, Sir."

"Captain Jett..." started Maddox. I didn't have his effortless way of conversation with generals. We were worlds apart, some days.

"I get it, Maddox," said Williamson. "It's something akin to MAAWS."

"Yes, Sir! But it's so much more. It's a game. It's a path, it's..." But I didn't have all the answers, except I knew it would lead to truth, so that's what I said. "The Fourth Wall is a path to the truth, for me personally, I mean."

Maddox went from red to purple.

"And for a CG, like me?" said Williamson. I could see his wheels turning. He got up and walked around the room. He looked at the map again. "You said you're a lawyer?"

"In my civilian life."

"A civilian life?" said Williamson. "I forgot what that's like." He got a laugh out of Maddox. I was relieved for the break in tension. I thought Maddox was about to explode.

"I live in a sea of red tape, you know," said Williamson.

"I can at least tell you that T4W is not more red tape, Sir," I said. "It's anything but."

"And you want me to subsidize your path to the truth? Did you come here to ask for money, Maddox?"

Maddox stumbled with his words. "I think we're mainly here to...talk about geography."

"Oh, yes," said Williamson. "Mars Station."

LTG Williamson called in his deputy, Major General Sanchez. Maddox later told me he wasn't bosom buddies with Sanchez, and years later I learned Sanchez's career ended with one too many toxic leadership allegations and a full investigation against him that resulted in a GOMOR and no more stars. I got to sit and listen to the melodic whispering of a three-star and two-star general. Sanchez smiled at me on the way out. I had a feeling that, now that I was floating in the stratosphere of modern warfare, with the generals, I was learning to fly in an alternate, more down-to-earth way learned by all mid-career Army officers.

LTG Williamson winked again. "Well if you want to be *the* man, then you'll be *our* man," he said.

I'm sure I was giving a big, expressionless stare, at that moment. It was reflected in Williamson's face. Maddox was nodding now, agreeing with the general. I met Yvonne an hour later in a courtyard behind the Canadian headquarters compound. She arrived before me. She was sitting alone in the dark. By now she knew my routine pretty well. She had her ways of getting into my head. She could do as she pleased in some ways, in ways of dreams, when I was vulnerable, but the way she came to me, in dreams, tip toed toward me, I didn't like her waiting in the cold, dark night like that. She looked like any other urchin on the base, ghostly. I could see she was uneasy, in pain, but the first thing she did was comment about me.

"Something or someone else is on your mind, as always," Yvonne said.

"I've got some Taliban-related homework, so I can't visit long."

A Black Hawk flew overhead. It illuminated our position. We kissed in the light of the helicopter. It was an important night, a night when I developed a stronger idea of parallel worlds, with wars in both. Yvonne was a part of this world and that one. And now the CG was giving me a wider berth to get things done in both.

I got a text message. There was going to be a dignified transfer ceremony at 2300 hours. The amusement park ride went along: pleasure, pain, fear, madness, and Yvonne's incredulous grin through it all. One last kiss and I went about my duties. The fallen were five: three Americans, two Australians. Their vehicle hit an IED in the road in Area New Mexico, in Desert Fox territory. Their party was ambushed. I later learned that the Taliban hung around for longer than usual, disrupting the extraction element. It made me sick. I lurched back to my shack afterward. Everything in the world was venom/reward/punishment/out of control/world gone wrong.

2D WAR

Stacked near my shack were canvas scraps, olive green on one side and creamy on the opposite side. I went through the scraps and found a rectangular piece, 40x24 inches. I rolled it up and took it to work. I used it to create a map of Afghanistan. I drew the boundaries of the five regional commands: RC-South, RC-North, RC-East, RC-West, and RC-Southwest (the newest, with Helmand and Nimroz Provinces split off from RC-South). I noted where I believed Mars Station was. Sugarbush was also on the map. It got a big red circle. Other flash points got dots. My magician card was visible at all times while I made the map. I glanced over at it often. It was a patchy creation, an old-fashioned approach to navigation, but the universe was sending me these messages to get back to simpler approaches. I put the map up on my shack wall, on display like gaudy artwork. I marked all over it with multicolored pencils, but mostly red. I didn't finish it on day one. Indeed, it's an unfinished art piece that I've carried with me all these years, like Leonardo da Vinci with his Mona Lisa, going back to Maddox's comparison.

"Reminds me of a love note," said Patty.

Red lines arched this way and that. I could understand why Patty saw my 2D war and thought of love. Perhaps savagely, like the sketch of heart broken and breaking further. I saw a triumph and a hand reaching to grab my throat and pull me from the abyss, simultaneously. My vigorous little lines...twisting like tornadoes, punishing and ripping up the paper slopes. It took a bit of taxpayer time to draw that map, but I knew it would pay off one day.

The map helped me drift off to wherever Digger had gone, that place in space where levitation and ectoplasmic entities are the norm, where I could fly again. It helped me ask the right questions. God help the sad soul who's too tired to ask questions. Beware your squares. With some good inertia in my bones, empowered in new ways by regular outings with Yvonne, just two months into my tour, I was able to bring a new world into play with this 2D approach.

I went back to the religious center, just to see if the place was open, with Major Nichols dead. Major Darby, another Brit, was his replacement. He had a little mustache but otherwise looked the same as Nichols. Where did they get these guys? Did the Queen have them stuffed away like coins in her pocket? Darby's smile was as big as Nichols's. He had a dark aura, like Nichols. This made me not want to get to know him as well. He was a marked man.

I went back to my work-shack, back to Bluebird's tracking system, in search of anything that might lead to Digger, or any other Sugarbush clues. Mangal was in there, somewhere. If Bluebird had synergy, I wasn't yet in touch with it, but I was well on the way with my offbeat theories. Keeping things clear on this journey required a basic approach, back to paper, and my map came in handy.

I met Yvonne that night behind Canadian HQ. I showed her my map. She touched some of the red points, traced lines. "What is this?" she said.

"My future...my immediate future...is in this map," I said. "The answers are here, somewhere."

Yvonne studied it. "Too much of your Army is here in your map."

"You don't like it?"

"Continue working on it. Make it yours. Do not let the Army make it theirs. Stay within your imagination, Thomas. It is where you will achieve what you want to achieve. Anything that was created by mankind was first imagined." She blossomed at that moment.

"I've imagined a door, more of a wall," I said. "So much of my war experience till now has involved the experiences of other people. I'll have to create a door of my own and go through it and keep going."

"This door you speak of," said Yvonne, "is not a door you have to open in reality."

"It could be, and I only have a vague idea of what's on the other side."

"You will succeed." She was so sincere. The air around her shimmered.

Back and forth, between the four walls of reality, I would not succeed. Nothing conventional would keep me going. Neither harmony nor lines. None of that would ease me. I was going to have to do some fumbling around in the dark labyrinth leading to the Fourth Wall, but Digger had been there before me.

EXCERPT FROM JOURNAL OF SERGEANT DANIEL G. RAMSEY, U. S. ARMY (ADVENTURE NAME: HISTORIANS)

The tall, skinny figures stand before Tydo and Remvi. (Perception check for Tydo – successful dice roll.) Tydo sees that one of them is holding a staff. "We must proceed with caution," says Tydo. "They are not of this planet," says Remvi. "What do you want?" says Tydo, but the figures do not respond. "Can you hear me?" he says, louder. The figure with the staff raises its arm (the alien looks neither male nor female).

Successful perception roll for Remvi: "I believe they are telling us where to go," says Remvi.

"What makes you say that?"

"Look."

Ahead, shimmering in the desert, are the spires of Outpost Bekun. Tydo makes a run for the figures. Who are they? Are they following them? But they disappear. "Were they figments of our imagination?" says Remvi.

"Or shadows of ourselves?" says Tydo. (Perception roll for Tydo is successful.) "This is Decrex. There are collectors everywhere, some more powerful than others, and some may possess artifacts that can penetrate our thoughts and turn us against each other. Be careful."

A portion of the sky goes black, just for a second. Both Tydo and Remvi see it. (Each rolls a D20; neither roll is successful, so nothing more is revealed to either Tydo or Remvi.)

They proceed toward Bekun.

A VISIT TO THE AIR FORCE SIDE OF KAF

Christmas Night. I went with Chief Snow and Major Twigg to the other side of the airfield, where the air forces lived and worked, not just the U.S. Air Force, but multiple others. Twigg was happy because he was going to have a big meal at the Air Force DFAC, which had a reputation for better food than any other place on KAF, and it was steak night. I aimed to have a real conversation about technology with some people with knowledge, and to that end, I hoped to find Haines. I had some of my drone notes/ideas stuffed into my pocket.

Snow was driving the little truck very slowly, as if he had nothing to go back to that evening. I was sitting on the passenger side, with Twigg in the middle. I stayed quiet while they talked about golf. I looked up at the stars. I found the constellation of Perseus, the Greek half-god, slayer of Medusa. I dreamed of having my own quest.

"Why the glum look?" Twigg asked me.

"Sir?"

"Nah. It's better that you don't tell me. I had a long conversation with Maddox about you. I know what you're up to."

"I'm fine, Sir. Really." The truth is, I didn't want to talk to Twigg about anything I was dealing with. Twigg had opened the door to this world and gave me some sort of an institutional go-ahead, as pushed down by Lieutenant General Williamson, but I knew Twigg wouldn't go along with everything. I had been studying Digger's journal. I was learning the lengths I would have to go. I knew the names of some of his contacts, from reading a draft of the investigation. He didn't have many friends, though he wrote detailed character descriptions in the adventures he was writing about. He frequently mentioned a man named Hammer. His notes contained chronicles of different games, each taking place in a different world and a different time, past and future.

I planned to skip dinner at the Air Force DFAC and walk around and look for Hangar 4D, where Haines said he might be. When we arrived at the DFAC, I told Twigg and Snow I'd meet them back at the truck in thirty minutes. Hangar 4D was down the road. I saw Haines and another airman smoking near the hangar.

"Merry Christmas, Haines," I said. "You invited me, remember? I'm Captain Jett."

"I did, Sir," said Haines. "This is Rogers."

Rogers nodded. In the hangar, I could see sparks. Sounds of metal on metal were ringing out. "What's going on in there?" I said.

I went inside. Haines and Rogers followed me. Two airmen were in the back of the hangar, fabricating something, I couldn't tell what.

"This is how we get our aggression out, Sir," said Haines.

Something twitched in my brain.

"Are you all right, Sir?" said Rogers.

"I just had an intense feeling of déjà vu," I said. "I had a memory of Haines saying that, like remembering a dream."

"We're dreams that can dream," said Haines. "Did you know that, Sir? We, as material beings, are the dreams of super-beings alive and well in dark matter. When we move, talk, fight, everything, we are acting as circuitry between these beings. Transmitters of knowledge."

I said nothing. *I've read such words before, LM, in Digger's Historians adventure.*

"Haines is an aspiring physicist know-it-all, Sir," said Rogers.

"Whoah!" I said. "It happened again. I need to sit down." I sat on a workbench.

"What happened?" said Haines.

"He called you an aspiring physicist..."

"I say that all the time," said Rogers.

I looked up at Rogers. I felt pain in my temple, enough that I remained seated another minute. "I know you," I said. "I know each of you." I was rambling. I could hear my voice as if from a few feet above, then I could see myself from above, and Haines and Rogers, and the other two airmen working on what looked like a bat-shaped drone.

Are you doing this, LM? Are you pulling me from my body? I didn't know you could do that. But I couldn't rise higher. I couldn't leave the hangar. I was not in control. I snapped out of it. All of a sudden, I was back in my own body. I stood up.

Rogers' phoned beeped. "Inbound heroes. Terminal Delta."

It was my seventh dignified transfer ceremony. I sent Twigg a text and caught a ride with Haines and Rogers. Three soldiers, two twenty-year-old specialists, and a thirty-two-year-old staff sergeant, killed by a VBIED. These things never got easier. There was a big group of soldiers from many countries, their Christmas spirit shifted toward death. I saw the Red Hands, but we didn't have a chance to speak. Standing at attention in our first formation of the ceremony, I tried not to make a move or make any expression, though my head was still hurting. It was cold as hell. I couldn't focus on the fallen.

Then it happened again. A force pulled my astral form from my body. I was floating above the formation and the C-17 waiting on the runway to receive the caskets. Perhaps I was getting used to all the back and forth, between death and life, the casual and mundane versus the surreal and horrific. *Who are you? Is it you, LM? And where is the rest of the world?* I remembered my magician card. I felt it in my pocket and pulled it out. The card was glowing. Its image was bright, crisp. More and more each day, I resembled the man on the card. Above me, three clouds were intertwining, forming one big cloud. Parts of the cloud stretched sideways into what appeared to be wings. Moonlight highlighted the edges, making the cloud look armored. The silence was eerie, and this thing wasn't helping things. *It is the universe sending a signal, and I am beginning to understand. I am beginning to see a monster before me. Is this what you warned me about, LM? Could this be the monster that attacked Sugarbush?* Descriptions of the monster included smoke and this kind of size, but also fire, and as soon as I thought of fire, the core of the cloud started glowing orange. Then the cloud exploded, and the air crackled with electricity.

By the time the ceremony was over, I was back in my earthly shell, but out of breath. I stood there, dazed. Two men approached me. Both were tall and skinny. Their uniforms were gray, and I could not determine where they were from, based on their uniforms. Their skin was gray. Their accents were European, but I could not be more specific. Then it happened again: another wave of déjà vu, though I knew I hadn't seen these men before, or even dreamed of them. Yet, it hit me who they were. They were beings referenced in Digger's Historians story. Their names were Fate and Hope. I even remembered which was which. Fate was a little taller than Hope. Their features were elongated. I remember wondering what their skulls must look like. Together, I called them the 'Travelers.' My idea, not Digger's.

"Greetings, Captain Jett," said Fate. "We've been paying attention to you."

I kept my distance from them. "In what way?" I said.

"We've been watching your transformation," said Hope, "which has been gradual, but today your energy spiked."

I had felt an increase in psychological energy. I was more open to chaos, in all its forms. "Who are you?"

"That is not important," said Fate, "at least, not yet."

"Then why should I listen to you?" I said.

"Lady Mist is saying you should," said Hope.

"Lady Mist," I said as if I'd forgotten her. "Where are you from, gentlemen?" They looked at me sideways as they whispered to each other. Was each a version of Death himself, seeking recruits? I was waiting for one of them to hand me a scythe. "What are you saying?"

"We were wondering what they find so interesting about you," said Fate.

"Who do you mean? Who is 'they'?" I heard someone call my name. I turned. Haines and Rogers were approaching me. When I turned back, the Travelers were gone.

RISE OF THE HORSESHOE CRAB

Maddox's office was twice as big as mine, but he devoted half of it to the Sugarbush investigation. I visited him the day after Christmas. I hadn't been in his office in a while. He preferred to come to mine. The Sugarbush half of his office had gone wild. He was under the full weight of the investigation. "Washington red tape demands that mess," he said, pointing to all the maps on the wall and papers and photographs on his desk. I could tell he didn't like dealing with the Pentagon.

"Who are all the civilians I've seen coming and going?" I said.

"CIA, State Department, the usual suspects," Maddox said, offering me the Sugarbush mess with an open hand.

"Why haven't they been talking to me, Sir?" I had zero Langley contacts at that time.

"I want you to focus on your missing man and your primary mission," said Maddox. "The Sugarbush thing is going to be a sideshow before you know it. It already is. I've got it under control."

"But General Williamson..."

"Williamson is Washington. Just think of him that way."

"I thought I already had him thinking my way," I said. I thought Williamson latched onto me. I spoke so confidently during our meeting, and Williamson acted like he didn't have a choice but to subscribe to my wild story. Was it my serious voice? The mere possibility of emerging on the other side of the fourth wall was revealed in my tone and posture.

"All right," said Maddox. He dragged a box from the floor. "If you want to be involved, you're going to help me with all this."

Maddox had some dossiers partly assembled. I thumbed through the scraps. "Sir, some of these people go way back. You're interested in anticommunist rebels? I was twelve when this guy hit the heights." I showed him a picture of a man marked <u>GTJ, date of birth April 1957</u>.

"That's Tiger," said Maddox. He liked code names, like me. "He's a pimp of teenage boys. He's involved, trust me. You'll want to add him to your game, or whatever you call it. Just go through it. Give me your thoughts."

"A pimp?"

"Taliban commanders, Afghan National Police commanders...we hear stories of some of them involved in bacha bazi." I'd heard of this. Bacha bazi, or "boy play," was a custom still being practiced in parts of Afghanistan, though it was banned by the Taliban when they came to power. "Are you ok? Your face is turning green. You look sick. Still having headaches? They should've sent your ass home for a while."

"I'm fine, Sir."

Maddox picked up a stack of paper. "You need to read this," he said. "I need to go to Jalalabad for a week. When I'm back I'll work on the final report."

I felt like vomiting. I clutched my abdomen.

"Go to the hospital," said Maddox. "You're going to be surprised by what you find. I'm going to send you home to Texas if this keeps happening."

The main reason I didn't want more medical treatment was that it would pull me away from the war and possibly cut me off from opportunities, but I did as ordered. When I saw the horseshoe crab collection at the KAF hospital, I knew I was onto something.

If there was any proof of aliens ever inhabiting this planet, it would be the horseshoe crab, more ancient than dinosaurs. Maybe in the fourth wall scheme of things, we are just guests of this creature. With its special blue blood and strange form, it is proof of aliens, not just their existence, but proof they are active agents from places beyond. I saw a stressed nurse rushing through a corridor with a glass canister of blue blood and a few large crabs, their tails coiled up against the glass. Rising, threatening to rise again: the horseshoe crab. The connection between psyche and reality was happening again.

I talked to a doctor, a man around my age. I didn't trust him for that reason alone, but he did help some. "You're not getting enough sleep," he said as he felt points all over my bare upper body. He had a big mouth and a big smile. "Like most officers, you're trying to do too much," he said, "You can't do it all." He looked pretty battered himself. "Any more stomach pains?"

"No."

"How are your bowel movements?"

"Normal." Another lie. Was that even a possibility with anyone? Considering what they fed us.

"Anything else?"

I was still haunted by Digger's notes: what he was dreaming about, games he was playing in his head in those absurd dream oceans. I was stuck in a crevasse of my own imagination, along with other characters: Eve (Name of Yvonne's Fourth Wall character) and Max (Maddox's character name), and we were on a quest for some unholy object.

"We..." was all I said.

"We what?" said the doctor. I could see flecks of blue in his green eyes. His eyes fixed on mine.

"I can see that you need rest," said the doctor. He placed his hands on my chest.

"The human body is no temple," I replied.

"The long and short of it is..."

"Just give me the short."

"Again...rest." The doctor patted my shoulder. "Turn off your imagination for a while. It's sapping your energy." In Digger's games, when his characters found potions while exploring, they stored the potions for later.

The doctor started typing on his computer. I noticed a bottle of blue blood on a little table in the corner. I could've sworn it wasn't there earlier, neither the bottle nor the little table.

"Do you ever feed plants with that stuff?" I said.

But the doctor didn't respond. He kept typing. He handed me a note. "You'll follow up with us next week."

I left the hospital with blue blood on my mind. It was freezing that day. The flight line was screaming loud, with jets going to and fro, some with deadlier payloads than others. After two months in Afghanistan, I was suffering from insomnia, and my few hours of sleep were filled with wild dreams, and in those moments awake under my sweaty-wet sheets, I had to endure the noise. I can still hear the slap of the A-10s coming in at 0600 hours on certain mornings, doing practice runs.

One morning I had a confrontation with another soldier in the shower room. He accused me of slapping the walls first thing when I woke up, just to wake everybody else up and piss them off, but it was those planes going by, their echoes bouncing around in space before coming back to our shack. I wasn't doing anything. I went toe to toe with this big man.

"What's your rank?" I asked him.

"Captain, and you?"

"Captain."

"You're the guy with the crazy map on the wall," he said. Is that what you're hitting? There might be a regulation against having that thing."

A skinny soldier at the sink stopped shaving and watched us. Another soldier, who could've been the skinny one's twin brother, had just finished showering. He stood there and watched, wrapped in a towel. If it weren't for the captain's big belly, I would've been right up in his face, though I barely reached his chin.

"I'm not crazy," I said. "Why would I bang on walls?"

"I don't know. Why would you?"

"Trust me."

"I don't trust you. There's something weird going on here."

Another soldier intervened. "Leave him alone, Dustin."

He must've been at that halfway point in his tour, not close enough to the end of the tunnel to see any light because he just punched me in the stomach without letting me say another word. I couldn't speak, anyway. He knocked the air right out of me. I went down on my knees. I went through a proper physical-response-procedure, to use a martial arts term. Again, studying Digger's game was effectively re-wiring my brain.

Until the first punch was thrown, I thought I might be dreaming, but when I hit the floor, I woke up. Dustin overpowered me at first, but I sprang up. I performed a quick etiquette bow. He grabbed my arm. I went through multiple circular movements. This left him vulnerable. I did everything to stay upright. I trapped his incoming arms. His attack was drunken. I avoided punching his face; I angled myself a bit much, allowing him to put his weight where it belonged in proper counter-strikes delivered to my solar plexus, not effective, plus chin strikes with his fat palm, but he lacked proper harsh angles. There was sadness behind his moves and madness. I locked his neck in my arms. With a proper pivot, I could've crushed his groin, but I didn't. Going airborne was also not an option.

"Stop!" he said. "Let me go!"

So I let him go. It was a messy situation. I *had* to let him go.

"You're crazy," he said. He left the shower room.

Dustin seemed to believe what he was saying about me. I looked into the mirror, saw all the blood, knew it was my blood, knew I was just a normal human on the wrong end of things, knew I wasn't crazy, because crazy people don't examine themselves in that way. Having all these divine encounters was no proof of insanity, no more than strings of shattered romances. A man needs monsters in order to be a man. I started humming a song.

The shower fight made me numb. I went through the rest of my routine in a normal/quiet way. I walked to my work-shack. I took my time, kept humming my song. Three British Tornados flew above, banking left, coming in for a landing. Three A-10s followed. I kept chattering to myself. I didn't have a headache, like other mornings. Maddox will be pleased I'm getting better, I thought. I could feel my heartbeat in my temple. I could feel the warmth of my magician card in my pocket. I bought a tall cup of coffee on the boardwalk. When I arrived at my work-shack, I further explored Digger's universe.

EXCERPT FROM JOURNAL OF SERGEANT DANIEL G. RAMSEY, U. S. ARMY (ADVENTURE NAME: HISTORIANS)

The Fury is not far from Nemog, a group of cities in hollowed-out asteroids. Rhoknol is flying a little close to a chunk of space rock twice the size of the Fury. "Watch where you're flying," says Peruvia.

Die roll / skill check: Rhoknol's piloting skills: FAILS. The Fury clips the rock, knocking them off course. Rhoknol must make another skill check to get back on course to Nemog's primary port. Complicating matters, their pet, Gher, an octopus-like creature, is having some kind of mental breakdown, thanks to the Fury hitting the rock. Peruvia hurries to the back of the ship to check on Gher and the Ilix. She sees that the Ilix is glowing yellow.

Notes/Personal Statement for Rhoknol's character sheet: He would like to understand who made the Ilix but eventually would like to sell it for a high price. He would like to sell it to someone who might continue to give him access to it in the future. He plans to hide it in a safe place before deciding what to do with it. He would even like to figure out a way to speak to it.

DON'T LOOK THAT WAY (RED HAND PATROL IN SANGIN PART 1)

A few days after Christmas it snowed, just a light dusting. The sun came out after the storm. The space heater in my office-shack wasn't working so well. I had to wear gloves while I worked, which wasn't a huge problem, since I was just scanning emails and reading reports. I turned to the Fourth Wall. I continued building character sheets for Max and Eve and everyone I knew, friendly and otherwise. I even made Bluebird into an actual entity, sitting on a cloud above the world. Then, crazy as it sounds, I started getting messages from Bluebird. Bluebird was picking up a lot of noise in Helmand regarding what the locals were calling *Druj*, pronounced drooZH.

I got the Red Hand involved, plus my translator, Kochi, and the next day we grabbed a Black Hawk and traveled to the outskirts of Sangin, in the Musa Qala district. The British won the battle of Musa Qala, years earlier, but their control wasn't firm. Much of the civilian population still supported the Taliban. Disinformation was everywhere. Bluebird had good eyes but needed the human element.

Ellington led the way after we landed. Redmond and Butler were with us. They were more used to being on patrol than I was. Sure, it was just one foot in front of the other, but still. "You know," said Ellington, "the Royal Irish Regiment mothership may not like us being with you. Mother likes us separate and apart."

"Bluebird likes me separate and apart, also," I replied. "So what?"

"Why do you like us so much, anyway?" said Ellington. "You have so many American assets to choose from."

I squatted and picked up a stick. "There's here," I said, drawing a straight line, "and here," drawing another line at a ninety-degree angle to the first, "and here," completing a three-sided box. "My colleagues and superiors are not as willing as you to fill in that fourth line."

"You might be surprised," said Redmond.

"This man is correct," said Kochi.

"Captain Jett's a loon," Ellington said. They were good people, people who liked magic light shows, and I was determined to give them that. "Keep a good eye on Jett, boys. One way or the other, you're going to learn something."

I wiped my eyes. The dust was making me tear up. Half a click away was our destination. We passed fat sheep and some ruins. I was on the lookout for any peculiar buildings, modern or ancient. In particular, Bluebird informed me about the ruins of an entry-level jihadist camp in the area. It used to be a camp for Arab mujahedin, not for the Taliban.

All the houses were single level. Wide-open drains crisscrossed the streets. We met with three elders at a house. We sat around on mats inside a garage without a door. The bright sunlight made everything stand out on the floor. I'll never forget the finely woven mats and bright colors of the pillows, like the pop-colored room of a child, but the men's faces were hidden in shadows. A boy entered the garage. He looked about twelve years old. The youngest elder in the room sprung up and started speaking to the boy. The boy spoke a few words. The man pointed at the boy then pointed outside.

The boy looked at me then turned around and left. We had school supplies. We always had school supplies.

Kochi was jittery. I pulled him aside. "What's wrong?"

"The man is making me this way." Kochi showed me his shaky hands. "He does not say what he is thinking, but I know what he is thinking."

I clenched my fists to show Kochi that everything was going to be ok. I tried to display an air of determination. The boy came back and stood before the old man. The old man did not stand up. Ellington was at my side. "We left cozy homes and warm women for this shit," he said. He often complained in general ways like that.

Kochi whispered in my ear: "He is Sufi Muslim, but he has become bad. He knows dark magic. We should be careful, or the devil will come."

"We came all this way," I said. "I could see he was bad right when I walked in the room. I don't care. It's what we came for. Did the old man see something we might find interesting?"

Kochi returned to the man. The boy stood aside, very erect. He stood on the tips of his toes. He was a bright-looking boy, with the world in his eyes, but he was somewhere else. The other men sat in silence.

"This guy's a creep," said Butler.

Ellington was annoyed, as well. "Reminds me of my crazy uncle that always had some showgirl around."

"I have a taste for metaphysics," I said. "I'll stay. You all wait outside."

Ellington, Redmond, and Butler left the room. Kochi returned to me, shaking his head.

"What did he say?" I asked Kochi. "Did he see something?"

"In his mind, yes," said Kochi. "He says he can see the dreams of his goats. He says they dream of predators at night."

"But they wake up alive?"

Kochi rolled his eyes. "The old man says that his goats all dream of the same monster."

"What do you think of him?"

"He is old," said Kochi. "He does not sleep well at night. He wanders."

"Dreams are contagious," I said. "Maybe I've dreamed the same dream. Maybe I also wander at night."

"Be careful," said Kochi. "He has cursed the boy. He will curse you."

I went to the man. "Describe the dream."

Kochi translated. "The man says: Do not trust its fingers. They put together illusions."

This was the kind of thing that brought me to Helmand that day. It was for a deepening of the labyrinth, not a solution to it.

"Ask him what we can do to find and fight this monster."

Kochi rolled his eyes again.

"Let's play, Kochi," I said. "This is how I do things. You need to get to know me if you want to help me. Understanding what's important to me is important for the mission. Let's play."

Kochi wasn't as interested in the forces of chaos as I was. He didn't grasp that I was searching for clues and a new way to go, attacking something by avoiding it, that kind of approach, for the sake of the puzzle and ultimate illusion, not the solution.

The old man raised his arms and sang something. Kochi translated, laughing as he did so: "We pray to thee, Allah, to help us be high and holy, and to fight for the right, and to teach us to love this new enemy, this monster that comes to our door."

"Why is he this way?" I said.

"He is Sufi. He wants peace among everyone. He is going bad, but he is tired. Tired of fighting."

"I might go bad if I was too tired to be good," I said. "I don't want him to want peace right now, though. I want him to feel like it will be too late to act one day. What's he saying now?"

"He says that great kings once ruled this land. He says there is ancient bad blood still flowing in this land." Kochi's voice was sing-song, just enough that I saw musical notation above his head. The boy was looking ahead with a dead face. "He is certain that all the elements of life are against you: air, fire, water, and earth. He is nervous because of all the weapons."

"Weapons?" I said.

Ellington came back inside, shaking his head. I could see the old man's mind was leaping. He was saying "Druj...Druj." He pointed outside, toward the desert.

"What is Druj?" I said. "Is Druj this way?"

"That's not enough," said Ellington. "Captain Jett may want to listen to folklore, but my bosses are more interested in the drug trade. Are there poppy fields out there?"

Kochi did his job well. He calmed down. He talked to the old man then pointed in the same direction the old man was pointing. Their hand gestures were the same, like two synchronized machines.

So we hiked that way, leaving the mash-up of mud-brick buildings behind us. There was a strange sound, like a human trying to make a horrible bird call. A child screamed somewhere, followed by a few laughs. These sounds were coming from all around us, even the desert ahead of us. Clouds above twirled above like dancing dragons. There was supposed to be a field two clicks ahead where poppies would soon be sown. I didn't like the path we took. There was too much sinking in places, too much soft earth, perfect for bombs. Ellington read my mind and took us off the path, right when I was eager to do so. Clouds were rolling in ahead. It was the kind of terrain that could make you feel like you were at the bottom of an ocean after the darkness fell.

"This is UFO country," said Redmond.

"Maybe Bluebird knows," said Butler. "Jett?"

"That's a good question," I said.

Bluebird knew all kinds of things, the whole gruesome story. Funny how, by way of a little decision-making algorithm, men can create a kind of Fourth-Wall machine, but they can't get there on their own. I had some cold, hard facts, but mostly I just had folklore, as Ellington called it. Bloodstained maps, reports and plans, everything like that. And somewhere around there was the site of a face-off between rival factions of Afghan Security Forces. Each group blamed the other for a fouled-up Sangin raid, even though they both came roaring along together. Allegations went from mild to wild. I'd read the report about it. It stated a sudden storm blew in and blew apart the party with sheet lightning. Some thanked Allah. Some blamed Allah.

"Would be nice to spark up a spliff," said Redmond. "I wish."

"Spliff?" said Kochi.

"I joined the army to get away from blokes like you," said Butler. "Now look at me."

"Let's focus," said Ellington.

We reached a ridge overlooking a valley and a dry riverbed. "The old man said it was flat around here," said Kochi.

"The map says it's flat," I said, spreading my topographical map on the ground. All around us were black rocks. They looked like meteorites. I saw something in my peripheral vision that looked like a horseshoe crab. I looked closer. It was a fossilized trilobite. There were a bunch of them in the rocks. We were surrounded by Cambrian sea creatures.

"We're going back and having a word with that man," said Ellington. "He's led us into a trap, for all we know. We should've brought him along. He needs to spill his guts."

"Hold on," I said. "Nothing looks like it belongs." I pulled out my compass and found west. "There should be some low hills right over there, but there's nothing."

I was just a lawyer, just a reservist, but I had done land

navigation many times. I even did it in my neighborhood back in Houston, to keep my skills fresh. There was a ridge, and the ridge wasn't on the map at all.

"Maybe it's a refraction issue," said Butler. "Maybe you'll still find your monster out there, Captain Jett. Maybe if you go far enough you'll find the Pillars of Hercules...a symbol for what lies at the edge of the unknown. On its gates are written the words *ne plus ultra*, which means 'no further'."

"That's poetic," I said.

"Poetry is beautiful," said Kochi.

"There's also the possibility that Captain Jett has lost his mind, the way I'm losing mine," said Ellington. "Let's go back, boys. There's no drugs here, not going to be any anytime soon." He picked up a rock and threw it.

"Hold on," I said. "I've got an idea. You've got your goals. I have mine. We can keep them separate. They're going to come together in the end, trust me. There's no running problem."

"Happy endings all around, huh?" said Redmond.

"I'll think about it," said Ellington.

Poor Kochi. He had no clue what anyone was talking about. Refraction. Optics. It was too much for him. He looked confused.

"We're going back and having a word with the old man," said Ellington. The Red Hands started back without Kochi and me.

Kochi turned and looked toward the horizon. "Like it says in the Quran," said Kochi, "God will shake the trunk of a palm tree, and it will drop fresh dates on you."

Ellington came back to us. "Don't look back that way," he said. "Captain Jett, if you want to believe in things that aren't there, then I can't keep putting my men at risk to help you. Your vision is this way, Sir." He nodded toward Sangin. "The old man knows something. I could see it in his face. I've got a sense of this game you're playing. It sounds very American, but I like your vision. You need me."

He was right. Without him, I was going to have to go rogue, and it wasn't even 2012 yet.

"Look over there," I said, pointing at the horizon, in the direction Kochi was gazing. "There should be mountains. We've got to figure this out. But we're nowhere near Mars Station. Something else is going on here. Next time we come, we'll bring more men. It's going to be a more hostile place next time."

"Everywhere is hostile, in the end," said Ellington. "You'll find your Mars Station, Jett." That smile. He was a true poet and crazy death machine.

"Let's bring sharpshooters," I said.

"You've got two right there," said Ellington with a nod to Redmond and Butler. "Runs deep in their blood. I'll tell them to put on their ancestral war paint."

Ravens were calling above us, a whole family of them, clouds boiling above them. *As in Digger's Historians notebook...when Tydo and Remvi are walking through the desert on the strange planet, heading toward Bekun, leaving their ship behind. They saw a black form in the sky...*

Things just got stranger once we were back in town. A woman was running toward us, sort of. Butler raised his weapon, but Ellington pushed it down. She was running from her burning house.

"Something creepy is going on here," said Ellington.

We returned to the garage. We found the old man sitting on the floor, playing a string instrument. The boy was with him, dancing, not for him, just dancing, snapping his fingers. The boy was smiling. He started singing.

Later that night, back in my shack, I wanted to see what happened to Tydo and Remvi. They continued toward Outpost Bekun. Digger went in some different directions here, as several portions had scratch-throughs. I studied my big map. It relaxed me. I let my eyes zig-zag. I closed my eyes and tried to leave my body and see the world from a higher place. I did see the world, but it wasn't my world. The terrain was mountainous. Two figures were hiking on a mountain far beneath me. I could see the trees moving on the other side of the mountain, not in the line of sight of the men. I couldn't get to them. The way ahead was more shadows than trees. I wanted to warn them, but they soon saw what was ahead. One of the men had a kind of tool that lit up the entire forest, brighter than any flashlight could. Things emerged from the woods. I was too high in the sky to see details, but it was as if shadows merged together and became sasquatch-like creatures. Whatever they were, the men did not run. They engaged the beasts with weapons unlike anything I'd ever seen, weapons that spit fire that wasn't fire, dayglow orange emissions...laser weapons?

I can say that the future of my mission was born that day, that night while I went through Digger's notes over and over. The next day I started developing the system which would help me make decisions. The universe seemed like a dream, but I already had a good fix on not just its visible pathways, but its dark side, with so many particles bent on opposing each other. There is a mirror world...a shadow version of the universe. Digger could see this.

THE PSY-
OPS GURU

I got a strange email one cold morning from a staff sergeant I didn't know: Are you the same Jett from Ft. Huachuca?

I answered yes.

Did you know Rivers?

I answered yes.

Five minutes later I was knocking on the door of a work-shack about thirty yards from mine, just around the corner, just down from Maddox's shack.

My old friend, Art Rivers, answered the door. Two other soldiers were cramped into the tiny space. Rivers' hair was full, puffed up. He looked like he hadn't shaved in a couple of days. Rivers and I went back years. I gave him a bear hug before he could salute me. We were grunts together at the military intelligence school at Ft. Huachuca, Arizona in 2007. I slept in the bunk above his. I knew this was his second tour in Afghanistan because we were keeping up with each other during his first tour years earlier. We stood outside in the sleety cold and talked.

"Captain's bars," he said, pointing at the rank on my chest. "Looking good, Sir."

"Likewise, staff sergeant. You've turned into a real psychological operations guru. Does it suit you? Or do you want to go back to doing analyst work?"

"You're still a mind reader, Jett."

Rivers was a reservist, like me. He had less of a civilian work life than me. He said he felt "invisible" in Kentucky and wanted to go back on active duty. He said he thought he saw me twice on KAF in the darkness: once on the way to chow, another time at a dignified transfer ceremony. We took a walk. I told him about what I saw in Sangin.

It was too soon to let Rivers in on my plan, and I didn't mention anything about my involvement in the Sugarbush murder investigation or the missing soldier. I just wanted him to focus on this one monster with me. It was fate that led me to Sangin, despite the minimal results, the mere whispers of Druj. It was good practice, getting the Red Hand to gear up and go along with me. Until then, I thought I might be alone in my particular little mission. Maddox was gone. I needed his advice on dealing with orders from higher command.

The universe was sending me signals, but mainly in dreams, but that was starting to change. I'm sure I did not see all the signals, which is true of most people. We entered Rivers' shack. Rivers introduced me to his small team, including the female sergeant who sent me the email. There were stacks of trifold pamphlets, literature for locals. Pamphlets on how to spot bombs. Pamphlets on dealing with domestic violence. All cartoons, people smiling, dealing with all sorts of agitation. Speaking of agitation, Rivers seemed strange. We went back outside. "You like our little operation? We pretty much do what we want, as long as we get results."

"So I'm out there doing what I want, and you're doing what you want."

"That's what this is all going to amount to," Rivers said. "Loner types doing big things, standing out from the rest."

I talked about Sangin. Rivers was hooked into my story of the Sangin boy. He talked about an old man he knew of in Kandahar City, a wealthy man who'd kept hundreds of boys over the years. The left side of Rivers' face twitched. When you live with someone for a short time, but in intense conditions, their mannerisms and movements imprint in your memory. The twitch was new. I pressed him about it.

"What's that?" I asked him, squishing the left side of my own face.

"My twitch? It was my first tour in Afghanistan, in 2008. My unit was on foot patrol in Ghazni Province. We delivered supplies and were heading out when I saw a group of kids playing some version of 'Simon Says.' When we got closer, I noticed that the leader of the group was a blind boy. He was toying with everyone else. He knew things no one else knew, and those kids knew it. It made me smile. I needed that lift. I was the lead man in the patrol. I picked up the pace back to the rally point, maybe more than I should have. My mind wasn't on my job. It was on that bunch of kids, especially the blind boy. Then we got hit. The blast was on the left. I felt the concussion of air. Everything was happening in slow motion. I had my eyes on the man in front of me then looked left and saw Private Lam flying through the air, nothing but deadweight. There were Taliban fighters up ahead and on the right. They hit us with fire before Lam hit the ground. He was dead before his crumpled body landed. Lying on the ground, I returned fire with my rifle set on full auto. I don't how that happened. I'm usually good about just keeping it on semi-automatic. I heard some screams. I know I hit someone. I never did see their faces. They weren't close enough. My ears were still ringing. I couldn't feel the left side of my face. And right then, a random thought popped into my head: making love to my girlfriend's best friend, seven years ago, right on her dad's favorite easy chair, both of us drunk on beer. We knocked over some shelves. As we moved, I looked forward to many times with her, but that was the only time. It was good, though. It was nice to be with someone without having to say goodbye later. As I was returning fire, I watched Lam go to heaven. I was sure that's where he was going. He just seemed compassionate and thrilled to have been chosen for something special, like he knew God. He seemed so loving, but I was sad when I later learned that he had no friends or family to accept his body back home. Anyway, now I'm stuck with this." Rivers rubbed his face.

When I told all this to Yvonne later, she got it right. I was so tired, off all around, but she looked at me with those penetrating eyes. She usually had such a soft voice (for a Russian), but not at that moment: "You can either choose to touch certain things or not. Be in a hurry, or not. You are headed one place, then the world takes you to another. This is what is called 'truth.' So follow your friend. Make him part of your game." Sometimes she came at me diagonally, but not this time. I shuddered.

And I did include him in my game, and all his bloodstained stories.

RIVERS TAKES ME OUT...THINGS GO TERRIBLY WRONG

Rivers and I had differences. For one thing, he was always smiling, and he described his home state, Kentucky, as a place he couldn't get back to fast enough. He had Kentucky like I had Texas. He claimed that his primary intention when he joined the Army was to just watch the fight and take notes. He should've been the writer, not me. Like everyone I talked to at KAF, Rivers had all sorts of theories about the murders at Sugarbush. And from the conversations we had during our days together, I believed he saw the universe in bits and pieces, as I did. Both of us were explorers.

On New Year's Eve, I went with Rivers and his team to a village north of Kandahar City. Twigg wasn't going to let me go at first, but I created a nexus with the local drug trade, not a false one, either, so anything he would have to report to LTG Williamson would be along that storyline. I sketched it like a story: A, B, C. The fiction I was starting to create was itself turning into a living system where the energy brought into it was transforming then dissipating into a different reality, sort of a damper effect. So the energy within my fictive world was more balanced than the real world, as in Digger's world(s), and it was starting to take over. Fourth Wall calculus isn't all that different, as it turns out. Pulses. Flashes. Angles. These are what you have to watch for. It's an intuitive kind of transcendence. I looked out the window of our tactical vehicle. The land was creamy. All the earthen colors were starting to make me sick.

"Do you remember that night in Sierra Vista?" said Rivers.

I'm not going into those details, reader, but going into all that history made me feel *low*. Other people's high points can be my low points. But I was jazzed when the gunner scratched some targets with the .50-cal. The bastards were not skittish about firing at our convoy.

So Rivers and I traded old stories and laughed. He laughed more than me. We bounced from one planet to another.

"Remember when you kicked Swope in the shin?" said Rivers.

"Not until now," I said.

"He wailed on you. He beat your ass."

"I remember."

"Why did you kick him?"

"I don't know," I said, "I just did." It was the sad truth. "That reminds me. I ran into Swope like I ran into you, right after I got to KAF. We passed each other on the boardwalk. I ran into him two years ago in Germany, too. Same kind of thing."

"I know he was here," Rivers said. "I guess you didn't hear what happened. Swope is dead. Got too close to some roadkill stuffed with explosives."

"Damn," I said. That was all I could say. I hardly knew Swope. I deserved the beating he gave me. I talked to him more the two times I met him outside of Arizona than I did in Arizona.

"Swope..." Rivers said. He laughed. He had memories he wasn't telling me about. "I'm going to Alaska when I get home. First, Kentucky, but then I'm going to Alaska. I want to see some bears."

"Did you know that black bears can be born with white fur?" I said. "You never know what nature will bring." I was going to follow my trivia with some witch stories, but I remembered I told him all my witch stories when we first met. "So you want to see some monsters," I said. I closed my eyes and went someplace far away. I wanted to see some monsters that day, regretfully.

Outside the village, we found a man pierced by a tree branch. The branch was a good six inches wide. It went right through his torso below his rib cage. His face was covered in black blood.

"That's not all blood," said Rivers. "That's his own shit."

What an evil smell. If it wasn't for that old man, I might've seen the place differently. Locals were blaming a new monster. Everyone was trying to figure out all these new holes in the war. Poor Kochi. Here he was again. He tried really hard to explain what was on people's minds. He just couldn't do it all the way.

"Kochi," I said, "Ask them what happened here when half of Sugarbush was killed last month." Kochi searched their faces to find the right one to talk to. He chose an old man deep in the crowd who looked like he didn't want to be bothered.

Sugarbush wasn't far away, but the more I traveled around southern Afghanistan, the more detailed the picture was becoming. Kochi explained to the old man what I was wanting to know. The old man didn't understand at first. Kochi showed the old man the date of the Sugarbush massacre on his pocket calendar. Kochi called the place by its actual name. Rivers and his team stood by. Once I started this random investigation, they stayed out of my way and provided support. Kochi came back, frustrated as always, but with the blood drained from his face. He started to talk, then paused and put his hand up, and walked away. It was his way of saying he needed to take a break when he didn't want to ask for a break. He stepped away.

"There's no denying that your translator knows more than us at this point," said Rivers. His leader, First Lieutenant Kay, was shaking his head. He didn't like me, and he didn't like where things were going, but he played along for the sake of unit cohesion because Rivers liked me and so did the other soldiers. "I'd love to be able to figure out something easily for once. This job..."

Kochi came back. "What happened then does not matter like now. What is now is vengeance. Someone, something, has a plan." Most serious look I'd seen yet on Kochi, like he was now a part of some internal scheme. That's the way he was. He wasn't a control freak, but he still liked holding cards.

The elder he was talking to came back with a boy. Kochi and the elder exchanged more words, then Kochi presented the boy to me. "This is Ahmed. He is blind, but he knows everything."

Ahmed was maybe eleven years old. He had energy, something shimmering within. He wasn't fazed by anything that had taken place or was going to take place. It was easy to see.

"Ask Ahmed what he saw," I said to Kochi. "You know what I mean."

Kochi and the boy talked.

The boy became excited. He hopped about and raised his hands above his head, indicating some large object. Kochi was taking notes but became frustrated and put his hand up for the boy to slow down, as if the kid could see the gesture. Without even understanding what the boy was saying, I could see his imagination was running wild. Mine was. I looked around the village. How do you survive in a place where virtually nothing follows a conventional model? My vector was zigging and zagging, but I felt like I was within closer reach of my dreams. I was learning every day, but it was hard, considering the model of my business, but that model, right down to the data, to the very core, got sucked into chaos, fury, but sucked in with the weight of its old paradigm, the training routines, and intelligence products. Then the response to the chaos was more of the same training, the same intel schemes, and that was going to be the case for this new murder, it looked like. Watching Ahmed talk, I was already starting to go through some of the reports in my head, reports I would need, stuff that Bluebird liked, worn so thin already by stuff I was already doing.

Some locals were now dragging the man's body toward us, the branch still through him. They had him chest up, so his head was jerked back, his bloody mouth open, hungry flies still all over his face. His eyes halted my imagination, then I got going again, seeing his parts half-eaten-away, a corpse of the future.

The old man was talking to Kochi again. The man was excited, like Ahmed. He pointed away, down the street. Kochi pointed in the same direction. The man walked away with the boy. Kochi came back.

"Where is he going?" I asked Kochi.

"He says he has something you need to see."

The man went into his house then returned with a piece of torn cloth and showed it to Kochi, who brought it to me. "He says it is a map that has been in his family for many generations. He says it is proof."

"Proof of what?"

"Proof of a different race of men that once lived here."

"Hocus Pocus," said Rivers.

I knew otherwise. The old man was talking to himself. The map was brittle. The script was faded. I let Kochi handle it. I didn't touch it. "What does this have to do with that?" I pointed at the corpse. Kochi translated. Kochi and the man had a long conversation.

Kay came to me. "Sir, we need to go. While you've been talking, my men dropped off the supplies."

"Soon," I said. I meant it. My head was bothering me.

We followed the old man to the edge of the village and into the desert. The boy stayed behind. Kochi and I lead the way. A cold front was blowing in from the west. Visibility was getting worse. No one wanted to be going deeper into the desert. Kay was grumbling to Rivers about how badly the weather was about to change. We walked down into a wadi. The slope was steep. The earth was loose like it wanted to slip right out from under us. The only sounds were dry grass crunching and tactical gear clicking and men breathing. Grape rows were on the other side of the wadi, rows and rows of bare vines and gray earth. We stayed on the edge of that spooky field. Kay was getting more and more restive. "This is not right. I don't like this sky. We're about to get hit. Remind me what we're doing here."

"Finding clues," I said.

"Chasing ghosts," Kay said.

We kept going. I didn't trust this old man, but my gut was telling me to move forward. All we could do was brace for the next big thing, whatever that might be. I knew something was coming, but I didn't come right out and say anything. My mind was wandering on the edge of a bad dream. The sky was going from gray to black and sunlight looked like moonlight. I had a vision of Kay blasting into twenty pieces.

The following is a portion of an unclassified statement of 1LT Matthew Kay taken on 1 JAN 2012: "We were moving west down the road behind CPT Jett and the translator, and the male villager. CPT Jett didn't fully inform me about where we were going. All he said was he "believed" he would find some clue about Event Q1.[1] The mission was accomplished, but CPT Jett said it was necessary to investigate Q1 since we had the chance. I was looking all around our position. It was flat desert. There were three typical single-level mud-brick structures ahead. Once we got within fifty meters of the

---

[1] This was an alternate designation for the Sugarbush massacre.

structures, we started receiving small arms fire, semi-automatic bursts of AK's. Hostiles were shooting at us from the rooftops. We were pinned down. There was no cover, and little concealment, so we went prone. The old man didn't drop. He was still standing when he got shot. I saw him crumple over like he got shot in the gut. I fired back at the rooftops, but it was so dusty I couldn't see anything. I just fired at the bursts I could see coming from their rifles. I think I got one of them. He stopped firing. Then another big dust cloud swallowed everything. SSG Rivers was ahead, with CPT Jett. People were still shooting. The dust storm was so loud that it drowned out the gunfire. Helicopters weren't going to be able to land in that. I got up and started looking for my men. Others were looking around. It was so dusty I couldn't see who was who. Since the old man was the only person I actually saw get shot, I went to him first. The translator was already helping him. He was shot through his abdomen, on his flank. He looked bad, but he made it out alive. SSG Rivers was down. CPT Jett was with him. SSG Rivers was shot in the stomach and toward the top of his rib cage. CPT Jett was applying pressure to the stomach wound. I got down on my knees and unpacked my pressure bandage and applied it to the hole beneath SSG Rivers' throat. He was choking but still trying to talk. I told him not to talk. He kept saying 'light,' but he was having a hard time saying that. SGT Bunker called in the nine-line.[2] I did all I could to stop the bleeding. I think CPT Jett did, also, but it wasn't enough and SSG Rivers died before the MEDEVAC arrived. My men did their jobs correctly, but we wouldn't have been in that situation without the direction of

---

[2] Way of reporting combat injury. Line 1. Location of the pick-up site. Line 2. Radio frequency, call sign, and suffix. Line 3. Number of patients by precedence. Line 4. Special equipment required. Line 5. Number of patients. Line 6. Security at pick-up site. Line 7. Method of marking pick-up site. Line 8. Patient nationality and status. Line 9. NBC Contamination.

CPT Jett, and I just don't know what we accomplished. One flaw was how SGT Bunker called in the nine-line. He reported that the enemy only 'may' be in the area. The fire had just stopped, so I thought it was strange that he didn't report in an affirmative way enemy forces were in the area. I later asked him about that, and he questioned me instead. He said, 'Didn't you see the tornado? The lightning? I'm from Oklahoma, and I've never seen anything like that. Those guys were gone. The lightning was like a big hand that grabbed them and pulled them into the sky. I said thanks to the Lord it was them and not me. That was the Lord watching us. He got all those bastards.' I asked him if he saw SSG Rivers go down, and he said he did and that he then saw SSG Rivers go 'up' into heaven as we were trying to save him. 'That was also the Lord's lightning, but it was different, and I wasn't afraid,' said SGT Bunker. Nothing Further."

Bunker's statement was even more descriptive than Kay's, but Kay's statement highlighted the conflict that was manifesting among all the characters (internal and external) I was dealing with. Some were in line with my schemes and those who needed better demonstrations of what I knew to be true about this war and all war. I used that statement as Exhibit A in my quest to convince higher command of the forces we were opposing, the forces that were just toying with us. I saw it in Rivers' dead eyes. They were wide open, seeing something for the first time, not seeing the last of the world, seeing a new world of infinite dimensions. I was a little jealous. He was gazing with spirit eyes, as if looking at a piece of art, and in some other form, beyond space and time, he was about to reach through and touch the aeon prior to this one, reach through the Big Bang sliver at the center of the universe, swim through the density of space-time as if it was nothing and touch the Fifth Dimension and unlock the density, the irregularities, see how it was all set up in the aeon before our own then slipped through a sliver and left an imprint on our universe. But I did feel partly to blame.

Gunmen were still shooting, running for their truck. The sound of gunfire diminished, a Doppler effect of retreat. Gunships were in the area. The gunmen weren't going to get far. The old man was still alive, groaning, coughing up blood. Kochi was helping him. The ringing in my ears returned. The meaty sounds of war were still coming through. The magical healing power of horseshoe crab blood was what I needed. That's where my mind went after Rivers was gone.

PROPHET OF THE IMAGINATION

Major Twigg made me stand at parade rest before him as he was sitting at his desk, studying a map. "I read Lieutenant Kay's statement," said Twigg. "He came to see me this morning."

"He could've steered us in a different direction," I said. "Maybe saying no to me wasn't an option, but he could've persuaded me. He knew that area better than me."

"The tornado was...just wind," said Twigg. "You outrank Lieutenant Kay. That was the dynamic."

"Yes, Sir. Well..."

"Psy Ops is not your team to play with."

"I was curious, Sir."

"Your curiosity got two men killed yesterday."

"One was an old friend," I said. "Did you know that?"

Twigg looked at me like I was an idiot. He continued. "If it was my decision, I'd order you to take a step back."

"But the Sugarbush investigation..."

"That investigation is not your responsibility."

"I see, so as long as my leash is kept short..."

"You're out of line, Captain Jett!"

He was right. "I went too far, too fast," I said. "I'm not taking this lightly. It won't happen again, Sir."

"Of course it will," said Twigg. "You've got a captive

audience in General Williamson and Colonel Maddox, but I'm going to start keeping a closer eye on you. I don't know what all you're telling them, but you have a wild imagination. So what was it all about?"

"Sir?"

"What was the old man trying to show you?"

"There were some ruins in the desert."

Twigg winced. "So? I don't recall any SIGACTS involving indirect fire or otherwise on those coordinates, but it wouldn't be unusual. Ruins of what? They could be ruins going back to Soviet days." He studied his map. "A training area or something."

"They were thousands of years old, from what my translator was saying."

"This isn't easy. I know you know I know there is strange stuff going on, but this is ridiculous. You need to focus on other things in Kandahar Province, like Mars Station and the tasks I've given you."

"But General Williamson and Colonel Maddox..."

Twigg shrugged his shoulders. That kind of body language was atypical of him and his kind, in general, but I got the message. "Wait a minute," he said. He opened a desk drawer and pulled out a file. I could see my name on the tab. "It says here that you used to be an archaeologist. I just remembered."

"I studied it in college. I've never done it for a living."

Twigg gave me a weary look. "If you're engaging in war tourism, it needs to stop. We'll send you home. I'm in touch with Major Dengler in the Planning and Personnel Office of Reserve Command all the time."

"That's not what I'm doing, Sir." I was fidgety. My ears were ringing. It came with increased blood pressure.

"I should've sent you home right after you were in that bomb blast."

"It is not affecting me, Sir." Even as I said that, I felt a sharp pain in my temple. *I am not the type for this kind of lingering thing.* I remembered voices. My monosyllabic responses sounded like someone else's voice. I was surrounded by bloody faces. I had a thought from the distant future: *This is the first and last time I'm doing this.* It was déjà vu. Future shocks were adding up. Explosion effects, not jolly times.

"Maddox says the same thing," said Twigg. Why would he bring up Maddox? I didn't think Twigg thought much of Maddox's opinions about anything. Now all of a sudden he was sweet on him. Nah, but that's where my damaged brain was leading me.

I redirected the conversation away from me to him. "I had a dream that Maddox was the victim of an IED blast, but his only wound was a six-inch gash in his head. He was asking that I be the man to sew it up, so we both had a couple of drinks and told some jokes to ease the tension, then I started working. He passed out during the procedure, but I finished the job."

"Then what happened, Captain Jett?" Such a facetious tone.

"Then I woke up."

"Well wake up now. That's all I'm asking. You're not right in the head, in my head, but we're going to let it play. General's orders, but I still need convincing. You're smoke and mirrors, Captain Jett. That's what I think. You're good at telling monster stories, that's for sure. Your file looks good. You have good OERs and a good reputation, so why do I feel this way?"

"I'm not making up anything, Sir. You don't have to make up monsters in this place. I'm not sure what to convince you of, since I'm not certain about anything, except that I am certain about how I'll find the answers. That part I'm making up, sort of. It's a new way of doing things with a little smoke and mirrors."

"You're turning this into a game, Jett, and I don't like it. Stay away from Lieutenant Kay and his Psy Ops unit. Don't use any other Army units. Go back to your office and put something together. I'm not seeing the connection between the ruins and the massacre. I say again: that is not your primary mission, is that understood?"

"Yes, Sir."

I took my time walking home that night, not sure how I was going to play at being either nice or naughty for the rest of the game. KAF had its own night beats, just like you notice in your own city after a while, with just as many sounds, just different volumes, oscillations. I had to learn to listen all over again.

I couldn't help thinking of the bigger picture, I mean a huge picture of two galaxies colliding, with the bigger galaxy consuming the smaller galaxy. My reality, my purpose, came back to me with other big picture thoughts about evolution and nature and how men are designed for conflict.

LEARNING
TO FLY

I started dealing with Twigg a little differently, knowing he knew my life story. I was a business student for two years at the University of Texas at Austin, but I lost interest in business and changed my major to archaeology, a deep interest going back to my childhood. It was a new vector. I was twenty-one years old when I started visualizing my future as a group of vectors. Once I got to Afghanistan, it was easy to see that, aside from all the chaos and conflict, everything was working out according to a grand plan in my life, yet the vectors of my life were at the mercy of the fog of war.

The next day was another day of strange encounters, starting with Kochi. When I heard a knock on my door, I thought it was a doctor making a work-shack visit. I'd vomited in the middle of the night, right as a helicopter was hovering above my home-shack. I think it was the heavy vibration that stirred my stomach. First self-diagnosis: nerves. Second (and final) self-diagnosis: upset stomach due to the greater than usual intake of pepper sauce the previous day.

But it was Kochi at my door. He had a one-foot square canvas map bag, the kind I had when I was a kid and would take with me on adventures. It was one of my first pieces of military gear. He handed it to me. My first thought was espionage...Kochi was sent by an overlord from the future to start pulling me deeper into T4W.

"What's this?" I said.

"Open it," said Kochi.

Inside the bag was the map that the old man was showing Kochi when we were attacked.

If Kochi was from the future, I wanted him to show me the future in a different way. "I don't know how I feel about this," I said. "I'm not going into all of the details, but let's just say that certain people want me to move forward with other things and not deal with Sugarbush or Mars Station or anything like that."

Kochi frowned. "Take it," he said. "Use it."

"What did that man explain to you?"

Kochi rubbed his temple. He looked confused. "By Quran," he said.

"Are you ok?"

"I do not like it." From the way he was rubbing his head, I assumed he meant the pain, but then he pointed at the map. "I do not like it. By Quran."

Some of the man's blood was on the map, but there were older, darker stains. The light in my office flickered. Shadows danced and fell back into impossible positions. "What are these symbols?"

"That is what I do not like," said Kochi. "When I was a boy in Kabul, there was a man on the street who would tell the children stories of ghosts and evil spirits...*jinn*. We thought the man was crazy and that his beliefs were from a time long before Islam, during days of ignorance. He talked about the end of days when forces of good and evil will face each other. One will destroy the other. We laughed at him, the way that he talked, but he showed us one of his many ancient texts. I remember the symbols from that text. Why would I remember this, unless Allah wanted me to? To this day, I believe the man was himself a *jinni*, sent by an evil spirit to watch over Kabul. He tried to test us, each day. I saw an automobile strike that man with my own eyes. I saw them carry his body away, but he was back the next day as if nothing happened."

The symbols didn't have the form and curvature of Arabic or Pashto script. They were grouped in strange ways. Some were interlocking. It struck me as higher-dimensional geometry. I guess it struck me that way because I'd started thinking of the Fourth Wall as a higher dimensional creation/aspiration. I turned over the map in my hands. It was brittle, but not too brittle.

"This map is a copy of another map," said Kochi.

"Look at the star shape surrounded by circles. Mean anything to you? Wait. Those aren't all circles. What are they?"

"Those are *jinn*. The man said so. The man told me about a dream, but he was afraid that what he saw in the dream would come for his family during the day. The dream sounded horrible, and I was afraid for him. These things...they sounded like things that only come out at night. He thought the dream, and other dreams like it, were connected to the map and that the real map once belonged to a living, real *jinn* here on earth."

"Did he mention anything about the murders?"

"Yes, but he quickly changed the subject to a strange man, perhaps your missing friend." Kochi always referred to Digger and other soldiers as my friends or companions. He did not say if this person was American. He did not know. He said the man was white-skinned and wearing strange clothes. He said the man was looking for something. He did not want to say. He described the mountains. He said the mountains were full of caves.

"Do you see them on the map?"

Kochi pointed to a group of tiny pentagons. "He said there were Taliban snipers in the mountains all the time."

Kochi left me the map and bag. After he left, I went into the command office and made a photocopy of both sides of the map. Twigg's office door was closed. Snow didn't even look at me. He was wearing a headset and staring at his computer screen and talking low, probably talking to his wife. I was about to leave when Twigg's door opened. It was Maddox. He didn't look happy. He didn't see me right away, but when he did, his face reddened.

"There's the pup," he said, pointing at me. "My office, now!"

I knew I was about to be grilled for something. First the sowing, now the reaping. I put the map and copies in the bag and followed Maddox. His shack was dark and dusty. He must've visited Twigg before coming to his own shack for the day.

"How was Jalalabad, Sir?"

"All right, but I spent most of the time in Kabul. Some twisted shit is happening there. Gang rivalries are complicating operations, but more on that later." He tapped his fingers on the desk and looked away. "What's going on with that girl?"

"The Russian?"

Maddox nodded.

"Her name is Yvonne."

"Her name is Ivanna Vasiliev, and she's connected to this man." Maddox opened a blue folder, a fresh folder right out of the box, with just a few pieces of paper inside. So wherever this was leading, it was someplace new, and he was getting me involved right out of the gate. He showed me a photo of a middle-aged white man. He looked like Mr. Rogers, from the television show. There was a matrix of bad guys on the wall behind Maddox. The matrix was a standard intelligence tool. He attached the photo to the matrix with a thumb tack, in a box labeled "to move."

"Who is that?" I said.

"Nikolay Vasiliev, also known as the Snow Leopard, or simply, Leopard. He is your girlfriend's father. I may connect him with a single line to Malak, but I'll have to put a big question mark underneath the picture for now."

"Don't forget Mangal, Malak's twin brother."

"Mangal? Who?" said Maddox.

"Something in Digger's notes, Sir," I said. "This will all go into my CONOPS for the Kabul mission."

"Don't make it confusing, Captain Jett, and don't lose yourself in Sergeant Ramsey's file. I'm aware of your concept, but there are some things going on in your brain I just don't want to know about. And if you're going to draft a CONOPS, then keep it to yourself. We won't even be in uniforms or driving tactical vehicles, not after what I just went through in Kabul. I've already decided."

"Who else knows about this? Is General Williamson involved in this, Sir?"

"I'm not telling you more," said Maddox, "not right now." His blue eyes popped, and that devilish grin was back. I'm sure he wasn't daydreaming about the same kaleidoscopic structures as me. I mean patterns in my neocortex were batshit.

"I'm just thinking about what kind of top cover we'll have, Sir."

"You leave that kind of thing to me, pup."

"Sir, why did you bring up Yvonne?"

"Maybe that was a mistake, or just premature. I don't have a problem with her, at this point, but the computers do."

"What kind of problems?"

"It's nothing," said Maddox. He patted my shoulder. "Go do...whatever it is you do together. Get to know her better and take good notes and report your findings to me. That's an order. I just need you to help me figure some things out. Once we collect more data, we'll go from there. You're a prior intel soldier."

"And prior archaeologist...attorney..."

"Captain Jett, I just got back and my whole body aches. It's probably from the dream I had of falling, only I didn't wake up before I hit the ground." Further evidence of Maddox crisscrossing astral worlds, thanks to his connection with me. "Keep an eye on your girlfriend, but keep buying her flowers." He started studying some paperwork. I glanced at the paperwork and saw a series of glyphs.

That night after work I walked by the barber shop. It was late, and the place was closed. It occurred to me that I didn't even have Yvonne's number. Everything was closed on the boardwalk, except for Tam Tam. Tam Tam was open but empty. I was hungry. I ordered beef stew and rice. Sometimes you just need a quiet place to think. I started thinking about how Maddox and Yvonne had changed, or my perception of them had changed, just that day. I was going to have to modify the character sheets I'd created for them. What a confusing dream. I needed to spend some more time going through Digger's notes to get some ideas, despite what Maddox said. This was going to be my first good-sized Fourth Wall expedition authorized (if in a dark way) by higher command, so I had to wargame it.

EXCERPT FROM JOURNAL OF SERGEANT DANIEL G. RAMSEY, U. S. ARMY (ADVENTURE NAME: MONSTERS OF L.A.)

Baz Buettner parks on South Hope Street in downtown Los Angeles, just up the street from Bank of America Plaza. As he is getting out of his car, he has an anxiety attack. Nearby, he once fought a huge amoeba-like creature with five pseudopods that wrapped around him. That night he was on his way to a movie shoot south of downtown. He'd stopped to check on a client when the creature blindsided him as he was walking across the street. Baz Buettner was a marked man in the eyes of the monsters of L.A. The movie shoot wasn't much fun. He was only an extra, though he did get to meet Ludwig Aachen, a movie director he'd been wanting to work with for some time. And tonight Dispatch had arranged for him to meet with Dr. Randolph, a paleontologist at USC.

Baz gets himself together and walks south on South Hope. The night is very foggy. (Listen check: the die roll fails, so he doesn't hear anything unusual. Then a perception check fails, so he walks right into thick fog ahead, without seeing anything unusual.) This kind of fog usually appears during times of high stress. He has powers of his own and can affect his environment. Dispatch knows this. Together, they try to control his powers. Dispatch and Baz are two of the many monsters in Los Angeles.

His cell phone rings. It's Dispatch. Baz likes the sound of her voice.

DISPATCH: What do you see?

BAZ: I see myself.

DISPATCH: In the fog? When was the last time this happened?

BAZ: You should know. You keep good records.

DISPATCH: I'm just seeing how well you're keeping up with these events. It's part of your therapy and recovery.

BAZ: For the sake of all Angelinos, I don't think you want me to ever recover. It would lead to early retirement from monster hunting.

CONOPS
FOR KABUL

I skipped breakfast the next morning and visited the religious center. When I walked in, a black woman in a U.S. Army uniform was hunched over, going through a box.

"Good morning," I said.

She turned. I saw the lieutenant colonel rank on her chest.

"I mean good morning, Ma'am," I said.

She stood up. Her name was Ferry. She looked solid as a wall. She had a welcoming smile but was not as open and welcoming as Major Nichols or Major Darby. She was wearing the same unit patch as me, so we answered to the same generals.

"Where is Major Darby, Ma'am?"

"God rest his soul," she said. "We lost him."

What the hell? *LM, I might need your help on this one. Ferry's giving me that look, same look that Drill Sergeant Newark gave me in 2007, when she was commenting on a crazy look I was giving, said "you have that look you get like you want to kill someone."*

"I'm sorry to hear that," I said. "I see you have some new literature, Ma'am."

She now looked perplexed, not by me I hoped. "One of our suppliers keeps sending martial arts magazines along with the normal Bible study guides and Korans and such."

"Mind if I have a look?" I got on my knees like a child in wonder at Christmas. "Vintage ninja magazines! Do you want these, Ma'am?"

"Take them all," Ferry said.

Pure joy. More secrets of the universe were at my fingertips.

"Wait," she said. "Leave me one. I may look through it."

I left her a 1986 issue of Black Belt with a pajama'd assassin on the cover.

"I can use this stuff," I said.

That perplexed look again. "Use it for what?"

"I'm planning something big."

"A mission? I'm intrigued."

I breathed a sigh of relief. She was like me.

"Just read the magazine, for starters, Ma'am." I gave her a couple more.

"Good luck with your plans," she said. "Man plans and God laughs. It is a Yiddish proverb."

Back at my office, I used a CONOPS template I found as a basis for my own Fourth Wall plan. The CONOPS I found was for a mission which involved two stops in one day: One village to deliver supplies, another to meet with elders, then back to the day's starting point. Maddox said I could name the operation, and I did: T4W. So it was no longer just an intuitive personal response to the fog of war. By order of higher authority, I was going to use the system to shape the whole operation.

I got Specialist Henry involved. I had him dig up some other CONOPS examples. I wanted my approach to be as comprehensive as possible. I had stacks of intelligence-related Army field manuals alongside my new (old) martial arts magazines. I was ready and willing to be inspired. I had my big, personal map. It was the basic model for the world of T4W. I gave my map a codename: Bandit, inspired by the map used by the band of robbers in the movie Time Bandits. On the map, I drew pictures of storm clouds and strange creatures, inspired by sixteenth-century sea charts. I added to the map as I shaped and re-shaped T4W. Bandit did not become part of the T4W CONOPS. I predicted the whole thing would be blown wide open in some way, then further dissected by the news media, up and down and all around, and I didn't want to see Bandit released to the general public through a FOIA request or some other backdoor.

I worked hard for days on the CONOPS. Regarding Yvonne, I did what Maddox asked. I started asking more questions. I went in for a trim one day, but she was busy with a colonel, so I settled on a trim from one of the Cambodians. I caught Yvonne after her shift. We watched Canadians playing soccer in the middle of the boardwalk. She looked great. She had her hair in a ponytail, thrown over her shoulder.

"Tell me about where you grew up," I said.

"That is out of somewhere."

"You mean out of nowhere." She was right. We were both so used to talking about our dreams, not our pasts.

"Moscow is so cold and gray."

"Did you live in a house?"

She laughed. "I lived in a tiny apartment in a huge apartment building in Belyayevo, outside of Moscow. Very boring. A house?" She laughed again. Twice? "But it is why I am who I am. Thousands of people lived there, but I saw more than that. I saw ghosts. I was very young. I would talk to them and invite them into my home. I thought they were alive. They said they were family or friends of my father, and I believed them. They stayed. They would never leave." Her eyes narrowed. "My mother lost her mind. She nearly killed herself several times. Later, when my mother was sick, I begged her on her deathbed to forgive me for the terror I brought her, but she said I did not bring the ghosts. It was because of my father, she said."

I thought back to what Yvonne told me about her sister

committing suicide live on the internet in that apartment. She probably saw the same ghosts as Yvonne.

"Let me show you something," Yvonne said. "Give me your book."

I pulled a small sketchbook from my cargo pocket. She started drawing in the sketchbook. She was both graceful and quick.

"What is this?"

"It is you," she said. "This is how you should dress."

"Like one of the three wise men?"

I was trying to make her laugh, but she didn't get the joke. "It is a simple disguise," she said.

"I trust you," I said. If I followed her advice to the letter, I would've resembled Lawrence of Arabia, whom I was starting to feel like. Yvonne drew some stars around the drawing. At that very instant, I conceived of putting together a photomosaic of Kabul POI (points of interest) and including it as an appendix to the CONOPS. This would become one of the most important features of the final product. Parts of Kabul are mazelike. Many commanders and planners have ripped off my ideas. Planning-tool photomosaic work as extensive as mine has practically become doctrine, and it all started with Yvonne's drawings. She touched a nerve.

My mind was popping. I had a vision of my team riding into town on horses. The population would be confused and terrified, seeing us as new villains in their lives, but we would open their eyes and minds and would find the answers to all our common problems in mystical treasures. Our vector would meet their vector, and the resultant vector would be beautiful and later represented in a piece of public art that would remind future generations of what happened in this place. Yvonne was a big part of it, but it wasn't just her. Signs were everywhere, passing overhead like a storm. I was feeling a need for them. All types of metaphysical elements were at play, and I later categorized them according to the most related CONOPS step, (steps for planning CONOPS: 1. State goals and objectives; 2. Identify strategies, tactics, and constraints that will affect operation; 3. Describe stakeholders involved and list responsibilities of those individuals and organizations; 4. Identify specific processes for conducting an operation, describe in more detail.) This wasn't true Army-style planning. This was, in part, a Russian barber's floating magical spells which were triggering everything that I was doing, everything magical about me, and powering everything that was to come. So her little sketch of me was the germ of so much more.

I pushed Yvonne's hair over her ear and touched her chin. "What about your father?" I said. "Tell me about him."

"He liked Afghanistan. He liked killing. He liked beating his own men, and he was beaten by his superiors. He had a kind face, but he was not kind. Do not let a kind face fool you. He told me strange stories of this place. He was here before I was born. I got all my powers from his side of the family. He saw the same things I saw. I can hear his voice clearly, to this day," she said.

"Is he dead also?"

She didn't answer.

WACKO

Ellington visited my work-shack. Another man was with him. Ellington was a big man, but the other soldier loomed large over Ellington, made him look like a skinny boy. His work-shack must've been huge. He wasn't a Red Hand. I'd never met him or seen him. He was the blondest Irishman I'd ever seen. It took me a half-second longer to spot/mentally process his rank insignia. He was a major. I stood up. "Good morning, Sir."

He didn't have that Red Hand pluck I admired in Ellington and the other RH. I didn't like his aura, blackish-purple.

Ellington answered for him. "I want you to meet Major Bodkin."

"A pleasure, Sir." I extended my hand. Bodkin sized me up for a second then shook my hand.

"After our last adventure, Ellington," I said, "I thought you might keep your team away from me."

Ellington shushed me with his eyes. I hoped I didn't interfere with Ellington's chances for covert action glory, where he wanted to be.

Bodkin gave Ellington a look and went back to sizing me up. Perhaps he saw something curious in my aura. "Your general is friends with one of our generals," said Bodkin. His accent was thicker than Ellington's. "They shared one of Saddam's palaces after the invasion of Iraq." His voice was so low he almost growled.

"Major Bodkin has seen them together, but I haven't," said Ellington. "They're apparently a couple of smiley blokes when they're together."

"They want us working together on your T4W mission," said Bodkin.

I was trying to keep a lid on the mission, but apparently, others were chatting. How goofy was I starting to look among peers?

"So you're the new Red Hand?" I asked Bodkin.

"Sort of," said Bodkin, "special assignment with the blessing of Her Majesty the Queen, but we're all part of the same Royal Irish Regiment family." Bodkin patted my cheek.

"Major Bodkin knows Kabul well," said Ellington.

"But I haven't been to Kabul in some time," said Bodkin. "I hear it's changing. There have been more suicide bombings in places that were considered safe. You should know, with all the expats and journalists on your payroll. Do you even know what kind of assets you have there?"

"I haven't gotten that far, Sir," I said.

"I've told Major Bodkin how you operate," said Ellington.

"In what way?"

Bodkin beamed. "Ellington told me you're an explorer. You see things in a different way. I see things in a different way, too. We may be after different things, but maybe we can help each other."

"This is going to be a small outfit," I said. "General Williamson has given me a wide berth, and Colonel Maddox works me like a dog, but to others, I'm kind of a pariah, like you said. We may all wear the same uniform, but..." I shrugged.

"Why the..." Bodkin mimicked/mocked my shrug. "That's life. Stand tall around the opposition."

"Easy for you to say, Major Paul Bunyan, Sir," I said.

Then he shrugged, for real this time. I didn't explain. That was the first and last time I was so cheeky with him, but he was right. Bodkin looked around my shack and the stacks on my desk. Bandit was on the desk, half-open, along with magazines and cutouts of people in extreme poses, or just general graffiti, nothing classified, all spread across a circle a meter in circumference.

"And this?" Bodkin found Yvonne's sketch.

"That's not my work."

"It's your Russian friend's," said Ellington.

"How do you know about her?"

"When you get going on this Fourth Wall you're always talking about, you can't stop, Captain Jett. It still sounds wacko to me."

"It does to me, as well," said Bodkin. He stepped closer. His breath was oppressive. "I've been there. I have no urge to return. You'll see."

"In Afghanistan?"

"And Iraq. And Belfast. I'm older than I look. What's that?"

Bodkin was pointing at Bandit. "That's work product," I said. I covered it with a ninja magazine.

"Not the map. I can see it's a map of the country. I mean the drawing on the map." Which did he mean? I held it up for him.

"Is that the figure of a man? What is he doing?" said Bodkin, so fascinated he whispered.

"Oh," I said. "That's a fighter, and he's in a very basic horse stance, like this." I demonstrated the *kiba dachi*.

"See what I mean?" said Ellington. "Wacko. Strange atop strange."

"No more than you," said Bodkin.

"He needs to meet Blind Butchy," said Ellington.

"He's not blind," said Bodkin. "I saved the eye, remember? You were there, Christ." Bodkin looked like he wanted to slap Ellington.

"It was dangling, Sir, hanging by threads, and you pushed

it back in with your finger, but Butchy is definitely half-blind."

"I saved the eye, Captain," Bodkin said to me alone. Bodkin patted my cheek again with his bear paw. "You can't help but admire Sergeant Ellington's respect for his superiors." Sarcasm was strong with all the RH.

"What was it like to put your friend's eye back into his skull?" I asked Bodkin, joining in the drinking-buddy banter.

"He's not my friend. He's an asshole. And it wasn't the eye that bothered me. It was all the headless bodies that were around him that had an effect on me that day."

"This is why I'm here," I said. "This is good stuff."

"I'm here," started Bodkin, "here in your office..."

"It's a work-shack, Sir."

"Your work-shack, that is, because of the drug trade in this country," said Bodkin. "Fighting season is over, but world hunger for the opium can't be slaked. When we're gone, years from now, locals will go right back to narcotics. The poison will just keep spreading. Ellington may think you're wacko, but I think you're onto something, and I'm closer to those deep American pockets than you are, with General Williamson. And this Fourth Wall you're so fascinated with? I can protect you from the things you haven't seen yet. We all need a friend to trust."

"Instead of some Russian girl," said Ellington, with a flowery edge on the last word.

"You've never met her," I said.

"Who do you think cuts my hair?" said Ellington.

"She's a bigger part of this than you know," I said, pointing at the pile on my desk.

"Bring her tonight, if you'd like," said Bodkin.

"What's tonight?"

"I can see you've been working hard to figure out this war and how everything fits together," said Bodkin, "but how well do you know your home base?"

"Just show up at Tam Tam, twenty-two hundred hours,"

said Ellington.

"Unless we're too late," said Bodkin. He clenched his teeth. "Unless you've given up on everything before getting a good start."

They left. Their visit put me off track. My CONOPS was still a skeletal work. Maddox wanted to meet with me the next day, and I was worried that all I'd have to show him would be this pitiful framework regurgitated out of others' templates. I was pretty sure my cutouts wouldn't interest him. I'd spent a lot of time creating Bandit, but Maddox wasn't going to be impressed with it. So I was stuck, and if it took a tour of the secret side of KAF, or whatever the Red Hand were planning, then I was game. Speaking of games, I went back to my character sheets. I started a new one for Bodkin. I added character traits to Ellington's since I saw a new side of him that day. I noted his swaggering ways around superiors. I made notes about Yvonne, just some thoughts, and attached the notes as an appendix to her character sheet. At that point, I didn't know how else to handle what other soldiers were thinking about her, since she had never mentioned her dealings with them. But I was suspicious. To fill in some missing pieces, I did what Digger did in these situations: I rolled some dice, again and again...on the warpath.

Then, of course, there were all the letters to Lady Mist, who was turning into a real queen in the pantheon of this game. I had to get her and Yvonne together. *But is that a good idea, LM? Did you ever see Ghostbusters? Was it a good idea to get the Gatekeeper and the Keymaster together? Two dangerous entities with higher, malevolent aims. Their evil mother was waiting to cross dimensions. They ended up as a couple of burned, mangled bodies.* In a cap-tilt to Yvonne, I sketched out a spring-force model of the universe, leaving a space for divine providence to fit. My whole day went on like that. It wasn't a complete waste of time, though. I built on what little information I had about Druj, the dark force the old man in Sugarbush mentioned. I wrote a (speculative) fact sheet, similar to other character sheets I'd written. In the Fifth Space beyond the Fourth Wall, Druj was becoming more powerful. Druj also made an appearance in my T4W CONOPS as an opposing force, alongside all the usual threats.

Digger's character sheets were much better than mine. His bad guys were carefully categorized by type of evil, whether blind evil or something more purposeful. His good guys had such descriptions as 'balls-out bold' and 'vengeful but loveable'. Having read portions of Historians and Monsters of L.A., I could see how he used his character sheets in crafting those worlds. His penmanship was better than mine. Altogether, he seemed to be much better organized than me. My superiors looked at him in the strict light of the UCMJ. Since Digger abandoned his post, everything was on the table, administrative or punitive measures. I looked at him in more of an intellectual way. Everything he wanted was free for the taking. He was so fractured, in many ways. What debates were left open for him? What was in question? Such questions were in his notes, and I was asking myself the same questions.

Maddox came by around 1900 hours. He had a grim look, but even that could be said about his regular stare. "You and I are not going to be involved in this one, but you need to be aware about it." He handed me a folder. There were images unlike anything I had ever seen in an Army file. I realized that I wasn't the only one creating unique written products. The photographs still haunt me. I saw kids without arms, alive and dead. A picture of an old man holding up his tunic, his *khet*, revealing three slashes across his stomach, then a picture of a boy's corpse with a hole clean through his abdomen, as if he was hit by a high speed old fashioned cannonball.

"Please don't say this is a friendly fire incident, Sir."

"I can't even say that a human did this," said Maddox. "It happened at Provo before dawn. A local sent us those pictures. If you were closely monitoring your email, you would've noticed the SIR I forwarded to you."

I looked at the title page of the report. "Where is Provo?"

"It's in RC-North, near Kunduz. Way outside of our AO, Captain Jett."

I stood up. I was hoping for more of a surprise-free day, but that wasn't the case.

"Don't even think about it," said Maddox.

I was thinking about my magician card. That's all.

NET
FORCE

Maddox wasn't impressed with the shock-horror ways of my Red Hand friends (even after everything we went through together). He seemed empathetic toward Yvonne in the beginning, but "she can go down her own road, and you can choose to follow or not," Maddox told me before our big adventure. A big part of how he judged others was by the company they kept. "Looks like you fell in with a rough bunch," he once said. Maddox oozed calm/cool when I first met him, but after knowing him a couple of months I could see he was suffering. Getting good intelligence was always a problem for him. Bluebird did a lot of dice rolling on its own (damn algorithms) and we all grimaced at the results (ergo I had to lean a lot on the Fourth Wall). It wasn't just that. It was like Maddox was absorbing all the pain and confusion I was going through after my own IED attack. All those demons he had been dealing with for years came to the surface. I especially noticed this after he returned from Kabul, and it was around this time he told me of his low-grade full-body chronic pain. When he came into my office and told me about Provo, it was as if he was trying to keep me away from the war by revealing just a sliver of new horror (with a sliver of new happiness and surprise that Bluebird actually delivered something he could work with). I was still dealing with some physical symptoms like headaches and ringing in my ears. I was dealing with more nightmares than I told him about, off in phantom places more often than not. I imagine Maddox had taken me under his wing because something similar happened to him. So when he went ballistic from time to time, I knew what he was going through. At the same time, he put up walls. He didn't seem to have a place. He still behaved like he was muscle, always having a hard time dealing with strategy and policy. No one thought Maddox was a touching guy, but I did. There was something touching about a man who talked about his daughters so much.

I weighed these things before meeting Ellington and decided not to tell Maddox what I was doing that night. I met Yvonne at the barbershop first. We walked to Tam Tam. It was cold, but a deeper chill was setting in, coming from Yvonne. She was having a bad day. She was worried about having to go back to Russia.

"The manager hates everyone," she said.

"Do you hate him?"

"No. I do not hate anyone."

I couldn't tell her about the Provo mass murder event, if you could call it that. She would hear about it soon, but not from me.

"I have not seen you in a few days," she said. "Are you still making your game?"

"I'm toying with various ideas. Reading hearts and minds, as you said. It's part of my mission, actually. Part of the American mission in general. You must think I'm a lunatic."

LM, are you in there somewhere? If I have to drag you out of there, I want to visit with you again, face to face. Yvonne gave me a blank look. Could she see my neurons firing? Awash in dark signals at that moment. I just liked being with her. The boardwalk was quiet. Nobody else was eating at Tam Tam. The only sound was the light spit of the empty grill. Gul, the owner, was watching us. I waved to him. I ate alone at the Lux earlier and wasn't hungry.

"Why did you bring me here tonight?" said Yvonne. "I already ate dinner."

Bodkin and Ellington were approaching from the other end of the boardwalk. "They are the reason I brought you here." I pointed behind Yvonne.

Yvonne turned. She looked apprehensive.

"Everything's all right, Yvonne. They're here for me, not you, but I need your help."

"I know them."

"I don't know the big man that well. I met him today."

"You do not want to know him," said Yvonne. "Now would be a good time to leave. If you had the chance to add him to your wargame, to toy with him, then you would not be sitting here."

It was too late. Bodkin and Ellington fell into matching struts, and with their long strides, they transected the length of the boardwalk in under a minute.

"You brought the girl," said Ellington.

I stood up for Major Bodkin. His expression was grave. (I later learned from Ellington that Bodkin's own brother was being questioned about their cousin's death in Dublin, called it a 'hit and run', and I thought he meant car death, but that's not what he meant.)

"Good evening," Bodkin said to Yvonne.

Yvonne smiled. She looked at me. She could be like a damper at times, absorbing energy and dissipating it as other energy, away from me. It was a gift. She wanted me to do my job as best I could.

"Follow me," said Ellington. Yvonne and I followed. Major Bodkin was behind us. We headed in the direction from where they came. We reached the main KAF road. A half-mile down on the right was the Poo Pond, but we started walking in the other direction, toward the British Sector. We had to wait for a convoy of tactical vehicles to pass before crossing the road.

"Where are we going?" I asked Ellington. "Does this have to do with that blind guy?"

Major Bodkin laughed.

"You never know who you might meet in this place," said Ellington. "You might meet them again on Lover's Lane."

After a couple of blocks, we turned off the main road. We zigzagged through smaller barracks mixed in with bomb shelters and shipping containers.

"I get it," I said. "We're going to that bar you've mentioned."

"Nah," said Ellington. "We just passed the bar. Around there is where we're going." He pointed at a group of shipping containers ahead. "We call it the Stash. It's our secret stash, get it?" Ellington turned and winked at me.

I looked at Bodkin. He smiled like he was listening to an old favorite song, just another madman in a sea of madmen. "Of course there are some visual codes you would have to know if you were on your own, but you're with us," said Ellington. He was a different person when he wasn't in the gym or in the field, and I thought if he ever got a chance to play the espionage game later he'd do well. "Just be careful, Jett. I wouldn't want to see your name in Army tabloids for bad reasons. You don't have to be outside the wire to hear things go bang in the night."

"I know you won't tell anyone," said Bodkin.

"I couldn't make this shit up," I said. Yvonne looked like she wanted to be elsewhere. She didn't speak.

"Take off your nameplate and rank," said Bodkin.

"Are either of you going to take off yours?" I said.

"That would be pointless," said Ellington. "Everyone in the place knows us."

The Stash was inside two connected forty-foot steel containers. No other containers were stacked on top. The containers were inconspicuous. One was labeled NSCSA, (National Shipping Company of Saudi Arabia). It probably made its way from Jeddah to Dubai then Karachi then several other places in Afghanistan before it ended up in Kandahar. Ellington sent a text and the front door opened and a young British soldier appeared. The boy didn't regard Ellington much but straightened up for Bodkin. Inside, the Stash was a hole. It was dark except for a few dim overhead lights, filtered red. Electronic dance music was playing. It was something familiar to me at the time because it lifted my spirits, but now I can't say for sure what it was. It wasn't playing so loud that it drowned out all conversation. Once my eyes adjusted, I could see that most people there were Brits. It wasn't just their uniforms. It was the variety of hairstyles. Brits were more relaxed than Americans in their hair-ways. It was a mash-up of tired warriors hiding in the dark, mole-like, keeping to themselves, just there to get away from the war, even if it meant a more dangerous kind of entropy within the walls of the Stash. Not that it would've mattered (or so I thought as I was walking around), but in close quarters like that, I thought of martial arts moves that would come in handy. There was little room for inertia. I made an inventory of objects that would be useful. There were bottles, plates, and trays. The chairs were either tall bar stools with backs or tiny wooden chairs, like the IKEA chairs in my kitchen back home that one of my fat-ass guests once broke, a warlock I didn't like. I hexed the chair, to be honest. The warlock was cursed the moment he walked into my house. Houston seemed like a dream. And this new place made it seem like I was part of my own Fourth Wall game. The surroundings and people were similar to setups in The Fourth Wall, and Digger's games, before mine.

Heads turned toward us. It was Yvonne. The men wanted her. So did the women.

"Our people are back there," said Ellington.

I made my way through the haze. I recognized Redmond and Butler. Ellington and Bodkin joined them. Further back were my new Air Force friends, Haines and Rogers, dressed in black uniforms I'd never seen. They saw me and nodded. Moving toward them I almost needed my ninja moves. People were pushing each other, pushing into me. An Australian was at the next table, a sniper, I believe, with his SR98 rifle leaning on the inside of his thigh, pointed downward. Further on, two women were kissing. Not the first time I'd dealt with this kind of thing on the base. One of the contractors in my own shack complained of staying in a different barracks, mixed, and hearing sounds of women having sex. The issue wasn't that they were having sex since they were of the same rank. The issue was that the barracks walls were tissue-thin and didn't even go all the way to the ceiling, so everyone could hear them. A man pushed the kissing women into me. They smiled at Yvonne. She stayed close to me.

Haines came up to me. "Are you going north?"

"Why would I do that?" I said.

"Word travels fast," said Haines.

"Am I going north?" I repeated. "You know it doesn't work that way. If I go exploring again they're going to send me home. Besides, RC-North is German territory."

"How's your German?" This kid was persistent. He reminded me of the one black kid in my neighborhood growing up, always a great smile, everybody's friend.

"My German is fine," I said. "I lived in Germany for a year. I don't have any friends in the German army, though, and I don't think they'd want me snooping around up there."

"Maybe I have some friends."

Ellington was behind me, hearing all this, cowboy cool.

"You're a dreamer, Captain Jett," said Haines. "That's why you came to us. That's why we let you in. Maybe we need you to step outside the gate at a time like this. Turn into the hardcore wizard-fighter you were meant to be."

That got Yvonne's attention. A higher power was in control of this whole scene.

"I got people killed the other day," I said.

"I know what happened, Sir," said Haines. "I've just never met anyone like you in the military. After we met I thought, here's a man who can connect...things and people, and forces, and he can carry souls." This whiz, Haines, suddenly granted me some poetic license in my mission, beyond what I already had: what little magic I brought to the table on day one; and the magician card; and the quiet approval from higher-ups.

"So now I'm Charon," I said, "the guide who leads souls across the River Styx, and the other side is waiting for me?" Perhaps Charon never actually knew what was on the other side, I thought. "How do you know what happened, Haines? Are we talking about the same thing?" I wasn't about to start talking about secrets I barely know anything about. Then again, he knew more than me.

"I've seen the footage," said Haines. "What do you think we do when we're not tinkering with things? I think I'll be a bird in the next life."

"I thought it was more like extrasensory perception," I said. "Either way, I've been given another big assignment, and it has nothing to do with anything going on in RC-North."

What weighed on me more were not the images of Provo Maddox showed me, but the idea that what happened there would remain a mystery. "You're encouraging a side of me that others are trying to temper," I said.

Haines gave me a puzzled look but had a good follow-up. "You're a fine American, Sir." Crazy Haines. He later told me about growing up on the streets of Los Angeles. He witnessed a murder when he was a kid. He saw a gang member tie up a rival gang member and curb stomp him.

"Don't, Haines," I said. "I'm here for hearts and minds. You barely know me, but you know that much. I'm told this every time I start to feel frisky."

Ellington heard that and laughed. Yvonne was no longer paying attention. She was watching the other women watching her.

"Do you want to go back to that?" Haines said. "Is that your world?"

The music got louder. We were almost yelling.

"What is this place?" I said. "Who sent you? The gods?" Flashback to the movie Time Bandits, the scene in which the boy fell out of the sky onto the minotaur.

"I get it," said Haines.

If he truly got the Time Bandits reference, then he was on my side.

Redmond came over. He was drunk. "Welcome to our world, Captain." He pulled me toward the other Red Hands.

"I'm leaving," Yvonne said.

"Stay a little longer," I said. My little comical nightmare was just going into high gear. I needed her. She looked so tired. I kissed her cheek.

"Yuck," said a woman at a nearby table.

"Yuck you," I said.

"I've got one last thing to show you," said Haines. He stepped away. At that moment I felt a push from behind. Redmond and Butler were fighting. Bodkin, bigger than both of them, tried to pull them apart. I went into a receiving posture called *hira no kamae*. I stretched my arms and bent my knees. Butler tackled Redmond. They slammed into several soldiers. The bartender tried to get involved but wasn't very effective.

"That's enough!" said Bodkin.

Butler paused. Redmond, the drunker man, kept going. I looked at Yvonne to see if she was catching all this, but she wasn't. Her attention was on an orb of light approaching us, a floating star. It wasn't making a sound. Tendrils of white light stretched from the orb. Everyone else was watching the brawl. The Air Force boys were in the back corner. Haines had a big smile.

The star landed on Redmond's neck. He jolted. His hands turned red. He let go of Butler. Butler howled with laughter.

Redmond's eyes looked like they were about to pop out. He looked like a startled donkey. His hair spiked up even more than it already was. He fell back. Everyone was laughing now. "Was that the American Air Force?" said Bodkin.

The orb released from Redmond's neck and flew back to Haines, who was waiting with a little box open for it. "Did that thing shock Redmond?" I said. "How many volts?"

The crowd was applauding. "It's more a matter of current than voltage," said Haines.

"What does he mean?" Yvonne whispered in my ear.

Redmond was shaking his head, struggling to catch his breath. "Fuck off, all of you."

Haines opened the box to show me, revealing a creature more bee than fairy, but made of metal and plastic.

"What is that?" I was whispering, talking to myself.

"That's Tinkerbell," said Haines. "Tink for short. Like I said: We tinker."

"It's a bee," I said.

"Anatomically, that's accurate," said Haines.

Bodkin was behind me. "You know these guys?"

"You know *him*?" repeated Haines, pointing at Bodkin. The music was still playing. Bodkin turned around and sliced his throat with his index finger and the music stopped.

"He's the one I wanted you to meet," said Bodkin. Ellington was tending to his feuding mates.

"We met already," I said.

Rogers took the box from Haines. The box was vibrating. "Why is it doing that?"

"The drone is recharging," said Haines, "using mechanical energy from the vibrations."

Rogers pulled out an identical box. "Tink has a twin," he said.

Redmond was still a little dazed, but he wasn't lashing out the way I might have in his shoes. Either the whole thing was staged on my behalf or he had previously been the victim of the Tink System.

"You satisfied?" Bodkin asked Haines. "You think it's ready?"

"It's his if he wants it," said Haines. Haines nudged my shoulder. "We'll discuss passcodes and protocols later, Sir."

I took a closer look at Tink while Haines explained her. She had six side legs and four shorter legs front and rear. Her head was nearly as big as her abdomen. The main lift came from a top rotor, while side wings provided further speed and maneuverability. Her panoramic vision capability was powerful, according to Haines. But she wasn't mine. She belonged to the Shadows, which is what I started calling my Air Force friends. They were true shadow-operating innovators and explorers.

There were Red Hands to my sides and rear, all of them, including sweaty/bloody Redmond, and the Shadows in front of me, each with a little box and big grin, and all would play big roles in my game...my mission...

"They are for you, Sir," said Rogers, handing me the boxes of drones. "You're going to need them more than us."

"Does the other one have a name?" I said.

"Blink," said Haines. "He's Tink's cousin."

"Tink's twin," said Rogers.

"So," said Ellington, "are you in, Captain Jett?"

The Fourth Wall, just a game at first, inspired by Digger's notes and Yvonne's meditations and my own magical wanderings, was coming to life, and all the players were acting according to the character sheets I'd drawn up. I had character sheets for the Shadows before that night, just not much information. I made everything up. But now magic was permeating everything. It was about time. I was starting to believe this world was false, or at least not a good fit for my game.

The music started up again. The women were dancing. Butler joined them. "If you do this, you'll need your translator and me, for muscle," said Ellington.

"Do what?" I said. "No one in this room is in my chain of command. I could get sent home for this. Hell, I could lose my commission and go to jail."

"You won't," said Bodkin. "We'll all be heroes. Think of it as extended planning for the Kabul operation. You've got plenty of top cover for that, don't you? I've got some pull with the general. I can provide smoke."

"Life would be simpler if we didn't have to take that approach, Sir," I said.

"Simpler, but not as interesting," said Bodkin.

"The Russian's got his hands in this, I'm sure," said Ellington. "You said your German is ok. How's your Russian?"

"Better, now that I'm with her," I said, bringing Yvonne to their attention, but I turned and she was gone. "Do you think she was jealous?"

"Bring her back," said Bodkin. "You're going to need her."

PART II

OPERATION HORSEFLESH

Dear Maddox:

You know where I am. You know what an important clue this is. It's not just a game. My (incomplete) draft of the CONOPS is attached to this letter. It may look like a game or a description of a dream, but it isn't. It will look strange to you, but if it was complete, and if I was there to explain it, you would understand. Don't send the cavalry after me just yet (or your crazy mother-in-law...is that something you mentioned or my imagination?). I'm not alone; I'm in good hands (or their hands are good in mine). For instance, Kochi is with me. He's having other issues. His parents back home in California are trying to set him up in marriage with a cousin who still lives in Afghanistan, and he's mad about that (the boy is in love with a different cousin in California, he's explained). He's coming with me. Will I be as inventive under fire as you? Time will tell. My headaches are not in control. I feel that I've been decaying. In the coming days, you should be contacted by various players, friends of my CONOPS construction. Read the draft. You'll see. I'll keep a log (action-packed) of what I see and whom I deal with. It will make the AAR much easier to write, with all its good parts and bad parts, like it's supposed to have, assuming you assign me that task, as well. I'll see you in Kabul. I promise. Keep talking. I'll pick up the chatter. I'm 'connected,' so I've been told, Sir.

P.S. The inventory I've attached to this letter is not connected with the CONOPS supply list. The intent of this inventory is to capture in writing some things I might need for this mission, in case something happens to us and people start looking for their stuff. Don't wonder about 'horseshoe crab blood.' I'll explain that later. If this doesn't work out I can always go back to my law practice or life as a trucker sounds exciting. Archaeology would be interesting, perhaps exciting, but the pay isn't the best. I've looked into all this! As you can probably tell! But for now, I'm gonna hustle, while the hustling is good.

V/r
CPT Jett

I put the letter in my office chair, where I knew Maddox would find it, but he found me first. He didn't even knock. He let himself into my work-shack.

"Where are you going, Captain?"

"Morning, Sir," I said. It was unusual for me to be at my work-shack at 0500 hours. Unusual for Maddox, too, but he was wearing PT clothes. "I'm just working." As with the letter, there was plenty more I wanted to say but didn't.

"I saw your light," said Maddox, wiping his sweaty brow with his sweaty shirt, despite that it was a bitter cold morning. "You look like you're going somewhere. You've got a full load. Every pouch on your pack has some kind of ammo in it, looks like. What's the matter?"

I guess I was embarrassed. Not for what I was doing, but for getting caught like this, and I was a little embarrassed for how short the letter was. I wanted to say so much more.

I handed Maddox the letter. He read it. "I told you to leave this alone," he said. "Show me this crab blood you mentioned. I have to know you're serious."

I opened a pouch and showed him the clear plastic bag of blue liquid, with its translucent corpuscles clumped together like galaxy clusters. You could hold the bag right up to your face for a full phosphene explosive show. Even if its healing powers were questionable, untested by gameplay, it diverted Maddox's attention from other more interesting items in my bag, like Digger's notebook and copies of investigative reports about Sugarbush.

"This is a goodbye letter," said Maddox. "This is not how an officer is supposed to behave."

"This is bigger than me," I said. "This is bigger than our mission. What if, after all the years of fighting this war, my mission will be what stands out as the binding force between all our cultures."

"If you fail, this will stand out as a big black mark on your career."

"My career, my life, is flat," I said. "I don't know if volunteering to come here will help me or hurt me. I just know it was the right thing to do, because of this. Sugarbush was one thing, but I'm going to Provo while the situation is fresh."

"I told you to focus on Kabul, and you were doing a good job with that. Stay here. Make yourself useful."

"If that's the way you feel, then why did you tell me about Provo at all, Sir? Bluebird would've glazed over it, may have even called it a weather event and I may not have heard about it at all. Maybe let the Germans handle it?"

Now Maddox was the one who looked ashamed. His face was beet red. He gazed right through me. I put on my fleece and a coat over that and grabbed my pack, my helmet attached to the pack. I'd spent hours putting it all together. "I don't want to forget this." Bandit was spread out on my desk. I folded Bandit up and put it in my coat pocket.

"You're going to need more than that," said Maddox.

"Then come, Sir. You haven't ordered me not to go."

"What is with you, Thomas? What is this need you have?"

"You may look around in your world and ask yourself why it is so," I said. "I dream of worlds that don't exist and ask myself 'why can't they be so.'"

Maddox was looking at the space on the desk where Bandit had been. He picked up my half-finished CONOPs. I felt like a caveman, alone in a dark cave, on the cusp of something great, like the next step in human evolution (or something bigger which I may never understand, no matter how hard I try), and Maddox looked like a caveman, contemplating fire for the first time.

"Goodbye, Sir."

I left the compound. Yvonne was waiting for me outside, bundled up. She had a small pack. I tended to see her as a wounded creature, someone who needed my help, but that was far from the case. We walked arm in arm to the terminal a couple of blocks away. Ellington, Haines, and Kochi were there, and seeing them in high spirits lifted mine and the winter gloom was gone. I wasn't lying about the part in the letter regarding Kochi's reservations about going up north. His cousin was in Khanabad, fifteen miles east of Kunduz, where we were going.

The C-130 trip from Kandahar to Bagram was kindly arranged through Haines' Shadow friends, with KAF-release paperwork for myself and Yvonne arranged through the Red Hands. Catching a big-bird was only slightly more difficult than catching other birds out of KAF. I wasn't leaving the whole theater. Oh, how I was already looking forward to that day, though, when the light in the bay of that C-130 would go from RED to WHITE. Yvonne was listed as a mission-essential asset since she was Russian.

I took a cat nap during the flight. Yvonne did the same, her head on my shoulder, and I had a cat-nap-dream where I visited a multipurpose complex in Moscow which I had visited in a dream years before. In the dream, I was acting as a guide, showing people around, from the grocery store to the concert hall, telling the group about my previous visit there (in the previous dream), when I went to a rock concert and got in a fight with some gang thugs and how all that almost turned into an international incident. I saw the same man in both dreams: a Russian warlock. I saw him in other dreams in those days, like an angel who went from dream to dream looking for astral treasures. This was happening before I went to Afghanistan, but it picked up once I was in theater. So with that dream-recall within a dream, it was as if my mind was doing exercises, training for some Russian leg of my adventure. The fourth wall is there, in my dreams, both the mountain and the snake in the grass.

When I woke up, I was dying to tell Yvonne about the dream, but she was still asleep, and since I was feeling rotten about dragging her along on my adventure, I waited till later to tell her. Haines and Ellington did the legwork once we got to Bagram. Haines was better connected at Bagram Air Base, but Ellington was the driving force. He wasn't just muscle. He took ownership of this leg of the Fourth Wall, which I designated Operation Horseflesh, after a character in Time Bandits who was mentioned as being the dead leader of the gang. Randall was his successor. Horseflesh is credited in the film, but he never appeared.

I made a pledge to myself not to fly during Horseflesh, not to even try. I wanted to learn new tricks, not depend on old ones. Kochi was fidgety, full of nervous energy, ready for a new role in a new adventure, no longer satisfied with being a side player. Yvonne served various functions. She was the yin force in the group, the female presence who could provide dark energy when we needed it. That would mean many things, but in the beginning, it meant that she was sort of a babysitter. In particular, I wanted her to help Kochi since all the negativity was coming from him. Still, altogether the net force for the mission was looking good so far. The sum of all the forces, our disparate personalities, and skill-sets, was looking workable. I didn't want to have to force anything with this crew. I wanted all responses to be natural and right. Starting out, our biggest problem was the lack of all the proper cold-weather gear. I had plenty of Army-issued gear, but the plan was for all of us to change into civilian clothes, just as we would if we were players in the main T4W mission in Kabul. Yvonne said she didn't need much heavy clothing, being Russian. The lone Texan in the group (me) was freezing. Bagram was almost five thousand feet in elevation, and it was January. Winds were sweeping snow across the runway when we landed.

While Haines and Ellington secured a vehicle and some extra gear, I took Yvonne and Kochi to the DFAC down the road, the same DFAC where I had my first meal in Afghanistan. Kochi got his favorite: chili-mac. Yvonne barely touched her food.

Back at the terminal, Ellington was guarding a pile of stuff.

"Where's Haines?" I said.

"Getting the truck," Ellington said. "Holy shit."

Maddox was coming toward us. He was holding an M4, and another rifle was slung across his back. He looked gruff, serious at first. My first thought was that he came to haul us in.

"I had to pull some strings," said Maddox, "but I made it on the flight right behind yours."

"Where are the MPs, Sir?" I said.

"We may yet see them," said Maddox. "I'm not giving you a full pardon, I'm just curious to see where you're going, and so is the commander."

"So it's official?"

"You're not in his crosshairs yet, but tread lightly, Captain Jett." Then he left me in silence for a while.

Haines scored a mid-nineties Toyota Forerunner. We changed into civilian clothes in a garage nearby. I'd brought some civilian clothes to Afghanistan, glad I didn't ship any home earlier. Ellington provided us with extra layers and even had something for Maddox. We would've looked cozy in a LL Bean catalog. I remembered to transfer my magician card from the breast pocket of my uniform to my new outfit. Yvonne had a couple of plain scarves to cover her head and face. Mid-morning we rolled out of Bagram Air Base and headed north on Highway 76, which split mountains. Haines was driving. It started snowing. All around, the land looked pretty chewed up, even with the light powder. "If we get stuck out here we're done," said Ellington. "We're on our own."

"That's why I brought Kochi," I said. Kochi was in the rear with our packs and ammo. Each of us had an M9. Yvonne's was thanks to the Red Hand. No way I could squeeze one out of my supply guy. Beneath Kochi, in a hidden compartment, were four M4 carbines. The extra rifle Maddox brought was an M-110 sniper rifle.

Kochi gave me a nervous look. He was less confident than the rest of us. Maybe he knew something we didn't. The north was much different from the south, with a different mix of ethnicities and languages. I pulled out Bandit. My notes and topographical lines for that part of the country were sparse. On Bandit, that section was still *terra incognita*, with little pictures of monsters riding the wind. I didn't erase or replace those drawings because I felt like we were being watched.

Yvonne wrote something on a piece of scrap paper. "Attach this to your map," she said. It was in Cyrillic. I had to read it a few times in order to figure it out. I could read Russian better than speak it.

"Appetite comes during eating?" At least, that's what I thought it said.

"It is an old Russian proverb," Yvonne said. She was telling me she was finally hungry, but she was also telling me to be careful what I wish for.

We stopped for some food at a makeshift market in Pol-e-Khomri, situated between rugged mountains along the

Kunduz River. We stood out as foreigners, of course, in our Western-style clothes, but we didn't draw attention the same way soldiers might. A cold north wind was blowing. There was a smell of meat cooking and spices, but also diesel exhaust and animal excrement, the smell of surprises around every corner.

A merchant treated me as German. He knew a little German. I know a little German. The German conversation between us was short, but here's a rough English translation (starting with some German):

Merchant: Guten Tag!

Me: Groose! (I only said this because just days before I was listening to "Don't Bring Me Down" by Electric Light Orchestra, and "groose" was something Jeff Lynne threw into the song. It means 'greetings.')

Merchant: Groose! (He apparently understood me.) How is the weather? The weather is cold.

Me: Good day, my friend. (No need to answer his question, since he answered his own question)

Merchant: Do you like good food?

Me: Sometimes.

Merchant: Do I have good food?

Me: Do you have a cow or a chicken?

Merchant: Eat good food here. (no answer to my question; he didn't understand)

The market was swarming with flies. So was the little plate of food he gave me. My stomach was just going to have to get used to it.

The merchant and Kochi exchanged words. Kochi came to me, rolling his eyes. "He says the town is divided."

"What's new? You told me that fighting is in your blood."

"This is new fighting," said Kochi. "I don't know how you would say it but...gangs inside gangs."

The merchant started talking in German again.

Merchant: "You go there?" He pointed at the busy main road then north.

Me: "Yes, there."

Merchant: "To the winter?"

Me: "Yes." I think he meant the clouds.

Merchant: "There are new bad men. You are good men."
He didn't look at Yvonne. She was behind us.

Me: "New bad men here?"

Merchant: "Yes, here, and all places." He gave us more
food and charged nothing. "Go. Go to the winter."

After our conversation, the merchant joined some other
men who were chewing hashish and giving us suspicious
looks. The market's many magnificent magenta objects
contrasted with the beige and gray of the world in a very
pleasing way. There were quartz crystals and brass plates for
sale, creating a Christmas tree effect. I caught Yvonne's
reflection in a shiny brass plate. I thought of growing old and
gray with her. I was looking forward to waking up with her in
the days ahead. I thought it would be painful not to wake up
beside her. I was starting to feel that she would be a light just
beyond my reach if I was ever in a dark place, somewhere in
the immensity of space. We could be lost together, fly together.
Sunshine was breaking through, but shadows were creeping
in. It was time to go.

Everyone was quiet after we left Pol-e-Khomri, in their
own dreamy space. The highway curved into a plain between
mountains. It was a decent paved road. The mountains and
plain were white with fresh, glittering snow, the mountain
spurs like teeth of a gigantic beast. It was a place of rugged
beauty. The merchant spoke of new bad men, but what did he
mean? Bluebird wasn't tracking any new bad men in these
parts. Provo happened, but that was an outlier. Anyway, I was
veering away from the Bluebird nest.

I am an archaeologist by training, after all, so I was looking
forward to exposing the evil substrate of anything I
encountered. A lawyer as well, I would cross-examine. My
approach at this point had become more intuitive. I wasn't

waiting for accidents to fill in the blanks. I was just letting every detail, every motion, permeate my decision-making process. That's what Horseflesh was going to be about. Ten years earlier, before the U.S. invasion of Afghanistan, this road would have been blocked by the Taliban. Instead, we encountered a squad of Germans. They were only stopping bigger trucks. They waved us through. Haines pointed at the NATO decal on the windshield.

Maddox had all the paperwork he showed me earlier regarding Provo. It wasn't much, just photographs obtained through open-source channels and topographical and satellite maps. Maddox thumbed through the photos. I noticed no classification markings on anything. Then it clicked. "That's your own private CONOPS," I said. "Not bad, Sir. Does General Williamson know we're here?"

"General Williamson is gone. He went on leave for two weeks." Now things were making more sense. That meant General Sanchez was in charge. I knew Maddox and Sanchez didn't get along, as I mentioned earlier in this book, reader. "And if Sanchez doesn't like any of this, he can kiss rectum east and rectum west." That was the end of that conversation.

As on previous occasions, Maddox behaved as if I was intruding a little too much, and maybe I was, but I acted with pure curiosity, without repentance for any odd thing I'd done to Maddox. But this was my world, despite some of its gaudy features. I wanted him to feel more welcome, so as a kind gesture, I unfolded Bandit halfway and let him look at it. He had seen it before, but I never let him handle my map. My theme was there. The core of the Fourth Wall, as a game/mission/mindset. In a world turned upside down, Bandit was a giver of life and love, an infinity of mystery. If anyone, other than me, or perhaps Yvonne, was capable of deconstructing it, it was LTC Maddox. Even if he saw it as some kind of maze, he would be able to find his way out. So I let him look closely at Bandit, just to get a better idea of the overall concept of what I was trying to accomplish during Horseflesh.

"What's our story going to be?" said Haines. "An airman. Two Army officers with their translator. An Irish soldier and a Russian woman. We need to come up with something."

"I say we're taking this defector back to the border," said Ellington, giving a nod to Yvonne. "We're almost there, anyway. What do you say, lady?"

"I say get me out of this car," she said.

"And where would you rather be?" said Ellington. "They didn't check us, so we're fine."

"They didn't check us because there's going to be another checkpoint somewhere ahead doing the job," said Maddox. "We need to get off this road. Kochi, what do you think back there?"

"Let me think a minute," said Kochi. Kochi was always thinking, and I was getting a bad vibe. His mood was already grim. He stroked his thin beard in such a delicate way as if it was an enchanted region. He worked so hard to grow it and was constantly worried about getting caught by the Taliban. They had strict facial hair requirements. It wasn't beyond them to beat someone publicly for a facial hair violation. "I do not like this road."

"We're playing a little jazz," I said. "Let's just roll."

Yvonne was on the verge of boredom and fatigue and blew mouth steam on the window and drew what I thought was going to be a heart but turned into a spike as we hit a bump.

"Share your thoughts, Kochi," said Maddox. "Spit it out."

I put myself in Kochi's shoes. We all must've looked so serious. Like a rib cage, or west Texas, this highway had lots of small side roads that went off to God knows where. Kochi's big, alert eyes scanned the roads. He watched each one fly by.

"Turn there," said Kochi. "Turn right."

Haines had been driving like a sad drunkard but woke up and responded to Kochi's sudden energy. Communication is a key element in the art of war, especially at times like this when the war got wacky. I didn't feel like I was part of a war, just caught in a fog. Kochi's road was smooth and straight and once we were on the road it reminded me even more of places in Texas I had visited and missed. I was doubtful about whether we should get off the highway, the path of apparent least resistance, even knowing that a German element might be ahead, blocking the flow of Horseflesh in some way, but I felt better as we drove along. Maddox had good instincts, so I trusted him, and as a group, I felt like we were going to harmonize, in time. It was myself I doubted. My headaches were back. The bright snow-white world around us wasn't helping. I sneaked a few sips of the horseshoe crab blood. My overall stamina score went up a notch. I noted it on my character sheet.

Haines slowed. "Look ahead," he said. "Looks like two men."

"They're carrying something," said Maddox.

The front man waved when we drove by. They were carrying what looked like a pipe, about four feet long.

"That's suspicious," said Ellington. "Would be nice to have some drone assistance, to see where they came from and watch where they go."

"Hand me my laptop, Kochi," said Haines. He stopped ahead and turned on the computer and opened his window. He opened his backpack and pulled out Tink and Blink. It was a given that Blink was the name of a male and Tink female. For Haines, there were technical reasons, but for the rest of us, it was because of how the words sounded. Haines held both in his left palm and keyed commands with his right hand. The bug drones took off with a whine. We watched their flight via split screen. They had a lovely view of the lunarscape. The men stopped and looked back at us then kept going toward the main highway.

"How fast can those things fly?" I asked Haines.

"Up to 20 kph."

"That's not going to be fast enough."

"No, but I can find a pattern through what's visible," said Haines. "It's like predicting the landfall of a hurricane, in reverse."

"I can do that on line of sight alone," I said. "Look how straight the road is."

"What if they haven't been on the road long?" said Ellington. "What if they're leaving the road soon?"

"Shit," said Maddox. "Man is born for trouble. Hurry up. I want to see what this thing can do."

The drones were two feet above the road. I almost got sick just watching the vid. "You're a reckless pilot, kid, you know that?" I said.

"They respond to their own moves and environment and self-correct. I'm less in charge than you might think. Their guidance algorithms are improved from previous versions. Trust me, Sir."

"Modern warfare," grumbled Maddox.

"Too much monkey," said Ellington. Of course, I had to note this off the wall comment on Ellington's character sheet.

"Wait," said Haines. "Look at those low flying birds. I don't like the looks of those birds."

From afar, the two vultures were just gliding along, but in Tink's vision, they looked as fearsome as dragons, and they were headed right for the drones.

"I'm picking up the people's footprints," said Haines.

"How?" Ellington asked.

"Patterns in shadows created by raised areas created by their footprints in both snow and dirt. It took a while. Both drones have to scan the same area. Their views are combined to create sort of a holographic image, then a program kicks in and counts shadow pixels, while standard visual software looks for patterns."

"Software that you wrote?" said Ellington.

"Not exactly," said Haines. "I'm more of a vulture when it comes to programming. I just look for cool stuff. Speaking of vultures, Tink and Blink are going to have company soon."

"Our other friends have stopped," I said. "Get down, Yvonne." The men put down the long object and pulled aside their cloaks and raised AK-47s and started shooting. Two bullets hit the back of our vehicle. Rounds splashed all around us.

"Move over there," commanded Maddox.

Haines drove back over the road to the right side into a low area. The men found concealment behind some dead bushes.

"What just happened?" said Haines. Tink's side of the screen was dark. Then some red and brown spots appeared. "Shit. The bird got her." We were seeing inside the bird's guts. Tink was bouncing around the stomach from wall to wall. Haines pulled up another window full of commands. He hit F5. There was a burst of white light. Blink was watching all the action. His video feed showed that he was circling the bird. The other bird was circling him. Then the vulture that swallowed Tink fell out of the sky.

Maddox and Ellington got out of the vehicle and returned fire. I wasn't as quick to move. Yvonne was quicker than me. She ran across the plain in the opposite direction of all the action and got behind a boulder. I returned fire alongside Ellington and Maddox. Haines and Kochi took cover in front of our vehicle. Ellington took out one of the men and the gunfire stopped.

"I think I got the second one," said Maddox. "I don't know." Maddox was at his most wily and surly when killing.

I observed the scene through binoculars. The first fighter who went down wasn't moving. The second fighter was down, but he was still moving. Haines rushed down the road to dislodge Tink from the bird's gut. I could hear one of the insurgents grunting. He stood up and started running. He fired at us while running backward, then turned and sprinted. "I've got him," said Ellington. He got up, whistling, took careful aim, and fired and the man fell forward.

"Where's the girl?" said Maddox.

I looked all around for Yvonne, but I didn't see her. With mountains on all sides, I lost my sense of direction. I called out for her. "She went this way," I said, nodding at a boulder-strewn plain. "I'll go look for her."

"This keeps getting better," said Maddox.

Yvonne was nowhere. I had seen her take cover behind a boulder. When I got to the boulder, there were handprints in the dirt. Like a good soldier, she tried to dig in as best as she could, but there was no other sign of her. I called her name again and a sense of foreboding rose within me. Then I found her footprints. I was up for the challenge of tracking her without drone assistance. I waved back at Maddox so he could see where I was going. He waved at me in response, then waved at Ellington. They ran to my position.

I scanned the horizon with my binoculars and saw Yvonne's cloaked form, hunched over, but just her upper half. I zoomed in. She appeared to be cradling something. I ventured after her. She wasn't alone. In her arms was an Afghan boy, maybe fourteen. His bright eyes darted. He was saying 'water' over and over. I gave him some of mine. "What happened?" I said.

"I heard him," said Yvonne. "I could hear his whispers." Secrets were swimming in Yvonne's eyes. Whatever it was, I didn't want to break the spell.

The boy was calmer after drinking the water. He slowly got up, with Yvonne's help. She wrapped her arm around his thin frame.

"We won't hurt you," I said. I waved to get the attention of Haines and Kochi. When they saw me, they came.

"Druj," said the boy. I didn't need Kochi to translate. The old man in Sangin said the same thing, talked about Druj as if they were super-humans roaming the land. I lifted the boy's upper tunic, to see if he was bleeding anywhere, but he wasn't.

"He is exhausted," said Yvonne. She stroked his long, dark hair.

"Where did he come from?" I said. "You just found him lying here?"

Kochi talked to the boy. His name was Ajmal. Kochi said that he had come from the mountains northeast of our location, that he escaped from two men. The men were part of Druj.

"What is Druj?" I asked Ajmal. Kochi translated.

The boy was on the verge of crying, then stopped himself and answered Kochi.

"Darkness within, darkness without," said Kochi.

"Careful with this kid," said Ellington. "You'll see what you want to see and hear what you want to hear."

Maddox showed Ajmal pictures of Provo. "Did you see this?" he asked. "Tell him, Kochi."

But Kochi didn't have to translate. Ajmal's eyes grew wider. "Druj," he said again.

"Was this your home?" I said.

"No," said Ajmal. He understood. "Gathering place."

"And murder place?"

Ajmal said nothing.

Yvonne helped Ajmal sit up and took off her coat and wrapped it around the boy. Mucus was dangling from his nose. He wiped his face with his sleeve. He spoke with such a low voice that Kochi was having a hard time understanding him.

Maddox interrupted. "We've got two dead that way and Haines that way on a road where we don't want to be."

"We cannot leave him here," said Yvonne.

I thought Maddox was going to have a brief psychotic episode, with that hot red look on his face. He gave me a look that said this was all my fucked-up-baby. "Get him to the car,"

Maddox said.

I left that to Kochi and Yvonne and walked with Maddox and Ellington back to the vehicle. Haines was deeply involved with something on the ground. He saw us coming. "I'm performing surgery on a bird," he said. His hands were bloody.

"I saw some rags in the truck," Maddox told Ellington. "Get them and the camera out of my pack and take some photos of those dead guys."

"What are we going to do with them?" I said. "You've got to be an idiot to go around looking that suspicious. Unless the men were trying to get shot."

"They're coming with us," said Maddox. "Check them for intel."

"There she is," said Haines. His drone survived the ordeal in the bird's stomach. The bird was ripped to shreds. Other vultures were already circling above.

We continued driving through the rugged terrain. Kochi and Ellington were stuffed in the back of the vehicle with two corpses. They were tiny men. If it wasn't for their beards, I might have mistaken them for children. They were wearing kohl eyeliner, common among the Taliban. Ajmal was up front. He knew the men we killed. They were his captors. At least, that was the story he gave us.

"This is just peachy," said Ellington. "Peachy keen. We can't turn them into any authorities. What should we do?"

"We're going to bury them ourselves," said Maddox. "Kochi, how long until we get to your cousin's?"

"Leave her out of this, Sir." Kochi was kind of stuck.

"You're the one that got her involved at the very beginning."

"She is a good woman," said Kochi. "Though it is not her house. The house belongs to my other cousin, also a good woman."

"How long?" Maddox wasn't going down that road.

"Thirty minutes. Please, Sir. They are good people."

"I'm sure," said Maddox.

"I see some mountains to the east," I said. "Maybe we can take the long way to Khanabad."

"Another detour?" said Ellington. "Look what happened last time."

"Yes, please," said Kochi. "It is better than my cousin's."

"And whatever monsters are waiting are the monsters God wants," I said.

"Praise to Allah," said Kochi.

"We'll take the long way," said Maddox, "but keep that monster shit to yourself, Jett."

The boy was looking back and forth at all of us. He kept quiet. Poor Ajmal. Perhaps he was on his way to his own epic adventure, then he got caught up in mine, my quest to master the Fourth Wall and enter the fifth dimension. Yvonne was quiet. She knew what I was doing.

"This was all part of Digger's game," I said. "Wrong turns and false leads were built into it."

"Is that supposed to make me feel better, or worse?" said Ellington.

"No," I said. "We're going where we need to be. We're going to show up with two dead bodies, bug drones, and a strange boy."

"And a tired woman," said Yvonne.

"Keep the drones secret," said Haines.

"Keep the bodies secret, please," said Kochi.

It was sick, but it was just the start of the whole mind-bending mess.

KHANABAD

Kochi's cousins lived in a compound on the south side of Khanabad. We parked down the road and let Kochi approach alone, to soften the blow of our arrival, an intrusion, any way you put it. We waited about fifteen minutes for Kochi to return. Longest fifteen minutes of my life. I felt naked without a translator. Eyes were on us, and the presence of the boy wasn't helpful. Maddox wanted to deploy the drones again, just to see what was going on. I felt bad for Yvonne, like I was there to entertain her but doing a horrible job. She said it with her eyes. Then there was silence. All we could do was brace for the next big thing, whatever that might be. I knew something was coming, but I didn't come right out and say anything. My mind was wandering. Kochi finally returned and all was well. His cousin-in-law was waiting at the gate when we pulled up. He was short and fat and had a fat smile. He was near Kochi's age. His age was hard to tell, with the beard. He spoke English fluently, like Kochi. His name was Omar.

Omar sold cars for a living. "Whatever you do while you are here, I will not bother you," he said. "Just let me have your car."

Kochi was embarrassed, but that's because Omar had been around Americans a lot, and it showed in his glistening eyes. This man was a merchant.

"Omar smiles too much," said Kochi.

"That's all he wants?" asked Maddox. "Just the car?"

"It is true," said Kochi, "and not even payoff money."

The compound was spacious. The main house had two stories. The courtyard was half-filled with cars. He had some Taliban favorites, a few motorcycles, even an old Porsche. "That is my honey," he said of the Porsche. He'd done plenty of business with the Taliban over the years. Omar promised he was not using his home as a place to sell the cars, though. On the other side of the courtyard was a building where the women worked. We parked the Toyota as close as possible to that building.

The issue of the boy and dead bodies was delicate. I have spent many nights tossing and turning about taking the bodies to Omar's, but at the time it seemed the best thing to do. Looking back, I still think we had no other choice. I was still trying to be comfortable in my own skin, knowing it was going to be all new skin down the road as events started unfolding and madness expanding.

Omar didn't want his home to become the scene of further crimes. I could understand that. All that blood...the whole plan was forbidden in his grand worldview.

I pulled the car up to the building.

"There she is," said Kochi. "My cousin, Jamila."

Jamila was a portly girl, early twenties. She was helping Kochi's other cousin and Omar's wife, Hafiza, with washing clothes. Hafiza did not like Kochi, or any of us. She completely covered her face the whole time we were at the compound. Jamila seemed to like Kochi very much, and she did not cover her face like Hafiza. She was open and courteous, like Omar. Omar invited us inside his house. Omar loved the US. His house was filled with American objects: Elvis Presley memorabilia; an old map of the US with Route 66 highlighted orange; a picture of himself with a life-sized cut-out of Ronald Reagan. "You like?" he said. "This was taken in Kabul."

We needed to distract the women so that we could

examine the bodies. Omar helped with the bodies and our weapons. The boy helped. He was no longer afraid of the dead men. Once inside the shack, Omar found some old sheets and rags. Maddox and Haines and I started removing the clothing of the men. The smell of blood filled the space. I caught a whiff of vomit.

"Hold on," said Maddox. "Look at these tattoos."

Each man had similar tattoos. They looked like Arabic script. I sketched the tattoos. Kochi entered the room, and he knew right away we were dealing with something different. "Those men are not Taliban," said Kochi.

"Al-Qaeda," I suggested.

"No," said Kochi. "I do not believe so."

Omar was muttering to himself. It sounded like he was praying. "The women," he said and left the shack.

Haines photographed the bodies. I sketched them. Ajmal was the most helpful one of the bunch. He told us his story while we cleaned and redressed the bodies in some of Omar's old clothes, to make them more presentable, in case the cousins found us. Kochi translated for Ajmal: "I am from Mazari Sharif. My family sold me to a man in Mazari Sharif when I was twelve. For two years I have been a dancer for him. He brings people to his house for entertainment. He smiles. People love his smile, as do I. I was not afraid of him until a month ago. He started beating me. He no longer prayed to Allah. He did not like to see me pray. Different men started coming to his house. They wore dark cloaks. I danced for them, but they did not seem entertained. The musician played different songs. I changed my dancing, but this did not help. One of the men had teeth of gold. He was very pale. He looked sick. He did not look Afghan. He looked bored with the dancing. I began to sing for the men. I sang about swimming in the river, on a beautiful day, and lying on the shore under the warm sun. Their expressions did not change. They seemed more concerned with other men at the gathering than with the dancing. All the strange men left before I was finished dancing. I did not stop. I am a good dancer. I will show you." Ajmal moved like a Siamese cat.

"You said 'Druj' when we found you," I said. "What did you mean?"

Kochi translated. "When I saw the monster, it was like a dream," said Ajmal. "I was looking at many men, but my eyes were playing tricks because I knew in my heart and mind that all the men formed one evil thing that was one moment a cloud, and the next a lion. I do not want to go back to that place. Druj is the invasion of all these men, as this one thing. Allah willing, please do not let it happen. This will be too difficult. Please. You cannot distinguish Druj from a flower, or a river."

Omar appeared with an old tape player. "Sufi mix," he said in English. He rewound the tape to the beginning and played a catchy tune with guitars and cymbals.

The music lifted Ajmal's spirits. He took off his sandals and twirled on his toes. He balanced like a bird on a wire. He spoke to Kochi.

"He is sorry he is not dressed better," said Kochi. I said nothing. I was lost in the dualities before me: the dancing boy; the dead men in their chairs; I was confused as to how they were connected. The still-cooling corpses were tilted a little bit toward Ajmal as if they were also watching him.

"This is grotesque," said Maddox. He turned away from the scene.

"Are they actually dead?" I said. "I swear I saw one move."

"Maybe they're just playing dead," said Maddox. "I've seen it before."

"That's brilliant, Sir. I'm going to use that. We're all playing dead, just to fit into each other's schemes. I'm going to turn the notion against itself. Like the fairy tales we grew up with. They transformed reality. I look at him dancing, and I see the universe oscillating."

Maddox had a great opportunity to chop me down to size for such strange comments, but he didn't. "I'm with you, pup. Do what you need to do."

Ajmal stopped dancing when Jamila and Hafiza entered the room and screamed.

I later found sketches in Digger's notes similar to the men's tattoos, except the explanation about the design was that it was similar to Vegvisir, an Icelandic compass symbol. I showed Yvonne. "This guy must be a shaman," I said. "This isn't random. Do you think he can tell the future?"

"I do," said Yvonne. "He brought us here."

Yvonne and I sketched together. She sketched Ajmal dancing, and I sketched variations of the men's tattoos. I found that drawing helped me enlarge and empower my place within the Fourth Wall. Drawing helped me notice things, like a hawk from above, but deep inside, and not just the surface of things. The drawings later made their way into my CONOPS. Maybe it was my sleep-deprived mind playing tricks on me, turning all cognition upside down, but the drawings in the Digger notebook, combined with my own drawings in my Fourth Wall CONOPS, combined with the sweet music we were making in that compound in that north Afghanistan town, with the boy dancing, and the dead men watching, seemed like it was all starting to come together. There was competition, and I was friction-force, causing motion, in terms of overall force required to move the future in a certain way. Merely, it was a sum of forces. The scene had a soul.

That night, a realistic dream collided with a fantasy dream: a fairy princess got it on with a quadricopter about her size, and that didn't go well for either of them. Their lovemaking ripped a hole in the fabric of the universe, but the dream got me thinking: It was a basic tenet of entropy that if no energy enters or leaves the system, then the total energy of a system remains the same. But what if...

PROVO

To go deeper into the fantasy, I studied Bandit when I woke up the next morning. I wrote notes on Bandit about Provo. The map was too small to accommodate all my notes for the north, so I drew asterisks and sub-numbers. For example: 6* (A practice that went back to my days as a waiter.)

Provo was only big news to our little group and a few others. Even the massive world media machine missed it. Since Taliban names and numbers were so difficult to track, Bluebird treated the incident at Provo as an outlier, a wicked little dream. Without significant loss of civilians, the incident was buried. Even in a political way, at that time, it was too remote to touch. But even further down the road, Provo was part of the glowing core of actions by friend and foe, Druj or terrorist. We left before sunup. Omar followed in his Land Cruiser, so we were a modern Toyota caravan. Ajmal came along. He couldn't stay at Omar's with the women. His participation in the game was now set. I even made a character sheet for him. Yvonne sketched a portrait of him in the corner of the character sheet. The dead guys had to come. I had a feeling they were going to affect the forces of nature, one way or another, as secondary vectors from outer space, in a mad way. We traveled south toward mountains. I was anxious. All these pieces of the jigsaw puzzle were being assembled, but I still didn't know what the picture was going to look like. I whispered to myself, *Where are you, little magician man? There you are.* I pulled out the magician card and studied it. Due to the presence of our dead passengers, we kept the windows cracked, even though it was freezing. Perfect for the dead guys, but not for the rest of us.

"What are you doing back there?" said Maddox.

"Figuring out how to keep myself entertained," I said. "Exorcising demons."

Yvonne snickered. "Liar," she said. "You want to be possessed. Your demons are more friend than foe."

"You're both making me nervous," said Maddox.

"How much longer till we get to the carnival on the edge of town?" I asked.

"Not far," said Haines.

Yvonne fluttered her eyelashes at me, struggling to stay awake, still so beautiful. The road started climbing and falling, then it just climbed. Burping sounds of the dead guys mixed with the car's hum, sounds I never wanted to hear again, though I have for sure . Yvonne fell asleep.

We arrived at Provo at dawn, the sun's orange glow beating back the moonlight/starlight. Like Provo, Utah, the site was situated in a plain between two sets of mountains. There were signs of human activity, dirt roads, building foundations, tire tracks tangling. There was little snow on the ground. Two sections were cordoned. The first section was to our left, down a slope.

"Where are the structures?" said Ellington. "There's nothing."

I pointed out a ruined wall and platform on the opposite mountain slope, but they looked ancient. Ajmal was still sleepy. His face was gray. Omar and Kochi propped him up like he was one of the dead guys.

"Martians are responsible for the desolation of this place," said Ellington. "I'm sure of it."

"I wasn't expecting much," said Maddox, "but I was

expecting more than this."

I remembered a reference in Digger's Historians journal. Something about a Plain of Reclamation. "What would the drones make of this place? Surely we could calibrate them to produce..."

"We don't have time for that," said Maddox. "Ask the boy where the houses are."

Ajmal told Kochi another long story. Kochi took notes and said that the boy had lost his mind.

"Can't you give us something more than the obvious bottom line, Kochi?" said Maddox.

Poor Kochi, such twisted words were beyond him. "Ajmal said there were compounds where there were now pits."

Ajmal yawned.

"Did they burn?" asked Maddox.

"The boy said they were taken away, piece by piece," said Kochi. "He watched it happen."

"What did they want?"

"He does not know," said Kochi. "He does not believe they wanted anything, except they believed it was a Taliban camp, and they wanted Taliban to be dead and their camp wiped away."

"Why did you run?" Maddox asked Ajmal directly.

Without Kochi's translation, Ajmal said, "They think I am Taliban."

"Are you?" said Ellington.

"Leave him alone," said Yvonne. She put her arm around Ajmal.

"You're our prisoner," said Ellington. "Do you understand that word: prisoner?"

Just like Digger's Plane of Reclamation passage. The characters all started fighting. They almost killed each other, whether human or some other magical being. The only thing that stopped them was an outside force. Outcomes and solutions in Digger's game were a bit *deus-ex-machina* for my tastes, but as a character in his game, formulating my own game at the same time, I thought that his solutions were fine.

"Captain Jett," said Maddox. "You're the archaeologist here. What do you think?"

"Maybe the Germans came in and cleaned up afterward as part of their investigation." The sole basis for this remark was my own memory of exploring the ruins of Tiryns years ago in Greece. Tiryns was the mythical birthplace of Hercules. Darkness was approaching, and I was the only one at the site at the time. The Germans had all left for the day, so I got to view their work up close. Good pits, very precise work, clean cuts all around.

We started down the slope toward the right-side pit. I saw some movement on the hill south of the site. "Did you see that?"

Maddox saw what I was pointing at. He used his binoculars. "Snow leopard...or something similar. What the hell is that?"

Ajmal started talking so quickly that Kochi couldn't translate everything. He hushed the boy.

"It's not going to come tear us apart," I said. "It's too far away. Take it easy."

"It is not that," said Kochi. "That thing is not...later I will explain. Jinn."

"Come on," I said, a skeptic of my own evolving powers. Then to myself: "What kind of new beasts are bursting forth in the world?"

Omar joined in the fussing. We reached the pit. Inside the pit were several levels. Maddox helped lower me down. Omar and Kochi and Ajmal were all going at it above me. I was losing patience. Time and luck were running out.

"Quiet," I said. I needed to think.

I didn't feel like digging, but I did feel like I was going to probe hidden realities. I saw more than what was actually before me. I saw piles of bones. I reached down and felt the earth. It was wet, with some clay, not much, good ground for digging. Ajmal climbed into the hole with me. The rest stayed above, keeping guard. Ajmal conveyed a range of emotions with his eyes, but mainly fear, or recognition of fear that he was intent to overcome. At that moment, just the two of us, I knew he was on my side, but he needed my help and I was going to help him. I've always had an intuitive sense of people's needs, hidden desires, and the fight against the void, deep within, a deep sense of those things. Like a blind swimmer, I made myself see these things, from a need to survive. I moved in the fluidity of the moment.

Omar and Kochi helped Ajmal and me out of the pit. "Why are you looking at me like that?" Maddox said to me. "You know everything I know at this point."

"Ask the boy, Kochi," I said.

I found Kochi's perplexed looks entertaining. I tried not to laugh. "Part of what the boy explains," said Kochi, "is that these men, the new terrorists, use the snow cats."

"The leopards? How?"

The explanation stumped Kochi. "To distract? Entertainment." I pictured a transformation of the animal from its natural state to something monstrous. This kind of thing was certainly allowed by my game and Digger's, but I was still having a hard time connecting it with reality, even though the creepy events were starting to pile up.

"Who's watching our cargo?" said Maddox. "Ellington, go back there."

Ajmal looked a little less worried than he did at the beginning of the day.

"Did they get what they came for?" I said, to no one in particular.

"Yes, but no," said Kochi. "They found death. They did not find all death they wanted to find."

"So they will come back for more," I said. "But what do they have to do with Sugarbush?"

"They are explorers," said Yvonne.

"We're running out of time," said Maddox. "You better put your mystical muscle to work and figure this out, Captain Jett."

The second pit was a football field away. It was rectangular, with levels, like the first pit, empty as well. I noted its dimensions. I could do this all day, explore and note everything like a naturalist, like Charles Darwin. "Kochi, didn't Ajmal say that there were entire compounds where we are now? These holes ought to be bigger."

Kochi nodded.

"We really need eyes in the sky," I said. "There's more than a few things going on here. I can't process it all. Haines, might you offer an algorithmic solution?"

Tink and Blink took flight. I asked Haines to control them as much as he could, but he couldn't. He had programmed them to make sense of data, to do what humans can't do. Not to mention the nanobots in the drones, which monitored and made minor repairs. The drones defied their creator, as I was defying my creator and my leaders. More than ever, I was being pulled toward something with a great invisible hand, rushing through clouds, with a bird's eye view of the universe. But this wasn't like any previous OBE. Monstrosities and uncertainties were ruling me as they do the whole universe, all for big reasons. Same with the dead bodies in the back of our vehicle. We couldn't dump them at Provo. I wanted to keep them with us throughout the adventure, like in the movie Weekend at Bernie's, though Weekend was not in my heart like Time Bandits.

I took Maddox aside. "We need to keep them, Sir."

"Keep who?"

"All of them. The boy. Omar. The dead guys. I'm sorry, Sir, but I feel strongly about them."

"They're going to start smelling strong," said Maddox. "They're getting there. So are you. You've lost your mind, Jett."

Just like in Time Bandits, when all the robbers ganged up against Randall, their leader, and said he was losing his mind.

Yvonne kissed me.

"You're killing me, son," said Maddox, his eyeballs to mine. He went to check on Ellington.

"You're staying, aren't you?" I asked Yvonne. I don't know what prompted me to ask that question, except that she felt so distant. I needed her more than ever, but her mind was elsewhere.

"We are looking for different things," said Yvonne. "I am happy you wanted me to come, but you brought me closer to Belyayevo, where I was a girl. I do not want to be back in that place."

"You seem lost," I said.

"Lost? Perhaps. Perhaps I do not want to be found."

"Are you in pain? Is this some kind of psychic attack that I allowed to happen?"

"Perhaps," said Yvonne, "but it is a sign that you are closer to where you want to be."

"I don't feel that way. I don't know why I'm here. What's done is done, as far as this place goes. You're in danger, being here. We all are."

"What did your friend have to say about this place? It is in his journal."

"He's not my friend," I said. "He's more of a ghost."

"Is he? Perhaps that is why you are stumbling. He is a ghost only in your mind. You must release him into the world. Face him and all your ghosts."

"I can say the same to you," I said.

Back at Omar's that night, I poured over Digger's journal and Maddox's intel, along with all my notes, which was a huge pile, and Bandit, which was like a life force, my skewed vision of the world on paper. At this point, Bandit was as good a map as any for the operation. I tasked Ellington with reading the news for bits about Provo, and to go through all the open-source materials he could find using Omar's computer. Haines was busy repairing Tink and Blink. They flew too close to each other and clipped their wings. Haines said their pattern recognizers were a bit off. I was the happiest I'd been since I don't remember. All sorts of strange elements were coming to me, falling into place, into a grand scheme that I couldn't yet see, except that it all felt right, even the bodies, which flew in the face of logic. I needed them, but if the dead men were going to be part of our team, they needed names: Franz and Karl. No German connection, except that we were on German turf.

Going through Digger's journal, I noticed some sketches that I'd passed over before, swirls and tumbling shapes, similar to the tattoos on the men. Digger was onto something. Maybe it was my sleep-deprived mind playing tricks on me, but when I compared his sketches to mine, I knew. I was working with his ghost in that north Afghanistan town. We were combining forces against devilry the world did not know (or hadn't known in a long time, geologic time). I was the friction force, causing motion. It was a competition, in terms of the overall force required to move the future in a certain way. The sum of all forces, whatever that might look like, was going to be the inflection point in my search, except I realized that the key wasn't going to be in Digger's notes. The key was Digger himself. The key was us, working together. The opposition force would grow without us, but we could empower it, enlarge it. This all felt so weird at the time. (And you, reader, are saying: human speak...please. I'm getting there...) Was the movement doomed to fail because of incompleteness? The pathway to truth I chose was nothing but switchbacks up a steep mountain. Every foothold felt like an unprovable element.

I sketched variations of the men's tattoos. The one shape I kept coming back to resembled a four leaf clover. Applying simple human logic, inadequate by its very nature, I connected shapes and patterns in the tattoos and sketches with the

Fourth Wall universe I was building and that I knew went way beyond what I could comprehend. (And so what? The Wright Brothers built and flew their first flyer without a full understanding of aerodynamics. They just flew!) Still, I barely had a modicum of rules to play by, and I had no idea of the monstrosities that were waiting and the rules they knew.

I set up a table in the courtyard. The night was quiet, except for the occasional howl of wind. The clouds were low, red and gray lights of Khanabad reflected. Ajmal watched me work. Could he see the madness around me? Or the chameleon me? Did he have a sense of taking imaginative paths, meandering, segmented motion, to arrive at truth, while watching the world arrive there through deep sleep? He was too young for such, but I think he understood me from the very beginning.

Omar and Kochi checked on us. Omar was walking in a very prissy way and had that startled-donkey look he sometimes had. Kochi was going along, hot-to-trot, too. I had every reason to mock, but as a guest, I went along with it.

Ellington joined us. "There's food inside."

"I'm not hungry."

"You haven't eaten all day."

"I need to figure it all out," I said.

"There's nothing to figure out," said Ellington. "We're avengers avenging the murderous rampage of bad men killing other bad men. I have a question. Why do these places have American names? Of all the names you could pick. You Americans are masochistic, deep down."

Yvonne joined us.

"Bad men killing bad men..." I repeated.

"That is all you people talk about, Thomas," said Yvonne. She turned up her nose at all our death-dealing. "Killing, all the time, killing."

"It's the general theme of our business," I said, "but my stories involve more."

"I am exhausted," Yvonne said. "Just from talking about it."

"Me too."

Yvonne put her head on my shoulder before I could put my head on hers.

"I could use some new magic tricks," I said.

"You have a death wish," said Yvonne.

"Maybe I'm just trying to have a little fun? There has to be something at stake, seriously, for there to be a little fun in this."

"Like death." There was her smile, back from the dead.

"Perfect," I said.

Haines came up to us. "Sorry for interrupting," he said. The drones were in his palm. "Loiter," he said. The drones came to life and twirled into the night sky. I could barely see them, even a few feet away, but Haines assured me they were keeping watch over the compound.

"Be careful, Tink and Blink," I said. "The night sky is full of demons. Angels, too."

"Their digital mapping systems will capture everything," said Haines, "maybe not demons and angels, but their sensors are pretty receptive. They point out ghosts all the time. It's all data. I've hacked the sensory systems of multiple flying insects, especially moths, to get to this point."

Omar and Kochi were laughing at Ajmal. "He thinks you have the power of invisibility," said Kochi, pointing at me.

"Why would he think that?" I said.

The answer was gameplay, all the way, a nod to the ninja in me, more to my past ninja dreams that got pulled into the Fourth Wall, logically. I had discussed the Fourth Wall with Kochi a few times. Now he was over there telling stories. Fitting Ajmal into the game was easy. I felt like I was doing the right thing. I imagine Digger went through the same arc of emotions. I could see how he visualized and quantified his imaginary world in his character sheets. My character sheets needed work. I made do with what I had.

Kochi said something to Ajmal.

"What did you say?" I asked.

"I told him to be careful. You make up the rules as you go along. You are like water, how you move."

"In the Koran, it says water is life," I said with a wink. He liked the quote but not the wink.

Bandit was too big for this game segment, so I sketched a smaller map, similar to drawings/mini-maps in Digger's Historians journal, of Outpost Bekun on Decrex and Nemog, the group of cities on the asteroids. Kochi had already played with me a couple of times, so he knew all about the motivation system I had created for the game. I let Kochi review the motivation list, which included things like greed and revenge. Kochi explained the motivation system to Ajmal. Apparently, the boy could read English better than he could speak it. He understood some of the words. My main reason for showing Ajmal the list was to see which motivator he would choose, as a way for helping me learn about the boy. He chose 'betrayal' from the list, which made me wonder if his betrayal went both ways: he was betrayed and also betrayed others himself. I could see that in his eyes, how he watched all the carnage, took it all in in a soul-searching sweep.

The gameplay was mainly for my benefit. It was a new group, with several new faces, and I needed to get a better sense of the group's dynamics in order to be ready for approaching shifts in equilibrium. Gameplay in my head: *Maybe that equilibrium was going to peak, or take a new form altogether, a new psychic empowerment. Maybe it was going to be a huge step in the evolution of our whole species, telling us everything we know is wrong.* I took Ajmal, Kochi, and Yvonne through the ruins of a building crushed by a fallen spacecraft. It was the stuff of nightmares. I chose such bleak landscapes for those early Fourth Wall games. Alien oil was seeping from the wreckage of the aircraft (I got that idea from the USS Arizona, its oil still seeping into the ocean, after all this time). Haines just watched. I asked him a couple of questions about topology which I thought were applicable. Ellington and Maddox were with the dead guys. As game master, I made adjustments for Ajmal, being new, and made the same for Yvonne and Kochi. Making up the scene as we went along, like Kochi said, I paused and sketched an idea for a building based on one of Digger's sketches. The concept was that the building was a platform or entry point into a larger base which I couldn't yet conceive, and I didn't want to until we were finished with this quick throw-down game. I then sketched it out in the sand and used pebbles for players.

Yvonne used a good bit of magic during the game. She whispered some spell. She said she was attempting to re-establish contact with a spirit guide from the past. I remembered she mentioned this being before: some protective force formed by benevolent ghosts from her childhood home, a multitude of spirits that joined into one entity.

"Why are you doing that now?" I said. "This is just a game."

"It is for later," she said.

"When you do that, you're going to reach into the underworld and bring back all your old demons, like your father."

Yvonne was dismissive of me. Between the two of us, she was the superior magician. Until now, I'd only been touched by this outer world here and there. Yvonne knew it well. Next to her, I was a con artist. "I need to face mine like you need to face yours," she said. "We have talked about that."

Ellington came over. "What's that you drew?"

"A layout of where we're going," I said. "This side building here...that's the drug lab."

"Are you war-gaming all this? Shouldn't Maddox and I be invited?"

So I took out his character sheet and gave it to him. He reviewed it and gave me a look. "You can embrace it or not," I said.

Ellington joined in with one more little quip: "Modern warfare."

Maddox had the same kind of comment, but the action wasn't completely beyond their imagination or training. Maddox left the presentation of mysteries to me. "Does this place exist?" he said.

"If it can be grasped by the human mind, then it exists, Sir. You're both stoked, I can tell."

After a slow start, I kept the game grounded in reality as best as able, but my mind was in a phantom landscape where every color of the spectrum was reflected. I got a good idea of where the players were coming from in everything they did. Ellington, for instance, loved machines/weaponry. I explained the motivator element of Fourth Wall character creation, and he loved that. He loved the logic and the role of chance and the dice. As they played the game, I toyed with them, all parts of my grand strategy. For me, it all came back to Digger. This started as his game. I was going to take it as far as I could, but it was still his game, so I had to inject him into it. Nobody objected. For them, it was just a little fun, unlike my own vision of the unfolding action.

The players left the circle, one by one, called by nature or boredom or fatigue, but I stayed and played and did some more mapping in the dirt. I envisioned a full Druj camp. I imagined its walls, the people (people from many countries, inspired by the makeup of my Horseflesh team), but I didn't know where it might actually be, if it be at all. My stars. I looked above for answers. Tink and Blink caught my attention, floating above me, their tiny electric eyes shining, twinkling with the rest of the stars, and dark stars that I could sense but not see, lots and lots of them.

THIS IS
THE FUTURE

I started my day by practicing some Shotokan Karate against my dead enemies. I looked them in the eye and moved into a low horse stance. I kept my hands in the guard position. I brought my left leg across my right then kicked with my right. I barely touched Karl's chin. I practiced that a couple of times. I went through some blocking and counter-attacking exercises. Franz and Karl sat there, stiff in their chairs. All this ninja stuff might seem silly to you, reader, but hand-to-hand combat skills are an important dimension of military life.

"I see shallow graves in your future," I said. "I'm inspired to write something. Yes...an ode to a pile of bones."

"Who are you talking to, Sir?" It was Haines. He went back to his computer in the courtyard. I sat next to him and unfolded Bandit. It was still dark and Maddox and Ellington and Kochi were still asleep on the other side of the courtyard, and I could hear Jamila and Hafiza inside the house, staying as far away from all of us as they could. Neither had children, and I didn't ask why.

"It's become man's best friend," I said.

"Sir?" said Haines.

"The computer. I'm not a complete convert to digitalism. There are other ways."

"Right...I'm just making some adjustments to the drones."

"Was there any activity in the night worth talking about?"

"Do we even know what would be coming after us, Sir?"

"No, we don't," I said. "Well, I have some ideas. It's as if the whole world has gone hazy. This is the future." I held up Bandit. "I know. It's an old school approach."

"The future is in the past?"

"I mean you have to rewire your mind, just to survive, and for me, that survival is more analog than digital." I was referring to my notes.

"You don't like Tink and Blink? Suit yourself. I'll take my chances with them."

"That's not what I mean," I said. "I hesitate to tell you everything I see. I'm seeing more each day. And the world is...I don't want to say. It's too early to say."

"It's hell," said Haines.

"It's not," I said. "It may be ghastly, but it's not hell. It's energy. Look at the bigger picture." I thought about it. "The bigger picture..."

"You've got that look you get," said Haines. "Lost in dreams."

Too many things were starting to frighten me, but I didn't know jack about anything. "You have any aerial shots of Provo?"

Haines pulled up a few on his computer. "I like this one," he said. "I adjusted contrasting tones." In the areas of topology and complex number theory, Haines had the finest mind. He had an intuitive grasp of complex spatial relationships.

"Look at that." There were blips and fuzzy spots that I knew had to fit into the bigger picture. I picked one. "There."

"That dot?" said Haines.

"That's a house."

"Maybe."

"And there's a road leading around the hill, straight to the house. Did we find any other structures in the area?"

"No, Sir. We didn't make it over the hill."

"Maybe we should." I felt I was controlling the space around me better, not telekinetically, but in understanding where things are or where they ought to be. There was more to Provo than we initially found.

PROVO

Later that morning, the whole crew went back to Provo, even the dead guys. It was cold and foggy. I had an out of body experience on the way there. Feeling lighthearted and lightheaded, I flew alongside our vehicles. I saw ruins all over the area I didn't notice before. Perhaps they were connected to Druj. I saw the Travelers again, the gray forms who approached me after the dignified transfer ceremony, like stress-induced ghosts. I reached for them, but they neither pitied me nor loved me. They were just there. I had a feeling someone else was in the sky with me. I checked my six and saw a man, just for a moment. I thought it could be my own reflection on the fog. Then he was gone.

After all that flying around, pain bubbled up in my head. It was my first big headache in a while. I kept flying. I thrust ahead of our convoy, over Provo. The headache brought forth strange vibrations all around. Provo looked different, but not so different that I didn't recognize it. It looked like a place I had visited before but in a dream. A ghostly mist was streaming out of a distant gorge that wasn't there before. I could feel seismic activity in the earth, though I was far above. Then the mere thought of riding around the desert with such a motley bunch, including two dead guys, pulled me, whipped me, back into the car. I forgot where I was for a second. I forgot I was in a different vehicle than Yvonne. Kochi was on one side, Ajmal on the other. Both had such goofy grins as if they were going home.

We found the house we were looking for. It was a tiny structure, surrounded by a low wall. A few goats were outside. A man was tending a small fire behind the house. With his withered skin and stringy hair and tight eyes and lips, he looked more Mongolian than Afghan. Kochi spoke to him alone a minute then came back to us. "He speaks Parachi, not Pashto," said Kochi. Parachi is an Iranian language. "I speak some Parachi. He said he is sorry we came back."

"He knew we were here before?"

"He was in the hills, watching us. He did not think we were with the military, because of how we are dressed and our vehicles and what we are doing."

"Tell him he doesn't need to be afraid," I said. "We just need to ask some questions."

"I told him that," said Kochi. "I told him to let us see inside his home. He says he will let us, and he has nothing to hide."

"Why are you sorry we came back?" Maddox asked the old man directly.

Kochi translated. "He says he is only doing what he was told. He does not like Americans, or Taliban, but these people are different."

We went inside the house. Yvonne and Haines stayed outside. Omar and Ajmal came into the house then left after a moment. There was only a small table and no other furniture. The floor was plaster, with a large, green rug. Some pillows lined the walls. The man was courteous. He offered us tea.

"The men you seek are not from here," said the man, through Kochi. "I do not know where they came from. Their skin is different, not like mine, but not black or very light, like his." He pointed at Ellington. "Now I must tell my keeper the truth."

"Your keeper?" I asked.

Kochi asked him that and more.

"Have you seen this man?" I showed him Digger's photo.

The man nodded, but his expression was neutral.

"He was here?" asked Maddox.

The man nodded again. He wiped his arm as if bugs were crawling on him. He talked a blue streak.

"What's he saying?" said Ellington.

There was rifle fire. I unholstered my M9. I could hear bullets striking the vehicles. I went to the doorway. I didn't want to draw fire to the house, even though I knew it was due to the old's man's betrayal we were being attacked. I could see Yvonne and Haines crouching behind a vehicle. I couldn't see Omar and Ajmal.

"Looks like the fire is coming from the other side of the vehicles," said Maddox. "I can't see anything."

"We can't get in the fight if we're here," said Ellington.

"On three," said Maddox, "we'll head for the vehicles. Ellington, you're going to the one on the right. Jett and I will stay left. One, two, three."

We burst from the doorway. I didn't start firing right away since I didn't have a target, but fire found us. There was a man on the far left behind a vehicle that wasn't there earlier. Maddox and I took cover behind the low wall. Ellington aimed and released a couple of three-round bursts, taking out the enemy. That just left the men on the fireside of our vehicles, and we still didn't have a clear line of sight.

"I'm rushing to the car," said Maddox. "Cover me."

I nodded and looked to my right and gave Ellington the signal for covering fire. Maddox ran forward and joined Haines and Yvonne. I fired at a spot of desert left of the vehicles. Ellington rushed to a spot next to Maddox and I provided covering fire. Yvonne was also providing covering fire with her M9. Then Kochi and I moved up together.

Shooting at us meant shooting at our vehicles. Poor Omar. I felt bad for dragging him into this. I could see him behind his own vehicle with his hands over his ears, his mouth and eyes wide. Ajmal was next to him. Omar's car was riddled with bullets. Glass went everywhere. Same with our vehicle. Glass shattered above us, fell onto us, then I noticed blood and brain matter. I looked up and Karl's head was hanging out the window. His tongue was halfway out of his mouth. His skull was open. An eyeball was about to fall out right onto my face. I scooted sideways. Dirt was flying up. They were now shooting at the ground beneath the vehicle. Ellington took a prone firing position and shot at their feet. When they fell, he shot their bodies.

"Wait!" I yelled. "Don't shoot their tires!"

"I'm shooting the people, not their tires," said Ellington.

"Let the man work," said Maddox. He gave me the quiet sign, index finger to lips.

"Let the others go," I said. "Haines, you have enough power in the bugs to track them?"

"No way," said Haines. "I mean, not in flight mode." Haines pulled his laptop out of his backpack.

One of the vehicles started. Ellington popped up and lobbed a grenade, but it fell short of the last vehicle, which was already backing up to leave. The grenade landed closer to the first vehicle. The blast tore into the tail of the vehicle. Metal flew straight up. The rear wheels flew straight out. I stayed on the ground till the other vehicle left.

"Just one guy," I said.

"I count two dead," said Maddox.

"I meant one guy is driving that car," I said. "Haines, you working that?"

"One minute," said Haines. He was pounding away at his laptop. Sweat was pouring down his face. Yvonne went over to Omar and Ajmal. "Drones are airborne," said Haines. "They've only got a few minutes of flight time, though." I glimpsed at the screen. The fleeing vehicle was going slowly around a bend, giving a chance for the bugs to catch up. Watching the world from their eyes was making me dizzy.

Ellington came to our position.

"Do the drones have the juice to even reach the target at all?" Maddox said.

"It will be close," said Haines. "I'll give them one minute then I'll cut the video to save power. Hopefully, they'll do ok with sound alone. They have very sensitive receptors that can hone in on the target and ignore unwanted noise."

"Brilliant man," said Ellington. "Now computer-generate a way home."

Kochi went into the house. Omar and Yvonne and Ajmal were huddled together. Ajmal nodded his head.

"Got it," said Haines. He did it. The drones attached to the roof of the vehicle. The view was shaky, then the screen went dark. "We lost video. They'll automatically go into sleep mode to save power, but when they wake up, I'll see them."

Kochi came out of the house. "The old man is dead," he said.

"Gunshot?" Maddox said.

"No. This was on the floor near his body." Kochi held up an empty bottle.

We swept his house and the site for evidence. I kept my eyes open for ancient objects that might litter the landscape, noticeable only to a trained archaeologist like myself, and I did find some potsherds. I kept searching and thinking. It felt like going back in time to my days of digging up Mayan ruins in Belize. Hunting artifacts kept me away from reality. It was my way of unraveling encrypted messages, sent by some long dead person. That's what the Fourth Wall is: decrypting the universe's messages.

Reality soon found me again. Kochi and Maddox undressed the old man, like Franz and Karl, and he had some similar tattoos, not as big. They looked incomplete. I think God places old sages all along my path to send me messages, only this time his man got killed. His man was Druj. Strange pick.

I spent some time alone on the hill. It started to snow while

I was up there. I scanned the whole area with binoculars. The mountains around us were lightly covered with fresh powder. I saw the snow leopard again. He was sitting on what looked like a ledge, but upon further inspection, I could see it was man-made, perhaps a foundation of a building. The area resembled a desert world in my mind where I built one of my memory palaces. I still visit the palace often. It is massive and as tall as a skyscraper, in a place where the sky is orange and the wind is constantly blowing. I've created many maps in that particular memory palace, maps of unexplored universes, complete with huge territories of dark matter, like our own universe. The darkness in my palace isn't a kind of emptiness, though. It is a created form.

Many maps came before Bandit. Let's go way back to when I was twelve years old. I grew up in Uvalde, Texas. Along with a couple of friends, I planned my first big adventure. We were going to ride our bikes to Ft. Inge, a Civil War era site, just ruins next to a dormant volcano on the edge of town. I had it all planned out. I made a list of the equipment I would need. I did some research at the public library. It was going to be a big adventure, but it never went beyond the planning stage, like so many other things in my life. But twenty-five years later, I was living a childhood dream.

Haines joined me on the hill. "Omar and Ajmal are burying the dead...uh, Karl and Franz."

"We're keeping the new guys, right?" That was a little too eager.

"You said that's what we need to do," said Haines.

"Need?" I said. "It's just a feeling. Sit down. Consider the potential energy of this closed system," I began, with a sweep of my hand. I explained my hunches in terms maybe he could understand, with the laws of thermodynamics and system mechanics. It was a disjointed representation.

Maddox and Ellington and Yvonne were below, each following different leads. When Yvonne disappeared for a moment behind a boulder, I was about to call out, but she emerged. I turned to Haines. His skin was glistening, tinged a little red. "You like the cold?" I asked him.

"I'm used to it, but I don't like it."

"What do you think?" I said.

"Whoever we're dealing with, they're skilled at deception. And they aren't Taliban or Taliban-trained."

"What proof do you have?"

"Just a hunch, Sir," Haines said. "I thought you'd like that."

I called the new dead guys the 'Sleepy Brothers,' because of how comfortable and sedate they looked next to each other in the car. Both were looking down at their blood-stained shirts. When we arrived back at Omar's, Jamila and Hafiza started wailing, arms in the air. They kissed Omar and Kochi. I must say, there was some real love in Omar's house. Kochi was the shy one. Haines made a b-line for the shed and started working. He was able to home in on the signal. It was coming from Kunduz, to the northwest near the border with Tajikistan.

Yvonne helped me spread out Bandit next to Haines' computer. So on one side of the room we had a tactical operations center and on the other side a morgue. The next logical step was to create a character sheet for the Sleepy Brothers. I only needed one.

Maddox saw what I was doing. "Again?" he said.

"The problem is that they're inanimate objects," I said, "so they get zero values for dexterity, strength, intelligence..." This was going nowhere fast.

"It is not a problem," said Yvonne.

All the way back from Provo, Maddox talked about doing an AAR. He jumped into it before we could prop up the Sleepy Brothers without them falling over and getting the floor bloody. He brought it up again, trying to pull me away from what I was doing. "Some things work, and some don't," said Maddox. "We practice, practice, practice until we get it right."

"In the real world," I added.

"What we just experienced was very real," said Maddox.

I held up my Fourth Wall folder. "So is this, Sir. So far, so good, on the simulation, but we still have a way to go."

"I know where you're going, Captain Jett."

Really? I didn't know where I was going. The Fourth Wall version in my hand was about unlearning old bad habits and discarding old versions of self. I could understand how it seemed sketchy to Maddox, but my method was just like doing an AAR, except it was more about firing new synaptic connections, deep inside, and in the end, the complicated illusion of life becomes less so. Vivid storytelling requires it.

I had to get some air. I sat in the courtyard alone. Yvonne joined me. "Are you tired, Thomas?" she said.

"A bit tired," I said. "Maybe I went too far."

"No," said Yvonne. "It makes sense, what you say. Maybe you do not say it exactly as you should?"

"I mean...I should not have brought you here, Yvonne. There's no clear way ahead. We start down one road, but it leads to a swamp."

"A swamp?" Yvonne looked about ten years old at that moment, but it was the child in her that captured me like I was captured by my inner child. "I cannot imagine a swamp," she said, "not in this place."

"If you could go anywhere, where would you go?"

"America," she said right away, "but where in America? That is the better question." She thought a second. "California."

"Los Angeles?"

"All over. San Francisco."

I looked up at the night sky, remembering the time when Rivers and I walked around Sierra Vista, Arizona, trading stories of drone/UFO sightings in the area. He said he saw a UFO the morning his mother died. He recalled that it didn't make a sound. His story made me think of another childhood friend whose mother died when he was very little, and the memory of hearing about it was itself a shadow within a dream. All these threads of dreams are wrapping around each other. Decoding it all, through the Fourth Wall, has become my life's purpose. The Fourth Wall guided me here to Los Angeles. They're guiding me, still.

Haines interrupted. "The drones are awake."

FLIES

Letter to LM (drafted in Kabul, 2012): The sandfly problem is out of control, but the way I look at it, things are getting better. I mean, it was worse in Kunduz. We got up there and saw all sorts of strangeness that I can't go into fully. According to my translator, there was a big outbreak at the time. Like the sand fly, Druj needs human blood to survive, to spread. So Druj and the sand fly spread in northern Afghanistan, side by side. I've seen the growth, the motion of the group, like oily water, in all things and the people, in the breakdown of facial expressions. I've taken what you taught me, piled on all I've experienced since then, made notes of as much as I can, and the Holy Land lies ahead. It will fit like a glove. The Fourth Wall is a tall wall. It gets taller each time you try to climb over it. Technology doesn't hurt. It may be a coincidence, but the Army is using Sand Flea jumping robots all over the place. They can hop over walls much better than me. Look it up. You think I'm making this stuff up? (end of letter)

We didn't have a Sand Flea robot. I was only kidding, but we did have Tink and Blink. They were in sleep mode all this time. They woke up in Kunduz. After all the planning the night before, all the meandering dialogue, the basic plan we came up with was to go up there in full force before dawn, which we did, with Ajmal and the Sleepy Brothers, too.

When we pulled into Kunduz, markets were just being set

up for the day. It was right after morning prayers. Kochi prayed on the way there. I caught the rising sun on his face. Poor Kochi was squeezed right up against the Sleepy Brothers. He was so drowsy he looked like a third brother. Kunduz houses were like little loaves of bread, stacked side by side, on top of each other, etc.

The story on our vehicles was that they once belonged to the CIA, leftover from Soviet days. Once we got to Kunduz we found a lot full of them. Tink and Blink were still attached to one of them.

Haines honed in on the signal, weak as it was.

"Does anyone know what we're looking for?" said Ellington. "I was too busy smashing heads at Provo to notice the make of the vehicle that got away."

We parked a block away. Omar was excited. "I know this," he said.

Kochi was yawning but perked up and talked to Omar. "Omar says he knows this car place and that it does good business."

Tactically, we were at a disadvantage. We stuck out, even with our tactical gear hidden beneath cloaks and local clothing. The clothes alone made us stick out. Ellington liked our costumes least. Ellington was serious about tactical gear, in general, and looked menacing in all his stuff. He knew he looked menacing. It was a big part of his total-scoundrel persona. Particularly he loved his sophisticated optical system, which he liked to joke was given to him by a time traveler from the future, which to me meant black market.

Yvonne stayed behind, the designated getaway driver if we needed one.

We climbed on top of a nearby house for a better look. Kochi and Omar had a conversation with the owner, who wouldn't help us, except he had a ladder we could use. We got a nice view of the whole city from up there. Dawn exposed thunderheads in the distance. Lightning flashed. No one was in the car lot. Dawn light made all the brown surfaces pop with color. At first glance, it looked like any car dealership you'd see anywhere in the world. There was a shed on the opposite side, which might have served as a repair shop. Ajmal was keeping watch below us. I was going to have a lot of explaining to do about him, either way, good day or bad day, but at the time we needed an extra man. In some ways, I trusted him more than Kochi.

"I don't know if that boy knows what he's doing," I said to Maddox, "but it sure beats crawling around rooftops like a bug."

"Let's spread out," said Maddox.

Haines gave me a look. He tilted his head several degrees. He was worried about his own bugs. He was sure he was going mad. I told him that was not the case. We spread out along the edge of the roof. Aside from all the cars, piles of cardboard boxes were everywhere. I asked Kochi if he could see any markings on the boxes. Kochi looked through binoculars at the nearest pile. "I see writing," he said.

"Alien hieroglyphics?" said Ellington. "Captain Jett will be pleased."

"No, my friend. It looks Cyrillic."

I was fidgety with my rifle. I was more used to reacting to the world around me than hunting like that.

Maddox moved next to me. He elbowed my arm. "Do you know what you're doing with that thing?"

"Haines, what are the drones doing?" I said.

"Sleeping."

"Wake them up," I said. "Ellington...optics." In addition to high-powered zoom, Ellington's system had thermal imaging and even recording/playback capability. Poor Kochi just had regular goggles.

"What am I looking for?" said Ellington.

"Alternating red micro-LED flashes."

"Tail lights?"

"Yes, tail lights."

"Well, just say that next time. For fuck's sake." Ellington grumbled to himself while he surveyed the lot. "Let's just go in there and see what we find. This doesn't have to be so sneaky and complicated."

Then Omar came out of nowhere: "Why do you have to be such a horse's ass about everything?" He must've heard that on television.

Haines used a laser device to better pinpoint the location of our drones. "We're in the right place," he said. "It's there." He pointed at a vehicle on the far side of the lot.

"You see that guy?" Ellington identified a hooded figure beneath the canopy of the central building. "He's dead still."

"He might just be still," I said, "or maybe our enemy is using corpses like scarecrows, kind of like what we're doing. They're as adrift in the void as we are."

"Very poetic," said Maddox.

A little cocky, honest, perhaps, in these pages and in life, but...

"Think I see them," said Haines. Then a muffled voice, followed by a sharp scream.

"That sounded like Yvonne," I said. I scrambled down the ladder. The stack of boxes I had used to climb onto the roof collapsed. The ladder fell and I had to replace it for the rest of the crew while keeping an eye out for action. Around the corner, I saw a vehicle speed away.

I had no idea why Kochi threw Ajmal the keys, but I later found out why: Kunduz was his town. He had a lot of bad history there. Maddox, oldest and slowest, was last off the roof, last to pile into the chase car.

The chase was on. Craziest ride in any car since Las Vegas 1998, what a great night of warped energies. Some pimp mistook me for someone else. I lost him in North Las Vegas, then ended up in a downtown casino, where I got to see Ray Charles perform an impromptu set around three in the morning and then won some good money playing craps. None of that would've happened without the pimp. Then in 2012, I got to see Kunduz in high speed, not a fantasy town, very brown, never ending nests of shades within shades. Under different circumstances, it would be a nice place for a contemplative bike ride. I saw lots of bright faces in the bazaar, good omens...except for Kochi's face. Poor Kochi was pushed up against the Sleepy Brothers again.

On the edge of town, edge of reality, edge of madness, we swerved to dodge an old Soviet T-62 tank. Its main gun was lowered. Ajmal nearly creamed a guy on a red motorbike, probably Taliban. They all drove those bikes. Kochi was so angry about Ajmal's driving. Kochi was Mr. On The Edge Of Madness. He shouldn't have handed the keys to the boy.

Ajmal dodged dust devils and chickens. He bounced between boulders. My headache was back. I was unable to dodge obstacles like Ajmal. In my mind, we were hitting everything. We hit a pile of rugs. It was one horror story swapping out for another. I could feel myself slipping away, or limping, or floating. I took a swig of horseshoe crab blood and everything was more than reality.

We chased them into the desert. We picked up speed on a straight road. I couldn't see Yvonne in the car, but I saw the man in the passenger seat reach to the back seat a couple of times. The car veered from the road to avoid hitting a burned up Russian personnel carrier. The car stopped on the side of the road. We stopped behind it. Two men exited the vehicle, followed by Yvonne. They let her go. She kept her distance but did not run. We got out of the vehicle with our weapons ready. The men were dressed in rags, some sort of dress-in-layers-approach to camouflage. They were smiling.

"She is your woman?" said the driver, a burned-red/brown white man with a German accent. He was a little strung out looking, older than me but younger than Maddox. The other man was wearing sunglasses and looked younger.

"She is our woman," I said. "Not *our* woman but *my* woman. Are you all right, Yvonne?" Without waiting for a reply, I said, "Why did you take her?"

Ajmal was furious. Kochi tried to calm him. "He is having, I don't know how you call it, a flash time."

"Flashback," said Maddox.

"Bad days," said Kochi. Poor Kochi. He said the strangest things at the strangest times. Poor Ajmal, too, so full of teen rage.

Yvonne's hair was soaked. She must've have been squirming and fighting back the whole ride. "Are you hurt?" I said.

She walked up to me and slapped my face. "You did this," she said. "You are a liar! All Americans are liars!" I had my own flashback to the summer of 2000, the island of Mykonos, when the young girl at the hostel desk let me use the house phone for (what I thought) was a toll-free call, and it wasn't, and her mother found out and entered the room and started screaming at me, said those same words, all for the equivalent of ten cents.

"Did what? Settle down." I tried to shush her, but she was having none of it.

"You did this, Thomas, or your witch in Georgia. The one you always speak of." She pointed at the other man in sunglasses, who hadn't said a word. "There is the demon you have been chasing! You made him appear."

The man took off his sunglasses. Then it hit me: this was the same soldier I locked eyes with, even exchanged a few words with, while flying around the cargo hold of the C-17 the day I arrived at Kandahar Airfield. It wasn't just his face. I remembered his pink aura and how it turned red when he saw me. Our eyes met again.

DIGGER
AND HAMMER

This is the point in the story when, in order to be fair to the other Fourth Wall players, I have to reveal some further points about my own haunted past. Before going to Afghanistan, I talked to multiple ghosts in my house using a Ouija® board, a Parker Brothers product purchased at Toys"R"Us. I was renting a room to a college student, and the whole thing was his idea. The following is an excerpt from a transcript of a conversation with an entity that referred to itself as Eve:

Me: What are you?

Eve: I am pure fire.

Me: When were you alive?

Eve: I was never alive.

Me: Why are you in my house?

Eve: To protect Harold from you. (Harold Haroki was a much friendlier ghost we'd spoken with earlier.) He does not know he is dead. He thinks you are his roommate.

Me: Yes, I have spoken to Harold. Why must you protect him from me?

Eve: Because you are a bad influence.

Touchy, right? So there you go. The enigma of ghosts and ghostly speaking, not such an enigma to me.

So when Yvonne implied that Digger was a demon, I really thought I was capable of making such a thing happen, and maybe the Digger who appeared in Kunduz was a demon of my creation. Maybe Yvonne was right. I mean, I know what it's like to be scolded by a ghost. It hurts.

Maddox recognized him. "Sergeant Digger," he said. "You have a lot of explaining to do."

"That's not my name," Digger said. "My name is Daniel Grayson Ramsey."

Maybe I did create him out of some magical process going on those few days. Maybe I conjured him out of thin air with my will alone, which is the very definition of magic. I was dazzled. Whatever was the official word on him before then, I shut it out. I struggled for a bit between the man before me and the one I created. This guy was both a sign from God and a reward from God. What else was stirring beyond?

The old Maddox appeared, the guy that looked at me sideways whenever I mentioned anything about sub-universes or game theory within the construct of Army missions. Digger was holding an M4. Maddox raised his rifle and aimed it at Digger, out of fear and anger, I suppose. "With authority from ISAF, the UCMJ, and as your superior officer, I'm taking you into custody."

"What about our deal?" Digger said. "You said..."

"There wasn't a deal," said Maddox.

"Then why did you send me all those photos?" said Digger.

"I was just seeing if you were paying attention." Maddox lowered his weapon. "Do you know anything about Provo?" Maddox's face was redder than Digger's aura.

Digger laughed. Yvonne was right. He was a devil. I was in awe. I outranked Digger by far, but I had built up such a mythology about him in my mind. On paper he seemed like a true kindred spirit, but standing before me was a man defiant of fellow rebels.

"Who are you?" I asked the other guy.

"Kristopher Hammer, Hauptman." Captain Hammer was German. No surprise, considering Kunduz Province was

German turf. He was as polite as our poor, fated KAF chaplains, in a severe way. My gut was right again: Later that day I learned Hammer was a former Lutheran pastor, so he was roguish, like Digger, like me. Digger and Hammer. Hammer and Digger. These two were kindred spirits in the Fourth Wall world, even when I tried to put them on different tracks. The Fourth Wall didn't want that. I later learned it was what brought Digger north in the first place. He wasn't working alone, not from the start. He met Hammer in an internet theology chat room before either of them was in theater. Each was a metaphysician with an interest in role playing games. Once they threw themselves into Afghanistan's strange war, the game was on. I thought I was so clever for coming up with the Fourth Wall as a guiding tool in the slippery chaos of war. For me, it was more of an art form and coping mechanism at first, though when I reached into the heart of it, its true anatomy emerged. It was serious stuff for these guys. They didn't need a catchy name for their system, like me.

"What is that thing you're wearing?" Ellington asked Digger.

"You don't like my cloak?" said Digger. "I'm cool and comfortable. It took you a while to find me."

"What made you pull over?" Maddox said.

"This screaming Russian and the dead men in the back seat," said Hammer.

"But we were chasing you in a Druj vehicle," I said.

"That was not the first thing on my mind," said Hammer.

I checked on the Sleepy Brothers. They were slumped over. I really wanted more active participation from them. I wanted to wake them up and get them in the game.

"So, let's get a few things straight," said Maddox. "Is there a hostage situation going on in that place?"

"Maybe," said Digger. "I don't know for sure."

"People of all ages and types are going into and out of

there," said Hammer. "Mostly leaving it."

"Living conditions?" I said.

"It's not a place to live," said Digger, "but it's not squalid on the outside."

"Weaponry?" asked Haines.

"Impressive, from what I've seen," said Digger, "relatively speaking."

"Relative to what?" said Maddox. He was in full blown 15-6 investigation mode, even though he played a big part in setting up Operation Horseflesh in the first place. It was as much his game as mine, at this point.

"This is not a new movement," said Hammer, "It is ancient. It is a movement going back thousands of years, perhaps, but the moving of the movement is new. It is the Russian. It is all his doing." He gave Yvonne another look.

"What Russian? You've got my interest," said Maddox, "but these people are out there killing our enemies, possibly, so what's the rush?"

"Because the rabbit hole goes much deeper," said Digger.

"Yes," said Omar. He'd been keeping his distance. "It is not a normal place for selling cars."

"But why all the strong-armed tactics and mystery?" said Ellington. "Are they trying to steal land?"

"Have you witnessed any torture?" said Haines.

"Stabbing of forearms," said Hammer. "Your boy may know more than us. Look at his..."

Maddox silenced Hammer with a raised hand. Ajmal was crying. "So outside, nothing," said Maddox, "but inside they're running around like wild animals." Maddox looked pleased with his thought.

"No," said Digger. "At least, we don't think that's the case."

"Then what the hell is going on in there?" said Maddox. "I'm going to close the book on this Provo thing before things get crazier."

"General dirty work," said Kochi. He looked pleased with

his thought, like Maddox. He sounded like a cranky sheriff in an old western movie. He was starting to speculate out loud, like us.

Ellington's face was beet red. "Show me some intelligent, civilized people around here," he said.

"You're looking at them," said Maddox. He realized his toxic tone was a bit much and kicked the dirt. "I don't know about any of this."

"The dangers of doing nothing outweigh the risks involved," I said. It didn't feel that way, exactly. I just had a sinking feeling that if we didn't do something...well the world heals itself in terrible ways. Traffic was passing by normally. In this land of the strange, people were out and about, living their lives.

"I don't know how much deeper I want to go," said Maddox. "Maybe we need some direction from HQ, get the CIA involved, that kind of thing."

"There's no time, Sir," I said.

"Maybe they are involved," said Digger.

"BND is involved, I am sure," said Hammer. "So let us put pieces together..."

Ajmal was still disturbed, not by anything we were talking about. He couldn't understand, and I could tell he was off in another world, another life. I motioned to Kochi and Yvonne to take him aside and help him. It was a surreal setting for a confab of international players, with the burned out Russian vehicles and vehicles of the living going by and dead guys close by.

"We need to get back to town," said Ellington, eager to finish what we started.

"We cannot go back to Port Delta," said Hammer. "Not right now."

"Port Delta?" I said. "Ah yes, I remember that you mentioned in your game notes that opposition forces are coming from what you called ports."

"There are many ports," said Digger. "They are all over the country. Who is the boy?"

Ajmal clenched his fists. "He is our driver," said Omar.

"We could use some help from the Germans on this," said Maddox.

"You will not be welcome at the outposts in Kunduz Province," said Digger.

"Why not?" I said. There were so many mysterious pieces to sew together. "We may be rogues, but we're not assholes."

"Because he isn't welcome," said Digger. He pointed at Hammer. "Neither am I. It's a long story, but his story sounds a lot like mine."

"Where have you been living?" I said.

"For the past few days we've been in a room around the corner from Port Delta," said Digger.

Maddox was sticking with business. "Captain Hammer, is there anybody in your organization who will support going in there?"

"Many, but it is the timing. They only want to watch for now. They have theories. So do we."

"We've got shelter and supplies in Khanabad," I said.

"We are staying here," said Hammer. "I like to be close to the border. I have been tracking members of Druj going across. They have ties in Tajikistan, Uzbekistan, Turkmenistan."

"Iran?" said Haines.

"Definitely Iran," said Digger. "It's an international group. These aren't ethnic locals or Paks."

"Who are they?" I asked.

"People from the countries Hammer mentioned, and lots of others," said Digger. "Russians. Various Europeans."

"What's the binding force between them?" I said. "Money?"

Hammer laughed. "There is always money, but these are people seeking power. They are not fools. They have been infiltrating populations, causing mayhem."

"What is the purpose of slaughtering whole villages? Innocents?" said Yvonne.

"You do not know they were innocents," said Hammer. He pointed down the road toward Provo.

"Nobody has clean hands in a war like this," said Ellington. "What do you think, Digger?" I said. "Your work got you this far."

"I think these are people who see what I see," said Digger. "I was called here, same as you."

"But in our case, you are the one who made the call," I said.

"No, Sir," said Digger, "I just opened the door. You found the way."

"And what is it you see?" said Maddox.

"Dark energy," said Digger.

It was further evidence of how connected the Fourth Wall was with Digger's own work. My work built on his. Gameplay was different, yet there was synergy between them.

"And you?" I asked Hammer.

"Druj is not so much an organization as an arrangement of nature."

"We need to get out of here," said Digger. "We're probably being watched."

"I agree," said Ellington. "Whatever it is we're going to do, let's do it fast."

Maddox and I rode with Digger and Hammer. Omar followed us. I made sure he drove back instead of Ajmal.

"Where are we going?" I said.

"Back to Kunduz," said Digger. There was a strange light around his body, brighter around his head, like a halo. Digger was a resurrected form for me, not for Maddox. If anything, he and Maddox now seemed cut from the same cloth, since they were communicating without my knowledge. Here I was trying to figure things out on my own, and Maddox and Digger had the keys all along.

"You make it sound like Druj is everywhere," said Maddox.

"They are," said Hammer. "Locals are more fearful of Druj, because they know the rest of the world isn't aware." Hammer turned and looked at the rest of us. "We did not talk about it earlier, but there are corpses rotting in the car."

"They're napping," I said. "They're the Sleepy Brothers, and they're here to help."

Maddox groaned. Digger smoothed it over. "Remember our adventure in the Wakhan Corridor," he said to Hammer. The Wakhan Corridor is Afghanistan's panhandle. It is very rugged terrain. They talked about busting up an opium stockpiling location deep in the mountains where no one with any sense would go, but they were talking about Druj. This was what we were dealing with. When I later explained their adventure to Ellington, he was more excited than ever. He would please his boss and see plenty of action.

We passed the airport and drove further north through Kunduz. There were mostly single-level structures, except for some buildings in the center and the blue and gray mosque with its dual minarets. People were out and about. Men were sitting in front of the bazaar, chewing hashish. There were dual parabolic arches in the bazaar. It made me think of MacDonald's. It was breakfast time, and I was really craving an Egg McMuffin®. Perhaps the whole thing was an illusion, everything except my hunger.

We reached a line of buildings on the edge of town. The only person I saw either way along that road was a young boy sitting at the south end of the buildings. He ran when he saw us. Digger and Hammer were occupying two of the buildings. One was a garage, big enough for both vehicles. They had two motorcycles. I had forgotten that Digger was into dirt bikes. He had done some professional racing at some level. There were photos of him in his notebook of him flying through the air on a shiny green machine. Inside, Hammer lit a couple of oil lamps. There was a mid-sized ringed hot-plate in the corner.

"What is this place?" said Ellington.

"It used to be a storage facility for all sorts of bootlegged media, DVD's and games mostly," said Digger, "but we bought them out and kicked them out."

"You paid them dollars?"

"Euros," said Hammer.

"I don't like it," said Haines.

"Nor do I," said Yvonne. She was calmer.

"The light of Allah is not upon this place," Omar said.

"You have no idea," said Digger.

Hammer turned up a lamp. "Is that better for you?" he said.

"It is better," said Omar, and after a moment looking around said, "I am pleased to be part of this great campaign."

Hammer said nothing. He looked at Digger then looked at Omar with the same blank expression as he did with Yvonne earlier. Yvonne was holding up just fine among us soldiers. She was no sheep among wolves, quite the opposite.

Omar gulped. His skin was milky. He looked at me for some kind of support or interference. I thought Omar had a point. The oil lamps were a creepy touch and created malevolent looking shadows and it was mid-morning, too early for all this. I felt like I was a jester in a medieval pageant. I changed the subject. Digger's story about the Wakhan Corridor made me think of something in his journal, a strange-upon-strange list of things, could've just been mnemonics, but it was worth bringing up, even if the collective world brain wasn't ready for it. I got the impression he was working on a theory through monster development.

Yvonne and Ajmal settled on the floor in a corner.

"First things first," I said, not quite ready to get into his monster list. I had my creations to think about. "Do you think the Sleepy Brothers will be ok in the vehicle?"

"They don't have a choice, Sir," said Digger.

"Now it's my turn," said Ellington. "Is Port Delta used for storing narcotics?"

"That is not our main interest and should not be yours," said Hammer.

"Speaking of drugs," I said, "your Wakhan Corridor story didn't make much sense. It's too rugged up there to move narcotics."

"Let me tell you something," said Digger. "You can throw sense away. There's a lot more going on than a little criminal conduct."

"More than a war?" said Maddox.

"It doesn't make much sense they'd be interested in narcotics at all," said Digger, "though there are some signs of that. Maybe it's a smokescreen."

"No fucking way," said Ellington, "not in this country. There's too much money at stake."

Hammer directed our attention to a map. It was nothing compared to Bandit, but it wasn't as if Digger was trying to play a part in an old childhood memory made fresh like I was doing. It wasn't necessary. The map and oil lamps and jumping shadows had a surreal effect, as if to prepare our souls for something stranger than anything any of us had ever seen in war. Hammer spoke in his sonorous baritone. "One theory is that Druj are followers of Angra Mainyu, the god of darkness in Zoroastrianism. If you are trying to think of something analogous, think Satan. They believe it is their mission to appease the evil lord and his army of spirits. Before the U.S. invasion, Druj were against al-Qaeda. During the civil war, they tried to make contact with western forces, but there were no western forces to be had and hadn't been for a long time. The U.S. embassy in Kabul closed in 1989."

"How do you know all this?" I said.

"The group is ancient, with ties not just to central Asia but to Europe. It appears the Germans are ahead of the Americans on this?" said Hammer. "Now is your opportunity to join the game."

"Give us all a break," said Maddox.

"But the Russians are ahead of us both," said Digger.

Hammer huffed.

"Hammer has his own theories," said Digger. "He believes the group goes all the way back to the Scythians, a group which prospered more than two thousand years ago in southern Russia. Our knowledge is in clusters."

"It is not just *my* belief. German scholars..."

"Let's see if I got this straight," said Maddox. "Are you saying that NATO forces have completely missed the existence of an opposing force at least as dangerous as the Taliban all these years?"

"Is it so hard to believe?" Hammer said.

"This country has always been a crossroads," said Digger.

"The Russians?" said Maddox. "Druj has foreign state support?" Maddox was pissed. He was becoming less suspicious of Yvonne, but he had no love for Russians, in general.

"Do not look at me like that," said Yvonne, not just to Maddox but all of us.

Kochi was in the corner, explaining all this to Ajmal as best he could, but Ajmal's English was better than he led us to believe.

"They are dark magic," Ajmal said.

"Dark magic men," Kochi said. He nodded.

Of course, that part wasn't so hard for someone like me to believe. "That's in line with some conversations we had with locals before coming up here," I said. They were obviously not a radical Islamist terrorist group.

"What a nightmarish mix," Ellington. "Call in an airstrike."

"We have many unanswered questions at this point," said Digger. "We don't know what Port Delta is."

"It's a storage facility," said Maddox. "We were there,

remember?"

"It is much more than that," said Hammer. "We believe there are tunnels beneath the building, a web of tunnels. There is movement in the area all the time."

"I'm betting it's a narco processing lab," said Ellington. He was clearly more excited about the whole operation, what with mere circumstantial evidence and all.

I found the narrative enticing, as well. It fit in so well with the whole Fourth Wall scheme. It was a cultish group in bed with an ancient dark force, sustaining itself through organized crime and drug trafficking, with multi-national players, some of whom were just shadows, in the literal sense...something along those lines. And, as Hammer said, it was much more. This is the approach that took root in my brain.

"Are there any more terrorist groups in the area?" said Haines. "What am I missing here?"

"You don't know everything we know," said Digger, "but that is everything in a nutshell. You're all just having a hard time digesting it."

"I can think of one thing missing," I said. "Every group has a leader."

"This one has several," said Hammer, "but they are figureheads more than anything."

"And we don't know which ones are real," said Digger.

This was where Maddox was one step ahead of us, for once. "Am I the only intel soldier here? We've got files on all this. We had a file on you, didn't we, Digger?"

Digger rolled his eyes. Clearly, he did not like being called Digger, but he eventually got used to it. "Then tell me what you've got on this, Sir," he said.

Maddox looked at Yvonne. "She's not going to like it."

Yvonne had to defend herself. I couldn't blame her. "This is a nasty business you are in," she said. "You ask me to come, then you accuse me of...I do not even know what this is about. I know Tajikistan is not far north. I can make it there." She really did start to leave, but I stopped her.

"Hear him out," I told her.

"Hear him out," repeated Ajmal.

"Let me guess, Captain Hammer," I said, "maybe you have a guy, maybe you don't, but you've made one up, or more than one, as you've gone along."

"Correct, Sir," said Digger, "just play the game."

Not a surprise. I did the same thing. It all made sense, but not to Maddox. He wanted his man.

"They can make themselves invisible," mocked Maddox. "Did you catch that? And you want to go after shadows."

"Invisibility is not that uncommon, Sir," I said. "It's a matter of making another person look through you. It's an old ninja trick. You mentioned having such a power in your notebook, Digger."

"I guess no one is going to call me Ramsey anymore," said Digger.

"I like Digger," said Hammer.

"I mentioned invisibility in some of my games that started to play out in real life," said Digger.

"You mean Historians?" I said. "And Monsters of LA?"

"And others," said Digger. "Are you surprised, Captain Jett? When we met you were invisible. Remember? And you're not the only one with powers." He looked at Ajmal and Yvonne.

"I'm taking notes of all this, so you know," said Haines.

"If there's an investigation," said Maddox, "your notes are going into my file. At least I won't have to be the IO for this one. I'm too involved."

As interesting as all this was, I was getting a sinking feeling that our paths would diverge in one way or many ways further down the road, but he was a firecracker. I wanted to listen. I had been listening to him through his notes for some time.

"Does Allah know of these things?" said Kochi. He wasn't the most devoted Muslim I'd ever met, so it struck me as a silly question. It was just his way of voicing fear. We were all afraid. A dark force more ancient than any featured in the modern dominant world religions was awakening, according to our new madmen friends.

"I hope Allah knows," Omar said.

"It can only help," I said. "It can't hurt."

"You boys are hanging on by a thin thread," said Maddox. "I should've called General Williamson by now, but something tells me he'd let you run with it. You've got a short leash, though. Where are we going with all this?"

"For now, Sir, just follow us," said Digger. "We've tried to interpret phenomena in the best way we know how. This isn't magic, but we've been using what people might think is magic to achieve an end."

"It is magic," said Hammer. "Sure it is."

"It is dangerous," said Yvonne.

"What do your superiors know about all this?" Maddox asked Hammer. "Let's call them up." He took out his cell phone.

"No phones," said Hammer. "Trust us. Trust in the process. I will make the call when the time comes."

"You want us to trust a supernatural process," said Haines. "That's what I'm hearing."

"Well said," said Maddox.

"Trust imagination, Sir," I said.

"Besides," said Digger, "we don't have much choice at this point. Provo was just the beginning."

"According to what?" said Ellington.

"According to my game," said Digger.

"Mine as well," I said. Whenever I ran game scenarios involving ambushes, where high rolls represented a shadowy monster named Narat, the high number hit every time. It was spooky. Had we chosen not to venture this far north in the first place, odds were that something like this was going to happen in RC-South again, similar to what happened at Sugarbush.

"I don't believe it," said Maddox.

"And I think it's all a big signal," said Digger. "Something else is coming."

"I believe it because I understand quantum theory," said Haines. He didn't wait for the quixotical looks. Kochi and Omar looked very lost. "According to quantum theory, particles are capable of being in two places at once, going in and out of existence, like magic. The universe is a far stranger place than we can possibly imagine, and when one particle on one side of the galaxy can disappear and reappear on the opposite side of the galaxy, you come to accept that there's a whole different level of reality."

Haines' little speech lifted my spirits. He put a scientific spin on my whole Fourth Wall plan, in a way that I understand now but didn't understand much at that time. He barely scratched the surface, but he was onto something.

"A very thin thread," Maddox repeated.

"It's mathematically proven, Sir," said Haines. "We're all descendants of the same thing, the same source of power. So I'm on board with Captain Jett."

Maddox smirked, a good omen.

"Any word from our little friends?" I asked Haines.

Haines checked on his computer. "They're back in sleep mode."

"Or they were found," said Maddox.

"Not likely, Sir," said Haines. "They use signal jammers and motion detectors, even in sleep mode."

"What about protections for Port Delta?" I said. "I didn't see much."

"Everyone in the surrounding area knows about them," said Digger, "but they don't understand who and what they are. They think they're an anti-Taliban group, so people tolerate them like houseguests."

"That's hearts and minds," I said. "And if everybody knows about them, then they know about you two."

"We don't make a sound, Sir," said Digger.

"You'd better be ready, just in case," I said. "What about firepower?"

Hammer sketched Port Delta on the back of a piece of cardboard. He identified good places for gun nests and places where he'd seen guard activity. "There is a house adjoining the property. It may not be their house."

"We need to take that higher ground away from them right away," said Maddox.

"Very risky," said Kochi.

Omar was pacing back and forth, waving his fingers as if calculating something in his mind.

"Never mind the house," said Digger. "The goal is to get underground as soon as we can. If we spend too much time above ground, they'll close up like a clam and we'll never get inside."

Maddox was fuming, and it wasn't just from Digger's insubordinate attitude. "Sounds like a trap," said Maddox. "I mean this whole thing. You lured us into this situation so you could carry out some kind of experiment, using government resources." Maddox went to the opposite corner next to Ajmal and Yvonne, as if staring out a window that wasn't there. He was making Ajmal nervous, and Yvonne looked annoyed. "This is that game you made, Captain Jett," said Maddox. "It's warped your whole mind. Don't forget the dead guys in the car."

"Don't forget beings from a parallel world," said Digger. "I don't have any proof, but..." The storage and toting of the Sleepy Brothers was connected to Digger's own game. This thing about beings from a parallel world was a less developed idea, but not a complete surprise.

"You're toying with me," said Maddox. "You, too." He pointed at me.

I stepped in. "If you believe us, that the game is somehow being projected in reality, then congratulations, Sir, you're starting to get the point."

"Druj is toying with us," said Hammer.

"What he means is..." Digger had to think. "They don't toy with anyone, nor do they control. They..."

"I knew it," said Maddox. "I've known it since the moment we had to get off the main highway after we left Bagram Air Base. It's the kid. He's one of theirs. And the dead guys we've been hauling around. The bodies are somehow bugged, or they have eyes on us."

Yvonne pulled Ajmal closer. "Leave the boy alone," she said. "You all are no saints."

"Forget trying to understand it all," said Ellington. "For now I say we just block it. Destroy it as we see it. Full understanding will come later. Knowing any more than we already know won't necessarily help us, at this point."

"Ellington is right," I said.

Ellington elbowed me. "You like that, Sir? Smoothest thing that's slipped off my tongue in a while, but I have a question. With all the infighting and tribal warfare in this country, why do you think the Taliban aren't more involved?"

"I have a theory," said Digger. "The Taliban may know but just want to leave the whole thing alone and leave it up to Allah."

"You mean, leave it up to people like us?" said Haines.

"That's too sentimental," said Maddox, drawing on his years of experience. "That's not the Taliban I know. There's got to be some arrangement, some kind of money exchange."

"I agree with Maddox," said Hammer, the other old timer.

"We're serendipitous soldiers at this point," I said. "I say we go along with it."

Even Omar was on board. He started clapping and laughing.

I took Kochi aside. "Why is Omar so happy all of a sudden?"

"He is excited that he will have the chance to kill some

Russians again." Kochi said this quietly so Yvonne wouldn't hear.

"But we must be careful," said Hammer, his eyes dreamy. "There is too much about the world that people think they want to know about, but they really do not want to know and ought not to know."

By the way, reader, this transcription is a summarization of the actual conversation, more elegant than the actual one. Digger and Hammer conveyed information in such a way that made me suspicious that they were holding back so much more, but it took me years to grasp the depth of what they were saying, and of course, I was suspicious about where they got their information. Bluebird's reliability was closer to a weather forecast, and I could say the same about Decke, my designation for the German equivalent of Bluebird. Decke in English is 'blanket'. I studied Bandit. I drew a flat-looking cloud in the top right corner, just above the Wakhan Corridor. It was supposed to look like a blanket. Hammer caught me drawing it. "That looks like a flying carpet," he said.

"Flying Decke," I said. Bluebird, all around, was focused more on lethal threats. I liked the German system a little better. I also liked the name. Digger joined me and looked through his notebook. "An old friend?" I said.

"No," Digger said. "No...no..."

"What's the matter?" I said.

"This is incomplete. I've got something for you." He showed me an updated character sheet for his game. I reviewed it. His own character could double in size, and thus strength. He was skilled with a short sword.

"Do you have a sword or is that just part of the game?" I asked him.

Digger grinned. "Get into the game," he said. "I won't be so mysterious, anymore."

I went outside and watched clouds roll over the distant hills. I did some thinking. I tried to connect Druj with

Sugarbush. Druj was a dangerous element in an already clogged and chaotic system, where it was difficult to discern friends and foes, but they weren't likely to be treated the same as more direct threats like the Taliban and al-Qaeda, even after Operation Horseflesh. I had attributed the Sugarbush murders to some kind of Taliban roundup gone bad, though I gave serious weight to Kochi's jinn theory. All the talk of shadows and monsters and forces I didn't understand or want to be involved in, more the latter. I had my own monsters to deal with.

Yvonne joined me. "The German man does not like me. Of all the horrible people...they should concentrate their anger on this group, Druj, or whatever they are."

"You don't know?"

Yvonne didn't answer. She had a sullen expression.

"I don't get the feeling they want to destroy Druj," I said. "They're explorers. If they're after anyone in particular, it's the Russian, and it's not because he's a bad guy. He's going to lead them to something more."

"They know nothing," said Yvonne.

"How do you know that?"

"Because people love stories like this," said Yvonne. "How do you say? Far-fetched."

"I'm used to it," I said. "I told you about my haunted house back home. But you're right. It takes a willing soul."

"But the boy..." said Yvonne. "Do not involve him."

"Be careful with that kid. He's full of surprises."

"I know," said Yvonne. "Ajmal is strong. He has a strong heart. Be careful about your comrades, and that man you call Digger."

"If Digger goes back he'll likely face court martial," I said.

"But Maddox knew he was here."

"And that might not work out so well for Maddox," I said. "Maddox is looking for his own kind of payday, and if he doesn't get it...let's just say that Digger is going to have to prove himself before this is over."

"Maddox did not look happy."

"Maybe he was happy, just for a minute, after Ajmal spilled his guts."

"Spilled his guts? What a horrible thing to say." Yvonne turned away.

"It's just an expression," I said. "Maddox is an explorer, too. Lucky for us, or we might all be in trouble, him too. I don't care what he says about having top cover. These guys all work for the same guy, and I'll bet that guy doesn't know about any of this."

For another minute we said nothing. She stayed mad, but she held my hand. "Can you keep a secret?" I asked her. She did not reply. "I've seen the endgame. I don't know if it's just for me, or this place, or the bigger choreography of space and time, or if it's just a reflection of something." I felt that at any moment I was going to wake up from some labyrinthine dream. I wanted to say so much more, and I knew Yvonne could see much more than me.

"I see fire," she said, "but not death. Fire is alive to me." This made me think of Eve, the ghost. Eve described herself as pure fire. I say "her" because Harold Haroki, the friendlier ghost, described Eve as female. Operation Horseflesh was a psychic event for Yvonne, in a different way than me.

Hammer poked his head out the door. "You should both get some rest," he said. "We need to be going soon before night starts creeping in."

Yvonne kissed my cheek and went inside. I stayed a while longer. Digger joined me. I had a hundred questions for him but asked none. Instead, I made a comment: "I didn't want to bring this up inside, but I know you can fly. You can be in two places at once, like me. I saw you in the sky as we were driving to Provo."

"Yes, Sir," said Digger, "but I didn't have that ability until you arrived in Kunduz Province. Much has changed in the last forty-eight hours. I like it."

BIG
BREAK

Operation Horseflesh was my first real chance to go beyond merely participating in observing the mysteries of modern warfare, clamoring through its surreal and trivial elements, and add to it with my own imagination, pass into the realm of the not just improbable but unbelievable. As a writer, lawyer, archaeologist, metaphysics enthusiast, it was a doorway, not just to the unknown, but to opportunity. Chaucer, Dante, Shakespeare, they all passed through it, and once I tasted the new energy, I wanted it to feed me more and more.

Before our mission to Port Delta, I studied Bandit again. I thought it might be the last time I would see my creation. I tried to stay quiet. People were sleeping. No one was sleeping soundly, though. Hammer had his oil lamps down to bare blips of light.

Yvonne moaned and stirred. I joined her on the mattress, next to Ajmal. I didn't feel that we would need Yvonne's help, but she couldn't stay behind. No one knew for sure whether we would return. Being with us was the safest thing for her and for Ajmal. Besides, if the talk was true about Russians in Druj, we might need her help. She moaned again and twitched. I touched her shoulder. I was entranced by the shine of her moist skin. Her eyes were busy beneath closed lids. I could tell she was in a dark place. I didn't do any more than touch her shoulder. Maybe she wanted to be in that place. She stirred awake and sat up, as did Ajmal.

"Sorry to wake you, Yvonne," I said.

Thinking back over everything I had experienced up until our time in Kunduz, I realized that Kunduz itself, in my Fourth Wall playbook, represented synergy. Synergy was like earth or wind or fire, one of those elements that could help or hurt, depending on the dice roll. There was no way to know the intentions of people near Port Delta. Would they swarm upon us or remain behind closed doors...in a deep sleep even? Same went for Druj. I thought at first that they should be treated as a different species, but then I realized that, as men, they had the same kinds of motivations and weaknesses. Except they all were not men. I was more concerned for the safety of Ajmal than Yvonne.

"Do you know how to use this?" I showed Ajmal my M9.

He understood me, and he nodded, but he was not very confident. There weren't enough rifles for everyone. He needed to know.

I didn't need Kochi's assistance with this part. I went through the mechanical features of the weapon, demonstrated the action, then let him try it.

Yvonne shook her head. She didn't like any of this.

"It is time," said Hammer. "We must go back."

Maddox assented to the German's command. I didn't feel ready, but surprise was going to have to be our best weapon.

It was late afternoon. Those who were still cat-napping got up. We all packed up, woke up the Sleepy Brothers, straightened them up in their seats (Digger and Haines had that duty), and off we went to continue the adventure. Just as we were leaving, it started raining. Haines was quick to get onto his computer and wake Tink and Blink and fly them to better cover. It took no time at all for street flooding to occur, so we took a different route to Port Delta. It stopped raining before we got near. We parked in an empty alley running perpendicular to Port Delta.

Ajmal and I did some reconnaissance while the others prepared the Sleepy Brothers for their big break (Omar's idea, actually). They were going to hit the big time, literally. The alley ended at the street along the western edge of Port Delta, to the left of the main gate. Ajmal and I crouched behind a parked car. Ajmal had his M9 and was ready for anything. At that moment, I thought of the boy's father, and that I was like a father to him. The main gate was imposing, the kind you'd see on any standard haunted mansion. There was a lone guard, a skinny man dressed like a local, just sitting in a chair, trying not to look like he was guarding anything, but he opened the gate for a truck when it left the facility. The wall was as solid on this side of Port Delta as where we were earlier. A woman walked by. Ajmal and I stayed dead still. She didn't see us. Then we went back and reported the situation. We all repeated the plan, like singing a little song. The singing contributed to our supernatural transformations, and it just felt good. The first step involved the Sleepy Brothers. The Sleepy Brothers could've been called the Stinky Brothers at this point. They were a little stinky from the very beginning, and death did not suit them.

"This will work, my friends," said Omar.

"It's going to work," I said. "I agree. I don't know. Maybe our luck will run out soon. If you get lost, just roll."

"Captain Jett is a psychopath," said Ellington, "but let's let him do his work."

Yvonne came to my defense with a truly disturbing distraction. "At least he does not worship dead family members, like some in my family."

I didn't know to what extent that was true, but I did know it was at least true for her.

"Fuck us all," said Ellington. "You're both crazy."

We placed the Sleepy Brothers in the front of the vehicle, with the taller of the two (designated SB-A in future Army reports) in the driver's seat. We connected his hands to the steering wheel with duct tape, but not too tightly. Digger wrapped tape around his neck and the headrest so he wouldn't fall forward. I put the vehicle in neutral, and we pushed it forward about thirty yards toward Port Delta. Hammer and Maddox and Omar ran ahead to the end of the alley. Omar gave us a thumbs-up. This is traditionally a Muslim insult, but Omar was liberal and adopted behaviors he knew we would understand. Haines and Kochi stayed back. Haines was able to reunite with the drones. He got them flying again right away. I couldn't see them, but I could see Haines' face following them up and up. Yvonne was driving the rear vehicle, which we planned to use as cover once inside Port Delta.

Omar distracted the gatekeeper, who revealed an AK beneath his cloak when Omar got close. In my report, I nicknamed the gatekeeper Tom Petty. To me, that's who he looked like. He had gray eyes and long blonde hair. He didn't look like an Afghan at all. Omar was having a hard time getting through to him. The man wouldn't talk to him much. Omar was doing all the talking.[3] When Petty raised his weapon all the way up, that was it. The talking was over. Maddox and Ellington moved forward, but they didn't have to. Omar didn't need my help, either. He was all over Petty. His punching was roundhouse-style, but he landed heavy enough that Petty couldn't get his AK raised in time. Omar landed a punch on the back of Petty's neck, and Petty collapsed. A bug appeared. Omar tried to swipe it away, but we yelled at him not to. It was Tink. Tink dropped a micro-dot bomb into Petty's open

[3] Excerpt from statement of Omar in report on Operation Horseflesh: "I do not speak much Tajik, but I thought he might be from Tajikistan, since I know there are groups of light skinned people like him, so I said what I knew, to see if he would respond. Then I spoke Pashto, to see if he would respond. I practiced what I would tell my wife about everything I had seen. The man looked dead, as dead as the two dead men in the car, the pets of Captain Jett."

mouth. There was a pop like a pistol firing with a silencer attachment, and Petty started bleeding from his eyes. Omar took Petty's AK and gave the thumbs-up again and I ran back.

Assuming they had a security camera system set up somewhere, it would only be a moment before a bunch of men were swarming outside. I motioned back for our vehicles and the others to move forward. "I go there with you," Omar said as we went by. I gave him the OK sign, made a circle with my thumb and index finger, but he wasn't as familiar with that sign and grimaced at me. I learned this means various lewd things, is a reference to a certain area of a woman's body, and can also mean the evil eye. Ajmal and Kochi came up behind us, then Ajmal motioned for Haines and Yvonne to move forward. Yvonne drove right up behind the Sleepy Brothers. Everyone was loaded down with tactical gear. We pushed the first car into the lot, just inside the main gate. Once inside the gate, Maddox went left. Ellington came up straight behind me. Digger went right. Hammer went left behind Maddox. Omar helped me push the vehicle forward a few more feet. This got the attention of the other guard at the door. He couldn't see what was going on. Maddox shot me a crazed look as I got SB-A out of the driver's seat and propped him against the car door, clamping him down, setting him up like the little plastic G.I. Joe toys of my childhood, just like we planned. That's what all this was, just on a much bigger scale: a big toy set. The Sleepy Brothers played the part well. Ajmal and Kochi stayed in the back and kept the gate open, so that we wouldn't be locked inside.

The guy at the door walked over to investigate. He raised his weapon. He stopped dead at the sight of the dead guys propped up, their arms straight and stiff, like mummies. He wasn't startled, as I thought he might be. He looked around, to see if anyone was pranking him. That was a bad idea because when he looked back he got a bullet in his temple. His eyes crossed. He flew back. I walked to him and kneeled and pushed back his face covering. He was pale as Petty, with a fat, fleshy face. He was white as a ghost, and it wasn't from any blood loss unless he was a vampire. "What do you think?" I said, "Swedish? Russian?"

"Whatever he is he doesn't look like he belongs here," said Maddox.

"Less chatter, my friends," said Omar. "More splatter!" An odd thing to say, considering there were no more targets.

"Any thoughts, Digger?" I said. A light breeze pushed across the lot.

Digger took a deep breath of Kunduz. "Everything's in flux," he said. "We're talking about a hidden society. I stress the word 'hidden.'"

"This is turning into a pretty typical James Bond film if you ask me," said Ellington. "Secret lair. A couple of inept guards. And a pretty girl." That part was true. Ellington winked at Yvonne. He smiled at me, no doubt proud of his loaded observation.

Ajmal and Kochi dragged the guard outside the gate inside and shut the gate. We gathered the bodies of the guards and the Sleepy Brothers and piled them next to the building. I didn't get emotional or anything, but I knew that would be the last time I'd be seeing the Sleepy Brothers. Then again, I've always been prone to melancholy ways. I gave my cheek a little slap and went back to business.

We were approaching the problem in stages. Truth was gradually appearing, but as if on a stage, a carefully choreographed presentation just for us. But that's what T4W was all about: trying to reach the truth through unconventional means, hidden dimensions.

We stacked on the door the way you're supposed to when assaulting a building of this size and unsure of the layout inside. It wasn't something we covered with Ajmal and Omar, but they looked like they'd done it a hundred times or had seen a hundred movies with that kind of action.

"The entrance might be booby trapped," said Hammer. "Watch out for tripwires." He pulled some wire cutting equipment from his backpack and stuffed it into his pants pocket. He reached all around the frame of the door for any wires but found none.

Omar kicked in the door on my command. He put all his weight into it. It was a little office, something you would expect at a car dealership, which is what the place was supposed to look like. There were a couple of wooden cabinets. There was a desk and some papers scattered on the desk and all over the floor. Arranged in rows on the desk were empty cans of Pakola, the Pakistani soda pop, Apple Sidra, and orange flavor. Ajmal found one unopened and helped himself to it.

"There's nothing here," said Ellington. "Maybe the whole thing is a trap." He posted at the front door and scanned the buildings across from the lot.

"Nobody sit anywhere," said Maddox. "Stay still."

Hammer and Digger took a knee. Things were quiet until Ajmal finished the soda and belched.

I could feel the floor vibrating beneath my feet, just a little at first. I knelt and felt the floor tiles.

"It's just a hunch," said Digger, "but I think something is down there."

"Haines, we are eventually going to need to establish some high voltage relationships here. Where are the drones?"

Haines set up his laptop on the desk. His fingers flurried. He wiped sweat from his brow. "If you want to see what Tink and Blink saw after dropping off their micro-dot payloads, come have a look." On the screen was a web of black lines on a green background, a bit like a first-gen video game. It reminded me of a *vidimus*, the design on a stain-glass window prior to being painted. Some lines were thicker than others. Buildings looked more solid on the screen than in real life.

"What are we looking at?" I said.

"The tip of an iceberg in a desert, Sir," said Haines.

Yvonne joined Ellington at the door. "Anything look familiar, missy?" he said to her, with kind of a snarl. He was sending a weird vibe, but to me, it was an irresistible flow of Fourth Wall fun. Yvonne did the right thing and stepped away, back toward Ajmal, who was off in his own world. He belched again. Omar and Kochi seemed more comfortable and confident, now that we'd survived the entry stage.

A security camera was in the corner of the room. Its little red light said someone was catching all this.

Kochi took me and Maddox aside. "Ajmal does not know this place," said Kochi.

Ajmal looked happy. Omar's good cheer was having an effect on the boy. "So he hasn't described a little building like this," I said, "but he has talked about being underground, being in caves, that kind of thing. He doesn't look scared to me. Yvonne, are you sure the boy said something about other children here?"

Yvonne gave me a strange look. "Ajmal never said..."

There was a wild roar. Hammer and Digger sprung up. We all raised our weapons. I could hear moaning, really perverse sounds, beating drums, and more staccato screams. The sounds were coming from all around, not just below ground. (I didn't immediately connect these stray animal sounds to reports of unusual creatures at Sugarbush or any aberrant behaviors in my comrades, such as Ellington's snarl a minute earlier.) We had unleashed a beast, but it was all too easy, and it was all part of a pattern, a grander plan of breadcrumb-laying.

Yvonne touched my shoulder. She would've loved to turn back at that moment, and if we did the world would be different.

Digger replaced his empty rifle magazine. He smiled, but I saw something else. I got a sense of the malignant machinations of his heart and other forces coming into play for him. Then, right where Kochi was standing, the tiles on the floor started pulling apart, but not so much apart as into each other, like playing cards. It was another aspect of Digger's game that was now coming to life, something I read in Historians, and I think that's what he was smiling about, not quite surprised by any of this. His game involved just as much activity underground as above ground and just as much activity on the sea as in the sky. The sheer variety of doorways in his nebulous world was astounding. One thing after the other was a form of transubstantiation.

Kochi didn't see what was going on behind him. He was focused on the tiles changing all around him and under his feet. I wished it was me or Ellington, the rogue. Kochi was too good a guy for all this. I felt bad for dragging him and everyone into this nightmare. The floor opened completely behind Kochi. There was a blast of cold air then, like a shockwave effect, Kochi was pulled down into the darkness. He screamed and fell.

"Kochi!" Omar yelled. He reached for his cousin. Yvonne had to keep Ajmal from going in after Kochi.

I couldn't see anything. It was a long way down, but it wasn't a straight fall. Kochi had rolled down a curving stairwell, concrete, with handrails on the wall. Then my eyes adjusted and I saw Kochi slowly getting up. "Kochi?"

Kochi gave me a thumbs up.

Maddox looked into the hole. "You ok, Kochi? What do you see?"

"It is a tunnel," said Kochi. "It goes both ways."

"Stay where you are," said Maddox. "We're coming."

"We need the drones," said Ellington.

"We've got one," said Haines. "Blink went down there as soon as Kochi did."

Poor Kochi, I was thinking, then right at that moment Ellington said, "Poor bastard."

We secured our gear and checked ammo. Omar and Ajmal got on their knees and peeked into the darkness.

What was going on in Alice's mind when she chose to walk through the looking glass? No matter, I walked through that barrier the moment I landed in Afghanistan, and this was just another Fourth Wall obstacle for our band of adventurers to overcome, but this was a real turning point in the game. Turn off my thoughts, game over, or roll the dice and keep going, with at least my career and reputation at stake, and as always, my life. And Alice didn't have a weapon and training for such a nasty business, like me.

I joined Ajmal and Omar on my knees, with Maddox and Digger and Hammer hovering over us. We told Kochi to hold tight.

Then Ajmal had some kind of mental breakdown. Ajmal started checking his body, his arms, and legs, patting and rubbing ferociously all over as if he was covered with insects. He took off his tunic, then his pants, until he was only wearing underwear, blue up front and white in back. Yvonne tried to calm him, but the boy racked his temple, and I was racking my brains trying to figure him out.

"Kochi told me the boy wasn't afraid," I said. "What is he doing?"

"He could jeopardize everything," said Ellington. He looked like he was about to pounce.

But Yvonne was successful in calming him down. She had a way with Ajmal that the rest of us didn't have. It wasn't so shocking: mad boy loves mad woman. She cradled him. He put his face in her bosom. She helped him put on his pants. This kind of thing was noted on Ajmal's character sheet. Being vulnerable due to past life experience gave him a dice modifier of minus-one in some instances, which he often overcame with great bravery and enthusiasm. From dancing boy to prominent role in Operation Horseflesh. He was delirious with revenge.

There was a loud snap as Ellington chambered a round from his fresh mag. "Make room," he said and started down the stairs.

"Night vision," said Hammer. We had four sets of the latest optical tech. It was beautiful stuff. The gunmetal and rubber surfaces shined even in the dark.

Ellington said "all clear" when he reached the bottom. One by one we proceeded down the stairs. I stayed at the end with Yvonne and Ajmal. Kochi was standing, rubbing his elbow and temple, but he wasn't otherwise hurt. "When I fell," said Kochi, "it was like falling for many minutes. Did you feel it?"

Maddox winced. These kinds of comments were getting to him, along with the cosmic mysteries.

"For me, it was like I gained something," said Yvonne. "One second I felt alone, and now I feel that I am on the right path."

I was racking my brains. "This is all part of a pattern," I said, picking up external symmetries all around me, opening up a seductive path of my own.

"It's about using time itself as a weapon," said Digger, "as a tool to disorient. You smell that?"

"It smells like burning electronic components," said Haines.

I gave Yvonne's hand a squeeze of reassurance.

Omar wanted some fancy gear, but we didn't have enough for everybody. "It would be nice to shed some light in this tunnel," he said.

"Not now," said Maddox. "We stay dark."

And so it went: the Fourth Wall began in a dark tunnel, in full, with a very different kind of energy transferal than I was expecting. A whole world of new forms was waiting ahead. We were ready to explore. I could hear moaning and beating drums, not sure if my companions could hear the same things. I had the feeling that a hundred tiny eyes were watching us...watching me, those same ghosts from all my travels going back two decades. *They are the ones that understand the deep order in everything. Come home, they say. Come home.*

"Are you ok?" I asked Kochi. He was fine. Ajmal was worrying me more than Kochi. "What do you know of this place?" I asked Ajmal.

Kochi had to translate some parts, but Ajmal explained: "I remember now. The more tunnels there are, the better it is for Druj. They are like rats, and some of them are true rats. Others are pure smoke, but they must all be stopped." Ajmal tried to describe the layout. Kochi was having difficulty translating. Ajmal was calmer, but he continued examining his arms and legs and wouldn't put his shirt on, the bruised, skinny boy. He could see things we couldn't see.

"We're not here to stop them, or overthrow them," said Maddox. "We're here to save the children, if there are children down here. That's as far as I'm willing to take your game right now. Ajmal is giving us conflicting information, but I'm intrigued. And it would be nice if we could shed some light on what happened at Provo. I don't know about rats, smoke, people that turn into smoke..."

"Some of us just want to find a way back to sanity," said Hammer.

"We don't belong here," said Haines.

"Don't be a pussy," said Ellington.

"I am a pussy," said Kochi. "We do not belong here."

"I'm going to see what's ahead," said Ellington. He adjusted his night vision goggles and started down the tunnel.

"I'm going with you," I said. "Yvonne, stay here with Ajmal."

"I am coming," said Ajmal. He tugged at Yvonne.

"My instincts are telling me that would not be wise," I said.

"Mine are telling me otherwise," said Digger. "The boy is one of us. We could use his energy." This is how the rift between Digger and me began, as if we were dueling masters in the same game, which of course doesn't work. Besides, Digger had been living his own game before I started the Fourth Wall. The systems were bound to collide.

Omar was fidgety. "I miss my wife," he said. He had his own mental bugs to deal with. Hammer and Maddox were more stoic. I was in the middle. Each adventurer had some kind of Fourth Wall obstacle to deal with. In Digger's game, obstacles were more speculative than in my version. Characters in his game came with not just your standard inventory of necessities, but a Pandora's box of baddies and demons, always hanging around, in a cloud above, or at least in a kind of thought bubble.

Digger and I nodded at each other, acknowledging that this was a turning point in the game, and for me, it was a pat on the back: the Fourth Wall was turning into more than a movement, more than a game. I was lost in thought a moment, then the group moved forward together, almost marching in step. Two night-vision goggles up front (Ellington and I) and two in the rear (Hammer and Digger). Old Maddox grumbled about being in the middle of the pack, with the woman and child, instead of the tip of our little crusade.

"There's another camera," said Ellington.

Down the hall was the telltale red LED of a closed-circuit video system.

"Why are they just watching?" I wondered aloud.

"Not our concern at this precise moment, Sir," said Digger.

"They are not watching," said Hammer. "They are toying. They want us to find them."

"If it is a trap, then it is a trap," said Yvonne, never at a loss for portentous words.

"Either way," said Ellington, "it sounds like we won't be dealing with a scrappy bunch, down here."

I shushed everyone. I could hear a faint buzz. Haines explained it was the drones swirling out there, but that wasn't all it was. We crept. It wasn't long before we came to a crossroads, two more tunnels running left and right from ours, like transepts, each a smooth shaft with dark sides, walls still wet as if freshly carved. In some places was a thin veneer of gold dust.

"They are looking for something," whispered Omar.

"So are we," I said. It was not the first time I'd visited such a realm. It was like being back in Belize, in the ruins at Dos Hombres, near Chan Chich, crawling through the darkness on hands and knees, with spiders and bats clinging to the walls, inches away. Except this time was more thrilling, and there was more room to move around. Natural energies of the system we were in invited memories like this. They came in a melodic flow.

The walls started to shimmer. In the glow of my night vision goggles, it looked like a field full of glow worms, their bioluminescence a distraction, an attractor, a disguise, and I came to the conclusion that everything I was seeing served a dual purpose. I took off my goggles. The light was a little better down here. It was even better further along. I touched the wall. Gold dust came off onto my fingers. The tunnel started to curve. The walls became brighter and brighter, with vibrant shades of orange and gold, taking shape as flowers, a pleasure compared to all the other dirty colors of the place.

"It looks like Andy Warhol was here," I quipped, thinking no one would get the reference, but Haines did. The flowers were big and bold, like the pop artist's.

"Marigolds," said Haines.

"Marigolds are symbolic of the Virgin Mary," said Yvonne.

"She's right," I said. "I've studied ancient religious sites with ruins of walls painted like this. They were ways for the privileged few. Pathways to the true light."

"We are all God's children," said Kochi.

"Which one of you is going to start preaching?" said Maddox.

"It's a distraction," said Ellington. "They want you looking at the walls instead of straight ahead. We're exposed. Who the hell are these voyeurs?"

"It is more of a test than a distraction," said Hammer.

We stayed close together as we moved forward into our new, haunted world. There was an acrid smell.

"You smell that?" said Ellington. "Drugs. We're standing in an invisible river of heroin." So his mind was tweaking on something different as well, like mine. He sensed what he wanted to sense. As Kochi mentioned, I felt like I was falling. Each step was like a giant leap on the moon, with a different gravitational feel. Ajmal crept closer to the front, closer to me. He had every reason to be scared of this place, and we had every reason to lean on him to help us, our separate universes becoming closer, more parallel.

"There's a light ahead," said Digger. It wasn't an artificial light.

It was an orb, surrounded by a pinkish nimbus. Not the first time I ever saw such a thing. I saw orbs from time to time in my house back in Houston, going up and down the stairs, and when I passed through cold spots in the house I would grab my camera and take a picture, and sometimes I was able to capture one. The orb started to grow in size. It went from the size of a grapefruit to the size of a basketball. It grew extensions, like ectoplasmic limbs. It darted around then multiplied.

It was like Digger's Triangle adventure, which only occupied a few pages in his notebook, but now it was playing out. His merry little band had to deal with darkness that thickened as they proceeded through it. They penetrated the darkness using a magical tool, like a light orb on a chain, except rays from the orb were more than just light waves, according to Digger's description of the device. It was a good tool/weapon. It tore through all enemies in their vicinity, ones impervious to bullets and bombs. Now I could see he had real enemies in mind. But it wasn't just Digger's game. My own visions were coming true. Specifically, the vision that came to me in Sangin, when I was looking into Rivers' dying eyes. Only, it wasn't entirely due to the efforts of my neurons. It was like a wind blowing through me, carrying my essence outward, like a force beyond nature, being selective about what it pushed out of me.

And now, all my comrades had doomed looks. Were their senses heightened like mine? By that I mean everything. The Fourth Wall activates patterns in the most ancient parts of the brain. Sounds were amplified, and all popping and bursting with terrible rage, these drifting dreams. Ajmal said something to Omar, who replied. Both spoke with trembling voices. Ellington and Yvonne were close to each other. I knew Yvonne didn't like Ellington that close to her.

I stopped, rubbed my brow, too many strange things hurling onto it at once. Maddox noticed. "Your head is acting up again?"

"It's neurasthenia, Sir. Just a general malaise. Nothing substantial." An insubstantial description intended to keep Maddox away from that subject for the rest of the adventure.

It wasn't just me. There was very little ambient light, but all my comrades had gray faces. I felt like they looked, on edge, and I was scared. The orbs floated, drone-like. They kept their distance. "They are not backing away from us," said Yvonne. "They are leading us forward." She took the lead. The orbs were thirty feet ahead.

The walls and ceiling had pimple-like bumps. The floor felt bumpy, and the bumps were getting bigger with each step, yet the floor appeared flat. The orbs went through a doorway, into a larger space, and I got a bad feeling as if watching a secondary dream turn into a nightmare, out of my control. The orbs dimmed and it went from dark to darker in the tunnel. Even when the orbs were gone, their enigmatic presence persisted, like ghosts of ghosts. The ground started trembling beneath our feet, just a little at first, but it steadily became worse and we had to brace against the wall. My mind went to a huge space of molten rock beneath our feet. I became sort of an astral-geologist. Yvonne and I exchanged looks. She was in the same place.

Everything was happening in slow motion, an effect of light from another dimension. I was being careful. I had vengeful ghosts in my life, even before that day. I was tracking all the projectile motion, from bullets' trajectories to blood, yes blood, not mine, and not just the objects, the corpuscles and dust and spit, but all the associated lines in space, acceleration vectors and velocity vectors, for this was what the Fourth Wall gave me, just as an appetizer. Tricks and tricks, more tricks. All of it integrated into some complex system, more sinister and horrible than I could have imagined at that moment, and more beautiful. What next? Monstrous insects? Absolutely, they were there, lurking in such symmetry.

Ahead, the tunnel started widening. The walls became bumpier. The pimples started bubbling. They grew bigger, extending, spike-like, to the point that we moved through the middle of the tunnel in a line to avoid getting scraped by them. If they weren't real, they were a group hallucination, but what could cause such a thing to happen? We picked up the pace to avoid any further ghostly encounters of the underground lair in which I felt more trapped with each second. We entered the large space where the orbs disappeared. It was too dark to tell how big the room was, but every sound we made was now amplified. It sounded like water was dripping from the ceiling. The cave was carved by man, not nature. The orbs were gone, but light lingered and there was a rancid smell that made me want to puke. Perhaps the orbs dissipated into mist, or they could've gone down the next tunnel. The entrance to the next tunnel was in the middle of the far wall, which was moving left to right. All the walls were moving. If I only had more time to reverse engineer this place, I thought. But in time I felt differently. The Fourth Wall is about losing all trust in the visual pathway to the brain. The world appears more chaotic than it actually is.

Omar explored to the left. He reached for the wall.

"Do not touch it," said Ajmal.

Omar jerked his hand back. He stood, frozen.

"Listen to the boy," said Kochi. "The jinn will devour..."

There was a flash and loud bang on the other side of the room. It illuminated the room for a second. The space was a beehive-shaped room, more of a cavern. It reminded me of an ancient tomb, the *tholos* I visited in Greece in 2000 (minus the floor covered in guano). Ellington, Maddox, and Haines took a knee and aimed their weapons. Hammer and Digger took flanking positions. There was nowhere to take cover. There was another bang.

Ellington stayed low and moved forward quickly, firing his weapon, firing at nothing, from what I could tell. We followed. I stopped telling Ajmal and Omar and Yvonne what to do. I was done with crowd control. Ellington was in a cloak of swirling gun smoke. "I think I got two of them," he said. He was getting a taste of war in the spirit world, liked it from what I could tell.

"You think you got them?" said Maddox.

"Shit," said Ellington. "They're not dead."

"One of them is, for sure," said Digger, his foot atop a man's severed head, his nose encrusted with blood.

"I didn't do that," said Ellington.

But when the smoke cleared we found two men sitting in chairs. They weren't holding weapons, but we all raised ours, thoroughly spooked, and I had a hunch that they knew secrets about this labyrinth.

Yvonne was amused, glad to have more people around who weren't shooting or trying to disembowel us. "Perhaps they are grave robbers who got a little lost?" she said.

"Are you saying we're in a grave?" said Haines.

"Untie them," said Maddox. He was the cool one.

"They are not bound in any way," said Hammer. "They are just sitting."

"Sitting quietly," Digger whispered. Digger was a strange

273

one, and what entertainment would all this be without a strange one? And all this time you thought I was the weird one, reader.

But Omar sprang into action. He knew them. He explained that they were local warlords but had been missing for weeks, and when Ajmal saw them he went nuts. These were the men who sold Ajmal to some different men, Kochi explained. They were both wearing black trousers and brown tunics. They looked at each other, then looked beyond our group at the tunnel where we'd just come from.

"Superman is not dead," said Ajmal. "Sleeping."

"What the hell does that mean?" said Ellington, always in search of the linear, in sync approach. "Kochi..."

"Looks like the Sleepy Brothers have come back to haunt us," I said. It made perfect sense, considering how things were unfolding. I was back at KAF again, seeing those phantom forms in little Romania, the homeless people, and back in San Francisco, in 1998, the people at the end of the pier. Monsters have always had their eyes on me. Those same haunted faces are everywhere I go. The men stared at us with blank eyes and an overall dead/drunk expression. I did not feel I was looking into the eyes of an enemy, but the enemy was with us.

"They don't seem to know we're here," said Haines.

"Careful," said Digger. "The more you look at them, the more you'll see them looking back at you." I thought this was a poetic comment on how weirdly kinetic and non-kinetic operations can intertwine and present a monster only soldiers see. Like I said, poetic.

Kochi and Ajmal talked a moment. "Sleeping in mind," said Kochi. He pointed at his forehead.

"I had an uncle that walked around like that," said Ellington. "Partial lobotomy."

Maddox stepped closer. "We're looking at a couple of sleepwalkers?"

"Not exactly," said Digger, "but they have lost their minds, in a way. We'll be like them, soon, Sir, able to see the core of reality."

"Their minds were stolen," said Hammer. Hammer accepted Druj in a German way, considering the myth of the origin of his own people involved emerging from a deep, dark forest.

Maddox was fuming, walking around in circles. "If this is all part of your mindfuck, Jett..."

"It's just as much my mindfuck, Sir," said Digger.

"I'll deal with you later, son," said Maddox. "Remember what I said...UCMJ action..."

"You think I give a shit about...?"

"You could at least act like you give a shit," said Maddox, knowing not to go down that road too fast, too soon. He...we...needed Digger. Sure, Digger was in another realm entirely, as was I, each of us swashbuckling through our fantasies, which were spilling out before us in real time. Our new corpse-like friends stood up and started walking toward the tunnel behind us.

Ajmal said something to Kochi. Kochi translated. "He says there are more children."

"Those aren't children," said Maddox.

I knew where this was going. "We've lost our sense of time down here," I said. "I can't be the only one who feels this way. Maybe I'm going crazy. Maybe I'm not."

"You are not going crazy," said Yvonne.

"The kid said there were children," said Maddox. "Others like him."

Ajmal nodded and pointed at the men. "Children of the dark," he said.

"For fuck's sake," said Ellington.

"No, listen," said Haines. "He's right. We're in one of the most volatile places in the world, historically speaking, yet we know so little."

"I'm not going to say it makes no sense," said Ellington.

"In Africa, you've got Boko Haram hiring children to fight. The world's a sick place. I'm just questioning the use of...zombies...in this kind of place. You see something like this and it's like something from a dream."

"Look at their necks," said Haines, pointing at little blinking lights embedded beneath the skin. "Radio frequency identification devices."

"God only knows," I said. "They could be farming them for reasons more sinister than we can imagine."

Digger and Hammer were the wiser ones about all this, but they were keeping quiet.

"Ajmal doesn't know everything," I said. "He had the strength of body and will to escape."

"Or they let him escape," said Maddox.

"Well," I said, "he's ours now, one way or another."

Ajmal gave a sad little look. The fog of war was back. How was all this possible? Did multiple magical acts take place without me being aware? Or was I the cause? Or was it some *brujo* from my past? There were a few. This was all some variety of revenge and had been from the beginning, and now it was coming at us so thick and fast. All the visions were conspiring to punish me and my comrades...maybe just for not seeing the true path or something just as out of reach of our limited imaginations. And it was all more than fate. Fate just didn't will this stuff to come my way, never has, never will. Oh well, it was certainly better than being in a war that could bore one to death. But war is what you make it. I'd heard others describe their dull days in Iraq or Afghanistan. They spent their wars in gyms, pumping iron, told me I'd do the same and come home with twenty fresh pounds of muscle. That didn't happen on my tour. But at that moment I had a different thought. *Oh, to be back at my KAF shack, sitting there in the dark, or to wake up as the rockets were flying in from far, far away, then to go right back to sleep, instead of here in this tunnel, in the middle of the madness.* My breast pocket was warm. It was my magician card reminding me it was there.

Omar read my mind. "To be a good Muslim, it is right to fear the darkness," he said.

The walls had flattened out again. The light in the room was coming from all around us, very faint, within the smoky air. It was hard to breathe. Whatever was in the air was crowding out our oxygen. It wasn't just me. Yvonne was straining. She looked dizzy. I grabbed her arm.

The light grew brighter as the smoke intensified, and the bad smell was back, gassy smells, from deep in the earth. More smoke was coming through a fissure in the wall. Smoke moved in hallucinogenic swirls and formed into a great claw and took a big swipe at us.

"Duck!" Digger pushed me and Yvonne aside. We both hit the deck. *Have I located God or has God located me? Nobody knows for sure. You just have to believe.* "I'm sorry," said Digger. "I think that was my fault. I was thinking of something one of the locals told me. 'A great arm is reaching into our country from the north' a man told me." Digger had a roguish look. While this sounds outlandish, in 2014 and 2015 NASA launched a number of new orbiting sensors to monitor the weather and claw-clouds were often spotted north of Afghanistan, mostly in Tajikistan and Turkmenistan. Alien/demon invasion theories exploded.

Ellington must've seen something worse (he did tell me before this leg of the adventure: "what you call scary and what I call scary are different"), because he started firing into the gloom, firing at the spectral walls. Ajmal and Omar hit the deck next to me. I rolled over and sat on my bum and fired my weapon from between my legs like I was firing my...well, you get the picture. That's not a bad firing position if you get everything right, but wearing a sports cup might help, dear reader. Except, I wasn't sure what I was shooting at. The wall was a luminous gel, just sucking up our rounds. Ellington was screaming a bloody war cry. The spirit was passed around. We all started screaming. I don't know if any of that was a smart way to go, considering how things played out, but the significance of the moment was that it sharpened us. We pulled together as a team. Until then, we were just people brought together by circumstances (or a brand of rebellion?).

Smoky, thin tendrils, ectoplasm-like, were coming down the walls like tears, reaching for us. Hammer and Maddox tossed flash-bang grenades, with no effect. All were firing, really laying it on whatever was encroaching upon our position, stuff that's beyond description, though I'm doing the best I can. If we weren't in such a closed system, I would've sat down to take it all in, write it all down as it was happening, with the idea that I could later put it within the confines of a mathematical model, come up with clever, publishable theories on multidimensional system behavior. I had a mind full of stars.

More humans launched at us from the tunnel ahead on the other side of the room, shooting at us with funny-looking AK-47s with oversized flash suppressors. At this point in the story, I have to distinguish between flesh and blood forms and dim/dull shapes from other dimensions, archetypal images of a multiverse I am just now starting to understand but convinced I'll never fully understand. The people were a little dull to behold at first, but the light orbs reappeared above them, and what I thought was a group of five dark angels was actually ten. All were in black, save for a few spangled pieces of clothing.

Maddox and Hammer opened fire on them. There was a lot of yelling. They were spewing into the room. I didn't hear one word of Arabic or Pashto or anything close. I got off some rounds but wasn't a good shot. Haines was a better shot than me. He took out several fighters. Omar and Kochi were together, taking cover behind our new zombie-friends. Yvonne was keeping Ajmal close.

Tink and Blink were flying in circles around the invaders,

dropping microdot bombs on them. When the bombs hit their targets, heads exploded, hands got blown off, and the fighters' weapons went flying. Just when I was starting to think Druj had some super-soldiers in the shadows, these average shooters came bursting in. Here were more vague riddles of the underground lair. We quickly realized they may not have been expecting to find us and that we were, in some ironic way, bizarre elements in their own reality, as scary to them as they were to us.

When the last man fell, we saw they were not all men. There was one woman and four boys Ajmal's age. He ran to them and inspected the bodies and started crying. Ellington uncovered the woman's face.

"She's not from around here," I said. I did feel stupid for saying that, but Yvonne backed me up.

"I do not believe it," Yvonne said. "It cannot be her..."

Flash-bang! There was an explosion behind us. Our escape route was now blocked by a pile of rubble. The walking-dead guys sort of looked at each other. That was their escape route, too. When I was a kid, I dreamed of having a dungeon to myself. So, in a way, my dreams were coming true.

"I say we put more holes in their skulls," said Ellington, "just to make sure they've met their maker."

"Any one of us could've triggered that blast," said Digger, "or maybe it was command-wire triggered."

"Digger is right," said Hammer. "They have been onto us from the start. If they wanted to kill us, we would be dead by now."

"But we had the tactical advantage of surprise," said Maddox, "until we didn't. The walls have eyes." He pulled his weapon to his chest, snug like a teddy bear.

"We have eyes, too," said Haines, pointing straight up at the drones.

Indeed, the walls did have eyes, with a field of vision including the backs of our brains, and my own vision was transforming. I could see ethereal lines, just as Peruvia could see when she used the Ilix in Digger's Historians game, sort of like when I visualized force fields for some of my martial arts awareness exercises, standard practices, but new abilities were rising, and a deep sense of epiphanies and raptures lying ahead. The secret was time itself breaking down all around us, if Digger's game notes were any kind of foretelling of the supernatural intervention at hand. Specifically, referring here to a magical tool described in Digger's Monsters of L.A. It was called MT, which stood for Mother Tongue, a wicked thing that could discombobulate your brain, in a temporal way, designed to take you out of the moment.

Yvonne stepped away from the group. I joined her. "I just saw a ghost," she whispered.

"They're not ghosts," I said. "They're... half breeds of some kind." Yvonne and I were two celestial bodies bound by a unique attraction. In the saturation of spectral absurdities, we were together.

"Not them," said Yvonne. "Him." She nodded at Ellington. "He is mist. Only half there."

Hammer and Maddox flanked the route ahead and waved the rest of us forward. We looked at Ajmal. I guess we all got the feeling that he knew something we didn't, and that was true. He didn't understand everything we were saying. We didn't understand everything he was saying, but I could see his thought bubbles, and he was as fascinated as the rest of us, not as perplexed by all the strange dangers. Port Delta was a rat maze, and we only saw a portion of it, according to my estimate. We stepped lightly, in a dreamy way. We had very little room to move. We were packed together.

Ahead was a door, half-open, framed by ambient white light, and I could hear synth music, just a slow pulse. It was like being in a horror flick with a John Carpenter soundtrack. As I didn't locate the source of the music, I now realize this was a Fourth Wall effect. I was pushing the music out of my body and mind. My memories and nightmares were mingling with my sense of adventure, all of it was pulling me forward. It was all-in-all such a strange world that we had become the apparitions, floating in the oozing darkness. We approached the door and entered a small room, suffused with soft light. As with the music, I could not determine the source of the light.

"See?" I said. "There's no one. The blast was a booby trap."

"This place lies," said Yvonne. "Ghosts lie to keep their stories alive."

Indeed, there were new figures in the spectral gloom that weren't there a second before. I reached out. I could see a current of energy flowing from my body toward those forms, not as if I was attacking, but as if I was feeding the forms. They were sucking my energy. Yvonne had taught me to visualize feeding on the light all around me, from all sources. This was the reverse. *Lady Mist, are you involved in this? Are you the cause of this energy radiating from me? Optical illusion or not, I'm getting lost in the illusion.*

"Whatever happened here, it happened," said Haines. "They're gone."

"Skeleton crew is all that's left," said Ellington, "and we killed them all."

"No," said Omar, "beasts are here. Jinn are among us."

"I believe this," said Kochi. "They can possess men, beasts, become things that are in-between, live in two worlds at once..."

"Please, Kochi," said Omar. "You are scaring everyone."

This didn't faze Maddox. "I'm more likely to believe Jett's crazy ideas than in some ancient devils," he said.

"It's true," said Digger. "Men can be born again. They can be born as monsters."

Ajmal was clenching his fists and had a menacing smile. He was dead set on dealing with the present danger. He was dealing with the paranormal effects better, because he knew the real-world danger better than we did, and that it involved real men with real fears and egos. Yvonne stroked his shoulder. His smile became more whimsical.

"Keep moving," said Maddox.

We entered the next room. Before us were huge glass panels with LED splash-backs. Ajmal tried speaking in English. He started saying something. "Druj uses...this is..."

But Kochi had to translate the rest. "He says that Druj uses light and reflective surfaces in ceremonies and in training. It is for mental stimulation. The mirror helps extend the self into other worlds."

The panels were on rails. Panels on the far side were supported by steel cables, hanging from the ceiling. Etched into the panels were various odd swirls, geometric patterns. They seemed incomplete. Lines were cutoff, jagged in unexpected ways. I was startled by my reflection in the nearest one and moved into a defensive pose.

Ajmal stepped forward. He looked mesmerized. Kochi had a talk with him. Ajmal pointed out a box on a control panel with a viewing portal. The box was facing the panels. You could adjust the height of the box, similar to a submarine periscope.

Kochi tried to explain: "After they administer the medicine, you look into that thing while others move around the panels. It creates...I do not know how to say..."

"It is like a mandala," said Yvonne. "It hypnotizes."

Kochi continued. Obviously, he didn't know what Yvonne was talking about. "It is part of the training here, though this is not a training facility, according to Ajmal."

Ellington looked into the viewer. He cupped his hands over the rubber portal.

"So it's a giant Viewmaster of sorts?" I said, remembering the toy from my childhood. You slipped in a disk and looked through the lenses and saw 3D images. "Give me a chance," I said. "I'll bet it's just as illuminating."

"Doesn't matter," grumbled Ellington. "We could be

looking at anything."

"What do you see?" Hammer asked Ellington.

"Infestation," said Ellington, "and you don't have to look in that thing to see it."

I looked through the portal. The image was black and white, with shimmering white arabesques all around its edges. It was hypnotizing, as Yvonne said. Reminded me of days when I was running around Houston with my witch friend, and we were spotting giants and dragons in pockets of darkness amid the downtown towers, then we'd go to a certain all-night diner and have mini food fights. This was no different, with a full spectrum of mystical mayhem coming and going. Maybe I was just seeing what I wanted to see. I saw men fighting, with lots of effective elbow action and lots of head strikes. Haines looked through the device after me. He compared the image to circuitry; he saw what he wanted to see. Maddox had a look after Haines. "It's an intelligence overlay," said Maddox. "That's what I see. Each panel combines with another. I get it."

"You get it in one way," said Yvonne. "But it is more than you see."

"I get it," Maddox repeated.

Digger had his turn. "We're wasting time," he said. "This thing may not be here to pull us in, but that's the effect. Bit by bit. Whatever is supposed to happen, we need to get to it..."

"Where do we go?" said Omar.

"Wait," I said. "It's not a waste of time." I pulled out my notebook. When your feet are planted in two worlds at once, you see everything differently. "Let me have another look. Omar, good idea. Get on that end." I motioned to the far end of the panel. "Yvonne, that one. Kochi, Ajmal, the one on the far side."

"For fuck's sake, Captain Jett," said Ellington. "What's on your mind?"

"I'm not trying to be a prick," I said. "It's just turning out that way. It's going to be great."

"Just make it fast," said Maddox. "I'm ready to mike-charlie[4] this thing and get the hell out of here." Get the hell out of Port Delta, with deliberate speed. That was his point.

How many times had I seen this kind of thing in my life and let the moment pass me by? But not this time. This was the way a mathematician saw the world, like an artist. It wasn't a soldierly way, but it was the new way for me. I thought of the tattoos. I knew there had to be some meaning. I had my sketchbook in my pack. I pulled it out. My imagination went into overdrive. I looked for patterns the way that Tink and Blink would when shooting across the desert. I lined up the drawings of tattoos, as best as I could, just in my thoughts. I directed my teammates in sliding the panels left and right into precise positions so that the shape was created via layering and appeared in the viewer.

Digger was as excited as I was. A similar moment was in one of his game scenarios (instead of glass panels, it was a key that changed shape to fit different doors, under different spells). Our key came to us in a much more interesting way, though. "The dead guys came through for us again," said Digger. "We should be thankful."

"Why is that?" said Maddox.

"Their tattoos. When everything you see is a dream, something real comes along..."

"Do you hear that?" said Hammer.

"A man's voice," said Kochi.

syem...shest...pyat...

"It is Russian," Yvonne said. "Someone is counting backward from ten."

I knew that much. The number one hit before we could comment on what Yvonne just explained, just when the lines matched up with my sketch.

---

[4] mike-charlie = MC = mission complete

There was a series of clicks and other mechanical sounds which echoed. A door opened on the far side of the room, revealing another room.

"Fuck," said Ellington, "I was hoping for daylight."

"You got fluorescent light," Digger said.

"Daylight is this way, too," I said.

Ellington was not timid. He jumped ahead again. He smelled what he was looking for. I had my radar system, he has his. More lights turned on when we entered the room, which wasn't really a room. There was a platform, a dock for loading and unloading material from small mining cars, a few of them on a rail nearby, electrically powered cars. Numerous rail lines extended down a huge tunnel, three times the size as any we'd seen yet. It was another sign that we'd discovered a real operation of some kind, of many kinds. Ellington was giddy. He found renewed purpose in the adventure.

"I knew there was more," I said, "but...I don't want to sound like I'm always the guy that..."

"Push it out, my fellow captain," said Hammer. I think he meant spit it out.

I finished the thought. "It would be nice to have some new dead guys to help us out."

"I can deliver," said Ellington.

"Count me in, too," said Maddox. "Goodnight, sweetheart."

Kochi nodded. He motioned to Ajmal and Omar, who were pissing in the corner, and they turned and smiled and nodded.

"Let's see about this place," said Haines. He opened his computer. We paused to drink water and check ammo. Lights down the tunnel started turning on. I could not see the end of the tunnel. Overhead lights started flickering. The cars made a loud buzzing sound.

"Is that your doing?" I asked Haines.

"Not me," said Haines. "You're the magic man, Sir."

"Did Tink and Blink find this place?" I asked.

"They should be waiting for us at the end of the tunnel," said Haines, "a half-mile or so away."

"Is this a tunnel or the belly of a beast?" said Omar.

Hammer was speaking in German into a small device. I presumed he was taking notes of all this. Decke was going to have lots of questions for him. I imagined all sorts of new, crazy Teutonic weaponry resulting from Horseflesh.

Digger was squatting on the other end of the platform. I joined him.

"Some huge machine dug this tunnel," I said, "or a massive gofer."

"Either is available to them," said Digger. Digger was a straight shooter, no games, and I said a quick prayer that we would not run into a giant gofer...then I took back my prayer and prayed that we would actually see such a thing, or whatever it was that killed at Sugarbush and destroyed Provo. It wasn't just smoke and strange animals.

"I want to show you something," I said. I opened Digger's notebook. I turned to a sketch of a map which he later developed into a larger playing surface, according to his own notes. "Look familiar?"

Digger studied the map. He raised his arm and opened his palm, presenting the dark tunnel before us. "The stuff just came to me, you know," said Digger. "Like it comes to you, dark brother, like the sun. It's real. It's us."

I saw the same darkness he saw, or so I thought. "What do you see down there, Sergeant?"

"I don't want to think about it," said Digger. He was tired of the creepy occurrences, like me. "What we think...becomes real. It's who we are."

"What makes you so sure? You might be losing your mind."

"How is your girl doing, Sir?" said Digger. "I have to say, she's easy on the eyes."

Yvonne was sitting alone at the other end of the platform.

She had been keeping her distance from everyone. "She's managing," I said.

"She's as much to blame as we are." Digger checked the magazine of his carbine. "She's the reason we're encountering all this, and she found a willing partner in crime in you, and now me."

"What do you mean?" Here it comes, I thought.

"What are you doing here, Sir?" Digger said. He didn't make eye contact, confident I would give the response he expected.

"I'm here to unravel the mystery about who...or what...attacked at Provo and Sugarbush..."

"I mean here in Afghanistan," said Digger. "Aren't you a lawyer?"

"I'm a lot of things," I said. "Where do I start? First and foremost, I'm an adventurer. Like you. But to answer your question, and I know where you're going with this, I was drawn here, the way a moth is drawn to the light."

"You found darkness, though," said Digger. "Now you leap from one form of it to another, the way we all do. You found her." He nodded at Yvonne.

"She's not your concern," I said. Of all the cutthroats I'd encountered, she wasn't one.

"She casts a spell," said Digger. "I understand, Sir. It's how she found us."

"She didn't find us," I said. "I found her. I needed a haircut. Like I found you. I was drawn here. Not hellbent, so to speak, just..."

"We feed off each other," said Digger, "but I don't think it's us. It's her. You're doing good, Sir. I was in your shoes, in a tiny little box, then I expanded my universe. I've dreamed of heaven and earth. I've been disillusioned. We're soldiers. We run fire drills, wargames, then something like this comes along and changes everything. And Maddox and Hammer have reason to be suspicious. Yvonne knows more, much more than she's told us."

Good for Digger, pouring out his guts like that. Yvonne didn't look suspicious to me, staring into the tunnel. I joined her. Not too close, though. Maddox told me to figure her out. Maddox was so heavy-handed about everything, but he gave me an order before we left Kandahar and I intended to follow it. My conflicting loyalties were coming to the surface.

"Who was the woman back there?" I said. "You knew her."

"She...was from my childhood. She was a ghost."

"She was bleeding. We killed her. I think *I* killed her."

"I killed her, too," said Yvonne. "At least, I thought I did...a long time ago. Since I met you, Thomas, many demons have risen from the dead. All this time, I thought I was winning. I was not. I give up."

"Then give up," I said. "So will I. We can be free, together. Wouldn't it be nice to go to California and be together and forget about everything like we talked about?"

"You should not give up," said Yvonne. "And do not give up your California dream, whether or not I am with you. And if things do not work out, do not be hard on yourself."

Maddox came up behind us. "We need to get going," he said. "I don't want to wait on them to blow up the room again. At least, not with us in it."

Haines climbed into the first rail car, really just a big bucket. I got in behind Haines, followed by Maddox, Digger, Yvonne, and Hammer. The first car was a little bigger than the second car. Ellington, Omar, Kochi, and Ajmal were in the second car. Haines drove. We moved forward and kept low. The car had headlights, not the best. Even with the new light, my eyes were playing tricks on me. I trusted my senses least of all, though. Twisted as my imagination was becoming, it was what we were going to need to get out of the situation. I spaced out, not going to lie. Horseflesh was turning to horse-mush. Each little encounter brought us closer (notice all our cunning comments), yet I felt like we were slipping apart, lost souls finding it hard to cope with simple universal growth happening all around us, except Yvonne. She understood occult anatomy better than any of us.

"What the hell is this?" said Maddox. Headlights were coming toward us. It was another railcar like ours. It was on the rail running alongside ours, going about the same speed, from what I could tell. We did not slow down. I saw three heads. The people looked right at us when the car passed by. The man in the back raised his weapon. Ellington turned and raised his weapon and took careful aim and shot the guy in the head and the other two in their necks before they could drop for cover. Ajmal reacted with a gasp. Hammer started speaking into his recorder again. Digger and Maddox were looking ahead. It was all kind of ho-hum. The end of the tunnel was coming up.

"Slow down," I said.

"I'm not doing anything," said Haines.

True, he was hands off, but the car did slow down rapidly. There were further grumblings and obscenities from Maddox. This was not a good sign. The end of the line was ahead. A large space opened up before our eyes. It was a circular chamber with several circumferential levels about ten feet wide and dual ramps going up to the left and right, connecting the levels.

There was a noise like thunder. Ellington leaped out and started firing. It seemed at first he was firing at nothing in particular, but I looked up and saw fighters streaming down both ramps. They were shooting at us. Kochi followed Ellington, blasting away. Everyone in my car leaped out and returned fire and took cover behind the boxes spread around the floor. Omar and Ajmal hunkered down inside the other car. Ajmal got a kill. I saw him peak over the side and pop a guy between the eyes. I put two people down right away.

Once the left side was clear, Maddox and Hammer started sweeping the ramp. They started taking fire from a higher right-side level. We provided covering fire from the cover of our boxes and several fighters fell over the side or down the ramp. Maddox and Hammer had their eyes on higher ground. The rest of us were in a fishbowl, squatting behind the boxes. Digger and I began sweeping the right side. He was a good shot, center mass kill shots and slow steady movements like you're supposed to do. I looked back. Yvonne was pulling her weight. She was providing covering fire. Fighters fell one by one. The ones on the highest level began to fall back into another space we couldn't see. Some of the lights went out. Tracer rounds illuminated the darkness. Our targets became humanoid shapes, barely. Then it got quiet. *LM, when it's this quiet, when I'm supposed to be on task, my mind starts wandering. I become a kid again and say a prayer for everyone in my life, not just me...I hear the call to prayer and am reminded of God's mysteries.*

I looked at the faces of the fallen as we went up the ramp. They weren't like the other foreign Druj fighters we'd seen, and they weren't dressed in all-black. They looked like locals. Not surprisingly, Druj did have plenty of anti-Taliban warlords and former mujahedin fighters available to recruit all over the country. Digger moved a couple of boxes together and crouched behind them, in case anyone else showed up. I went back down the ramp.

Ellington was digging around in one of the boxes, pulling out plastic bags and pouches of various sizes. He looked closely at writing on one of the bags. "It's in Chinese...I think..." he said.

"Let me see that," I said. It wasn't just in Chinese. There were multiple scripts and a label in Cyrillic on the other side. I squeezed the bag. Some kind of liquid or gel was inside. Inside the box were also a bunch of clear plastic pouches. The liquids in those bags were of various colors. One was blue, the same as the horseshoe crab blood I was still carrying. There was some luminous pink stuff. Ellington and I grabbed a few pouches. Ellington's face said it all, said the same thing I was thinking: fantasy goop. Would we fight over it? Behave like figures in a Greek tragedy?

"What the hell is going on down there?" said Maddox, on the top level more than thirty feet above our heads. "We're clear."

Ellington tore open another box and threw it aside. More bags fell out of the box, even more colorful than the ones in the first box. It was like watching an old Skittles® candy commercial... "Taste the Rainbow®"...and a kaleidoscope it certainly was. I didn't trust my senses, but I couldn't ignore them, though my budding psychic abilities were filling in the blanks in odd ways. The walls were bubbling. A red fog started spreading throughout the room, so much that the dark space between drew my attention, the framework of it. Arms and torsos took shape. Vile creatures with heads on ropes, swinging their own ropes around. Digger was smiling. He had even bigger ideas than me.

Yvonne gripped my arm. She was not smiling. Her lips were trembling. Sweat was pouring down her face. "I think..." she said, then gasped. She pointed a trembling finger.

"Breathe, Yvonne," I said. "You're in a place...come up for air."

A boy appeared on the top level. His face was pale, his cheeks smudged. He had blonde hair. He looked no older than thirteen. He was dressed in a black long-sleeved shirt and black pants, like a tiny Druj fighter, but without a cloak.

"Anton!" shouted Ajmal. He waved at the boy. The boy did not wave back.

"*Nyet*," said Yvonne. "Anton..."

When children appear in my dreams...it's a sign, for sure, but not good. And it's always some kid from twenty years back that I never saw again and stayed the same age in my dreams. So when I saw Anton, I saw a ghost from my past. So did Yvonne. Ah, the illusions that knowledge provides, the endless mysterious swamps where we plunge into darkness we see as light.

Yvonne ran up the ramp. I ran after her. The boy started singing. Yvonne stopped dead. "That's Tili Tili Bom," she said, "a frightening song Russian parents sing to their children to make them sleep. In Russia, when children don't fall asleep, they are threatened with nightmares to make them sleep. My mother would sing it."

In my eyes, the boy was more ghost than a living boy. "He is your little brother, isn't he?" I said. He looked like a stoic lad. He was just standing there. He was just...a thing...like all the recently appearing ghosts from my past, a thing more inside me than before me. To Yvonne, he may have looked real. He had sharp, blue eyes, but my mind's eye saw shark eyes, a mysterious monster. Tink and Blink were flying. It would've been nice to have their point of view. Haines looked worried (for his pets, I presumed).

Anton reached for Yvonne. She dropped her weapon and walked closer to him.

"Careful," Maddox warned her.

Yvonne was just a few feet down the ramp from the boy. They spoke to each other in Russian. Must've been the magician card in my pocket, plus the Russian language book I studied during intel training at Ft. Huachuca in 2007, plus the Russian woman I dated in 2008, because I understood a lot of what they were saying, even though they were whispering. She was lost, then found, that was the gist of it, each was saying something like that and each had their own point of view of it. *LM, this is wonderful. I've created something out of nothing, this initiation into all sorts of mysteries. That's true magic, and you are to thank, in part. Some of this goes back to my card reading with you. I'm going to bring him home one day, your magician...*

Anton offered Yvonne his hand. She kissed it. It didn't seem right or real, because from where I was standing she looked too far away to touch him. It was as if his arm grew twice as long. Then, as if we were in a mirrored funhouse, everyone's bodies started morphing, lengthening, except Omar became even squattier. Haines' worried features stretched into bliss, and I felt bliss, too, like the whole world could heal itself. Trigger-happy Ellington went off again, setting off a chain reaction of small arms fire, all on our end. The boy just stood there. I don't know what everyone was shooting at. We were all spooked. Yvonne was in the field of fire. "Stop!" she yelled. She stood in front of the boy. From where they were standing, we all must've looked like...prisoners. Her powers grew in that place. Mystic leanings turned into bulldozers. An orb of light appeared and entered my brain. If this is goodbye, I thought, then she left without saying goodbye. The boy was looking at me as if he was saying hello. Somewhere between illusion and reality...

Digger was no longer crouching behind the boxes on the ramp. He was standing and giving me the same look I was giving him. His body was transforming, *like everything in the room, LM, or maybe it's the red fog, it's folding around him, the air is rippling, if it's a question of sanity or insanity, I'll have to choose insanity, just to get through this, this has nothing to do with tolerance, it's about survival, and how can I believe that my Yvonne is the alpha in the room when it's a fellow soldier shocking my brain like this, that smoke, I'm on fire...*

"You have the power to change what is happening," said a man over a loudspeaker system. He had a Russian accent, though not thick. The boy's lips were moving, but it wasn't his voice.

"Who said that?" said Maddox. "Show yourself!"

But he didn't show himself. "This moment has been coming a long time," the man said. He wasn't talking to us, though. He was talking to Yvonne. I could tell by her expression. She was the prize, the target all along.

Yvonne was standing next to Anton. Light in the room was faint, but Yvonne and her little brother didn't look much alike, except for their small noses and small lips. It was just one more element in the grand scheme. In war, I was no longer surprised by anything. Indifference had begun setting in even before Operation Horseflesh. There were the daily rocket attacks, the stories of soldiers maimed by IEDs, stories that had their own kamikaze momentum. It's a voodoo system, and soldiers are prey. I realize now that my indifference was growing from a strengthening clairvoyance. I'd already transcended the Fourth Wall and didn't even realize it when it was happening, though I discerned pockets of dark matter were in the room, coming together. I could've taken a more heavy-handed theological approach at that time. It would've been perfectly normal. I mean, it was easy to spot the devil in every little thing, every twist of light. If there is any sort of theology in Druj, it is light-centric, not just in the ancient sense of light versus dark/good versus evil, but in the sense that darkness doesn't just oppose light, it twists light. The darkness is organic/manipulative. Believe me, the first step in believing in all this is to overcome your fear of it.

Yvonne was radiant, though. She wasn't the type to run home in times of trouble, but she looked like she was arriving home, with family there to greet her, and here was her little brother, present in a physical way, though pale and scrawny.

"You have met your brother," said the ethereal voice, "and now you have new brothers, and I have new sons. I've been waiting for this moment for a long time. Let us celebrate."

"Nikolay," said Maddox, making connections with collected intel faster than me, and right (in part) about Yvonne and about what kind of devilry Operation Horseflesh was going to uncover. I was just a player in Maddox's game like he was in mine. "It looks like Druj is a family business," said Maddox. He slapped a new magazine into his rifle. Maddox had his family of demons like I had mine.

I grabbed Maddox's arm. "Let him talk, Sir." If what Digger was saying was true, then there had to be a better way out of this mess than bullets and blood, and maybe I could save Yvonne in the process. This was a seductive, dark force that I empowered just by dealing with, along with Digger, and we needed some negative entropy in our lives, just to slow everything down. What the hell made all this? Did I really play a part? I closed my eyes. A massive reprogramming of the world around me was in order. I closed my eyes and tried to fly out of my body but couldn't. I envisioned the man in my magician card flying through outer space, with dark matter particles smashing into each other all around him. For just a moment, my toes felt numb. I couldn't feel the floor beneath me. I opened my eyes and looked down and it looked like I was levitating two inches above the floor, though it was hard to tell.

"You have Russians and a mix of Europeans," said Haines. He looked around the room. He was always looking for more action, like his drones.

I was grounded again. "Did you just see me..."

"This is all part of a cult dedicated to what?" said Ellington. "Illicit trade in biochemical slime?" He squeezed the bag still in his hand then pocketed it and lit up the room with gunfire. He went crazy. Hammer started adding fire, blasts of light from his weapon creating harsh, angular shadows. What a ride, though. It was like being in a whirlpool, danger and destruction and all. No wonder Druj wanted us on board for the ride. We were Spartans, and I had the Fourth Wall and willing, active players. Who was playing whom? Digger was having just as much fun as me.

"I'll tell you what you have," said Ellington. "You have swine." Ellington charged up the ramp. I followed him, along with everyone else on the floor. The firefight that followed, if you could call it that, was among the strangest and bloodiest I've ever seen, and I've been in some strange fights, even here in Los Angeles, involving all the stuff that NATO brass had such a hard time stomaching for such a long time, not just my creations, but Kochi's jinn, all of it, all the same, from one dreary world to another.

Kochi had Omar convinced of the jinn stuff, and when red fog reached down along the ramp ahead of us, Omar started screaming. Ajmal was also screaming, but it was because he was excited about the fight. So much rage had been building in the boy. I was afraid, too. My game elements were becoming real. The red fog was something I pulled from Digger's game, actually. I'd drawn clouds in red pencil on Bandit. Except this red fog wasn't fog at all, but blood in suspension, of viscosities thin to thick, long tongues of it, and we ran smack into it. It was a bloody welcome wagon from Nikolay Vasiliev. I quickly figured out what a sneaky player he was.

"Is this your Leopard, Sir?" I asked Maddox.

"I suspect it," said Maddox. He started blasting the fog, with no effect.

Hammer and Digger were slapping the fog away with their hands, having more success. They had seen this kind of thing before.

Yvonne and the boy started backing away, into the red fog, out of sight. "Stay where you are!" I told her. "We're coming!" But she didn't reply, and when we all reached the top platform, Yvonne and the boy were gone. Nikolay was a cackling lunatic.

"What now?" I said to Digger.

"You can see what I see," said Digger.

"Well, I think we should put our heads together," I said.

"I'm tired of this shit," said Maddox. "You two have been hiding your whole card this whole time. Now we lost a member of the group. Are they coming after each of us?"

"Just two more of us, Sir," said Digger. He looked at Ajmal. "Maybe three."

"Then we stay together," said Hammer. He said something

into his little device.

"Consider this," said Digger. "They've been playing us all this time. But the rest of you don't have to be here. For me, the game started last year. I knew these guys were here...everywhere. I'm the one they're after."

"Then why were you conspiring with a German army officer?" said Maddox. "He's not the one that pulled you up here?"

Hammer stepped forward.

"Leave Captain Hammer out of this," said Digger.

"Look here, you little piss ant," said Ellington. Those were the last words he spoke.

Hammer defended himself. "Lieutenant Colonel Maddox, in a moment you may be taking your words back." Hammer continued speaking into his device. His hand was cupped over it. I couldn't understand what he was saying.

"All right," said Maddox. "One thing at a time, but when...if...we get back to Kandahar you're going to have to..."

At that moment Ellington was torn in half. The lower half of his body just dropped.

His upper half swiped sideways as if connected to a zip line, bumping into Haines. His bloody guts spilled out. Poor Kochi was standing nearest him and received the most blood splatter. Ajmal was splattered, too, but he was already covered in blood. Ajmal was still shirtless. All his skin was slick with blood and sweat. Ajmal screamed, a real belly yell like you'd hear from a grown man.

Everyone hit the deck. Maddox grabbed Ellington's lower body. Ellington's face was facing me. He'd been cut along the stomach. His blood was milky around what was left of his stomach. I touched Ellington's face. His lips were still moving. His eyes looked alive, even after a few seconds. I was going to miss all the banter and borderline antipathy between us. We were like rival gang members going after the same thing. I started to pick up Ellington's upper half, but he was jerked out of my hand. Darkness itself pulled him into other darkness.

Kochi had a look of horror.

"What is it?" said Omar.

"This is the work of Ifrit," said Kochi. "Ifrit is a kind of jinn, made of smoke."

"We are getting out of this horror house," said Hammer. "Follow me." Even though we couldn't see well through the red fog, Hammer sprang to his feet and rushed into it and started providing covering fire for the rest of us. Ajmal and Haines and I jumped at the same time and ran for the bursts of light coming from Hammer's rifle.

Going back to an exercise in one of the ninja magazines I studied before Operation Horseflesh, these were "water" moves. The idea was to slip over opposing forces and get them to slip by me. My reactions were quick. I didn't hesitate when facing the fog or any associated creatures. I was just as fine with ghosts and goblins as I was with real people, treating both with the same stone cold moves.

"This changes nothing," I said. I was determined to move forward but a little jealous of Ellington for whatever boundary he had just crossed. Looking at him, I could feel this crossing happening. I was working hard to test my own boundaries. I was looking at the bigger picture. So should you, reader.

The darkness came alive. I didn't have to think about it.

We were bumping into each other. No route looked more inviting than another, but we did pick up the pace. The air was fresher. "Yvonne!" I cried out, but she didn't answer. We all stopped shooting. During that pause, the only sound was our breathing. "She's not gone," said Digger. From the echoes, it sounded like we were in the middle of another big room. I put on my night vision goggles again. Ambient light confirmed it was a large space. The ceiling was fifty feet above our heads. It was another storage space of some kind. Kochi and Omar used their liquid light sticks. The floor was littered with dead bodies, slick with blood.

LM, I'm seeing things that just can't be there. Digger looks twice as big. His rifle looks like a sword. Why would one need a sword down here? I don't care what happens, his work inspired me and all this. All this started as a game, then the map came, then the game and map came together. I made people on paper, and those people merged with real people, then new people showed up. This is no different from the ghosts in my own Houston house. I invited them, all thirty of them. I invited the ghosts and monsters to join me here, too. I admit. How else was I going to figure out the mysteries of Sugarbush and Provo? I knew the game was here, all along. All I had to do was imagine hard enough, and the solutions would come together, one by one. This is why I volunteered for the war, to discover powers I knew I had but couldn't tap, until now.

A large closed door was ahead, to the outside world, I hoped.

"Recall your drones," I told Haines.

"Why, Sir?"

"Because we're getting out of here." I removed my goggles and put them in my pack.

"But Yvonne..." said Ajmal.

"Let's go," said Digger. "I'm with Captain Jett on this."

"She might as well be dead," said Maddox.

"She's not dead, Sir," I said. "We'll be able to do more for her once we get out of here."

"Did anyone see the thing that got Ellington?" said Haines.

"I saw a hairy arm," said Hammer, "twice as big as a normal man's."

Kochi and Omar did not like this and shook their heads. "By Allah...be with us, Allah," said Kochi.

Hammer and Maddox were glaring at me and Digger. "Why the mad looks?" I said. "If you think Digger and I are to blame for this mess, and I'm not saying we're not, you should also be looking at Kochi. He's had evil jinn on his mind since we set foot down here."

The ground started shaking. This triggered something in Ajmal. He said something that I interpreted as meaning "Get the fuck down." He crouched and raised his weapon. We did the same.

"Now you have really pissed them off," said Kochi.

The remaining red fog on the other side of the room started gathering together.

I felt intense heat, but there was no fire. It was our body heat. We were all feeding off each other. "Keep going, Sir," said Digger. He had a sly grin. "It's your ability. It's your game now."

It was my game all along, actually, but that one little comment said a lot about Sergeant Digger. He thought he was the game master. Of his game, that was true, but we were getting through Horseflesh with my own system. Digger helped bring out my abilities, and for that, I will be forever grateful. This particular ability, 'heat shield'[5] was conceived on paper, listed with other powers in one of the first Fourth Wall outlines, modeled after outlines of the law, from my law school days, then became a thought construct, and now, as I was achieving the transcendence I'd been searching for all along, we repelled creatures that I barely could have imagined a day earlier.

First, the Mul. A Mul is a shape-shifting beast twice the size of an average man. It usually appears with horns curving down from its cheeks and brow. It has yellow eyes and a large snout. The Mul roared. The room shook. We were thrown about, made suddenly insignificant in this environment. The room itself was as much a shapeshifter as the Mul...or as much as me. I fell to the ground. Everything in the room looked bigger. Even Digger hovered over the action like a statue of a

---

[5] Referred to the same way in Army reports concerning Operation Horseflesh.

construct of the Fourth Wall in my mind at that time, version 1.0, so to speak, but Druj was drawing me deeper into the unknown. It was a new enemy with so many mysterious parts, if you could call Druj the enemy. I was breathing with new life and a better understanding of the pantheon of madness before me. With such ease I was able to detect all the wrongs...detect whether they would all add up to a right along the rest of the way. Part of me did not want to see these creatures torn apart, but I knew that if we didn't, they would shape-shift into some other malevolent forms and terrorize, and my commander was not going to allow that in his AO.

When the lights came on (inside and outside), I turned and saw the near-dead guys we released. They were moving at a good clip, moving a little better than the Sleepy Brothers (RIP) and their corpse predecessors, Karl and Franz (RIP). Vengeance...a powerful motivator. They both grabbed AK's from fallen Druj guards we'd popped on the way out. They were as excited as (near-dead) kids at Christmas.

Still holding Ellington's remains, Maddox examined the bodies of the Druj fighters. "They're definitely human, but they aren't local." Maddox had traveled far and wide. He had the experience and credibility to talk like that.

"It is a fair mix of Germanic types," said Hammer.

"They're everything," said Digger.

Once we were over the hump of bodies, we ran like hell up the embankment, guns blazing...playing into Druj's hands, still, the beasts guiding beasts in an ethereal dance. A couple more Mul creatures were behind us. These weren't like vampires. They didn't mind the sunlight. Ajmal was the fiercest of all of us. He screamed a war cry and cut a hand off a Mul. Before the Mul could come around with his other hand, Omar got him with a short sword, stabbed his leg so he couldn't run after us. It worked. Omar didn't kill the Mul. It fell back and cried in pain.

Turns out it was a rat-infested place. Hundreds came up

the ramp behind us. The sun was up in full, but still low. There were still dawn colors. We stood together, galvanized with incredible energy, all new animals with new knowledge of the latticework of magic in the world all around us and beneath our feet, and I had a sense of hidden mysteries. How does one express the entropy of confidence itself? Old ways of thinking seemed unnatural. The moon was still out. It was a crazy-looking moon. One of the many ways to tell if you are in a parallel world is to look at the sky. The celestial bodies will be different.

I expected to see more buildings, but our adventure had taken us far outside Kunduz. Before us was a spooky graveyard of military vehicles. They all looked Russian. A thin rainbow arched across the grayish-yellow sky. A web of lightning followed. Shooting stars shot across the sky in impossible parabolic trajectories. I pondered a moment. The lightning was something I hadn't seen since my godform meditations, all the godforms arguing, Krishna in his Universal Form (Vishvarupa), Shiva, Kali, to name a few.

Snow glistened on the mountains to the south. I put a bullet in a Druj fighter, just to have some extra clothes available for Ajmal, but he refused them. He had his cloak of blood, happy boy. We took cover behind an old Russian T-54 tank. There were some explosions behind us, near the door. (It was the front door to the facility. We had entered through the back door in Kunduz.)

As a criminal organization...should I say criminal? Let's say dark instead...As a dark organization, the Druj outfit in Afghanistan was lacking in the real-world weapons department. This was a bunch still going through growing pains (despite the thousands of years on the rise) and it showed in the human elements. Sure, they had AKs and machinery, but they were devoting mystical resources elsewhere, in an effort to preach their universal message, no doubt, and their front-line fighters at Port Delta suffered for it. Some Druj fighters came out of the warehouse and ran toward our position. We were covered. It was suicide to run at us like that. Hammer mowed them down and then spoke into his little box as if he was keeping good notes to write a German version of this story, some Bavarian swan song about a meaty swan. *LM, My story is going to be better than his, with things within things within things, like one of those Russian dolls, but what's going to be at the core? Like all epics, it may just go on and on till the day I die, assuming I get out of this place alive. I'm looking forward to the day when I just start having fun with all this, without seeking explanations for every little thing. I'm sure explanations abound...there's electro-magnetism, for instance. You know, LM, that I've got certain...talents. Will you promise me that you'll educate me further? I've been building you up into something wild. Mystery is your bread and butter.*

Ah, those first Fourth Wall moments...these talents are easier to deal with now, but back then I questioned all the glow, the overall hammering of the glow emanating from my body during fights, and the Russian tanks and vehicles looked like they were melting away before my eyes. And since then I've studied dark matter theory, the structure of the universe, all this is connected...

Druj fighters were behind several wrecked Russian vehicles. They started receiving fire from forces up the road. Maddox looked at Digger and me. "It's not us, Sir," Digger said.

Hammer went around to the other end of the tank and used his binoculars to see what was happening. "That is the German Army," he said. "Units under Task Force Kunduz."

Ordnance was exploding, sending Druj fighters and chunks of vehicles into the air. I just laid back a second and took a sweeping view of all the carnage. It took me back to basic training, during a night fire exercise when we were crawling across a muddy field full of barbed wire and booby traps, with live rounds shooting overhead from a SAW mounted on a tower, but I just turned over on my back and marveled at the beauty of the tracer rounds zipping above me, and the stars were out in full. I imagined I was in the sky, zipping around, dodging fire, a crowing Peter Pan.

A vehicle was coming up the road. Like a crazy man, Omar started running toward it, in panic mode now that he was above ground. He was waving his arms, looking for a friendly face, then he ran back to us behind the tank. "There is bad news," he said. "Yvonne was the driver of that car. The man was with her. And the boy. Is he real? He must be a jinn."

"Of them all, he must be," said Kochi. The truck raised a cloud of dust. Ordnance exploded behind the truck, lifting more earth, but the truck kept going. "They are going toward the river," said Kochi.

"The border of the country," said Haines.

I ran in the opposite direction, back to the mouth of the underground facility where the truck was still running. A .50 caliber machine gun was mounted in the back. The driver was dead, lying on the ground. Ajmal's kill, I think. I got in the truck right as a German shell exploded a few feet away. The blast force closed the door so hard it would've severely injured my leg if I was slower to climb inside the truck. My ears were ringing again. *LM, Timothy Leary said that people have to go out of their minds before coming to their senses. Going forward seems ridiculous. It would be perpetuating the abuse of my team by the chaos of war, you can't just stop now, for that's what this life is: keeping the ship steady as you can as you speed toward oblivion. Is all this an elaborate hoax? Some of this stuff has to be a hoax.*

I picked up my comrades and we chased after Yvonne and her family. Kochi and Digger squeezed up front with me. The rest were in the back, along with the half-corpse of Ellington.

"Where are they going?" I asked Kochi.

"There is a bridge at Shir Khan Bandar. They must be going there."

German tactical vehicles were on both sides of the road. Soldiers were engaged with entities of smoke and fire, more Druj wards which were feeding off our energy, Digger's and mine. Hammer cheered his comrades as we passed them. Kochi was freaked. This was the jinn invasion he warned us about. I was starting to feel like it was all largely my fault, but I was still mad with delight and fear. This Druj creature which was smoke, in addition to feeding off my own imagination, fed off the smoke of its own body, sort of like the velvet spider which feeds her young by regurgitating liquid then allows her young to eat her, also consistent with Digger's Konfex, an insect-like creature mentioned in both Historians and Monsters of L.A.

Decke sources were more progressive in interpretations of this smoke, linking it to Provo and Sugarbush, which was not within Germany's AO, which led me to conclude that Hammer's connection with Decke was stronger than he indicated. The Germans were fighting hard. I yelled at the boys in the back of the truck to duck. I heard rounds hit the truck. Digger was starting to get creepy. He just laughed when we were getting hit by friendly fire. "Watch them devour," he said. "They are so beautiful. Why is everyone shooting at them?"

To the right was a flat expanse, but something was rising up in the middle, as big as a four-story building, like a school of fish, a spherical body of smoke and ash and dust. I thought of it as an energy orb, but as it got closer I could see that it had flesh. Arms and legs started growing from the cloud, now more like a giant flaming boulder, fleshy bits notwithstanding.

Omar was having a 'blast' with the .50 cal. He became braver and bolder as Horseflesh progressed, and now he was battling on wings of flames. He came close to being killed by crossfire. Targets exploded, becoming red clouds. Getting shot by a fifty has the effect of...well you'll just be shredded, no exaggerating. A .50 caliber round is like a decent-sized hot dog.

Clouds were moving in from all sides. The morning turned dark. Omar aimed at the giant ball. It was growing bigger and bigger, feeding on itself, but its fleshy parts were being ripped apart in the normal, human way. Much of it was gelatinous.

We were a quarter-mile from Yvonne's vehicle when two more trucks broadsided us, trying to run us off the road. We got some help from German helicopters. They fired rockets at the trucks. One of the trucks was hauling a trailer, which somersaulted over the front of the truck. I swerved to avoid crashing into the wreckage. I had no illusions about making it out alive. I was just living second to second.

The smoke and dust was intense. Despite all the shape-shifting, I tried to keep my cool. "I can't see anything," I said. But I had seen a lot at other times. "Digger, see if there's anything helpful here." I pulled Bandit out of my pack. I remembered drawing some topographical features in this area of the country.

"This area should stay pretty flat until you get to the river," said Digger.

"But it isn't," I said. "We're going to hit a wall of earth if we're not careful. Look closely."

Digger held Bandit closer to his face. "It looks like you drew a canyon," he said.

"We are close to the river," said Kochi.

Omar and Hammer were still back there blasting away.

Haines knocked on the rear window of the cab. "Drones?"

I said no, but Maddox was nodding yes, and then I said yes. I decided it all was part of a well-orchestrated Druj scheme to isolate our little band. I slowed down to give Haines a chance to work. I put my hand up. I didn't want him to release Tink and Blink just yet.

I turned onto another road, serpentine and narrow. It rose into hills then dipped down. It looked like we were back at Provo, but instead of mountains at the far edge, there was a dark wall as big as the cliffs of Dover. I felt like we were back at Provo, doomed to forever live in a terrible loop. The area was shrouded in snow, untouched, didn't look like forces had trampled through anywhere. We got out of the truck. All I could hear was the hissing of the Panj River, down the road, not in view, but I knew we were very close. It was a white and gray and brown world. It looked like an old quarry, with giant boulders, and my mind went to caves, and back to Provo. *LM, Stop this teasing. Am I the one crafting this world? I know I'm not supposed to fully understand the Fourth Wall, but am I crafting it to be a trap? Not for Ajmal and Omar, please. They are innocents. I just want to present the Fourth Wall to the world, that's it. And Ajmal, no one knows his secret nightmares, but he doesn't deserve to die as a player in my fantasy. He deserves the chance, at least the chance, to build a world out of his own fantasies. He deserves to weave time and space on his own terms, like me.*

I wondered what could be inside those walls: gnomes? My mind went there, thanks to a gnomes pop-up book from my childhood. Reader, don't think of this comment about my pop-up book as an odd outlier comparison, for the Fourth Wall is very much a pop-up world, a world built upon those underground gnome worlds I entered when I was just a little guy, amazed and astounded and unsettled in unusual ways, then and for the rest of my life. Have you ever closed your eyes and imagined a galaxy eating another galaxy? You should. It's happening.

If Yvonne was with me at that moment, she would have warned me that I was more likely to sabotage myself than an outside force. I could hear her saying that, and in her absence I found love. I loved her ghost. *Like I love your ghost, LM...*

I saw the landscape with my new vision, its once hidden dynamics. Where there were once large boulders, there were now huge piles of dust and debris. Druidic circles of smaller stones surrounded the debris piles.

Ajmal and Kochi were babbling. Kochi translated: "He wants to know if humans are doing all this. He wants to know what is real and not real."

"It cannot be real," said Omar. "That would be silly. It is jinn."

Haines rolled his eyes.

"Yes, jinn," said Kochi, then explained all this matter-of-fact to Ajmal, who said, "Oh, shit!"

Helicopters were circling our location, keeping their distance. I turned to my new German brother in arms. "Do they see all of us, Hammer? Or just you?"

Hammer wiggled his little box, big as a micro-mini-2006 cell phone. "If they come now, the game will be over. I know you do not want that."

"I think it's time," said Maddox. Poor, old, Maddox. But he was right.

The helicopters shifted course and strafed targets over the hill, unleashing hellfire I didn't want coming my way. I saw smoke to the left. It was coming from inside the rock face.

"Yvonne's inside the cliffs," said Digger. "We've got to move that way or those things will cut us to pieces."

"They're not trying to kill us," I said.

"That's what I'm afraid of," said Digger. "Did you notice that creature was half flesh?"

Fire was coming from the top of the cliffs. "Get to the walls," said Haines. "We're fish in a barrel."

We rushed from the cover of the truck. The cliff bulged in places. The fighters above wouldn't have a clear line of sight in places if we were directly beneath. We hugged the wall and moved left. Rounds splashed at our feet. I felt for the horseshoe crab blood, or what was left of it. I paused the game and went through my whole inventory: M9, M4, ammo for both weapons, water pack, first aid kit, etc.

Dirt fell onto my head. They were straight above us. A rock hit Kochi in the head. Blood streamed down his face. We moved faster, into the open a bit. Ajmal, his aim improving exponentially, fell to the ground onto his back and shot up at the top of the cliff and a Druj fighter fell nearly on top of him. He had to shift his body to get out of the way. The Druj fighter was light-skinned, with blond hair and aquamarine eyes.

The wind changed direction. The sky exploded with thunderbolts and it began to rain. I grew up in South Texas, and I've never seen a storm form up within seconds like that. The horizon was purple. More clouds were rolling in.

"Over there," said Kochi. "Look!" There was a crack in the wall. Maddox and Hammer provided covering fire while the rest of us rushed for the crack, thirty feet away. I provided fire for Maddox and Hammer. Maddox was screaming, but it was more like hysterical laughter. All the action felt different without Ellington. He would've just punched through that wall. Oh shit, I thought. We left him in the truck. He'd have some fun, get ugly, then do it all over again. That's what he would've done.

All the noise did not follow us inside. My eyes adjusted to the dim light, most of it coming from the place we entered, but some more was coming from a place ahead. It was a little more illuminated here than in the last underground facility thanks to refractions of hazy storm-fueled light outside and residual electricity from lightning.

"Oh, shit," said Omar.

There was Ajmal, all bloodied again, with bits of Druj flesh rolling off his body. He was propping up a Druj fighter, the back of the fighter leaning against his leg. The man's neck was bloody. Ajmal had sliced him nearly ear to ear with his knife. The man was still twitching, so I gave him the butt end of my M4. Omar smeared more blood onto Ajmal's face and patted him on the back. Omar searched his clothing and found more of the pink stuff. Ajmal, in a frenzy, grabbed the bag from Omar's hand and poked it with his knife, and sucked the glowing pink liquid like an ancient Mayan warrior eating coca leaves before a battle.[8]

LM, these musings help me cope...dreaming of a route out of here, the dream being the key to see through entropy, when will you respond? Wait, I still have that magician card. God only knows the full spectrum...On the one hand, this is a game, but on another, it's a game that is creating me, its creator, as the game goes along. Want to join me? Isn't chaos the natural state of the world? Get away from the peace and quiet. You want to...I hear your whispers...

New stew of Druj madness: led by Ajmal the Terrible, bloody boy. I could feel the darkness encroaching. There was no sign of where Yvonne and her family might be, so I decided to let the chaos rise around me, and she would rise above it. She would ooze up through the cracks, in some form, then turn into something else, and in a moment of passion I'd let her in. When Ajmal offered me a taste of pink stuff, I didn't refuse. I could feel vibrations all around me, great and small, in the air and in the ground beneath my feet, the living universe revealing the secrets of creation. I became aware of higher dimensions, not something I could see. Nature is full of infinite causes, said Leonardo da Vinci. I could see them all. The Fourth Wall had already presented to me many mini-epiphanies up to that point. The pink stuff was life changing. It was just a deep intuition, not like the Nazis, all high on Pervitin all the time.

Hammer and Maddox looked normal. Both were big men to begin with. It wasn't just neurochemicals messing with the

---

[8] Excerpt from statement of Ajmal in report on Operation Horseflesh, translated from Pashto: "Captain Jett and Sergeant Digger grew as big as the monsters that came to my village. I looked down and saw that I was big, as big as the others, and Omar was growing, except he was growing fatter, also. I did not feel out of control, though. Instead, I felt that I could burst through the rock cage of that day." Reader, if you think this stuff was ketamine, think again, though I met a British soldier who took K during a battle and told me about his wild trip.

flesh and blood around me. Emotions were coming into play. Fear was making a big run for my brain. Yet it was all circular: the strong belief in these creatures as children of entropy/the fog of war, the belief that I could somehow control the fog of war with the Fourth Wall, was causing this release of chemicals, similar to a placebo effect, shows that I had deep faith in my system and Digger in his own. His system was interacting with mine. When would our systems collide? *LM, I can see it: GOD IS A SPIRAL. And God is beginning to creep all around...*

A sudden blast of cold air nearly knocked me down. There was a fissure in a wall ahead. I could feel Yvonne's presence nearby, then I heard her. She was singing that creepy Russian lullaby again: Tili Tili Bom. Something was in that song...a hidden clue to her secret nature, her torments.

I ran forward. Ajmal was close behind, the brave, bloody boy. Kochi was screaming in Pashto. Poor Kochi, no longer. Like me, he was king of his own little messed up world. Hammer and Haines joined in the screaming, and the dark symphony was reaching a crescendo. Haines got Tink and Blink involved, but they weren't as fast and motivated as me to see what was ahead. The wall ahead was shimmering. It appeared real, but the split rock surface was oily. I touched it and my hand slipped through. The air on the other side was cooler. Ajmal plowed through the gap. I went in after him. Ajmal was falling forward. I grabbed the back of his pants, pulling them halfway down his ass. His ass was the only part of his body not stained with someone else's blood. He turned and grabbed me around the neck. He felt like family at that moment. He looked into my eyes with such intensity. His nose was bleeding. I don't know how that happened. We were on a small ledge. Another second and Ajmal's momentum would've carried him into the gaping, dark chasm before us. Our combined screams echoed throughout the space, bouncing back at us from the far side, where Yvonne was standing with her father and brother. Smoke was swirling around them. Yvonne raised her arms, but not to welcome us to her nightmare.

LM: *Explain your brain to me one day. How are you projecting your haunted life into my girl, Yvonne? I want to get you girls together one day and observe the sinister interplay between you. I can see you, wreathed in smoke next to her in this hall of mirrors. Though I think you're more alike than different, even mirroring each other in some ways, right down to your speech patterns, even though you're from Georgia and she's Russian...*

Yvonne was growing in size, like Digger and me. The air all around her was bubbling. Tink and Blink found their way into the chamber, but they were soon swallowed by dark swarms of something. Druj bug drones? Yvonne waved her arms and continued singing the lullaby. She seemed to manipulate the swarm. What else would her ancient craft allow? The boy, Anton, was singing Tili Tili Bom again, along with her. The proud father, Nikolay, was standing behind them in silence. He was a thin, pale figure, so pale the dim light of the space reflected from his cheeks and his balding head.

Hammer was right behind me. He broke the moment in an unexpected way. "Show us our fallen man!" he yelled. The boy reached for something in a shadow and brought out a bundle and unwrapped the bundle and raised above his head Ellington's severed head.

"Do not believe what you are seeing," said Kochi, right behind Hammer, startling us both. "These are jinn, and they are playing tricks."

The whole creepy idea put me off balance. I almost fell into the void and this time it was Ajmal who grabbed me. My head started pounding. My old war wound found its way into this stew. Maddox patted me on the shoulder. I didn't even see him. "Are you here? Wake up, Captain Jett." His voice sounded far away. Yvonne's voice sounded closer than his. My comrades were yelling. They were all on the ledge, now. Their voices dissolved into the noises rising from the deep.

Nikolay came to his daughter's side and clapped. "Great things were happening between you and my daughter, Captain Jett," he said. "Look at her. Isn't she beautiful?"

Maddox spoke up. "I feel like I know you, Nikolay. Or is it...Leopard?"

"An inaccurate *nom de guerre*, because a leopard stalks more carefully than me, but this is out of my control. My business requires greater boldness."

"He is jinn," whispered Omar in my ear. "He will do anything to control you."

Ajmal yelled something in Pashto at Anton. Anton responded in Russian. Each boy had a snotty nose on a steely-gray face.

The wall to the left illuminated in green and blue. The wall to the right responded, like a mirror image. Or the images were feeding off each other. This was what was happening between Digger and me, and between Yvonne and her family, and I could've just laid down and watched all the madness, but I had a part to play in it.

"We do not wish to hurt any of you, or your forces outside these walls," said Nikolay.

"Your little warlock has got the head of my friend in his hands," I responded.

"You will see your friend again soon," said Nikolay, "but this kind of thing takes work, and I cannot do the work without my daughter."

"Lies," I said. "You've been doing just fine without her. Yvonne, don't you see what's happening?"

"I do," she said. "Do you?"

"I see a great magician," I said, "fooling us all."

"Do you mean me or her?" said Nikolay.

I raised my weapon.

"Careful, Captain," said Maddox.

I didn't want to hurt Yvonne, but we were at an impasse.

This time it was Yvonne who shaped the space around us. My weapon started heating up. The metal was so hot I had to drop it. The sling kept the weapon from falling into the chasm, but I could feel the burning metal when the rifle brushed against my hip.

"It's all in your head, kid," said Maddox. It was half true. The brain processes information differently beyond The Fourth Wall. Maddox raised his weapon. Just as he pulled the trigger, he fell forward into the great hole. A burst of rounds shot straight up as he fell onto a narrow bridge I didn't see before.

"Maddox!" I looked for a way down to help him. Maddox was moving, struggling to hold onto the bridge. I grabbed the ledge and tried to lower myself. I slipped and landed wrong and slammed into a hard surface. A sharp pain was in my temple, a burning in the back of my head. I could even feel it in my nose. I started seeing things I know weren't there: my life force projected as several angels flying around us. Like a dream, I just knew it was my life force. I reached out for Maddox and shook his leg. "Are you ok, Sir?"

He moaned in response. When I shook his leg again, he rose up on an elbow.

"This can't be happening," he said, out of breath.

I peered into the gloom. There was a latticework of crystal beneath us. Nothing looked manmade. Smoke was swirling around the crystal. Above us, on the opposite ledge, I saw Anton looking down at us. He reached down, but not with an open hand. He was pointing at something.

"Make it stop, Captain Jett," said Maddox. He was pointing, too, at the creature writhing in the shadows far below, similar to the mysterious form we saw above ground earlier, but this one looked hungrier. It circled below like a shark. Like a shark, it had a beaklike face. It moved through the fingery crystal forest.

Maddox and I both tried to stand. We teetered over an abyss so deep and dark that I thought it had to be an illusion. The shadows cast on the walls were from impossible beings, coming up from below us, like flying skeletons. The whole scene gave a sense of vertigo. Some might say this was all id-based stuff in my head, difficult to tell what was real versus what was created in my mind and projected, but these intimate shadows of my thoughts were overlapping with my developing magical awareness, and experiencing war was sweeter.

Maddox fired his rifle, set to full-automatic, spraying the alien arms, the snapping claws. I joined him. *LM, when I get home, I'm going to look for your neon witch doctor sign.*

Blasts of our weapons created a disco-ball effect. Our comrades on the ledge were firing their weapons, too, and on the opposite ledge, Nikolay sprayed the creatures with his weapon, not an AK-47 like the other Druj fighters, but some kind of laser weapon which shot orange streaks of light.

The creatures below, about five of them now, hard to tell how many were in the furious swarm, were rising higher and higher. The situation kept evolving in unexpected ways. Each second there was a new shadowy villain to deal with. Nothing was black and white. Everything was running counter to established ways of thinking about what you normally find on a battlefield. Digger was yelling at the opposition. He wasn't just all talk, some feral hog with magical powers. He used those powers, and stuff exploded. Even Haines was getting into it. Not like Digger. He had his drones, his little menacing dolls.

"If you are going to kill us, then do it!" Hammer yelled at Nikolay. "Send your demons after us now!"

Nikolay fired more orange bursts at the creatures. They

loitered, in the drone-speak.[9] "They are ready for you, Captain Jett!" said Nikolay. He was urging me but leering at me. His English was flawless. "Let my son and daughter help you."

Yvonne didn't say anything, but I could hear her voice in my mind. *Life is muddy, not black and white, and just as you figure out one puzzle, new puzzles present themselves, as in warfare. It is space itself that is out of whack. I embrace what is elusive. The Fourth Wall helps you see what is hidden, without having to dig it all up.*

Then Digger piped in, completing the triangle of energy, just enough to make something big happen. "They are Charges," said Digger. "Charges were wards of a shadow world gone crazy. Our fears are projected in them. They are manifestations."

Just as God was talking to me through Yvonne (via LM...prior to that via the doomed corps of KAF chaplains, the ninja magazines, the stories/circumstances of others. I mean, God can warp space, shape matter-energy to shape space-time), God then spoke to me through Anton: "If you have the power to create it in your mind, then you have the power to destroy it."

This was kind of preaching the gospel to a world gone wild. For extra measure, Popeye the Sailor Man style, I finished off the horseshoe crab blood. The effect was different than before, probably because of the pink stuff coursing through my veins. I saw Legion/Leviathan. It reared its ugly head, dark dreams of deep sleep...the ugly head. How well can you really control your fear? It is built in. But I was more at ease with...the ebb and flow of my fear. Its defining features,

---

[9] The drones, by the way, were loitering above all this and captured some interesting footage, conflicting images that the Army couldn't figure out, so I turned some of the images into abstract art pieces, in consultation with Haines and the U.S. Air Force, of course, some of which now hang in the homes of some Hollywood stars I won't identify.

inflection points, the vectors of those points, well-established regularities, though imaginary. It was Fourth Wall clairvoyance, ultimately, something more than I'll ever understand. Not a gift, I assure you, reader. At least, not a gift among all the beautiful gifts of God to normal folks. It's a ruinous thing. But if this is what the universe wants of me, then how can I refuse?

Maddox and I were teetering over the abyss. We were grabbing onto each other while trying to kill the spectral whale. The moment seemed to last forever. I could've whistled a whole song in that long moment. I lost my balance. My foot slipped off the bridge onto a crystalline surface a foot below the bridge. I was able to hold onto the bridge. The surface beneath my feet shattered. The shards fell onto the face of the beast rising from the shifting geometries below, and further below that was a boiling surface, black and brown, orange here and there, and here and there a burst of wind from within the earth. Nikolay's weapon was leaving behind a shiny, viscous plasma.

Yvonne was up to something. While Maddox and I were ducking a great swinging spectral arm, Yvonne was waving her arms, as if she was trying to keep the beasts at bay. Then it was my turn. I concentrated on the air around them and around the crystals. I imagined it was syrupy, that it could be pulled apart by a puppet master from afar. This was how God worked, right? Even if such a thought is preposterous, it was a big step into a new world for me. It was working. At the moment I thought of peanut butter...what it must look like inside the mouth.

At the height of this encounter, I was filled with guilt over things I'd done and things I'd left undone, the way the prayer goes, plus for things I did and didn't know. Some things were almost on the table, and I wanted them all the way on the table.

"I had nothing to do with Sugarbush," I said to nobody in

particular. "Or Provo."

Maddox tried to grab my arm, but I didn't let him. I couldn't even look him in the eyes.

"You experimented," said Nikolay. "You opened your mind and invited a different power to take hold. I am thankful. You returned my daughter to me."

"That was a chance encounter," I said. Not the whole story, I knew that.

"Such is life," countered Nikolay. "Life begets life...and look at all the other lives you've touched. Wherever you go, you bring chaos. You bring life."

Then that's the essence of this, LM. It is the struggle, simply that. Oh, the contradictions. After all the struggling to understand, the digging for knowledge and grasping and holding on, at the end is a fistful of sand that drains through your fingers. It is fine, this sand, very elusive and pure as new snow, out of our control, and if you didn't give me the ability to control, you gave me sight. Is this why you torment me? Because you have much more to show me?

Yvonne wasn't steady. She looked seasick. Maddox was screaming at her to stop all this. My comrades behind me on the ledge were screaming at the beasts below, shooting in a wide circle, escaping into the fantasy by trying to tear it apart. Despite that our bullets ripped the beasts apart, sending flesh and blood against the mirrored crystals, the beasts reached for us, their mouths gaping, wider and wider, releasing a wind that had to be from a place deeper, outside of them, within the earth. My psychic powers weren't as developed at that time, but there was oblivion in their monster minds. The way they moved was odd. I think they were half-blind.

The bridge started shaking. On the ledge above, all my comrades were having trouble standing. Digger and Kochi both jumped onto the bridge. Kochi grabbed onto me. Digger was holding onto him. For my part, all my ninja self-education helped. I took up a defensive stance. Even with all the interference beneath our position, the ectoplasmic fingers reaching upward and all the weight leaning on me, pulling me forward and backward, and gravity working against me, I found a nice, low center of gravity. It's all about energy distribution, seeing vectors in the space in front of you, setting up the world around you as a simple motion diagram. Then you can be that mad-hungry ninja you've always craved to be.

Maddox turned his weapon on Yvonne.

"Please, Sir," I said, pushing down the barrel of his rifle, not that he would've been able to get off a clean shot, with all the shaking. Poor Yvonne, I mean I was glad to see her reconnect with family, but I didn't want to see her magical face obliterated; it's called *abductio ad absurdum*, Latin for "reduction to absurdity."

Kochi slipped and fell. Half his body was dangling over the edge of the slab into the creature's big yawning mouth.

Nikolay was smiling. "You can win back my daughter, Captain Jett," said Nikolay. "Ask your friend."

"Who are you?" I asked Nikolay. "And who are *you*?" I asked Digger. I locked eyes with him. The space between us got bigger. I tried to shape the air again. Nikolay was looking down at me with a blank/dead expression.

The earth shook. I had forgotten about the battle happening outside between the German Army and Druj forces. Something crashed against the wall. Pieces of the wall fell to the floor and onto the bridge from above us. It was concrete. We were in a huge bunker, not very well built, hastily built. All for what?

Daylight broke through the falling wall. This was going to be our way out. Anton reached toward us, offering his hand. He was such a small boy. I didn't want to pull him into the abyss. Before I could decide what to do, Ajmal beat me across the bridge, his skinny muscles were gleaming with blood and sweat. He was luminescent, glowing.[10]

Ajmal grabbed Anton and pulled him down. Anton fell onto Ajmal. They rolled around on the bridge. Ajmal mounted Anton and punched his face over and over. Tink and Blink got close. Their video footage revealed how intent on revenge Ajmal was and helped clear him of any charges of collusion with the enemy. I knew he had a vendetta all along. Ajmal was a strong kid. I felt like he could write his own ticket anywhere he wanted to go. I was still questioning whether Druj was friend or foe. After all, I was keeping a beast as big as a ballroom at bay with powers of clairvoyance and telekinesis long-simmering, used here and there over the years, but achieving fruition in a warzone, *in part thanks to you, LM, my Georgian witch. Keep your faith in me alive.* But I couldn't keep fighting this thing forever. There were too many distractions. My Russian girlfriend and her father had turned out to be...a one-two punch. But you know what? I looked at all the people living parallel lives around me, put them all into the context of my own, put them within the context of my whole study of entropy itself, a big reason I was in Afghanistan, the main reason, actually, and I wasn't completely upset. I wanted to see how far all this could go, and I was willing to let Yvonne go as an experiment, just to see what would happen, just to let serendipity continue to rule my life. It wasn't a dream. It was a necessity. Miracles were emerging, and I needed that in my life. There's time for redemption, and saving those you love, and I wasn't sure this was the time.

I watched the boys fighting. Anton was as bloody as Ajmal. Still buzzing with crab blood, Yvonne and her father looked like angels to me. Her little brother looked like a little devil,

---

[10] Excerpt from statement of Ajmal in report on Operation Horseflesh: "Since I was a child, I could shine a light in dark places, just by thinking about it...the light, but also the dark, because there is no light without dark. When Druj found me..."

but that didn't make me want to kick him over the ledge into the mouth of the Fleshux, my new name for the monster. It was just one of those odd, random thoughts that come to you during a battle. FLESHux. You'll think the strangest things. You'll remember stuff from years ago when you were a kid. I could've just as easily given the creature a name that better reflected its rank smell, the miasma drifting up from it. The thing was huge, but the name I gave it implied that it would shrink down and slowly eat its way into your brain.

My eyes came to. Yvonne and Nikolay were gone. Shadows were collapsing in the gloom, pulling a disappearing/invisibility trick, the kind of thing that gave such an air of mystery to the Sugarbush massacre, with nothing to track. Anton was now Ajmal's prisoner, both boys demoniacal and covered in blood, little piss-ants full of blood lust. That's the way Nikolay wanted it, a nice trade, Yvonne for Anton. It was still their game, too.

"Kochi!" I had to reach back and touch him to make sure he was real. "Grab the boys. We're getting out of here." Omar helped Kochi. Haines was in charge of the drones, and I had to believe they were the main chroniclers of all this activity...go for it, sonar scanners. And Hammer, well Hammer was chanting incantations.

Digger, with something to prove, lunged ahead, short sword in hand, ready to track down Yvonne and Nikolay, or their ghosts. But the Fleshux wasn't done. It brushed the underside of the bridge as we scurried across. Digger, Omar, Kochi, Ajmal, and Anton were able to climb up to the other side, but the arms of the beast blocked the rest of us. The beast's tentacles flared, teased before us. I employed a modified *Oni Kudaki* ("demon crusher"). I squeezed a tentacle then shot at the base of the tentacle. Digger jumped back onto the bridge to help us out. He chopped up the fleshy parts of the beast with his sword.

Maddox was in a state of disbelief. In a way, I was glad this was happening, glad to have the opportunity to redeem myself. He must've thought I was a complete nutcase. Once we found Digger, though, I knew it was only a matter of us putting our heads together to come up with some freaky solutions to freaky forces, except it was in Druj's kitbag all along to lure people like us, not just Yvonne. And it didn't hurt that Digger and I were in the Army. For Druj, it was a make-your-enemy-your-friend kind of thing.

The energy current of my martial arts moves was no longer invisible. I emanated a light of my own, great ribbons of it. *LM, this feels like a gift. I know it can't be you alone, or Yvonne alone, maybe it's the two of you together pulling this off somehow, affecting the world around you the way Digger and I affect it, with your collective willpower. I am your faithful guinea pig.*

While Digger and I were finishing off the Fleshux, Ajmal was on the other side of the room, hopping up and down like he was about to piss his pants. He was perched on a rock, looking out a crack in the wall, narrow as an arrow slit in a medieval castle. He waved at us to come. Tentacles were swinging wildly around us. Digger wasn't exactly a champion with his sword, but he was holding his own. In the end, it was Anton who saved us. I guess without his dad and sister he felt abandoned and didn't like his chances of survival. He stood on the ledge and manipulated the air so that mirrored flat-square surfaces appeared. It created a collage effect. He looked like he'd done this before. The arms stopped moving, stalled just long enough to allow Digger to chop them to bits, though Digger was thrown off by all the mirror images, and his short sword turned to pixie dust. We were both already covered in gore. Now blue blood started splashing us. I already had a taste for the blue stuff, but this was a new type from another world. They say the best approach is to fully immerse yourself in the system you are trying to master. I had to pick and choose. The Fourth Wall was presenting lots of paths to me at that moment.

The rest of us climbed from the bridge to the ledge. The remains of the Fleshux fell into the deep, dark pit. Its blue blood tasted funny. I wiped my mouth on my sleeve. I smiled. Anton smiled back. He was a different little man without his master, his father, pulling his strings, the man in the box, the Wizard of Oz. I looked at Anton and saw Yvonne's ghost. I reached for her, reached right through her, and patted the boy's cheek. His expressions were the same as Yvonne's. I said a quick prayer for him and her. Here I was questioning someone's mortal self, but Yvonne questioned nothing. She still had me. She proved us all wrong, especially Maddox and Ellington, God rest his soul.

Speaking of Ellington, I asked the boy, "Where is our head?" I really did say *our* head.

"What do we do with him?" said Maddox.

"He's in the truck, Sir," I said. "We'll get his head and go from there."

Haines chimed in. "I think I saw..."

"I don't mean Ellington," said Maddox. "I mean the boy."

Ajmal wasn't done with Anton. He took another swing at Anton, pushing him against me. They brawled. Omar and Kochi pulled them apart.

"Brothers fight," said Kochi.

"Brothers?" I said.

"That is what Ajmal said," said Kochi. "He called this boy his brother."

Omar went back to the crack in the wall. "I see them!"

Anton bolted for the corner. We followed. There were stairs leading to a door. I opened the door. The sunlight was blinding. It was cold. The cold hit me again, reminding me of the very real world. My stomach ached. It was the blue stuff upon blue stuff upon pink stuff. Now I longed for the release of it all, and the light was a sign of a new day, and my head was banging, the discotheque effect, again. I hadn't yet found a way to control the light of the world, upon me in a night that was going on forever. *But that's ok, LM. I now have a good reason to learn multiple systems. The Fourth Wall isn't the only game in town. Who's to say God got it right the first time? Like in Time Bandits...the whole purpose of the map was to go through time to fix all God's mistakes. All I know is the Russian man has my Russian girl. I came to Afghanistan as the receptive, reticent hero, and this is what I got. A trade might be the best thing to do...Anton for Yvonne. If these are higher-dimensional beings, they clearly aren't all that comfortable in this dimension. I have my honor. I've never known this kind of feeling. I'm going after her, coming after you, too.*

The door opened onto a small platform on the side of a steep slope. Metal stairs snaked down the side of the red, cracked hillside to the Panj River. A gust of wind swept across the broad plain of Tajikistan across the river and shook the platform. The geology was wrong/awkward. Chalk it up (again) to Bandit, my wanderings and doodling and my need to be a merciless destroyer of interdimensional beings, my new goal in life.

There was barely enough room for us on the platform. Ajmal teetered and almost fell. I grabbed the back of his pants to keep him upright, exposing his bottom, once again. Haines and Omar were in the same predicament, holding onto each other, both of them responding to each other's giant, startled look. Omar's brown face turned red. Tink and Blink were hovering above Haines' head. I pointed at them to remind Haines where they were. It was at times like this when I missed Ellington. He would've said we were fucking fucked.

"Where's the kid?" said Maddox.

I knew he was talking about Anton since Anton was more of a kid than Ajmal. Anton was halfway down the stairs, the excited little man. God only knows what his plan was since Yvonne and Nikolay were nowhere in sight. When I made character sheets for all of us as Operation Horseflesh got going, I left some empty boxes at the end of the sheets for unexpected powers. I created a few extra boxes on my own sheet because I was confident in my own potential. Now I was staring out onto a vast plain in Tajikistan, a country where I wasn't allowed to go, but my future was across the river. I could still feel the rush of adrenalin, but I knew that Horseflesh was about to end, and the adventure would continue in some other way without me. Like at the end of Time Bandits, when all the robbers left the boy behind to fight evil on his own, and then the boy woke up, as if from a dream.

But we weren't done yet. If it wasn't for the strange sphere, hovering over the plain to the right, almost out of sight behind a hill where the river curved...I mean it reminded me that I was between worlds. There were explosions northeast of our position. I could just see the sphere's surface, an orange light that moved more like amniotic fluid and suspended within were massive chunks. Death was palpable. The sphere was still within the Afghanistan border, but mostly out of sight due to the curvature of the hills. It was coming from Shir Khan Bandar, where there was a bridge crossing the Panj River.

"Captain Jett," said Maddox. "I want to know if you planned all this." He was serious. He sounded desperate. If Maddox was desperate, it was stemming from his belief that I was desperately detached from real war.

My response was serious. "Yes, Sir. All of it." A serious, but dreamy, response. Except I wish I wasn't so honest. My response went into the 15-6 investigation later. Going back to the invisibility conversation, I suppose Yvonne and Nikolay might have evaporated into thin air. That's what seemed to happen inside the hill and Port Delta earlier, but the effect was a positive one. It made me think that anything was possible, that I could fill in those boxes on my character sheet as I pleased, and as a Fourth Wall game master, I could do the same for my comrades and enemies alike. Was this not what Druj wanted of me?

My team started down the stairs without me, as there was no going back inside the hill, even with a battle raging around the corner. All the elements were within my sensory range: fire in the sky, water below, earth at my feet, wind in my face, all of it churning, and I could see everything. It was the psycho-sexual energy within me, the push and pull of subconscious and conscious elements. It was something I learned from Yvonne. She taught me that people have to have answers to their puzzles. For instance, the air was like oily water, but I couldn't pull it all together, at least not with the speed required at that moment, and that's when I saw Yvonne's face. She, herself, was a puzzle without an answer.

There were three small boats in the river. Upstream, on the shore, a man was watching his goats. Another man was with him, washing something in the river. They were bundled up. The men saw us but turned to watch the sphere. It was growing, becoming chimerical. There were faces in the sphere. They were spitting and hissing at each other, as much as at us. It was a real paradox, or like a hydra, if you need more of a mythological comparison. Later reports/intelligence products referred to it as a Fleshux, though I didn't at first. It was more of a cousin. However, to make monster hunting in the Army simpler, I eventually called it a Fleshux.

A helicopter appeared. It was a German NH90, with two .50 cal Gatling mini-guns in the side doors. The helicopter circled the sphere then came in for a gun run. As for the fleshy parts of the sphere, it was effective. The attack shredded the skin and blue guts, shiny like the guts of an adolescent pig. The forms within its forms became more defined at the moment before annihilation. The beast moved backward, away from the helicopter, deeper within the border of Tajikistan. Both the goatherds prostrated themselves before it. I was both sickened and amused by all this, since Digger and I were to blame, at least in part. It was like a dance, something you'd see in a comic book, but I remember thinking of the Danse Macabre slideshow we watched in elementary school music class each year at Halloween. Ghosts flew through the air and danced among the graves and none was too scary, except I remember a picture of one lonely ghost, a close-up of a ghost and that scared me a little.

Kochi came back up the stairs after me. "Do not let her seduce you, Sir," he said. Everyone else was waiting for me down by the river. I'd spaced out a bit. They took cover behind a ruined platform, as the helicopter's fire strayed our way.

At that moment, I had an out-of-body experience, the way I did at Provo. Provo seemed like ages ago, and though we had seen so much since then, my answered questions only led to more questions. I could see a dust cloud rising in the desert. I could see the world from the vantage of...hyperspace. I don't know how else to describe it. I was zipping around, stretched. I was a force of nature, a tool. I looked back and saw, far, far away, my form standing on the stairs and the rest of my team below. The beast was vaporizing, piecemeal, becoming what it was meant to be: a smokescreen. A tool! Like me. Yvonne and her father were in a car, moving deeper into Tajikistan. *LM, I can see you. Is that you? Are you there? Have you ever been? Or just half-in-half-out, like my love for Yvonne, like all the other creatures and clairvoyant visions and astral nuisances. I mean, it's always been my fantasy to...*I could feel my feet leave the ground. I flew back closer to myself. Just for a moment, I was physically suspended several feet above the ground. Kochi and Omar were pointing at me.

An explosion sucked me back into my body. The helicopter crashed into the river. Druj had Stinger missiles, but it wasn't that. (Apparently, during the time the CIA was buying them up from the Taliban, Druj was also collecting.) The sky was significantly darker. It was the beast. It sucked in all surrounding light, in its death throes, the way a school of fish does in a large net, when the water is so bloody from spearing, hacking, but also milky with sperm, the last gasp for life, but it wasn't just the beast, it was me. I was full of light. It burst from my body, from my fingers, my eyes. I knew at that moment how Yvonne must've felt when she was grabbed from this world by her father. She could never go back. She could only go forward. It wasn't just a bold act of imagination. It was empowerment from an outer realm.

Hammer and Kochi and Maddox jumped into the river to save the crew of the helicopter. That was my opportunity. I had to confront Yvonne alone. I had to see her in this new way, to understand why she made this choice, and it *was* a choice. She had broken away from her family before, but she was now going back.

I ran down the stairs to the shore. I jumped over huge hunks of flesh that had fallen from the monster and landed on the shore. I bumped against some monster flesh and my lower half was blood-covered. I was getting up there on the blood-smears, but not anywhere near Ajmal. He was the champion that day. He had his so called "brother," Anton, in a headlock. Other earthen mounds were along the shore. I wanted to dig. I was probably the only one that noticed they were manmade, and I speculated about their origins, even in the heat of battle. The only other one I noticed noticing me was the goatherd. Everyone else was busy. The boys were hacking away with knives at a fleshy tendril, shot off the beast but still wiggling on the ground. Haines was chasing something. I figured the drones were darting like fireflies, just out of his reach. Hammer and Maddox were tending to the crew of the helicopter. The only one I couldn't see anywhere was Digger. Was he invisible? I left my pack on the shore. I made sure Bandit was tucked away, but not the magician card. That stayed in my pocket. I plunged into the Panj River and swam for Tajikistan. The goatherd was watching me swim. I prayed for Yvonne. I prayed I would reach terra incognita intact. I prayed for Anton. I could hear him laughing. My comrades sounded like they were celebrating. When I reached the opposite shore, I pulled myself up on a slab and caught my breath. I could see up the river better, to the northeast. There was a ferry boat docked on the Afghan side of the river. The wind picked up. I had to keep moving so as not to feel the chill, though I felt eyes upon me. I looked back and Digger had spotted me. He didn't wave or anything. He let me go. I had to continue this game on my own.

For hours I walked in a straight line, straight north across a swathe of desert, deeper into Tajikistan, far exceeding the scope of my mission and orders, especially now that I was an invading force of one. I bypassed the border town of Panj-e Payon, to the left, and kept going across the arid plain, feeling and looking severe, like an old west outlaw, minus the horse. I thought I saw a couple of riders, two twisted, dark human/animal forms with agonized faces, but it was probably just a cold winter mirage effect.

Ghosts haunted these plains, just as my home. I'm sure Eve and the rest (there were twenty-eight others, according to Eve) were having a ball in my absence, and for the second time that day, I thought of the Danse Macabre Halloween slideshow from my childhood. In a flash, I saw them all. The poltergeists in my Houston house were now shapeless, shifting pockets of desert air, floating in the mist before me, while other entities I'd communicated with over the years, with the help of multiple witches I'd known, were coming toward me out of the purple distant mountains. Each ghost was in hysterics, to some degree. These were not exactly enemies. After all, I lived with the beasties, but I had to keep my distance. If these were human enemies (back to my ninja magazines here) I would create a sense of fear and exploit it with a diversion and combination attack. I would feel and exploit the shifting energies inside my body, nature around me would act in response. I saw the ghost of Ellington, or at least the upper half of his body. The battle where he met his doom flashed in my head. The second or two before he split apart were surreal.

Then his blood and guts spilled out. I tried to mentally construct a way out, or forward.

The sky above was dark, darker still on the horizon. Spheroids of light drifted all around me in the gloom, but I could make out LM. She was like the rest, like a mirage, or a hologram. Being near these forms granted me simple understandings. Reader, I present them to you untainted with reflection/hindsight: Linking up with Druj was the only way to save Yvonne and myself; that's what was going on in my head; and the dead should bury the dead, just like Jesus said. The various forms enlarged, and I could see inside or through them, like windows. I saw a whole new world. I saw at once its inner space and outer space. It was all the same.

I was dead tired, with a heavy feeling, feeling like dead weight, but I held up the magician card and started running toward LM. *I told you I'd give this card back to you, LM. Look at you, lording over me with such a hungry smile.*

It wasn't LM's smile. It was Yvonne's smile. But it was the old Yvonne, or at the least the lady I'd come to know at KAF, with her well-constructed fake persona. Each of us was living so many half-truths, and somehow they all crisscrossed and became truths. It was the entropy of this place. I established my own special cunning dialogue with it, just to survive. It's not that I was afraid, as fear is circumstantial, moment to moment, and in a moment like this, not what you might think. This thing, whatever it was, was just looking at me. I had no idea what it was capable of. I was scared I would enrage the specter. Thunder rolled. Distant lightning illuminated the mountain crags. And in the other direction, I could hear more helicopters going up and down the river. They were searching for me, perhaps? I hoped not. I hoped that they were mopping up Druj stragglers and any other of their kind. It was so far away. God only knows how I could hear it.

Here in Tajikistan, the ghouls were everywhere. I kept my cool, though. Never in my life, before then or since then, have

I been frantic around paranormal entities. Life has tried to beat me down with them, throwing them out at me like a belt-fed machine gun, but I keep cool, always. The entities started encroaching. More were pouncing down at me from interdimensional portals. Shadows closed in, and I was careful not to step on any, not afraid of harming or offending them, but this equilibrium I had achieved was delicate and depended on the ebb and flow of evil in all its forms, all around me, for light cannot exist without darkness, but I danced like a madman on both platforms.

As in the Danse Macabre slide presentation I mentioned earlier (and for the third and final time in this volume, reader), these ghouls danced around me. They were celebrating, a big tangle of them. It was easy to see, and each was a window into its own little world. Then I heard that creepy Russian lullaby again. I took the magician card from my pocket and raised it above my head. It was such a heavy burden. It was moist and its edges were frayed. "Take this from me, Yvonne," I said. "Are you there?"

Yvonne listened. She couldn't be cruel. I didn't want to see her go, but at the same time, I didn't want to see her come back with me and watch me suffer through the rest of my tour while battling her own inner turmoil, now brought to the surface by her own blood, visitors from an illusory past. That's when I realized that my card wasn't hers. I couldn't just give her my pain. I had to vanquish it on my own, on the terms I had established through the Fourth Wall.

I wasn't far from the highway. I could hear passing cars. I could see rising dust a half-mile away. But the area was about to get drenched. A big storm was coming. I wanted it that way. My lips were parched. I was thirsty. After all this action, I was thirsty for more, and I would let the dead bury the dead. *You're right, LM. I took the card from you. I just saw Yvonne in the mist and thought...It's silly, but I thought I saw you for a second. No, stay where you are. Stay there. You're better off...*

I heard an approaching vehicle. I turned. I still couldn't tell. A small, dark shape. My head was pounding, but I was out of horseshoe crab blood. I didn't have Bandit, where my next escape was waiting, lurking in the map's fringes, where I'd drawn all those monstrous forms, lurking hot-button topics. The blast from the past, the not-so-distant Afghanistan War, waiting for me, was hurting my head again. I would just have to deal with it. *It's too soon to say goodbye to the world, LM. I have more to give. This game, this system, whatever it is, is an excavation of sorts. The Fourth Wall...what kind of a name is that? Will I ever escape this fantasy? I will find beautiful things. Truth is beauty, and that is what I'll find. I thought I might run into you out here. My knees are getting weak. As it stands, this is a sad ending.* I was saying goodbye to an old self. The end of one life and the beginning of another. War brought together all my fantasies, their colors like a thermonuclear blast. *With other mysteries ahead...show me the way, LM.*

I examined the card again then put it in my pocket. I looked down at my body. It was emanating light, the same light that defeated the Fleshux.

The dark form was closer. It was a motorcycle. It stopped. It was Digger. "Good to see you, Sir," he said, getting off the bike. "Figured you'd be in hell by now. We've been looking for you. It's going to be dark in a couple of hours. You're going to freeze your balls off out here."

"Why did they send you?"

"It's poetic, don't you think, Sir? Missing sergeant is found, then sets out to find the captain who's also gone missing."

"I'm not lost," I said. "I'm found. Finally found." *And look at all that I've found.* "Look at them," I said. "Aren't they beautiful? They are profoundly beautiful."

Digger looked around. He pulled a bag from his pocket, something he brought with him, not something we found at Port Delta. He took a swig. His throat glowed yellow. "There's nothing there, Sir. Just the desert. It's amazing, though."

I sat on the ground and put my face in my hands.

"It's your head again," said Digger.

"It's just my old self," I said. "I'm saying goodbye to my old self. This is what it feels like."

"Did you get to the end?"

"The end?" I said. "I hope not. I hope this is just the beginning. Besides, I have eight months left in Afghanistan."

"No, Sir," said Digger. "I mean the end of my game, when you had a chance to play it."

"It seemed to have no end, which I liked."

"You didn't get how all the characters are being watched, all the time?

"That's the gamemaster's function," I said. "I've been trying to serve that role during Operation Horseflesh. Look how everything turned out."

"That's not what I mean," said Digger. "I created an entity in my game that was unnamed. It sometimes took human form. It affected the gameplay for other characters, but they didn't know it was there. It made them see the world as it should be seen."

"If players didn't know it was there, then how would you expect them to defeat it?"

"Because it wasn't an enemy to be defeated," said Digger. "It was simply a force at play."

"If it was doing harm...if it couldn't be defeated..." I was mumbling.

"Being an enemy to be defeated by the characters wasn't its purpose," said Digger. "Dealing with it was just part of the game."

I said nothing.

"It wasn't something natural," said Digger, "in a sense that it was from this world."

"It was living in some kind of parallel world," I said. "Yes, I did experience it." I stood up. "What have you done? What have *we* done? What have we unleashed?"

The forms around us came together. My heart was pounding. Were they the ones that didn't belong here or did I not belong? I searched all the faces but I didn't see Yvonne.

Digger looked around and nodded. Now he saw the things I saw. "We didn't make these beings or these people," said Digger.

"Yeah, but...we have a power," I said. "In each of our encounters at Port Delta, we were feeding off one another. Druj was feeding off of us. This is lunacy."

"I felt the same thing."

I turned to go.

"Where are you going?" said Digger. "Home is this way." He pointed south.

"You and I are kindred spirits." I invited him my way with a little wave of my hand.

"She's this way, Sir," said Digger. He was sure in smile and posture. "I mean the path to find her is south. Let's get back in the fight."

"She doesn't want to be found," I said. "It's just a theory." The other forms had turned into a light fog that started to pull away from our position, but I could see into Digger. He was a window, like the others. This was a sad ending for me. "I just feel that...if she knows someone is out there looking for her, attempting to love her, then that's what we'll keep doing. She'll be the magician, not us. She can help us both. Maybe we'll both find purpose in our lives. Maybe if you help find her you'll be closer to the unknown world you barely touched in your game. You'd have to be a bastard to think she was placed at KAF by Druj to subvert me, somehow."[11]

---

[11]This is where I stopped writing this section for the night. I went to bed and had many strange dreams. I dreamed I was studying a great book of Indian culture, history, and language, and I was sitting next to an Indian man and his young son. "Harami," I said. "Harami," the man repeated.

I found myself between two worlds. Yvonne would want Digger and I to continue experimenting to confirm this higher dimension of our universe we'd unlocked. To do so we'd have to strip it bare and be mad scientists. The Fourth Wall would be my guide, my map. I snapped out of it. "Mars Station," I said. "Do you know where it is?"

When Digger spoke in parables and told stories, it told me he knew everything about everything, but in an intuitive way, like me. He went back to one of his games, played out in real life before he met Hammer. "I had just left FOB Ripley in northeast Kandahar," said Digger. "Instead of a map, like you've been using, I had my character sheet in hand. I figured, go this way or go that way. I couldn't decide, so I let the dice decide. I figured, there was a reason why inspiration found me. It's what led me to Hammer, then to Kunduz, then to you."

"How?"

"Yvonne was a dice roll. Should we take the strange girl alone in the car or not? So we took her. You chased us. Here we are."

LM, Should I summon the wind now in order to blow me away from here? It's going to take mind-bending experiences just to feel normal again.

"You want to borrow these?" Digger had some dice. I didn't want to make it too complicated. I selected a twenty-sided die. I blew on the die. *LM, if you were here you'd perform some spell or conjure a spirit to affect the outcome of the roll. I'll do neither. I'll just ask for your help.*

And help I got. The wind picked up. I rolled the die on the ground. The wind blew sand over the die. It looked like an eight, though it could've been a three, or even a five. The die shook a little. A one appeared. How did I miss that before? So now it looked like an eighteen or fifteen. There was so much

---

This is a Hindi word and means 'bastard', but I had to look that up the next morning. I do not speak a word of Hindi.

sand in my eyes, it was hard to tell. The die was dirty, also.

Either way, the next thing I knew I was on the back of Digger's bike, heading back to the border. Wind in my hair, I could live like this, sucking up a drifter's delight, this is the life, I thought. The effects of the crab blood were wearing off. The wind was clean, and just wind alone, not the fetid breath of a Fleshux or any other trans-world monster. Helicopters were circling the area near the border crossing where the Germans had fought hard against Druj. There was wreckage and carnage from an even bigger encounter between monsters and German forces, great piles of smoldering flesh, and too many dead humans. German soldiers were walking around, scattered, collecting what they could and photographing everything. What was it all for? I felt bad. It was all a result of my quest for unearthly encounters, mystical pleasures. I guess it was bound to happen, eventually.

I spotted Hammer and Maddox talking with another German soldier. Haines spotted us on the bike and held up my bag. I was looking forward to making some much-needed additions to Bandit, a flurry of new sketches and symbols, to make it look more like a descendant of the *mappae mundi*, the glorious and symbolic family of maps popular in the Middle Ages, somewhere between truth and fantasy, like the Fourth Wall. I didn't care if the form was off. Bandit was a powerful meditative tool. Yvonne had to be on the map, somewhere.

Everyone was celebrating, not Ewok Return-of-the-Jedi style, but like Germans, with their more primitive dance moves. The Germans were as bloodied as my Horseflesh mates. Those guys were tired but smiling. Omar was always smiling, anyway. Helicopters were flying in formation. Apaches. So it wasn't just German forces. Americans had joined the party. It was a dream. A magnum opus of a dream. I didn't see any hidden meaning in it. I was all done with that...for the day, at least. The river bluffs were the river bluffs. The sky was the sky, a milky sky that was not of this earth. It was a beautiful sight. Throw yourself into the dark, reader. Graze like an animal. You'll see beautiful things afterward.

And the half-dead were protecting the dead. The half-there prisoners we freed in the belly of Port Delta found their way above ground and came to us, like loyal dogs. They were guarding Ellington's lower half. I mentally started preparing myself for all the questions that were coming about what happened to his other half, and they did come.

DIGNIFIED TRANSFER CEREMONY

January 23, 2012. Back at Kandahar Airfield, I was once again in my multi-cam uniform and glad. It was late at night, and all the Red Hands were gathered for Ellington's dignified transfer ceremony. I didn't get to meet all of them. They were more interested in Haines and his robot bugs than in me. Apparently, news traveled fast about what happened in the shipping container nightclub before we left. (They had no clue at the time of the trans-dimensional battles they were about to get sucked into.) There were bagpipes a-plenty. Other than the music and the wind, it was somber, but you could hear a few jokesters in the group, Ellington's prodigies. We'd arrived at 2200 hours. We took a Black Hawk from Kunduz to Bagram Airbase, and from there took a C-17 to KAF.

I had been to many dignified transfer ceremonies, but this one hit closer to home since I fought side by side with Ellington. It was bitter cold, that night. In a way, I was jealous that Ellington wouldn't have to go on in this world wasting time and pretending. We program ourselves then fill in the blanks with experience, over and over, and that's not just our souls. Our brains are the same: we fill in the blanks with stuff that may or may not be real. Hallucination or not, it doesn't matter. It's all about patterns. The Fourth Wall is something like that. I don't understand everything that it represents or could become. It's the attempt to understand that's important. It's about getting into nature's core.

There was a big crowd that night. Maddox found me. "Digger is in custody," he said.

"And the boys?"

"Anton and Ajmal are being held together."

"I thought Ajmal was going to live with Omar?"

"That's the plan," said Maddox. "Maybe later. There's some kind of connection between him and the Russian kid."

"What about Captain Hammer?"

"He's with his people, not too happy, I'm sure. The DCG has already appointed another Investigating Officer. General Williamson is still on leave. He might not like that move."

"I thought you said you were the IO, Sir."

"Get this," said Maddox. "It's an investigation of my investigation." He was relaxed. Nothing could phase this guy.

I, on the other hand, was seriously considering rediscovering the KAF container nightclub and getting lost in there. "It's time for the microscope on all of us," I said.

"Something like that."

"If I'd never met Yvonne," I said, my voice trailing. "If I hadn't gotten all those ideas...those crazy ideas..." A tear rolled down my cheek for the first time since 1999 when my dog died. I almost cried in 2007 when I saluted the Stars and Stripes for the first time. I just felt a salty queasiness emerge in me.

"If you hadn't met that witch," said Maddox. "If this, if that..."

"You still think I'm crazy, don't you?"

"Fog of war, pup," said Maddox. "That's all it is, but no, you had to invent meanings, purpose."

"There are a hundred billion neurons in the brain," I said. "That's the best you can come up with, Sir? I've developed a system the Army can use. It's..."

"When the general's man comes knocking, that's the story. Fog of War. It's simple as that. It's the real enemy. It always wins. Don't worry, pup, General Williamson likes you, remember? You'll turn out all right."

"I know how the general will want the end of his investigation to look. He'll want it nice and tidy, with lessons learned and recommendations for improvements."

"You have any?"

"The CONOPS I was drafting," I said. "There lies my redemption."

"He may want your map."

"Bandit? He can't have it. I'm not done with it."

"It's government property, government ink, you're here on orders. I'm guessing the Army will win that one."

"I won, Sir," I said. "I already won. He can't have what's in my mind. I'm not done creating it."

"You never will be finished," said Maddox, wise Maddox. He was right on that one, but there were so many other things he didn't understand.

"You know, I'm approaching the truth in stages. It's there. Under the circumstances, I think I've done well."

"That imagination of yours never quits."

"All you have to do is look closely, Sir. It's all there. Detecting all the points, gathering all the wrongs, is easy. It's getting them to add up to a right. That's the challenge. I don't know what the Fourth Wall is. It's so many things."

"General Sanchez wants a briefing tomorrow morning at zero nine hundred hours," said Maddox. "I'll do most of the talking, but there will be blanks you'll have to cover. I can try to postpone."

"No, Sir." I rubbed my temple. "I'll be ready."

Kochi and Haines joined us. Kochi's cheek and chin were bandaged, slashed by the coarse tendril of a Fleshux. His skin was darker, still stained with the blood of the beast. When a

Fleshux sprays it's like an octopus inking. The rest of us suffered other minor bumps and cuts. Ajmal was the bloodiest, but it was the blood of others. Haines was in a darker mood than when I last saw him. His eyes were glassy. Turns out, from what he later explained, he had already been meditating on the science behind the Fourth Wall, quantum physics, and such.

"I love chaos," I said. "Don't you, Haines?"

"I want to live a simpler life," said Haines. His dreams never came true.

Then there was Ellington. The bagpipes called. A group of soldiers formed up into two columns and marched out to a waiting plane. Sadly, Ellington wasn't the only one being honored. Another soldier died that day in a firefight with the Taliban in Kandahar Province. It made me remember there was another war going on. It was the war the rest of the world knew. But everybody's war was different. There are realms only within the mind of a soldier, fields of shadows and shattered souls, and we all know places that don't exist for civilians. We're all double agents...heroes in the shadows. I stepped away in order to be alone. I hadn't been alone in months.

Soldiers were marching toward the plane in time to the bagpipe music. The plane's tail ramp was down. Airmen were waiting. It was the same kind of plane which brought me to Afghanistan, not so long ago. I remembered having the OBE in the plane that first morning and looking Digger in the eyes, and when the ramp dropped and I saw the gray early morning sky, my metaphysical evolution began in full.

Now my whole idea of war was turned upside down, yet I couldn't feel the ground beneath my feet. I flew straight up into the cold night. I couldn't go down. It was no more my choice to take flight than it was the choice of the poltergeists in my house back in Houston to litter my kitchen floor with cutlery and pots. I wasn't in full control. I wasn't like Peter

Pan. Peter Pan could backstroke above clouds. I was still a neophyte, though a bloodied Fourth Wall angel ready for the next flight. I couldn't go backward. I had to fly forward. I hovered above the dual columns of soldiers. They stopped fifteen feet in front of the ramp and turned to face each other. *I will dream about this, LM, and to dream means to be alive. To stand atop this wall, to look left and right, to be the connecting force, in this war and this world, that is my purpose in this world, all is permissible atop this wall. Jesus said to let the dead bury the dead. The man he was talking to needed to bury his own father, but Jesus basically told the man to forget that and join Him, because the Kingdom of God was more important. That's The Fourth Wall...it's more about entropy than war. But T4W is my creation, one little clown car on an endless road jammed with clown cars. You may be the only person in the world to do it, to see war in that special way, but that doesn't make you wrong.*

The music stopped. All got quiet. A man read the names of the dead.

"Sean Ellington, thirty-five years old, of Belfast, Ireland...Richard Victor Jones, twenty-one years old, of Knoxville, Tennessee."

The other guy was just a kid. He's the kind of guy I need to explain all this to, someone with their whole life ahead, someone who has time to act. There's still time for me, LM. You had enough confidence in me to let me steal your little magician. Now a talismanic image that will be part of every mission to come, right here in my front pocket...but for now, wind is licking my brow and I have wings...

Then I saw them: the twin gray beings I saw at the previous dignified transfer ceremony I attended. They were looking up at me. Their mouths were open. They looked like they were screaming, but I didn't hear anything. I did hear someone in the group below say *come back...we need you, now more than ever...*It sounded like a woman. It sounded like

Yvonne. I don't know, could've been my imagination. I thought, there's someone who needs to come back to the world. *She's not like you and me, LM. She needed answers. I can go my whole life with beautiful, strange puzzles without answers. Most people can't.*

The bugler played taps. All stood at attention and saluted as the flag-draped caskets were loaded onto the plane. I was used to the visual field below me, with its vulgar, disordered riddles in a picture incomplete, so far. What would Jesus do? So many people ask that question. So I did what Jesus would do. I flew higher. This was all permissible beyond the Fourth Wall.

It was after midnight, a new day, with new hidden meanings. I flew forward and upward, closer to the moon and stars. I guess I was Peter Pan, after all. Second star to the right and straight on till morning, he liked to say. Peter, you see, just said anything that came to his head,[12] but the night ahead was long, dark, and so many dark days were ahead. *Don't look down. Relax and breathe rhythmically. I've been having an identity crisis, all these years, so please (a second please, so soon?) forgive me. No, don't...please...I take it back. Forgive nothing. What do you call this feeling? I have no name for it. Now, years later, I don't pay attention to all the mysteries, there a moment then gone, my memories of war now half-truths, but there's one point of light out there, beyond the beyond, still defiant. A candle flame. I see it. I see it.*

---

[12]A quote from J.M. Barrie's wonderful book, *Peter and Wendy*. Reader, please read it. Have I ever asked you please?

ABOUT ATMOSPHERE PRESS

Atmosphere Press is an independent, full-service publisher for excellent books in all genres and for all audiences. Learn more about what we do at atmospherepress.com.

We encourage you to check out some of Atmosphere's latest releases, which are available at Amazon.com and via order from your local bookstore:

The Embers of Tradition, a novel by Chukwudum Okeke

Saints and Martyrs: A Novel, by Aaron Roe

When I Am Ashes, a novel by Amber Rose

Melancholy Vision: A Revolution Series Novel, by L.C. Hamilton

The Recoleta Stories, by Bryon Esmond Butler

Voodoo Hideaway, a novel by Vance Cariaga

Hart Street and Main, a novel by Tabitha Sprunger

The Weed Lady, a novel by Shea R. Embry

ABOUT THE AUTHOR

Scott Petty is in the U.S. Army and is a veteran of the War in Afghanistan. His prose and poetry have been published in numerous literary journals, including *3Elements Literary Review*, *805 Lit+Art Journal*, and *War Writers' Campaign*. He is also a film actor, appearing in *The Challenger Disaster* and *Washington's Armor*. Please visit www.tspetty.com for more information.

Made in the USA
Las Vegas, NV
09 December 2021

36621671R00208